HER MAJESTY'S EYES
AND EARS

THE ADVENTURES OF
DRAKE & MCTROWELL

Perils in a Postulated Past
HER MAJESTY'S EYES AND EARS

By
DAVID L. DRAKE & KATHERINE L. MORSE

Drake & McTrowell
San Diego, CA

Cover design by David L. Drake
Front cover art by Jake Rieman
Back cover art by Katherine L. Morse
Book layout by Katherine L. Morse

Published by Drake & McTrowell <www.drakeandmctrowell.com>

Print edition ISBN 978-1-950849-02-4
Printed in the United States of America.

TABLE OF CONTENTS
HER MAJESTY'S EYES AND EARS

THE METTLE OF YIN

BY MR. DAVID L. DRAKE

The two figures at the bottom of the gray-white granite tower were busying themselves around two dark brown worktables they had pushed together. Dr. Edmond Pogue, the young scientist-for-hire, had his right arm buried up to the elbow inside a tarnished oval brass chassis, trying to unfasten the internal components of a still-operational leg component of an Electric-Powered Automated Crawling Transport, or EPACT. His assistant, Sarah Slate, who had been in his employ for less than a week, stood nearby holding a clipboard and a Birmingham fountain pen, cataloging in extreme detail the parts Dr. Pogue removed, so they could reconstruct the contraption. The table was already littered with pieces of machinery, mostly brass, but all tagged for identification. She was anxious to see the next piece emerge. But to be fair, she had been anxious about every nut and spring Dr. Pogue had carefully removed. Dr. Pogue seemed to be taking a few extra seconds this time, which made it hard for Sarah to be patient.

"Doctor, what do you think you've found?"

"It seems, Miss Slate, given the cramped area for this internal leg-structure-to-chassis connection, it called for something other than a hex nut since there's no room to wield a spanner in this corner of the body cavity. The hardware feels like a wing nut, but with all my might, I can't seem to loosen it with my fingers. It may have an internal spring to keep the connection under tension at all times, but I cannot feel a set screw or some other mechanism to free the tension or release an internal spring. Maybe if I can get a better angle ..."

Dr. Pogue removed his arm, which was surprisingly clean given that he had been reaching inside of a mechanism with many moving parts. However, as both scientists knew, brass is a wonderful metal for gears since it didn't require any oil or grease lubrication but instead acts as its own lubricant where brass met brass. Hence brass being the preferred metal within clocks and watches.

Dr. Pogue removed his lab coat, revealing a gray waistcoat, a dapper French blue shirt, and a striped blue and red silk bow tie. "I'm afraid the long sleeves are getting in the way," he added and rolled up his sleeves on both arms for good measure. He hopped up and sat on the table with his legs dangling off and reintroduced his arm into the body of the contraption.

Dr. Yin Young, Dr. Pogue's steadfast colleague, watched the undertakings from the landing at the top of the wrought iron staircase. She quietly crossed her arms and silently shook her head in disapproval.

Frustrated, Dr. Pogue again removed his arm, mockingly growled, and made a face at the brass object. "Doctor," Sarah pleadingly offered, "perhaps I can give it a try. My hands are smaller than yours, and perhaps I'll discover some way to extricate the fastener."

Dr. Pogue flashed his "Sure, that would be fine" face at Sarah and added verbally, "Be my guest." He hopped off the table, and she handed him the clipboard and pen. She climbed up onto the table in a sitting position, right where Dr. Pogue had been previously. She sank her arm up to the armpit into the EPACT and instantly started making a series of eye movements while holding her tongue just slightly visibly between her lips, both of which indicated which way her hand and fingers were working on the wing nut.

Within a few seconds, she let out an "Ah-ha!" and produced the brass fastener with a flourish of her hand. "It was easy! There are only six degrees of freedom, and I figured I would try all of the unexpected ones given the nut's shape. It turns out that a pushing and twisting motion works!"

"It's as if whoever constructed this contraption wasn't using a standard set of tools. In fact, I've noticed that this entire construction is more reminiscent of da Vinci than Babbage or Faraday. The storage of energy is achieved primarily with springs, although these crude moist electrostatic cells are used to maintain a modicum of current. Now, let's take a look at those odd little platters ..."

Yin distinctly heard a tap-tap-scratch-scratch on the door. She looked down to make sure that the doctor and his aide were engrossed in their disassembly activities, verifying that they wouldn't notice her retreat out of the tower. She hurried down the hall to the door, which she pulled open. Although it was ten o'clock in the morning in June, a late fog had settled in the area, giving a gray, unfocused backdrop to the scene at the door. Outside, standing in the stone entryway, hunched a man wearing a ragged, stained tunic covering his head and torso.

She started the conversation. "We're alone, but only for a few minutes. What news do you have?"

The figure before her stood up straight and slid his hood back a bit to reveal the face of Sergeant Fox. He spoke in hushed tones. "All went as planned. Ishild was captured alive. The Queen is satisfied enough to move forward with her plans. Drake agreed to Her Majesty's deal."

Yin nodded her understanding but retorted, "There's an issue. The doctor has unexpectedly employed a woman assistant - an American - who may not fit into the plans. Her name is Sarah Slate."

"We'll need to deal with that. I'll pass the information along."

With that, Sergeant Fox pulled his hood forward to hide his face again, hunched back over, and shuffled off into the fog. Yin closed the heavy door but stood for a few seconds going over what she'd heard. She tightened her lips and nodded to herself, mentally confirming that all Fox had reported was indeed good news. Then she went to the kitchen to fix Dr. Pogue's mid-morning cup of Darjeeling tea.

At the base of the tower, the scientific enquiry continued. Carefully holding two of the platters, Dr. Pogue examined their surfaces. To Sarah he exclaimed, "Look at this! Delightful! The platters are as strong as metal but made of something that won't conduct electricity. And see these tiny holes? These are played like music box platters! Ho ho! Those fine wire brushes go over the surface as the platters rotate, passing a small electrical charge to the metal contacts below the platters, indicating which activity the brass creature executes. This diaphragm over here detects whistle tones and controls which of the dozens of platters rotate. Different sets of platters can be rotated at the same time, causing a multitude of different movements to be executed in tandem. It's all quite simple enough but gives the impression of deliberate acts, which is the not at all the case!"

Sarah smiled at his discovery. Dr. Pogue reached into the brass belly again, loosening a retention clip on a set of tiny pneumatic brass whistles. While doing so, he heard the sound of air rushing out of the whistles but heard no tones. The other EPACT sprang to life, rapidly crawling out of its open crate, down to the floor, and up onto the two worktables with its disassembled compatriot. Edmond and Sarah jumped back to give the creature room and to see what the second EPACT could possibly be doing. Even though it only had three working legs, it gave its full effort to its new task. It reached inside the disassembled EPACT, feeling around quickly and precisely with the tips of its legs. Then it started to explore the tabletop surrounding the EPACT and discovered the parts that were laid out.

Then the operational EPACT did a most miraculous thing. Using miniscule pinchers on the tips of its legs, it grabbed the parts in the correct order and started the process of reassembling the gutted EPACT. Sarah and Edmond stood and watched, both awestruck and amazed. The EPACT stripped the label off each part and slid it into place without hesitation. The pace at which it performed this task was that precise speed at which one could see each step happening. But it did so at a rate so fast that it was hard to believe the assembly could be performed. It mesmerized the two scientists.

Suddenly, the operational EPACT started to just search the tabletop over and over. Dr. Pogue, quizzical look on his face, realized he was still holding the two platters. "Oh, yes, here you go," and he held out his left hand, placing the two platters near the edge of the tabletop. The operational EPACT lightly touched the surface of the platters a few times, verifying what they were and their locations and crawled an inch or two closer. It wrapped two of its legs around the platters and Dr. Pogue's hand. "No!" Edmond shouted and pulled his hand back violently. This jerked the EPACT forward. Rather than letting go, the EPACT leapt up Dr. Pogue's left arm.

Yin was preparing the tea service when she heard Dr. Pogue's scream of pain, which was immediately followed by Sarah's scream of shock. She was off like a shot, sprinting to the tower. She burst through the tower door and dashed down the stairs. She was confronted by Edmond with an EPACT latched onto his forearm, wielding razor sharp blades that extended along the length of each leg. The EPACT was in the process of cutting gashes into the breadth of Edmond's arm from his biceps down.

Chief Inspector Erasmus Drake sat at his desk, trying his best to fit back into his job at Scotland Yard. He was wading his way through a stack of cases that had been placed on this desk since his departure the week before, but his heart wasn't in it. Surely this wasn't how the Queen saw him helping the Empire. Then he flipped open a case file that he had expected to see but hoped he wouldn't. It was a new case, open and shut within a couple days, of a chemistry professor who had devised an acid so strong it could liquefy any non-organic material. The professor had created an acid bomb to be used against a rival university. He had planned to actually melt their chemistry building to the ground for no good reason beyond spite. Luckily, he was apprehended. But the cause for the sudden change in the professor's behavior was, of course, imbibing Green Fantasy. Erasmus knew that he needed to do something to address this and was starting to formulate a plan when his door opened and his superior, Bartholomew Horner, walked in.

Bartholomew neglected all niceties and started the conversation with, "Let's talk." They had a complex discussion in which Bartholomew revealed that, yes, he knew Erasmus was specifically requested for the regatta. It had been clear to Bartholomew that he didn't have any real choice in the matter when he was requested to send Erasmus. Bartholomew also revealed that he had received notification that Erasmus might be called out for other assignments in the future. As Bartholomew put it, "When the Queen asks for Erasmus Drake, well, she gets what she wants." The conversation ended quietly, and Horner departed.

Erasmus thought about his upcoming dinner with Sparky and how much we wished he were there already. Actually, the dinner was with Sparky and Lord Ashleigh, but it was her that he was thinking about. Perhaps he would bring that bottle of port he owed Lord Ashleigh; that would help the evening's festivities along.

In a single motion, Yin leapt and kicked the EPACT with the side of her foot, sending it flying across the tower into the granite wall. It fell to the floor without any additional movement on its own. Yin pulled a linen kitchen towel from her pocket and wrapped it around Edmond's arm tightly to the point of making him wince. She bit the middle of the loose end of the towel, ripped it, and tied off her makeshift tourniquet. Without hesitation, she took a hold of Edmond's good arm, his right one, and picked him up across her shoulders in a manner that a member of a fire brigade might use; she took hold of his leg with her other arm for control and balance. She turned and marched up the stairs in a display of strength that Edmond never would have guessed possible from her normally demure demeanor.

She immediately marched him out of the front door and into the street, shouting for a cabriolet. Not seeing one, she stepped in front of a cart drawn by two horses and demanded the driver take her and her charge to the Westminster Hospital. Her tone and determination won him over; she deposited the doctor in the back of the cart, hopped in, and off they went.

Sarah was shaking violently. She retreated until her back found the granite wall, and she sank down to the floor. What went wrong? What went wrong? She couldn't comprehend the sudden turn of events. Her tears flowed freely down her face as she sobbed to herself.

A Port in the Storm

By Dr. Katherine L. Morse

As Lord Ashleigh's coach approached the curb outside his townhouse, McTrowell spotted a carter unloading several trunks, her trunks, the ones she had stored at Western & Transatlantic before departing for the inimitably eventful regatta. How did he do that? She was certain they had taken the most direct route from the airship port and that Virat hadn't tarried. Logically, he could only have managed such timing if he had arranged for the trunks to be delivered in anticipation of her need for new lodging and her acceptance of his offer. She was beginning to feel rather like a pawn in a multi-layered game of chess. Although the moves always seemed to land her in a more advantageous position, so she wasn't sure she had grounds for complaint.

As they descended from the coach, Lord Ashleigh explained, "The guest room is on the third floor across from Anu's room. I hope you will find her an acceptable maid. She was my mother's favorite handmaiden at my father's court before his death."

"I don't mean to seem ungrateful, but I haven't much need for a maid."

"You are so like my mother in such delightful ways. I look forward to introducing the two of you in the near future." He stopped to pick up the mail from the console table by the front door and retired to his office to handle his personal affairs, whatever those might be.

She climbed slowly to the third floor, hoping that the luxuries of the house included a large tub. She wanted nothing more than a long, hot bath. The guest bedroom was quite generous, with charming dormer windows facing the square. It was tastefully decorated, but neither feminine nor masculine. The only personal touch was a small oil portrait in a round frame on the dressing table. It showed a couple in sumptuous, richly-colored Indian clothing, but the woman was fair. They were seated unusually close to each other for a formal portrait and smiling, as if being in the immediate company of the other was the most splendid possible situation in the world. These could only be Jonathan's parents. Then it dawned on her that this must be the room that his mother used when she visited London. She felt doubly honored for the use of the accommodations.

Anu had opened all the trunks that weren't locked. She hadn't touched the contents that weren't clothing, just left the trunks conveniently located where Sparky could reach them. She was just finishing up transferring the clothing to the wardrobe. "Would ma'am care for a hot bath?" Had Sparky fallen in with a den of Indian mind readers?

"Yes, please. Thank you, Anu."

Considerably refreshed from her bath, she stood in front of the wardrobe staring vacantly at her clothes. It felt odd to have the choice of all her clothing, though her wardrobe was somewhat limited for a woman of her means, and more than half of it was strictly functional. She barely managed to assemble an outfit suitable for a leisurely dinner in a respectable home. Once dressed, she began looking through her other belongings. With the mystery of her mother's situation resolved, the regatta behind her, and no new assignment on the horizon, she felt adrift. After twice inventorying her trunks without finding anything to capture her attention, she headed down to the sitting room to peruse Lord Ashleigh's library. Surely there would be something interesting there. She had only scanned the first shelf of legal volumes when Virat materialized with the silver tea service. He poured her a cup of chai and left it on the small pedestal table next to the bookshelves, departing as silently as he had arrived. Right then, den of Indian mind readers it was.

She had just stumbled on a refreshingly graphic and brilliantly illustrated text written in a textual language she didn't recognize, but whose physical tongue was unmistakably clear, when she heard a knock at the front door. She looked around the corner of the sitting room. Virat opened the front door to reveal a young Asian woman. Although the style and cut of her clothes suggested that she was of a neat disposition, she was somewhat disheveled at the moment and the front of her dress was stained with what Sparky's experience led her to conclude was dried blood. She didn't mean to stare, but that's just what she was doing when the young woman made eye contact with her.

"You are Dr. Sparky McTrowell." It wasn't a question. "You are required at Westminster Hospital."

"Why?"

"Chief Inspector Drake sent me."

McTrowell felt her limbs go cold and numb. "What has happened to him?"

"Dr. Pogue's life requires you."

It took Sparky a moment to realize the implication that it was Edmond Pogue and not Erasmus Drake who was injured. She snapped back to normal. "Right away." She dashed up the stairs two at a time. She snatched up her leather duster and Gladstone bag. She was back down the stairs and out the front door in less than a minute. The mysterious messenger was already waiting in a cab at the curb. The cab took off the instant Sparky boarded.

"I am Dr. Yin Young. I work with Dr. Pogue. He was attacked by one of the EPACTs. I have taken him to the hospital." She stopped abruptly, folded her hands in her lap, and bowed her head with a hint of weariness. Sparky didn't think she would get any more information out of her sudden acquaintance.

Nor was she surprised to find Drake waiting for her at the entrance to Westminster Hospital. She followed him in without prompting, and he led her to the surgery. Drake cautioned, "I must warn you that his injuries are quite severe."

"I'm a physician. I'm sure I have treated worse." While her boast proved to be true, she had only treated a more severe maiming that was the result of a battle. Tragically, this was not how she had ever imagined her first meeting with Dr. Pogue would be, not that he was likely to remember it.

৯৯৫৯৫৯৫৯ 🙂 ঞ৫৫৫৫৫৫৫

Drake was waiting for her when she exited the surgery. He offered the crook of his arm. "Your friend will live, but I had to amputate his arm," she explained wearily. "Anything less would have put his life at risk. I'm sorry."

"I heard you say that my friend will live." He lightly took her hand from his arm and kissed it. "Thank you." He gave her a moment to grasp his appreciation. "I believe Lord Ashleigh is expecting us for dinner." She just nodded. They bid a quiet farewell to Yin and rode back to Berkeley Square in silence.

Lord Ashleigh was waiting for them in the sitting room when they returned. He didn't like the solemn looks on the faces of his friends when they entered. "Virat has told me some of what happened. My ... resources have provided additional information. How is your friend, Dr. Pogue?"

"Dr. McTrowell has saved his life."

"But at a terrible cost," she added dejectedly.

"Perhaps you should ask him if he considers it a fair price when he recovers," Drake replied gently.

Sensing that nothing more productive was to be said on the topic, Lord Ashleigh decided to change the subject. "I expect you're both quite hungry. Dinner will be served in a few moments."

"Yes, dinner. I had almost forgotten. A gentleman always pays his debts." Drake reached inside his coat and produced a bottle of Porto Rocha.

"An excellent choice, my friend." Lord Ashleigh punctuated the compliment with his customary smile and wink.

"I'm of a mind to smite both of you for the cheekiness of wagering on my honor. And, as it's my honor, I don't see why Lord Ashleigh is receiving the port instead of me," Sparky quipped. Then she attempted to scowl at both of them, but it came out as more of a smirk.

Lord Ashleigh replied archly, "You received both the scarf and the return of the kiss, which I believe was more than satisfactory." And he made no effort to hide the fact that he was smirking. "Besides, I intend to share the port."

They passed the evening meal in companionable conversation, discussing various goings on of mutual interest in London. Lord Ashleigh kept mostly silent, allowing Erasmus to regale Sparky with his knowledge of the city. The viscount simply enjoyed them enjoying each other's company. When they retired to the sitting room, Virat had already poured three glasses of the port. Ashleigh raised his glass, "To an unlosable bet." Sparky didn't even attempt to scowl this time.

They were nearing the bottom of their glasses when Drake asked McTrowell, "How are you finding your new accommodations?"

"Delightful. The room is quite spacious and has wonderful light. It's on the third floor, right above Lord Ashleigh's."

"The most secure location in the house," added Lord Ashleigh. The remark was directed at Drake, and Ashleigh wasn't smiling. She glanced between the two of them.

Sparky set her glass down and rose to her feet. "It also has a large bed that looks quite comfortable, and I think I shall avail myself of it. Good evening, gentlemen." They both rose, and Drake kissed her hand with a familiarity that suggested he had been doing it for years.

"Good night."

Her nightgown was laid out on the bed, and Anu appeared as soon as Sparky entered the guest room. "May I be of service, ma'am?"

"No, thank you, Anu. Good night." Anu crossed the hall to her room and shut the door. Sparky had been staring out at the lights of London for a few more minutes when she noticed the light under Anu's door go out. She closed her own door, changed into her nightgown, and dropped into the bed. It was as comfortable as it looked.

She had expected to fall right to sleep from the exertions of the day, but her mind was racing, going back over everything that had happened over the last few weeks. She listened to Lord Ashleigh bid Erasmus good night and turn in for the evening. She heard Virat tidying up on the first floor, locking up, and then climbing to his room on the second floor, below Anu's and across from Lord Ashleigh's. The house was asleep except for her. She was restless like the city outside her windows.

She began doing multiplication tables in her head to try to get her mind off higher, more vexing matters. She was just getting to nines, her favorite, when she was jarred back to wakefulness by the sound of soft footfalls on the stairs between the second and third floors. She breathed slowly and evenly and opened her eyes just enough so she could see but not enough that someone could see her eyes. She replayed in her head the sounds she had heard earlier. There was no way there was anyone on the second floor except Lord Ashleigh and Virat. What was this treachery?

She heard the latch to Anu's door open. She slipped out of bed as quickly and silently as she could manage and went to her own door. She pressed her ear to the door and heard Anu's door close softly. Still doing her best to maintain her stealth, she opened her door, tiptoed across the hall, and put her ear to Anu's door. She heard voices. She couldn't understand what they were saying, both because they were speaking a language she didn't know, but also because they were speaking in whispers. She had only ever heard Virat speak a few words, but she was certain the voice wasn't Lord Ashleigh's. Despite her inability to understand the words, the tone of the conversation was clearly affectionate. How could Jonathan not know about such a clandestine assignation in his own house?

She heard the male voice say, "*Śubha rātri, mērē chōṭē pakṣī.*"

THE IMPOSSIBLE CHALLENGE

BY DAVID L. DRAKE

The heavy wooden door slammed in the entranceway, and Sarah jerked her head up. How long had she been sobbing? And had she fallen asleep from the exhaustion of doing so? She looked around the laboratory with her red-ringed, gloomy eyes. Nothing was moving. No EPACTs were trying to kill her. But the doctor was gone. And she had done nothing to help.

Yin appeared at the top of the spiral staircase and bolted down at the same speed as she had earlier that morning when Dr. Pogue was in desperate need of assistance. She approached Sarah with an air of conviction to which Sarah was unaccustomed, and it added to her frightened state. Sarah jerked her hands reflexively into a defensive posture.

"Get up, Miss Slate. I need you now." Yin's speech pattern was quick and sharp, and her words came faster than Sarah was used to, having grown up in Aspinock, Connecticut.

"Beg your pardon?" Sarah stammered out, trying to get her mouth to work correctly after all of her sobbing.

"Get up and come with me. Dr. Pogue needs your assistance. Bring your notebook and pen. You'll need it."

Yin took Sarah by the hands, abruptly pulled her to her feet, and practically lead her by the arm to her note-taking tools. Yin then guided Sarah to the stairs, up out of the tower, and out of the front door, all the while explaining the situation with Dr. Pogue.

"When we arrived at the hospital, most of the surgical staff was at a medical symposium. I put Dr. Pogue under the immediate care of the nursing staff and went to Scotland Yard to ask Chief Inspector Drake for assistance. He recommended Dr. McTrowell, an excellent field surgeon. I was able to get to her residence and immediately acquire her assistance. She spent three hours addressing Dr. Pogue's wounds and was forced to amputate his left arm just above his elbow."

"Oh my! How … dreadful!" Sarah stammered while being led to a waiting cabriolet. "How absolutely dreadful! What sort of help do you need me to provide?"

"Simply put, I need Dr. Pogue whole again. You and I will design a new working arm for him." With a light push, Yin guided Sarah into the vehicle and then followed her in.

"What?!?" Sarah couldn't comprehend the request. It was stated so simply, as if she were being asked to help prepare a family meal. "I'm sure there are a number of prosthetics on the market …"

Yin and Sarah sat facing each other in the cabriolet as the vehicle moved along smartly. Yin's face was gravely serious. Yin repeated her words, "I need Dr. Pogue whole again. He must be able to continue his work at the same level of capability and precision. I need you to do your part to make this happen."

Sarah was stunned. Her first thoughts were to ask to be excused to return home to Connecticut. She didn't have the schooling to improvise machinery. Then she thought about Dr. Pogue's influence on her education and how she had devoured his papers. And that he had been sitting on the worktable that very morning. And how he was now lying in the hospital, crippled.

She pulled herself up and with a sober tone asked, "How is he now?"

"He is sleeping off the ether Dr. McTrowell used to anesthetize him. He may be awake, but groggy, by the time we get to the hospital."

"Very well, I will see this endeavor through. But …," she was hesitant to ask the obvious. "How can you assist?"

Yin sat up straight. "I was one of Dr. Pogue's top students when he taught at University. He asked me to join him when he left and took up his private practice. I have been doing so for the past three years. Most of the papers that you have read from Dr. Pogue have my name on them. I am his co-author, Dr. Young."

"Oh my! My apologies!"

"No offense taken. Dr. Pogue saw your interest and hired you on to help. Two assistants are one too many. He asked me to take a 'break' for a while, giving you the freedom to expand your horizons. I needed the rest. We were not trying to deceive you. I've been impressed with your knowledge. Now we need to put it to work. This is the hospital. Watch your step."

Ashen. That was the word that Sarah couldn't get out of her head when she saw Dr. Pogue's complexion. It was obviously due to blood loss. It made him look like a ghost of the Dr. Pogue that she had only just met. She wondered if she would ever meet the previous version of Dr. Pogue again.

He was lying in a hospital bed. White sheets. White room. The smells of medicine and soap. His sheet and blanket were pulled up to his neck, sparing Sarah the view of his missing arm. His glasses were off, adding to the effect of looking not quite like himself. His eyes opened slowly, and he licked his dry lips. A squint, and he rasped, "Yin? Yin? Could you put on my glasses? I can't see a bloody thing."

Yin scooped up his glasses off a side table and placed them on his face. Despite her best efforts, they looked a bit crooked.

Edmond continued, "Am I in the hospital? If they used ether, which I can still smell, it knocked me out cold!"

Yin didn't sugar-coat the news. "Doctor. They had to amputate the arm."

Dr. Pogue didn't even flinch. "I feared as much. When I saw the sharp edges on those legs, I knew I was done in. Is Sarah all right?"

"I'm here. I'm unhurt," Sarah answered from the other side of the bed. Edmond tried his best to look in her direction just using his eyes, giving away the fact that he wasn't ready for head movement yet.

Yin's serious look returned. "Dr. Pogue, we need to talk privately. I am going to ask Sarah to step out for a moment and have her return when we're finished."

"Well ... of course," agreed Edmond, even though he wasn't sure what was to be discussed.

"Sarah, if you could, it would be much appreciated," Yin requested. Sarah was surprised by the politeness after the direct conversation in the cabriolet. Yin held open the door for her and, after Sarah passed through it, quietly closed it.

Sarah wasn't one to dawdle away her time. She spent the next ten minutes walking the hall and thinking about how such a mechanical arm might be built, controlled, and fastened to a living person. Weight issues. The number of degrees of freedom of movement and how to provide power to each. She had only ended up with a mental checklist of things to be resolved rather than making any real progress when the door reopened.

Yin was smiling and motioned her in. "Sarah, let us take some preliminary measurements." The three of them worked together into the night until the nurses shooed the two women away so that Dr. Pogue could get some rest.

Erasmus checked his pocket watch right after leaving Lord Ashleigh's home. Eleven minutes after the hour of ten. Even at that hour, he preferred to walk the streets of London rather than hailing a carriage. Tock, tock, tock; Erasmus' cane made its usual strident meter on the cobblestone sidewalk. Walking gave Erasmus time to think and observe. Supper with Sparky and Lord Ashleigh had been wonderful, and he enjoyed breathing the night air while rolling over the evening's conversation in his mind. London was still abuzz with its pubs and eating establishments going strong, some with music and song, others filled with laughter from bawdy stories, and still others with quiet polite company dining at white linen tablecloths with flickering table candles, just visible through well-kept windows and lacy curtains.

After a half hour of walking, Erasmus spied an unexpected scene. On the other side of the street was an apothecary fully lit for business with a number of customers inside. The scene just didn't look right to the Chief Inspector at this hour of the night. His curiosity got the best of him. He crossed the street.

The bell on the door tinkled as if it were midday when Erasmus entered. The other patrons gave him a quick look but went right back to their business. Five bleary-eyed men queued up at the register begrudgingly waited their turn. Erasmus hung back in the aisles to see what was drawing these men to a late-night shopping spree at this establishment.

The clerk behind the counter looked tired. "How many bottles?" he asked in a manner indicating it was the ump-teenth time he'd asked the question that day.

"Two, and make it quick."

The clerk reached down and pulled two bottles of Green Fantasy from somewhere under the counter. He clunked them on the counter, and money exchanged hands. This process, with some minor variation on the number of bottles, repeated itself for the next four customers and another two who came in while the original transactions were taking place. Erasmus was indeed shocked to see this product being sold openly and at a rate that would have made any bar happy. After the last customer left, Erasmus approached the clerk.

"How many bottles?" the clerk asked in the same noncommittal tone.

"Evening, sir. I am Chief Inspector Drake, Scotland Yard. May I ask a few questions?"

"Ask away. I have nothing to hide. And if you're asking about my feet, they're ready to fall off. I've been on them for twelve hours, and I've got another half hour to go."

"Why are you open so late? And when did it become legal to sell Green Fantasy?"

"I never heard that it wasn't legal to sell. We sell all sorts of controlled medications here. But as long as the purchasers are of age, you know, adults, we can sell it to them. Most of the customers for these bottles come at night, so I've been staying open until eleven o'clock. I'm going to have to hire someone to spell me if this keeps up."

"May I ask how many bottles you are selling?"

"Well, I've sold about 400 bottles today. I'm getting a new shipment in tomorrow."

Erasmus was visibly stunned. Knowing what a small glass of Green Fantasy had done to him, what was the effect of pouring all of this drug-laced absinthe into London? He made a plan to hunt down

Mr. Alistair Bennington Rutherford and find out why this "elixir" was being distributed so freely and express his obvious concerns regarding it.

"Well, do you want a bottle?" the clerk asked innocently.

Erasmus' first thought was to immediately reject the idea. "… Uh … er … no …" That was far too hard to say. It was as if his mouth and mind were not really in agreement, but his mind won this time.

"Suit yourself. Evening, Chief Inspector."

"And a good evening to you, sir." Erasmus turned, crisply slapped his bowler back onto his head, and walked out of the shop. He was upset. He wished he could stop this commerce but wasn't sure it was in his power or part of his job. He headed toward Ye Olde Cheshire Cheese and his flat, thinking, *"Mr. Rutherford and I will be having a most serious conversation!"*

GOOD NIGHT, MY LITTLE BIRD

BY DR. KATHERINE L. MORSE

Sparky felt as if she were trapped in a permanent nightmare state, or the world had stopped turning, and the night dragged on forever. Every time she opened her eyes again, it seemed as if no time had passed. When she opened them for what she judged must have been the twentieth time, she was relieved to see that neither of her fears were to be realized; the light was starting to change. Unfortunately, it meant she would be facing a busy day with almost no sleep.

So it was that she was awake when the door across the hall opened and closed quietly, and the sound of soft footsteps receded down the stairs. Well, there was one of the first matters of business for the day. She lay there listening for a few more minutes. As she expected, the door opened a few minutes later and she heard Anu go in and out of the washroom. Anu headed downstairs a few minutes later. Sparky decided to stay in bed for a few more minutes. She didn't want to reveal that she was already awake. Perversely, the next thing she knew was that she heard sounds in the washroom again, and the sun was higher in the sky. After not being able to sleep all night, she had fallen asleep as soon as she had intended to get up. She rattled her head back and forth a few times to clear out the cobwebs and made for the washroom herself.

Anu had just filled the basin with hot water and set out fresh towels. The third-floor washroom was tight quarters, so there was no getting around Sparky as she stood in the doorway.

"Good morning, Anu," she said as brightly and nonchalantly as possible. It was a good thing she was a skilled pilot and surgeon, because she was not a very good actress.

"Good morning, ma'am," said the crown of Anu's head.

"It looks like it's going to be a sunny, beautiful day today."

"Yes, ma'am."

Although Sparky was a fairly petite woman by western standards, Anu was even shorter. Sparky had to lean over sideways to see Anu's face.

"Are you quite well, Anu?"

"Yes, ma'am." Although she seemed discomfited by the questioning, she didn't display the level of distress Sparky would have expected from the victim of a terrible assault. But then Sparky couldn't claim to be an expert on the Indian way of thinking or acting. She let Anu pass.

Cleaned up and dressed for a day's work, she joined Lord Ashleigh in the dining room. He'd already eaten a few bites of his breakfast, but he was mostly focused on consuming the day's news. Virat materialized to pour Sparky a cup of chai, and she avoided looking at him.

"Good morning, my dear friend. What would you like for breakfast?"

"I'm actually not very hungry, and I must get to the hospital to attend to Dr. Pogue."

"I'm sure Dr. Pogue will appreciate your dedication, but it would be unwise to proceed on such a strenuous endeavor without benefit of breakfast. At least that is the advice I hear from medical professionals." He winked at her over the top of his newspaper.

"Very well," Sparky replied. Virat disappeared, presumably to fetch her morning meal. "Lord Ashleigh, I must speak to you about a delicate private matter of considerable urgency."

He put down his paper and smiled broadly at her. "Does this involve Chief Inspector Drake?"

"No, I hope not, but I fear it may." Ashleigh looked very confused at her reply. "It concerns Virat and Anu."

Ashleigh let out a booming laugh. "I'm pleased to see that I didn't underestimate you. You'll be just perfect."

Now it was Sparky's turn to be surprised. "I beg your pardon. Whatever do you mean?"

"I will explain later. Please continue."

She turned over his two previous remarks in her head a few times and could make no sense of them, so she proceeded.

"As I lay awake last night, I heard someone enter Anu's room. I'm almost certain that it was Virat. You have not mentioned that they are married, and I would expect that, if they were married, they would share a room. I attempted to question Anu this morning, subtly, but she acted as if nothing had happened. I suspect that she is too frightened to report a crime as she is a foreign woman in this country and probably has no reason to trust that she will receive justice, but rather would find herself without home or employment. Regardless, a crime is a crime."

"Dr. McTrowell, first let me assure you that no crime has been committed and that Anu is completely unharmed. I will explain, but first you must swear that you will never repeat what you heard last night, nor what I am about to tell you because I assure you Anu's very life depends upon it."

She nodded in agreement. The door opened and Virat appeared with Sparky's breakfast. She and Ashleigh sat in silence until he left again.

"Virat's family has served my father's family for generations. Virat was like a beloved younger brother to my father. They played together. They studied together. They trained together as soldiers. My father trusted Virat as he trusted no one else. By the time of my birth, my father knew the true nature of his first wife and her son, Vijay Deva, of whom you have heard me speak before. The instant that my father heard that I was a boy, he summoned Virat and charged him with my constant care and protection, knowing that my life would always be in danger. He told Virat, 'Teach him the ways of all weapons, both steel and human, that he may survive when we are both ashes.'"

"The nobility of his service to you and your father does not excuse what he has done."

"A little patience, good doctor; you have not yet heard Anu's story. As a young girl, she was sold to my father's household by her poor parents from the country. She was treated like a stray dog by the women of the household, which broke my mother's gentle heart. She took Anu as her personal handmaiden. I expect she felt some empathy for Anu's position as a young woman far from her home. When the other women weren't around, she would share her favorite treats with Anu. She would wear a magnificent sari once or twice, announce that 'it didn't suit her complexion,' and then alter it to fit Anu. Of course, this only served to make the other women of the household more angry and jealous. But there was nothing they could do because my mother was not my father's first wife, but she was my father's favorite wife, and Anu enjoyed her protection.

"My mother is not the sort of woman to let someone else raise her children. Although I had a nursery, I often played in her quarters. She attended my lessons, sitting quietly in the corner embroidering while I conjugated French verbs. She read me German fairy tales and showed me English picture books so I would know about her family and history. So, you can see that Virat and Anu were in each other's company almost daily. I would sometimes see them looking at each other, and my mother smiling at the situation, but I didn't understand.

"My mother's generosity and care for Anu's health and grooming had the predictable effect of causing a skinny, dirty village girl to bloom into a beautiful, graceful young woman. Virat was not the only one to take notice. My older half-brother began to covet Anu. He demanded her for his harem because, of course, she was not highborn enough to be his wife. Only my father's love for my mother kept Anu out of his clutches. By that time, I had matured enough to recognize the characters in this drama. The servants in the maharaja's court may not marry without his permission. My father could not give that permission without defying his heir's desires and incurring the wrath of his first wife. Theirs was a political marriage. She was the daughter of the maharaja of the neighboring kingdom. Keeping peace with her was essential to keeping peace with her father.

"We were at a stalemate. My mother and I conspired to give Virat and Anu time alone together, but there was only so much we could do. They could never be truly alone, because if they were discovered, it would have cost Anu her life and Virat would certainly have been exiled. And there was the ever-present threat of war with my half-brother's grandfather. My mother and I prayed that Vijay Deva's attention would wander.

"And then the unthinkable happened; my dear father died suddenly and unexpectedly. No sooner had my half-brother ascended to the throne than he demanded that my mother surrender Anu. My mother pleaded that she was in mourning for my father and that losing the company of her beloved handmaiden would be too much, but this excuse only forestalled the inevitable and further infuriated him. I should also say that Virat would no longer leave my side for any reason, fearing for my life. A fortnight after the coronation, I went to bid my mother good night as was my usual practice. The instant that her other servants weren't looking, quick as lightning Virat leaned over and whispered something in her ear. Just as rapidly, he regained his former pose. Although I had no idea what message he had delivered to my mother, his training had firmly impressed upon me the knowledge that I should behave as if nothing out of the ordinary had happened. My mother moved as if to stand, and then slumped back in her chair.

"'Dearest Jonathan, I fear I have completely exhausted myself with the trials of the last few weeks. Would you and Virat be so kind as to aid me in reaching my bedchamber.' Virat and I each supported her under her arms to guide her to the next room while Anu followed solicitously behind as always.

"No sooner had Anu closed the bedchamber door behind us than Virat whispered to my mother, 'Ma'am, I have heard whispers among the servants that Maharaja Vijay Deva has lost his patience with your stalling. Your very life is in danger.' She nodded sadly. I heard Anu sob behind us.

"'Very well,' my mother replied, 'I will do what must be done.' We exited her bedchamber because to stay any longer would have been to reveal that something was amiss.

"The next day at court, my mother approached my half-brother as he was granting audiences. 'Maharaja, I acquiesce to your expressed desire.' I'm rather proud to say that she made the word 'desire' sound like the filthy thing it was. 'As Anu will have no more opportunities to visit her brothers and sisters, I request your permission to take her back to her village for a final visit.' She also made 'final visit' sound like a death sentence. To deny such a reasonable request would have been to reveal his avarice, so he agreed.

"As my mother was departing the room, Virat said to me, 'Deva Raya, as your mother will be away in the country, perhaps you would you like to go tiger hunting.' I was so stunned by this suggestion that I almost forgot all his training, but he had used the tone of voice that signals, 'ask no questions; all will be explained.'

"I recalled my training and replied as expected, 'Yes, that would be thrilling.'

"When we were safely in my quarters he explained. 'Your mother is preparing to escape with Anu. She is going to Anu's village to get a head start.'

"'How do you know this?'

"'You are not the only one whom your father had educated in the ways of the court.'

"'Then why aren't we going with her?'

"'That would raise suspicion. She will take several days to prepare and pack, secreting the most valuable of your father's gifts to her. You and I must leave at daybreak. Pack only those things most precious to you. The rest you will never see again.'

"'Why am I taking my precious belongings on a tiger hunt?'

"'We are not going tiger hunting. I have signaled to your mother that we will aid in her escape. We must leave immediately to secure safe passage to England before your brother suspects anything. If we fail, it will cost all of us our lives.'

"At that moment I became a man and understood my father's sacred charge to Virat. He had foreseen such circumstances and put this plan in motion even before I was born.

"The rest of the tale is mostly concerned with logistics. We have arrived at another stalemate. My mother and I maintain the fiction that Anu is with her in Kirk-Linton while Virat is here in London with me. My mother writes once a year to my half-brother that she is in poor health, which she is not, and that the company of Anu is the only thing that keeps her alive. As my mother is an English subject of noble birth, my half-brother cannot very well petition Her Majesty for the return of something so inconsequential as a servant. Unfortunately, if Anu and Virat were to be married in a manner that would be acceptable to our culture, my half-brother would almost certainly hear of it. For such an offense, he could petition Her Majesty, and I fear there is nothing I could do to protect Anu.

"So, they live as husband and wife in my house under my protection. And now they are under your protection as well."

Sparky thought about this charge for a moment. She had been entrusted with many secrets in her life, but none more precious than this one. She looked up from her cup of chai, savoring the romantic heroism of the story, smiled and said, "Virat used to say a great deal more."

A Few Failed Experiments

WRITTEN BY DAVID L. DRAKE

Erasmus adjusted his gold and black cravat in the mirror and deftly pinned it in place to his starched, white, wing-tip collared shirt. He slipped on his black waistcoat, buttoned it, and walked across his sizable room to complete his outfit with his black frock coat. The gas lamp near his doorway provided a steady, yellowish light throughout the studio. Before donning his badge, he turned and looked about, wondering if Dr. McTrowell would find it homey or empty and drab. Perhaps it could use a few more pictures and more places to sit. And his living above a noisy pub, what would she think of that? Hard to say. Being from the Americas and the wilds of California, it would be difficult to determine if she would mind it at all. On the other hand, she has done a great deal of traveling about the world and might find it bourgeois, although she had never shown those types of airs and was rather down-to-earth. Perhaps he should buy an exotic rug to show that he was refined but not stuffy, and a rug might muffle some of the sound from downstairs.

Erasmus pondered the room with his new way of looking at it for a while, mentally rearranged it with new furnishings a few more times. Finally, shaking his head, he slipped his chained badge over his head, took his bowler and cane in hand, stepped out into the hall, and quietly closed the door.

Erasmus walked a great deal and practiced his fencing to the point where he had gained a good deal of strength and size to his legs. This meant that each morning he made the decision if he was going to scamper noisily down the hall stairs, tramp down them with authority, or quietly steal down them with restraint. Because he was in a pensive mood, with both Sparky and Mr. Rutherford on his mind, he thought the best approach was to proceed quietly and allow his head to continue on with its thinking.

Ye Olde Cheshire Cheese wasn't open for business yet not being a morning food or drink establishment. Erasmus normally passed through the door at the bottom of the hall stairs, rounded the corner, left Ye Olde Cheshire Cheese by its front door, and relocked it after he left. Today he rounded the corner toward the main entrance and stopped in his tracks at the uttering of a single word, syrupy and slow, which strangely commanded attention.

"Erasmus."

Erasmus turned and, without surprise, spotted Mr. Alistair Bennington Rutherford sitting at one of the dining tables, alone, well dressed in a full suit, totally at ease within his surroundings, legs crossed, and fingers interlaced and resting on his uppermost knee. Erasmus walked toward him without hesitation, but he was more drawn by Alistair's unvoiced request for him to join him rather than his own desire to hash out his concerns with the man's business dealings.

Before he sat down, Erasmus noticed that Alistair looked more mature, wiser, and self-assured than he had a week or so before. Rutherford exuded a sense of calm that filled the entire pub. As before, he made Erasmus feel slightly uncomfortable with his own internal sense of hazard and risk despite presenting no outward menace.

Erasmus slipped into the chair across the table from Alistair, placing his bowler and cane on the table. Alistair's minimal movements seemed trance-like. There wasn't a fidget or lean to show that he wanted to say something important; he simply followed Erasmus with his eyes. Erasmus felt as if he were sitting with a strange beast that neither cared nor worried about his presence, but watched him simply because he was the most interesting thing in the room at the time. This caused Erasmus to relax. His breathing slowed. He became more aware of the sounds within the room: the gas lamps' subtle hissing and the minute creaks of the floor from the morning temperature change, while the sounds in the street disappeared from his perception. The room containing the two men was the only thing that mattered.

Alistair spoke. "We need to talk." Pause. "We need to see this enterprise progress together."

Erasmus tipped his head slightly to indicate his upcoming inquiry. "Why me?"

"You are unique." Pause. "You see, and you understand." Pause. "You are not blinded by … the power, the control."

"Why would you say that?"

"Simple observations. Our interactions in your room. My contact with Sam Colt and his description of your letter. Your resistance to misuse of my elixir. Your treatment of Professor Farnsworth's situation. Your concern over the line of customers at the apothecary last night. Your innate sense of order that you are willing to set aside to have a civil conversation. You are unique, Erasmus. I would like to discuss with you the direction of the future."

Erasmus realized that Alistair must have talked to the apothecary clerk late the night before or early that morning. And he had communicated with Sam Colt? Now this was a thorough man to have followed up on the conversation regarding the Pocket 1849 revolver. "Well, I am concerned about the product you are selling. Its effect on your customers is visible and disconcerting."

"I want you to understand my approach. I apologize that it's philosophical in nature and a bit early in the morning for such musings, which are traditionally reserved for late night brandies and cigars. My studies and research have come to a singular approach of which I would like to hear your impression. Allow me to set the stage." Alistair rose to his feet and took the posture of a professor who was about to unleash his standard daily lecture, which included a cocksure stance traditionally reserved for a cut-and-dried lecture on science or math fundamentals. He started, obviously enough, from the root of his thinking.

"We are in a transitional period, moving from an agricultural age through an artistic renaissance into an age of industry and science. The world is now divided into those peoples who are making this transition and those who are not. A divide will form where nations that use manpower or crude machines to access food and resources will be left in the literal dust of those that are applying industrial-level muscle and processes to move their goods, and thereby their economy, forward."

The pause that followed was clearly not to give Alistair time to think but to make sure that Erasmus was right in step with what Alastair had said so far. He proceeded after a quick glance at Erasmus' face. "Technical innovation will fuel the nations that have embraced the age of industry. Engineers and scientists will drive the transformations, while mankind will be tool builders and maintainers rather than beasts of burden. All tasks will become more and more automated. Communication and shipping will quicken to the pace that are not even imaginable now. Companies and nations will realize that having all the world's people raised to this level of advancement will be better for all economies rather than having severe technical divergence between peoples. I could go on and on about how this will be mankind's self-supported advancement, but the important characteristic is this ..." He paused again and locked eyes with Erasmus for emphasis.

"We have previously enslaved our fellow man both directly and indirectly for manual labor. A horrible misuse of our brethren. The society that has the greatest technical advancement will be the first to pull itself forward into the future. But the scientists are the backs on which these advancements need to be made. My goal is to provide the elixir that allows these men and women to speed along this path. We must make sacrifices to get to this future."

Erasmus squinted and tipped his head slightly again. "You are sacrificing your customers to achieve a better world state?"

"Ah, you misunderstand me from a statistical point of view. I have improved the elixir since you have been out of London. The issues previously seen involved approximately one quarter of the clients. Now only one in ten suffer the ill effects, and the ability of the elixir to lubricate the mind is still fully present. But even those who have issues still contribute greatly to the technical cause; their discoveries and inventions are just as usable for the future as from those who had no ill effects. Unlike the misuse of manual laborers, where the spent shell of an oppressed man did not improve the lot of his fellow worker, each engineer and scientist leaves a legacy of advancement that others can further improve upon. At a societal level, it's a just price to pay."

"You are probably right," Erasmus stated flatly, to which Alistair responded with a faint smile. "However," Erasmus continued, "you may be fueling a new social class of technocrats who will not use their discoveries to improve the world, but rather use them to fuel a stratification of those who can dominate the laborers, perhaps control the flow of capital, and attempt to topple monarchs to gain power over others. You cannot count on the ubiquitous goal of a better life from all by those with knowledge and power."

"Bravo, Erasmus. You have read your Marx and Engels. I like how you wove in the struggles between the classes. What I have left out is that engineers and scientists rarely act as a class but rather let the goal of innovation drive them forward. A rare few want to control others with their inventions, but that type of control requires social interaction. Typically, they abhor it. Give them an intractable problem and they are happy. Give them people to govern and provide for, and they recede back into their laboratories. The real issue is how those who want power will misuse the technology, is it not? And that isn't something we're solving today. I'll be working that issue tomorrow."

"You are willing to act on your ideals, but I am concerned about your execution. I have seen your Green Fantasy customers, and they do not bode well for the future. They shuffle about, single-mindedly seeking your 'elixir.' They are building dangerous inventions to fight off their demons. This does not build a better society, Alistair."

"A few failed experiments. I'll help them via other potions I'll create. Like Professor Farnsworth. I'll help them as I will him. Meanwhile, I have improved the elixir. You don't see the thousands of customers who have increased their mental capability and capacity over the last week. London will be the birthplace of expedited technology."

Erasmus smiled. "You may be an optimist, but I hope you see things as others will. A son of a wealthy Baron selling a product that causes many to become dependent on it. You may as well be slapping a colorful label on laudanum, morphine, or powdered opium and selling it without cautions. You speak of a better world, and yet, it looks worse in the present due to your efforts. Alistair, the product is not ready for the world. You will create great misfortune. You must try to put the genie back in the lamp."

"This is why I discuss these things with you, Erasmus. Your advice is pedestrian, but your reading of the everyman's opinion is helpful. I was able to convince the association of apothecary owners to accept my elixir, and I'll resolve these minor setbacks. I'll see this through. Thank you for the conversation. You may go now."

Erasmus was shocked at being dismissed. He had hoped to talk sense into Alistair to halt the sale of this product for all of the obvious reasons. Instead, he was disregarded. But the reality was that reason wasn't enough to sway Alistair. Erasmus stood and declared, "Alistair, you give me little choice but to take action as a member of the London constabulary to stop the sale of Green Fantasy. I ..."

Alistair cut him off mid-speech. "That is not going to happen, my good man." During this pronouncement, Alistair swung a single finger in a lazy arc to show his dismissal of the issue. "There's nothing illegal about this commerce, my aspirations, or my principles. I appreciate your wanting to play the foil out of misapplied convictions, and it would be entertaining to have you as a nemesis, but I'd rather you remain a friend and see me through this. We have much to do."

Erasmus stood in shock while Alistair retook his seat. How could he be part of this endeavor? Should he venture outside the law to stop him? Or find some minor legal reason to shut down his industry? Or, worse, was Alistair fundamentally correct? And finally, how could Alistair possibly consider him a friend? "I will take my leave, but I want the conversation to continue, Alistair. We do have much to do to resolve this." Alistair made a faint nod to acknowledge Erasmus' statement.

Erasmus' bowler found his head, although it sat a bit higher than usual due to Erasmus' still-swollen head and taped dressing over his healing wound. His cane firmly in his fist, he walked sternly out of Ye Olde Cheshire Cheese's doorway, locking it behind himself with no concern that Alistair was still inside. Erasmus thought to himself, *"I am no longer alone with this issue. I wonder what Her Majesty would think of this development."*

PROBABLY BETTER

BY DR. KATHERINE L. MORSE

Lord Ashleigh offered the use of his coach to take McTrowell to Westminster Hospital to check up on Dr. Pogue, but the walk wasn't long and would take her through St. James's Park, giving her the opportunity to clear her mind. And she wasn't sure she was ready to face Virat quite so soon after the despicable accusations she had leveled against him, even if he didn't know.

Unlike the day before when she had arrived by carriage, she entered through one of the side entrances because it was closer to the park. She had taken care to dress in a more physician-ly fashion, rather than her usual pilot's gear, so as to minimize questions and interference from the hospital staff. As she approached the corner to the corridor on which Pogue was convalescing, she spotted an odd protuberance at eye level. She slowed her pace to give herself time to identify it. It was a man's shoulder and a very large one at that, which accounted for its visibility from around the corner while the rest of his body was hidden. Shoulders that wide were an uncommon feature. When she thought of the last man whom she had met who sported such impressive ones, she stopped in her tracks. Why would he be here and loitering on this ward for that matter? Whoever it was must have noticed the cessation of her approaching footsteps because he slid slowly and silently behind the corner. She thought for an instant. She shifted her Gladstone bag to her left hand so her dominant hand would be free. She took a few, soft steps to the left so she would approach the adjacent corridor at a more obtuse angle, allowing her another second or two to assess the situation. She put on a nonchalant expression and strolled around the corner.

"Sergeant Fox, what a surprise! What brings you to the hospital today?" He was wearing an expression that she suspected was remarkably similar to hers, which was to say, forced insouciance.

"I'm visiting an ailing friend."

She looked up and down the hall. "Here in the corridor?"

"Um, I'm waiting … for another friend to join me." There was an uncomfortable pause. "And what brings you to the hospital today?"

"I'm checking up on Dr. Edmond Pogue, a colleague of Chief Inspector Drake. He suffered a seriously injurious insult yesterday." She watched his face closely. It didn't register surprise so much as concentration, as if he were trying to wriggle out of a predicament. She decided to show him a little mercy. "Well, good day to you, Sergeant Fox. I hope your friend is on the mend."

She headed into Dr. Pogue's room without looking back. Of all the things she anticipated seeing in the room, the sight that greeted her eyes was completely outside her expectations. Pogue was propped up in bed by a mound of pillows, and the bed linens were littered with mechanical drawings. The woman who had identified herself as Dr. Young the day before was standing on one side, conferring with Dr. Pogue about one of the drawings. On the other side of the bed was a young woman McTrowell didn't recognize. The young woman had various measuring devices, including a tape measure, calipers, a metal ruler with very fine graduations, a protractor, and a French curve. She was taking an inordinate number of measurements of the stump of Pogue's left arm and scribbling them in a precise hand in a small leather-bound notebook, which she set back down on the bed after taking and recording each measurement. No one in the room noticed Sparky's arrival. She shut the door behind herself firmly, the sound of which caused the room's other occupants to finally look up and notice her.

Yin responded first. "Good day, Dr. McTrowell. Thank you for coming."

A flash of recognition crossed Pogue's face. "Ah, Dr. McTrowell! Excellent to meet you, so to speak." He thrust out his still functional right hand for her to shake. Unable to imagine another course of action, she put out her right hand as well, and he gave it a vigorous pumping. "I understand I have you to thank for my continued existence on this plane."

"Yes, I suppose so. I only wish my skill had been sufficient to save your other limb."

"Oh, pish posh. We'll have a new one worked up in short order, and I'll be as good as new. Probably better." He made a sweeping gesture to include the other two women in the room and all the paraphernalia of their complicated mechanical undertaking. And he smiled from ear to ear. Sparky had never met another individual with such a sunny, optimistic outlook on life. She leaned forward to get a good look at his eyes. They didn't appear glazed, but not all patients suffered that side effect of morphine.

"Dr. Pogue, I am encouraged by your optimism and energy, but I fear some of it may be a result of the opiates. As it has only been a day since your injury, I suggest a more restful convalescence for the next few days until I can be more certain of your recovery. I'm sorry, but I'm going to have to ask Dr. Young and Miss ...?" she gestured to the earnest measurer, who had stopped her measuring, but was staring intently at McTrowell.

"Oh, I'm forgetting my manners again. Miss Sarah Slate of Aspinock, Connecticut. Are you really Dr. Sparky McTrowell?"

The rapt attention was a little unnerving. "I know of no other, so I can only answer in the affirmative."

"I've recently read about your mechanical surgical assistant. I would very much like to examine it."

"It is currently in London, so I believe such an arrangement can be made. However, ladies, I must ask you to let Dr. Pogue get some rest."

Pogue responded cheerily, "We were mostly done for today anyway. You must come back tomorrow as we will need your input on the means for attaching it."

"I beg your pardon, attaching what?"

"My new arm. We are progressing swimmingly on its mechanical design, but it will require the skills of a surgeon to attach it once it's constructed." There was no rising inflection to indicate that he meant his last sentence as a question. Apparently, in addition to his complete certainty that he, Dr. Young, and Miss Slate could design and build a mechanical replacement arm, there was no doubt in his mind that McTrowell was just the surgeon to affect its integration with his body and that she would agree to do so without hesitation or inveigling. And she found that, in fact, she could not find the will to deny his implied request.

Accepting defeat, she turned to the other two women. "Ladies, if you would be so kind." They began collecting their drawings and notes. As she observed the tidying, McTrowell glanced down at the notebook in which Miss Slate had been recording her measurements. On the right-hand page was a fair drawing of the remainder of Pogue's left arm with extension lines and numbers to two decimal places. But what captured her attention was a drawing on the opposing page. It was a very precise, colored drawing of four daisies with their blossoms clustered together in the center.

She glanced away before Miss Slate noticed her staring. When she looked up at the white wall above Pogue's head, she saw the ghost of the image. Without the clutter of the rest of the notebook to obscure her vision, she realized that the daisies had been interlocking gears. This Miss Slate was a curious sort.

Yin swiftly organized the scattered drawings from the bed and slid them into a satchel. She picked up her shawl off a chair and turned to Sparky. "Good day, Dr. McTrowell. I will see you tomorrow."

"Good day to you as well. Rest well, Dr. Pogue."

As they exited the room, Yin and Sarah turned left to head to the front of the hospital, and Sparky turned right to retrace her steps out the side entrance. Sergeant Fox was standing right where he had been when she entered Pogue's room. Even out of uniform, the man was clearly incapable of not standing at attention. She walked right up to him and said, "I hope your friend's tardiness is not interfering with your plans for the day."

"I beg your pardon."

"Your friend. The one whose arrival you were awaiting before going to visit your ailing friend." She struggled to keep her mouth from twitching up into a smile. Fox was as loyal and valiant as they came, but he lacked the subterfuge of a spy or a confidence man.

"Um, yes, he seems to be late."

"Good day, Sergeant Fox. Undoubtedly we'll be seeing each other again very soon."

PEOPLE OF THIS ILK

BY DAVID L. DRAKE

In the midday sun, the streets of Shadwell were busy with the comings and goings of the wives of the lascar, the South Asian seamen and fishermen who had immigrated to the area. Their husbands were usually off working on cargo ships of the East India Company, so it appeared as if women were the only citizens of this London district. With the rarity of Asian women in London, it was common for a lascar to take a wife from the local area, even though they had been originally hired in Bengal, Assam, Gujarat, or Yemen.

The skirts, jackets, and shawls of these pedestrians were clean, but worn and unfashionable. They usually walked in groups of two and three, running their errands in a communal spirit.

The hansom that rolled by looked slightly out of place with its glossy black exterior and red highlights. The klip-klop of the carriage's steed seemed a tad brighter than the heavy-hoofed clomping of the workhorses that stood, heavy-legged and tired, in the street with their rugged carts loaded high.

Inside the hansom, Yin and Sarah kept up their conversation regarding the mechanical arm design, but they both knew that what they had so far was too heavy, too simplistic in its functionality, and it would be too hard to maintain. Yin stayed positive, but she was insistent that they meet an impossibly short schedule for the design and prototyping. Sarah was trying to keep her spirits up, but it was clear that she was doing less inventing, and more reviewing Edmond's and Yin's sketches and notes.

The hansom pulled up to Dr. Pogue's repurposed warehouse, where the ladies hopped out with rolled up designs tucked under their arms. Sarah trailed Yin, trying to keep up. She let out a long sigh and followed her into the building.

80808080⅄🎭 ᘉᘐᘉᘐᘉᘐ

Erasmus was running late to work. The long conversation with Alistair had thrown off his schedule. He wasn't worried about arriving late; he was worried about crazed mad-men strung out on spiked absinthe. Given that he was already late, Erasmus decided he should stop by the Westminster Hospital and check in on the good Dr. Pogue. This would be the first time he would see Pogue conscious since the accident. At Trafalgar Square, Erasmus took a hard right and headed toward the hospital.

Erasmus entered Edmond's hospital room quietly in case its occupant was sleeping. Instead, he found the scientist seated with pieces of paper of varying size strewn across his hospital bed, each with some meticulously drawn detail of some complex mechanical contraption. Edmond looked up and smiled.

"Erasmus! You're here! Delightful!"

Erasmus was much more solemn in his response. "Edmond, I cannot tell you how sorry I am for getting you involved with those dangerous contraptions." Erasmus held his bowler close to his chest with both hands. He had the sincerest look of concern on his face with a touch of sadness.

"Erasmus, old man, it was I who took unnecessary risks. I'm glad that you sent these metal monsters my way! My team and I have learned so much from them. Incredible workmanship! Combinations of mechanical techniques that I've never seen before. I'm just very happy that I'm the only one who was injured. If Yin or Sarah had been maimed, I would be beside myself." Edmond stopped and looked hard at the Chief Inspector. "Hello. Something else is bothering you. Erasmus, what's the matter?"

"I see a storm rising that I wish to stop, but I don't know how. There is this chap, Mr. Alistair Bennington …"

"Rutherford! Yes, I know him. He contracted with me to do an analysis of a product that he wanted to sell in a professional fashion, and I was familiar with the process to get it approved by the association of apothecary owners. I think Yin and I completed our analysis while you were still in Paris."

"You know him!?! Edmond, I am very concerned about what his product will do to society if it continues to be available. I planned to take the matter to Scotland Yard or higher, if need be. I fear my concerns will simply fall on deaf ears."

"No need to worry! Let me tell you what I discovered. Mr. Rutherford sees this as some special elixir, but it's not much more than a simple mix of commonplace compounds. True, there is a good mélange of stimulants combined with the depressant alcohol, and of course the wormwood, but nothing that will turn normal men into beasts, I assure you."

"But I saw a line of people in an apothecary that looked half dead and …"

"That's mainly the effect of the alcohol. You can see the same reaction if you mix strong drink with practically anything: milk, fruit juices, or even carbonated water. Some percentage of the population doesn't handle it well. However, Mr. Rutherford is on a quest to find those that the mixture makes hyper-intelligent since it seems to affect him that way."

"But does his mixture not have that effect on everyone?"

"That's what Rutherford claimed. My investigation involved analyzing the concoction chemically. In addition, my colleague, Yin, and I interviewed about 300 of his customers. The vast majority of them have fundamentally the same reaction as one would have if they had drunk absinthe: a heightened sense of awareness combined with the relaxation of the alcohol. For some, this allows them to concentrate. For a rare few, it seems to intensify their thinking beyond their normal faculties. My guess is that only one in 200 or 300 experience this effect. Mr. Rutherford seems to be one of these rare few, and he seems to be on a hunt to find more people of this ilk."

"That is incredible," Erasmus offered. But he wondered to himself, *"Should I let Edmond know that I seem to be of this ilk?"* He mulled it over and thought that he should share this information with Pogue but in his own way.

"Have your tasted or tried the mixture?" Erasmus queried.

"Not much of a drinking man myself. I tasted it after determining that it wasn't dangerous. I did not ... treasure ... the flavor. It smacked of a candy-coated vodka drink stirred with a licorice stick. Gave me a small headache that I wouldn't want to duplicate any time soon."

"Well, Mr. Rutherford visited me, and I experienced the effect that he was looking for."

"Delightful! I must study you!"

Erasmus worried to himself, *"That is not the response I had hoped for."*

Four is Too Many

By Dr. Katherine L. Morse

Esmeralda Pogue lacked the stalwart, charitable disposition of the society matrons who contributed their time and energies to improving conditions for the ailing by volunteering at hospitals. She could not even remember the last time she had set foot in a hospital. She would dearly have loved to retreat back the way she had come and gone for tea with a friend, but there was no conscionable way for her to continue to shirk her duty to care for her brother in his time of need. She had even made a special trip to Tom Smith's on Goswell Road in Clerkenwell as soon as they opened that morning to acquire a brightly-colored tin of Edmond's favorite nut brittle. She did her level best to make her expression match the gay colors of the candy container. With her visage thus set, she opened the door to his hospital room. It looked like his lab had been transported but without the dreary tower.

There were drawings and instruments strewn across the bed and bits of metal of various colors fashioned for performing functions she could not possibly fathom. She couldn't open the door all the way because its arc was blocked by a worktable cobbled together from a pair of mismatched spindle chairs, each with several spindles missing, and a door that had obviously been many colors in its life, judging by the clashing shades peeking through the cracks and scrapes. One of its rusty hinges was still attached. It was piled with more drawings, bits of metal, tools, and what looked like a small steam engine clamped squarely in the middle. *That can't possibly be dangerous to operate anchored to a dried-out slab of wood,"* she mused to herself.

And for a man who had always been completely hopeless with all of the suitable matches that she had brought around in recent years, her brother was remarkably surrounded by women paying acute attention to him. Of course, Dr. Young was there. Not to be outdone by Yin's attention, Miss Slate was there as well, fiddling with some small leather straps around the stump of Edmond's arm. In the opposite corner sat a fairly handsome woman wearing tragically unflattering clothing that made her look like a frontiersman in a skirt. The as yet unidentified woman was jotting something in a small, leather-bound notebook using an elaborately enameled red pen. She spoke without taking her attention away from her writing.

"I most strongly suggest that you design the apparatus so that it connects via embedded cleats. If I attach the whole apparatus surgically, he'll need continual assistance to perform many daily functions such as bathing." She continued soto voce, "Not that it appears that he will lack for such aid." When the two women fussing over Edmond didn't respond, she continued as before. "In addition, it will need to be removed and reattached surgically every time it needs a major repair or replacement. I can't promise to be around for all such occurrences, and the shock to Dr. Pogue's body will almost certainly shorten his lifespan. Finally, the bone is more likely to mend around a small cleat than a large rod or pylon."

This last bit was just too much for the delicate Miss Pogue, to hear her brother's body discussed with such scientific coldness as if he were one of his own infernal lab experiments. She made a noise like a field mouse gagging on an oversized seed. The seated woman responded first, springing from her chair and dropping her writing materials on the seat. "Are you all right? Are you choking?"

"No, thank you, I'm fine." They stared at each other for an instant until Esmeralda recovered her manners. "I'm Miss Esmeralda Pogue, Edmond's sister."

"Ah yes, I see the resemblance." No doubt she meant it as a compliment. "I'm Dr. Sparky McTrowell."

"You're the woman who saved Edmond's life!"

"I think 'women' would be more accurate. If not for the quick thinking of Dr. Young, your brother would have been lost before I got to him." Only Yin noticed that Sarah froze with a pained look on her face at Sparky's praise of Yin's lifesaving presence of mind. Completely oblivious to the little drama taking place around him, Edmond perked up and smiled at his sister.

"Hullo, little sister. Delightful of you to come visit! What's that?" He nodded toward the tin in Esmeralda's hands that she had almost completely forgotten.

"Oh, yes, I brought your favorite candy from Tom Smith's." She opened the tin and offered it to him. He grabbed a large slab off the top of the pile and stuffed it in his mouth.

"Shplendith!" he gurgled through a mouthful of crunchy nuts and caramelized sugar.

The room was now so crowded that the only direction for McTrowell to go was back to her chair, but what she really wanted to do was depart. "I had hoped that your brother would rest in the hospital for a few more days to recover more fully, but it seems there's no keeping him down or dissuading his 'visitors.' Dr. Pogue, you may return home, preferably before you burn down the hospital or the nurses suffocate you out of frustration."

"Huzzah!"

"This is not leave to spend all night working in your laboratory. You must still rest. May I count upon you ladies to see to this prescription?" The other three women nodded enthusiastically, or rather Sarah and Esmeralda did. Yin bowed her head once and immediately began organizing the various metal components into the crates stuffed under the makeshift table. Sarah began hastily collecting the littered drawings and calculations. In her nervous carelessness, she knocked her own notebook off the bed and onto the floor between Esmeralda and Sparky. It flopped open to the page with the picture of the interlocking daisies that Sparky had spied the day before.

Sparky picked it up and held it open. "Miss Slate, this is a peculiarly interesting sketch. I'm curious as to its inclusion in your scientific notebook rather than a personal journal."

Sarah stood pinned to the spot for a moment, excitement and caution chasing each other across her face. "It's a test pattern for a new weaving process I've conceived. I had been attempting to design the loom from the abstract concept, but I found I couldn't accurately visualize outlier conditions, so I drew this pattern as a practical example."

Before Sparky could formulate a response, much to her surprise, Esmeralda spoke up. "A new weaving process? What does it do?"

"As yet, it doesn't do anything since I've not completed the design. Nor do I have the resources to build the loom," Sarah admitted.

Even after all her years with her brother, Esmeralda never ceased to be exasperated by the literalness of people of his ilk. She raised her eyebrows in the gesture that she had trained Edmond to understand to mean "And?"

Apparently, it worked on all scientific sorts because Miss Slate continued. "The resulting fabric should present a different image when viewed from different angles. In the case of this drawing, it would appear to be a cluster of ordinary daisies from one perspective and a set of interlocking gears when viewed from another. This drawing illustrates how it might appear when viewed directly, but the use of color in the sketch helps me see what it should look like from opposing views." She held the notebook up flat at eye level and then rotated it 90° to illustrate her point. "You can see how this is a valuable tool for determining the requirements for the loom."

Sparky nodded up and down crisply. There was more to Miss Slate than she had originally surmised. Esmeralda nodded once, rather more sideways than up and down, hoping that neither of the other two women would seek to confirm her level of understanding of the mechanics of the loom. The part she had understood was plenty to awaken an intense, and mostly personal, interest.

"Miss Slate, would you care to be introduced to someone who has the interest and wherewithal to build your loom and make your fabric?"

In her excitement, Sarah nearly flung the notebook at Esmeralda's head. She had to flap about a bit to catch it before it hit the floor again. "Oh, yes! Who is it?"

"His name is Charles Howgill."

Just One More Thing

By David L. Drake

The warehouse was an old, wooden structure nestled in between other old warehouses. Its sides were once painted some nondescript off-white color, but almost none of the pigment was left on the weathered walls. The boards had a tired patina from long exposure to sooty air. The two halves of the heavy double door in the front of the building sagged on their hinges just enough to prevent the doors from closing properly. In this eastern end of London, there wasn't a great deal of activity, and from the triangle-shaped opening between the doors, it was easy to hear the give-and-take of three angry men inside the warehouse.

Inside, the three stood in a circle, still dressed from a recent meeting. The tallest of them pointed a finger at the skinny, frizzy-haired man in an accusatory manner. "That meeting was a disaster! They needed the limestone to complete the building façade, and we have no way to deliver. They're planning to take us to court for throwing their entire building façade repair project off schedule. Their investment in our workshop in Paris has all been lost! You are destroying our business!"

"You are, as zay say, not very bright, Monsieur 'edgley," the frizzy-haired man stated flatly. "Ze EPACTs are ze result of ze investment. Wis zem we can do ... many sings. Forget about ze limestone deal. We 'ave approximately 450 EPACTs, and wiz a leettle work, we can 'ave more here. Obviously, we can 'ave ze EPACTs do ze assembly. And as for machinery, well, we can ..."

"Oh, great! You want to thieve it! Here in my city! And I suppose you want to misappropriate the raw materials, too!"

"It does not matter, you fool. I know governmentz ... ozzer governmentz ... not your silly Briton ... zat would pay a great deal for what I ... I am SO sorry, WE ... 'ave invented. Money eez not so much an issue. So, we zhould get started. First ..."

The sturdy man, who had been silent so far, tried to chime in. "I know you two are working on the business end of this, but the EPACTs we have still need a great deal of repair. I thought I would ..."

"Shut up! Just shut up, Mr. Martin," Mr. Hedgley yelled. "Don't you see that we aren't going to fix our problems with EPACTs, whether they are restored to perfect running condition or not." Turning to the other man, he continued, "We're facing financial ruin unless we can get some legitimate job for our EPACTs!"

The twig-like man leaned in and lowered the volume of the conversation. "I zuggest ... you start listening to me."

"Why?"

"Because of two singz: I am ze only one here wiss good ideaz, and I control ze bugs!" He pursed his lips and blew an odd set of three tones.

Out of every conceivable nook and cranny of the junk-filled warehouse, an army of EPACTs sprinted to the middle of the cavernous building. The carriers extending their forearms menacingly with their paring knife edges exposed. The cutters raced across the backs of the carriers, their rotary blades spinning. They were clearly targeting Mr. Hedgley and Mr. Martin and stopped inches away when the twig-like man whistled a final tone.

Both Mr. Hedgley and Mr. Martin curled up into their best standing fetal positions, one leg on the ground and the rest of their limbs protecting their delicate faces and torsos, with just one small slit of an eye to peek out at the oncoming terror.

"Zee? I am now zeir master."

Mr. Hedgley relaxed enough to put his raised foot down and straighten out his jacket with a sharp downward tug on its lapels. He cleared his throat to regain his composure. "Actually, we now understand a bit about the action enhancements that you installed. And since you feel that you can threaten us with our own devices, I think it's time for this." He pulled a two-barreled pitch pipe out of his jacket pocket quickly and blew it hard. The result was immediate.

Every EPACT turned on its neighbor, ripping off legs and rending brass plates with a horrendous sound. The cutters were slower moving, but still inflicted an incredible amount of damage to all nearby EPACTs. Mr. Martin screamed like a little girl. Mr. Hedgley smiled wickedly. "Since they have some limited goal-seeking capability, I added a simple command to determine the champion through survival. I did it in case of a situation just like this. Monsieur Punaise, I believe this is the end of our relationship."

Monsieur Punaise stared out at the metallic carnage for a few seconds while the sound of dozens of buzz saws grinding on metal sheets filled the warehouse. He reared his head back and howled like a mad man. Then he bent forward with a raucous laugh. He followed this by putting his index and little fingers in the corners of his mouth and blowing a dissonant set of tones. The EPACTs stopped in their battle and froze. "Would you like to zee what happens when I instruct zem to work in tandem against a common enemy wiss no command to halt zem? My whistle will be ze second to last sing you'll 'ear."

Mr. Hedgley smirked. "I'll bite; what's the last?"

"Zose funny wet sounds zat people make when zey are trying to breaze srough zeir own blood."

"Oh, you're all so overly dramatic. If you want to abscond with whatever is left of our investment money, do so. The limestone mining, which was your idea, was both foolish and a failure. We are tired of trying to do business with a March hare. We're leaving."

Both Mr. Hedgley and Mr. Martin started to look around for reasonable footfalls between the entangled contraptions to make good their leave.

Monsieur Punaise countered, "Not zo fast. I need you two for just one more sing."

WARP AND WEFT

BY DR. KATHERINE L. MORSE

Esmeralda Pogue was keeping up most of the conversation as she and Sarah Slate crossed over the Thames via the New London Bridge to High Street and wound their way through Bermondsey to Rotherhithe. "Mr. Charles Howgill is a self-made man. Although he has no title, his banker's wife, who is a dear friend of mine, assures me that he has quite a tidy fortune. He lives in Hatton Garden," not that Sarah had any idea what that implied, "but he can certainly afford a more stylish, up and coming neighborhood. All he lacks is the right sort of wife to raise him to the station which his good fortune affords him." Sarah was quite certain she knew what that implied.

The carriage rattled past a series of foundries on Rotherhithe Lower Road before halting in front of a small, newly-built cotton mill. It had a brick exterior and a small profile that was three stories high facing the road. It stretched far back from the street. The door through which they entered was unremarkable, rather like a mouse hole in the side of the enormous blank, brick wall whose only other opening at street level was an enormous, wrought iron gate. Though the latter was more impressive in size, it was as functional yet undistinguished in design as the one through which they entered. The only marking on the door was a street number. It gave no indication of what lay behind it.

Esmeralda rapped smartly twice and opened the door without waiting for a reply. Sarah was pleasantly surprised to discover that the interior was as plain and practical as the outside. It was not at all the sort of place that she would have expected her new friend, the elegant Miss Pogue, to frequent. But a frequent visitor she must have been because the clerk at the desk just inside the door greeted Esmeralda without need of introduction.

"Good morning, Miss Pogue." His tone was bland, but his eyes hinted that he found her tedious. Fortunately, only Sarah was looking at his face.

Esmeralda was gazing past the top of his head. "Good day. Is Charles in?" *Charles?* Sarah squirmed a bit on the spot where she had planted herself. Esmeralda was obviously on very familiar, practically intimate, terms with Mr. Charles Howgill. Miss Pogue was even leaning toward the other door in the room as if she were not going to await permission. The clerk was the sort of man who took Shakespeare's advice about the better part of valor to heart each day. "Of course, Miss Pogue, you may see yourself in." Esmeralda already had her hand on the knob by the time he finished.

The interior room was only slightly larger and marginally better decorated than the exterior office. The middle-aged man behind the desk lifted his eyes, but not his head, from the ledgers spread out in front of him.

"Charles, dearest, may I have the pleasure of introducing you to my new friend, Miss Sarah Slate, from Connecticut? She has a keen interest in weaving."

"Miss Slater, from Connecticut?" He was suddenly paying considerably more attention than when they entered, apprising Sarah's features very carefully.

"Miss Sarah Slate, Mr. Howgill," Sarah corrected him.

"My apologies for mistaking your name."

Anxious to keep the focus of the conversation on her desired topic, the impatient Miss Pogue continued. "As I was saying, Miss Slate has a keen interest in weaving. She believes she can design a loom to create clever cloth that presents itself differently when viewed from different directions."

"Interesting."

"I have proposed to Miss Slate that we should start a small concern together." The look on Miss Slate's face suggested that the use of past tense in the sentence was only accurate from the perspective that the sentence had just been uttered. "Closely acquainted as I am with the finest dressmakers of London and all of their fashionable patrons, I should be very successful at introducing it in all the right circles. It would almost certainly be even more desirable if it were priced dearly."

"Interesting," but the tone of Howgill's voice suggested that it was less so with each new utterance.

"Sarah, dearest, would you be so kind as to show Mr. Howgill your drawings?"

Sarah withdrew her notebook from her carpetbag, opened it to the page with the daisy drawing, and held it flat. "Do you see how the drawing is colored to reveal a different image when viewed from different angles?" She repeated the 90° rotation action with the level book. "You may have to squint to observe the desired effect as this is only paper and ink. The challenge with cloth is that warp and weft shift, disrupting the continuity of the directional pattern. I believe the stability of the pattern can be achieved with a blending of fibers to create slightly flattened threads rather than round ones. The sides of the threads are died different colors and a precise, tight weave prevents the threads from toggling." She was practically breathless when she finished her explanation, and her eyes were shining. She looked Howgill directly in the eyes but could not read his expression. "Unfortunately, a mill that can spin such thread and create such a precise weave does not exist."

"Yet …"

"Excuse me?"

"It does not exist yet. Although a moment ago, when you were describing it, I could see it in my mind." And now the expression on his face was perfectly clear. He was smiling for the first time since the two women had entered his office.

Esmeralda cleared her throat, perhaps a tad petulantly. "Can you imagine how fabulously striking a dress or costume made from such fabric would be? A costume of the sort that one might wear to a masquerade ball such as the one tonight at Kensington Palace?" She was dearly hoping he was getting her hint about the evening's festivities, but his attention had wandered off in thought as he stared fixedly toward the corner of the ceiling. When his attention returned to the room, he gave no indication that he had heard what she had just said.

"Miss Slate, are you familiar with the operation of a mill?"

"Yes."

"Would you like a tour of mine?"

"Why, yes, I would enjoy that very much!"

"This way to the blowing room." He opened the side door of his office that led directly to the first floor of the factory, motioning for Sarah to precede him. He very nearly followed immediately behind her when the sound of Miss Pogue's heels marching smartly toward him reminded him of her presence. She smiled tightly at him as she also passed through the door. There was no way she was giving up that easily on an eligible suitor and a business opportunity.

When Miss Pogue and Mr. Howgill rejoined Miss Slate, she was looking about but with more of an assessing eye than a look of wonder. When her gaze settled on the cotton bale breaker, she stopped, put her hand to her mouth, and frowned in frustration.

Howgill approached. "Is there a problem, Miss Slate?"

"No. I was just thinking that there is not enough room in here for the unpacking of the other fibers alongside the bale breaker."

"This is my only factory in London, but I have another larger, more up to date one in Carlisle. And I own more land immediately adjacent on which another mill could be built." Esmeralda made a mental note about the accuracy of the information provided by the banker's wife. And then she sneezed from the cotton dust in the air.

Sarah nodded at Howgill in understanding and continued surveying the blowing room. She stopped and cocked her left ear toward the bale breaker. She listened for several seconds before turning to face him. "One of the bearings in the bale breaker is wearing out."

He opened his eyes wide in astonishment. "You have very perceptive ears! We have ordered new parts that should be delivered tomorrow. I think we should be fine until then."

"I don't share your certainty on that point, Mr. Howgill. The pitch of the whine has changed since we entered a few moments ago."

He opened his mouth to dismiss her concerns but stopped himself. "Are you quite certain?" She sniffed a couple of times. He thought that a rather rude way to answer his question. And then, even more strangely, she whirled around on the spot before dashing behind the willowing machine. She emerged with a bucket of water, the contents of which she immediately dashed into the exit chute of the bale breaker.

The foreman rushed over to disengage the machine from the belt drive while unleashing an unholy stream of curses. Howgill screamed, "Good lord, woman, have you lost your mind? Do you know what it will cost me to repair that machine, not to mention the lost productivity?"

The foreman was frantically yanking handfuls of sodden clumps of cotton out of the exit chute. After freeing more than a dozen handfuls, he pulled out one that was singed along one edge. Howgill's mouth dropped open. "Oh, Miss Slate, I owe you an apology. You have just saved my factory from going up in flames! How can I ever repay you?" Esmeralda swallowed hard. She didn't like the direction this was going. "There's a masquerade ball this evening at Kensington Palace. Your friend, Miss Pogue, and I have invitations, but I confess I have been less than enthusiastic about attending. Would you do me the honor of being my guest? Perhaps as a small repayment of the debt I owe you?" The minor conflagration in the bale breaker might have been extinguished, but there was smoke pouring out of Esmeralda's ears.

"How very kind of you, Mr. Howgill, but I haven't anything appropriate to wear," Sarah demurred.

"I'm sure Miss Pogue can help. Esmeralda, dear, do you have something suitable that Miss Slate may borrow?"

Esmeralda snapped open her fan and began flipping it frenetically to cover her face, hoping to hide the fact that her complexion was turning the same shade of purple as the fan. The nerve! He had never before referred to her in the familiar manner, but now he had deigned to do so to ask a favor for a woman she would not have considered worthy to be a rival for his affections. She nearly choked as she responded, "Of course."

"Very kind of you. Miss Slate, I will collect you this evening at 6 p.m. Where shall I call?"

"I am lodging at McCreary's Boarding House for Respectable Single Ladies."

"I will collect you there. And now if you ladies will excuse me, I must see to repairs of my bale breaker, but thankfully, not my entire factory." He beamed at Sarah as he took her hand and deposited a light kiss on the back of it. Esmeralda felt like she was going to faint.

The ride back across the Thames passed in stony silence. Esmeralda was seething, and Sarah was so dazed by the whirlwind of the day's events that she failed to notice. When the carriage deposited

Sarah at the boarding house, Esmeralda said, "I'll have the dress and mask delivered presently," and drove off without another word. Once the carriage was a block away, she leaned out the window and said to the coachman, "Bingham, we'll be stopping at Maricela's Trapeze on the way home."

The costume Bingham delivered later that day was like nothing Sarah had ever seen before. The teal silk taffeta perfectly complemented her dark hair and fair skin. The bustle had a clever little pocket that accommodated the spray of peacock feathers packed into a separate box along with a domino encrusted with blue, green, and hazel crystals to mimic the "eye" in the peacock tail feathers. The effect on the mask was made perfect by the attachment of some wispy brown barbs from more feathers. The box contained two other marvelous gems: a fascinator with a single peacock feather anchored by a stylized brooch in the shape of a peacock feather bejeweled with the same crystals as the domino and a fan of the same taffeta as the dress, not surprisingly hand painted to look like a peacock tail when opened. Despite her elation at the elegance of the costume, she spared a moment of sympathy for the poor peacock that must have given up absolutely all of its feathers for the making of the ensemble and another moment to be grateful that Esmeralda hadn't sent along a peahen costume that would have been more appropriate for her sex.

Sarah struggled a bit to descend the stairs at ten minutes before 6 p.m. She was unaccustomed to maneuvering in such voluminous skirts and petticoats, and Esmeralda was a tad taller than she. She was congratulating herself on her safe arrival in the brightly lit foyer when the landlady bustled in dressed in attire that was even more colorful than Sarah's, if such a thing were possible. Sarah wondered if such a shade of red were appropriate for a woman of Mrs. McCreary's age, but it certainly matched her mood.

"My dear, you are a vision of splendor. Are you off to some fabulous soiree?"

"So it seems. It's a masquerade ball at Kensington Palace."

"Darling, that is the very definition of fabulous! Have you arranged for a cab?"

"No. Mr. Charles Howgill, the industrialist, should be calling for me on the hour."

"Mr. Charles Howgill, the industrialist? He sounds positively eligible."

"Yes, so I hear. He is very nearly betrothed to my friend, Miss Esmeralda Pogue."

Mrs. McCreary winked at Sarah in her vibrantly colored splendor. "Perhaps not after tonight." And then she pinched Sarah's cheek for good measure.

Precisely on the hour there was a crisp tapping on the door. The landlady handed Sarah a key. "If you should return late, please be quiet. I need my beauty sleep. If you don't return until early, please make plenty of noise so I can be elsewhere and pretend I didn't know you were out past a respectable hour." She winked conspiratorially at Sarah before opening the door. After quickly sizing up the properly dressed gentleman on the front porch, she stepped back to reveal her tenant hidden behind her.

Howgill stood stock still, staring at Sarah in rapt amazement. "Miss Slate, you are absolutely stunning." He held out his elbow for her to take. Neither of them noticed Mrs. McCreary smiling knowingly at their backs as they made their way to the carriage.

It seemed to Sarah that there were more servants than guests at Kensington Palace: two footmen to help her out of the carriage, another one to hold the umbrella to shield her from the evening drizzle for the few feet between the carriage and the awning, a bevy of ladies' maids taking ladies cloaks and their male compatriots relieving gentlemen of their hats and coats. Another servant floated toward them carrying an ornately embellished tray cramped with flutes of goldenly bubbling champagne. Charles turned to her, "Would you care for a glass of champagne?"

"I can't say, as I've never tasted it."

"Then nothing else will do." He retrieved two glasses as the tray with the servant drifted past. "I advise a modicum of caution. I find the bubbles go right to my head." He watched her take a gingerly sip, focusing all of his attention on her. As she looked back at him, she considered that she might have misjudged his age when she met him that morning. He seemed not much past thirty years now that she looked at him closely.

Growing a might uncomfortable with his fixed attention, she began searching for something distracting. She spied a gentleman dressed in relatively unremarkable clothing, but wearing a strikingly sinister mask. It had a protruding brow and a long, upward swept nose with flaring nostrils. Its deep red color gave it a devilish aspect. It also matched the dress of the woman standing next to him. Rather than wearing a mask on her face, the woman was wearing a dainty hat with a harlequin mask affixed to it. Sarah nodded in their direction, "Do you know who the man in the red mask is?"

"It would be almost impossible to say given the completeness of the mask, but the woman next to him is Grand Duchess Almaza, the noted crypto-zoologist."

"Are you acquainted with her?"

"Sadly, no, but she published an excellent article last month in 'The Zoologist.'"

She was struggling to think of another suitable topic, when a wave of silence followed by a murmur rippled from the entrance toward them. They both turned to face the source of the crowd's fascination directly. The assemblage parted to reveal Miss Esmeralda Pogue in a costume immediately recognizable as Botticelli's *The Birth of Venus*. Certainly she wasn't naked, but her dress was nearly the exact shade of her alabaster skin; the outline of Venus was hand painted on the silk of her dress; and the bottom tier was a ruffled sea foam green. Her long red hair was somehow fastened around the dress to cover the painting on the dress as it did in the original work. A soft pink, patterned drape flowed from her left shoulder. A pair of tiny winged angels bobbed from a wire frame whose base was hidden under her hair. An enormous scallop shell fanned out from her bustle, necessitating the parting of the crowd. Her escort wasn't wearing a costume per se. Only a madman would have come to such a gathering impersonating an admiral of Her Majesty's Royal Navy. The uniform was undoubtedly real, and several people in the room recognized him, although Sarah wasn't one of them.

Sarah suddenly felt very plain as Venus washed in on her half shell. Esmeralda and her escort halted their promenade immediately in front of Sarah and Charles. Charles stood up very straight and looked her directly in the eye. "Miss Pogue, you certainly have a talent for drawing attention to yourself." He turned to the admiral and shook his hand firmly. "Sir, I trust you will have a pleasant evening. The Perrier-Jouët is a marvel." Sarah noticed, much to her relief, that Charles had deftly, but politely dismissed the new arrivals who moved on. Neither of them noticed a dark-haired, dark-skinned man in a kurta and turban closely observing the exchange from the cover of the more elaborately disguised guests. Charles turned back to Sarah.

"Sarah, may I call you Sarah?"

"As you wish."

"Sarah, have you ever been to Cumbria?"

DANCING IN THE LAB

BY DAVID L. DRAKE

The June midday sun shone on London's district of Shadwell. The streets bustled with noontime errand runners and stocky cart-loading laborers. Erasmus sat uncomfortably in the hansom cab he hired to take him to see Dr. Pogue and, merely out of nervousness, glanced again at the address for Edmond in his logbook. This was his first visit to the doctor's laboratory, and it seemed like a longer and bumpier ride than he had wished for. Then he plucked out his pocket watch and gave it a quick look. It had been four minutes since he last looked at it. Why did he dislike these carriage rides so much? Today's theory was that having someone else steering the vehicle made him feel like he had lost some control over his life for the duration of the ride. But that was silly; he could redirect the driver at any moment. His fingers tapped the top of his cane. Only a few moments longer.

Erasmus had seen Edmond in the hospital a few days before and promised to come by his place to understand the mystery of Mr. Rutherford's concoction. Edmond had been released by Dr.

McTrowell, and he was supposed to be resting at his combination residence-laboratory. Knowing Edmond, the chance of finding him actually resting was as likely as Ireland becoming tropical.

The hansom came to a stop in front of the converted storehouse. Erasmus felt the gray granite walls and tower stood out impressively from the surrounding building, and it took him a second more than usual to hop out of the vehicle as he gawked at the edifice. Pressing a number of coins into the driver's hand to cover payment and a tip, Erasmus turned and strode up to the building's heavy door. He had only tapped the knocker twice when it swung open to reveal Yin's smiling face.

"Good day, Dr. Young. You look cheerful!"

"So glad you're here, Chief Inspector. The doctor was expecting you. I'm just glad that Edmond is back home. He's down in the laboratory. I'll lead you there."

With Yin leading the way, the pair traversed the main hallway to the tower, down the wrought iron staircase, and finally to the floor of the laboratory, where Edmond was working on a brass contraption on one of his worktables, lost in his activities. Yin simply cleared her throat to get his attention. Dr. Pogue spun around and snapped out a heavily gloved hand for shaking. "Drake! You're here! Delightful! Delightful!" He then looked down to his own hand and realized that it wasn't properly uncovered. Just as quickly, he stuffed the tip of the middle finger of the glove into his mouth to aid in its removal, bit down, and whipped out his bare hand again for shaking. Erasmus shifted his bowler and cane to his left hand and gave Edmond's hand a hearty shake.

Edmond was already compensating for the lack of a left hand, Erasmus thought. "How are you doing my friend?"

Edmond opened his mouth to speak and deftly caught the falling glove in his hand. "I have been busy! I have so much to catch up on. But I am so grateful that you could take the rest of today to help me expand my study of the 'Rutherford Phenomenon.'"

"I'm glad to help, but I have never been studied before."

Edmond and Yin were wearing mustard yellow lab coats, both equally stained and smudged from their work. Yin rounded the table, pulled a smallish hammer out of her lab coat pocket, and proceeded to finish closing the rivets on the brass contraption.

"Erasmus, you're in good hands; I assure you. But first let me show you what we're working on. Here's a prototype of my replacement arm! Yin and Sarah did the preliminary design, and I've added some touches. It's not complete, but we need to test some concepts before we know if we're going in the right direction. Our biggest problem is weight. This simple version is 35 pounds and still needs many of the finger controls and a better extension capability. Did you know that my right arm is only ten and a half pounds? Approximately. I'd like to get this down to a closer weight. I'm hoping to finish the prosthetic in ten weeks, but Yin asked if we could try to do it in less. Given that we are doing it on our own time, it will delay our other efforts."

Edmond spoke as if he was merely fixing a penny-farthing. Erasmus looked around and saw all of the other efforts that were underway but disregarded. They were from many of the sciences: mechanical linkages, botanical cross-pollination, high-pressure engines, and multi-colored chemicals. In addition, wooden crates sat scattered on the floor in the back of the laboratory, the ones Erasmus had sent to have their contents analyzed.

After the look around, Erasmus paused and then agreed, "I am ready for what you have in mind. How should we proceed?"

"Erasmus, have a seat. I've put a great deal of thought into this since we last talked. I have a bottle of Green Fantasy. This is Mr. Rutherford's latest variation, which seems to have less of a negative effect on its recipients. I had thought of giving you just a little and seeing what the effects are, but that may be problematic. Most reactions to medication are not linear with respect to amount. If I give you half of what Mr. Rutherford did, I probably won't see any effect. What I would like to do is give you the same amount I did with my other subjects, which is eight ounces."

"That is about twice as much as I had last time! Are you sure that is safe?"

"I do believe it is. From your own story, you only had the most intense response for a little over five minutes. This will allow me to compare you to my other subjects. It will also allow me and Yin to observe your reaction so we can see if we can determine whether the mixture is really having an effect on you, or if you are just relaxed into concentrating on the task at hand."

Dr. Pogue poured the green liquid from the bottle into a graduated beaker. Eight ounces. Erasmus stared at it. Was he really going to go through this again? "I must admit I am nervous. I do not want to end up like one of those half-awake, corpse-like opium smokers."

"My preliminary analysis says that you won't. Yin, are you ready to take notes? Erasmus, please begin."

The Chief Inspector picked up the beaker. It looked harmless enough. It smelled of sweet candy. He remembered the taste and the instructions Mr. Rutherford had given to let it roll around in his mouth. He mumbled to himself, "I enjoy new experiences, I enjoy new experiences, …"

He took about half a mouthful, which was only about a third of the beaker's contents. While turning it over in his mouth, he looked at Edmond and then at Yin. Then he stood and looked around the room. He swallowed. His attention focused, and his concentration accelerated.

Erasmus woke up in a soft feather bed covered with linen and blankets and a cotton pillow under his head. How long had he been asleep? Did he black out? He had a bit of a headache but was otherwise no worse off. He sat up. He was still in his clothes but wearing a white lab coat. He got out of the bed and looked around. He realized that he was in Edmond's bedroom and had been allowed to sleep until he woke. At the window he pushed aside the cotton curtains to reveal a midday sun. What had happened?

Erasmus made his way out of the chamber and down the hallway to a kitchen. The kitchen made him realize how hungry he was, but he would deal with that after he found the others. From the kitchen, he entered the main hallway, turned right, and headed toward the laboratory. From the landing on the stairs, Erasmus could see Edmond toiling away at one of the worktables. It had five or more bulbous glass containers either being heated or having some liquid deposited into them from coiled glass tubes. Erasmus descended the stairs.

Edmond turned, and exclaimed, "You're awake! Delightful!"

"Did you not expect me to awaken?"

"No, no, I didn't expect you to be awake so soon! You're having trouble remembering? You went to bed, or rather we lead you to the bed, at six o'clock in the morning! You've only slept six hours. Astounding!"

Edmond turned and patted Erasmus on his back while reaching out and shaking his hand. "You've done me a great service."

"How is that? Wait … let me see your other arm!"

Dr. Pogue was wearing his yellow lab coat, but a gleaming brass left hand was visible at the cuff of his sleeve.

Erasmus was beside himself, "Impressive!"

"Impressive? You built it last night! From parts from the two EPACTs! See these fingers? They are shortened versions of the EPACTs' legs. Watch this."

Edmond whistled a simple three-note tune, and the hand closed into a neat fist without a single part rubbing or scuffing. He looked at Erasmus and wiggled his eyebrows. He whistled a two-note sequence, and just the index finger extended to make a perfect pointing hand.

"Great, isn't it? This is your work. Well, Yin and I assisted you, but you took over the laboratory." Edmond took off his lab coat as he continued. "Yin was exhausted, so she's still sleeping. Take a look at the leather yoke for my shoulders and top of my torso. It fits perfectly."

With the lab coat slipped off, Edmond revealed the leather harness that went over his shoulders and tied in the front of his chest. Attached to the top of his remaining left arm was a slim and shiny brass arm. It had pinkie diameter-sized holes in it, as if it needed cooling vents. But then Erasmus started to remember the entirety of the previous day and evening. The holes were to reduce weight, and he'd placed them in a staggered pattern so the brass exterior retained its strength. And the power wasn't from steam, as originally planned. Instead …

"Erasmus? I lost you there for a second. Are you recalling the design? You know you didn't draw a single picture. You just described out loud what you were thinking while you were building. The driving force comes from a stacked set of storage cells you removed from Professor Farnsworth's electrical discharge pistol backpack. The functional activation is through the audio input controls from the EPACTs. You reused some existing operation disks and manufactured a number of new ones. And then we set them to frequencies that I can whistle."

"I remember. I drew the yoke pattern onto leather for Yin to cut out and rivet into shape. We destroyed a couple of perfectly good tool bags, did we not?"

"I have a working mechanical arm, my good man! It's only 11 pounds and twice as strong as my right one! What do I care if I lost a couple of replaceable leather bags?!"

The men hooted and did a little jig right there in the laboratory. Yin, bleary-eyed, padded into the room in a kimono. "You two are noisy. I thought you were going to let me sleep." The two men laughed and played with making the arm do a number of simple movements while Yin went off to get properly dressed.

After a half hour of celebrating, Erasmus remembered his hunger. "Let us go out and get a meal. Can we put a jacket and glove on your right arm and give it a test run outside?"

"Delightful!"

Edmond trotted up the stairs to fetch his overcoat and gloves. Yin and Erasmus followed. Yin was now fully awake and extremely happy. Edmond was able both to put on the jacket and glove and to conceal his metallic prosthetic arm.

Outside on the street, the three discussed where they could go to celebrate. An open cabriolet was headed smartly up the street toward them. Erasmus spied it first and waved, but the driver was oblivious to his signal. Without thinking, he pursed his lips and gave a sharp whistle. Edmond's left arm shot up and punched its owner in the jaw, knocking him out cold.

Erasmus and Yin turned to the doctor, who was now lying flat on the sidewalk, unconscious, his left hand still making a fist and aiming at the red spot on the side of his face. Erasmus thought, *"Well, I guess it still needs some work!"*

AUNTIE CATHERINE

BY DR. KATHERINE L. MORSE

"Good morning, Mr. Littleton."

"Good morning, Dr. McTrowell. What can I do for you today?"

"I need to pop up to Stirling for a day or two. Do you have a ship going to either Edinburgh or Glasgow?"

"The Aelian is departing for Glasgow tomorrow morning at 9 a.m., and Abercromby still needs a co-pilot. I can't pay you a full pilot's wages, but all the paying seats are full."

"Abercromby's a fine pilot, so I won't have to do much but keep him company. And get paid for the pleasure. That will do nicely. Thank you."

"Unfortunately, I don't have a returning ship for another week."

"Then I shall have to return by train. The co-pilot's wages should cover that cost, and I'll be no money out of pocket for the trip. Very good, thank you again, Littleton."

As she had expected, the trip to Glasgow was uneventful. She only had to do a bit of spotting. And since the weather was lovely and clear, it wasn't much more than sightseeing from the air. She collected her wages at the local office of Western & Transatlantic before heading to the train station on foot. It was conveniently close by, and she only had her Gladstone bag since she was just staying overnight. The train ride gave her an opportunity to reconsider Her Majesty's letter. Maybe the Queen didn't really know and was just trying to spook McTrowell into revealing the whole truth. If that was the case, Sparky had just played right into the Queen's hands with her trip to Stirling.

There was almost no one about on Broad Street, which suited Sparky's purposes just fine. There was no immediate answer when she rapped the knocker at number 30. Perhaps she had made a tactical error by trying to hide her plans. If no one was home, she had risked discovery unnecessarily by coming to Stirling. She was just contemplating whether she should plan to stay another day or two and make some quiet inquiries when the door opened. The face of the older woman who answered the door lit up when she saw the visitor.

"Czarina! What a lovely surprise! Have you come for a bit of a stay?"

Sparky winced a bit. No one but her maiden aunt called her by her given name. Even her mother had acquiesced to calling her Sparky, at least to her face. "Hello, Auntie Catherine. Sadly, I'm only here overnight as I have business in London. May I come in?"

"Oh of course, dearie! It's been so long since I had a visitor, I'm forgetting my manners." Sparky felt a twinge of regret. Her paternal aunt was all the family she had left besides her mother, and she went years in between visits. And her aunt didn't have any family other than Sparky ... Czarina. "Would you like a spot of tea?"

"That would be lovely, thank you. I flew to Glasgow from London this morning and came over on the train. It feels like I've been traveling for days though."

"Well, aren't you the grand adventurer?"

Sparky rubbed her eyes. Yes, she felt a lot like a grand adventurer these days, and it wasn't always to her liking. The smell of the tea lifted her spirits. It wasn't the spicy delight of Virat's chai, but it brought her back to the times she'd spent in these environs as a child. Her aunt fixed a cup of tea for Sparky just the way she had when she and Sparky had sat reading adventure stories together years before. McTrowell thought it criminal that her father had gotten to go off traveling, an experience that had been almost entirely wasted on him, while her aunt had had to stay home and care for their father as his health failed, and he died. She was sure Catherine would have had a better appreciation of the larger world than her dissolute younger brother. She took a sip. "Auntie Catherine, has anyone been about lately asking about Grandfather's 'arrangement?'"

"Isn't it funny that you should ask. A big fellow came by not much more than a month ago asking about Da and *bràthair*."

"A big fellow? Can you describe him?"

"Nearly as wide at the shoulders as he was tall. Brown hair and very blue eyes. Stood up quite straight like a military man. Easy on the eyes, if you know what I mean."

"Aha. I know exactly what you mean."

"Is he a beau of yours?" She smiled wistfully at the thought of her niece having such a fine young man.

"No, he's more of a colleague or an acquaintance. He's a bit young for me and not really intellectual or worldly enough for my taste."

"So, is there such an intellectual or worldly gentleman?"

"There might be. Perhaps we can discuss him over dinner." She smiled slightly on the outside, but broadly on the inside. "For the moment, I'm more concerned about your visitor."

"Your grandfather may be gone more than a decade, but I kept my promise to hold his dying wish. I told that young man I hadn't seen your brother since Da passed. He asked if the two of you were close, so I told him I wasn't sure anymore, but you were when you were younger." And then the two ladies had a great laugh together. "Dearie, you must be terribly peckish after your long journey. I was working on a proper shepherd's pie when you arrived." Sparky let out a happy sigh at the thought of her aunt's shepherd's pie with its savory chunks of tender lamb and crispy mashed potatoes on top. "I thought that might pique your appetite. Let's have some supper and you can tell me all about that intellectual, worldly fellow of yours."

Sparky felt delightfully rested as she left her aunt's house the next morning. She had forgotten how blissfully quiet it was here, far away from the chaos of London. Her aunt had fortified her with cream scones, strawberry jam, clotted cream, and several more cups of tea. After two helpings of shepherd's pie the night before, she felt like she wouldn't need to eat again for a week. She kissed her aunt on the cheek.

"Thank you, Auntie Catherine."

"You take care, dearie. And don't be a stranger."

"No, ma'am." She made a promise to herself to keep her word.

The train ride back was going to take longer than the flight up, so she settled into her seat, pulled her notebook and enameled pen out of her Gladstone bag, and began drawing graphs of the encounters she had had over the last month. Abusir led to Drake, but she didn't detect any causality there, only correlation. Drake led to Pogue, a clearly intentional relationship. Pogue led to Dr. Young, which was also clearly intentional, but there seemed to be a missing connection there. Dr. Young was entirely capable of pursuing research on her own. Why did she stay working with Dr. Pogue? If it wasn't wholly for professional reasons, was it personal? Or was there some other influence of which McTrowell wasn't aware? Jonathan Lord Ashleigh clearly had a business relationship with Wallace, but he also had his mysterious "resources" and an uncanny way of turning up with just the right resources at just the right time. Wallace was the only one who made perfect sense; he was clearly motivated by money. As annoying as he could be, it was a relief not to wonder about his raison d'être. And then there was Sergeant J.B. Fox, who was far too integrated in her life for no readily apparent reason. She was not a strong adherent to theories of coincidence. Her pen hovered over the nodes and arcs that didn't form a connected graph. Who was the puppet master?

When the train reached Carlisle, she closed her notebook and stared out the window, hoping that focusing on something other than the frustrating page would provide some insight. She gazed idly at the passengers disembarking and boarding. She saw something that caused her to sit forward in her seat and press her face and hands to the window. There was a well-dressed, obviously well-to-do gentleman preparing to board the train, an unremarkable event in itself. But he was offering a hand up to Miss Sarah Slate! What was she doing in Carlisle, and who was her unidentified companion? Sparky was still wondering about the new passengers and staring into the space they had just vacated when she saw something astoundingly more noteworthy. Boarding the train a discreet distance behind the pair was a man in very ordinary clothes intended to blend into the crowd. What did not blend in was the remarkable width of his shoulders.

"Well, Sergeant Fox," she thought, *"the game is afoot."*

THE BIG DATE

BY DAVID L. DRAKE

Sparky trotted up the steps to the front door of Jonathan Lord Ashleigh's row house and, before she even reached for the knocker, Virat opened the door with both a smile and a bit of a bow. "Well, hello, Virat!" Sparky cheerfully exclaimed. Virat scooped her Gladstone bag out of her hand and proceeded to take it upstairs. Anu was standing in the sitting room with a tray of hot chai tea that she must have poured as soon as the cabriolet dropped Sparky off.

"Was your trip satisfactory?" Anu enquired.

"It allowed me to get a bit of business done as well as see my aunt. Oh, thank you for the chai. It smells wonderful!"

Sparky pulled off her gloves and jacket and settled into an armchair that was much more comfortable than the train accommodations. Anu handed Sparky a cup of the steaming brew.

Anu continued. "The Chief Inspector of whom you have spoken stopped by earlier this afternoon to see you."

"To see me? Oh, I'm sorry to have missed him. Was it urgent?"

"Not in the usual sense. He wanted to ask you to accompany him to dinner tonight. He was practically shy in his confession of his request. Would you like the particulars? I wrote them down on this card."

Sparky eagerly held her hand out, but batted her eyes and feigned, "That Chief Inspector, what a bother. Well, if I must!"

Anu wasn't quite used to a guest play-acting with her and withdrew the card slightly with a perplexed look. Sparky quickly apologized. "I'm sorry, Anu. I didn't mean to confuse you. Yes, I'm very interested in the specifics of his offer!"

Anu handed over the card, and Sparky eagerly looked over Anu's perfect handwriting.

If it would please Dr. McTrowell, Chief Inspector Drake would like her to accompany him to a restaurant located in Clerkenwell in the Italian style of cuisine. The Chief Inspector will arrive to escort her at half seven in the evening, tonight, if the offer is accepted.

"How thoughtful. I'll need to select a dress. Can you have word sent back to him that I accept his offer?"

Anu gave a slight bow while saying, "Right away ma'am." She set down the tray and went up the stairs toward Virat. In a moment, Virat descended the stairs wearing an outside jacket and carrying a cap. With a slight smile toward Sparky, he zipped outside to deliver the message.

Anu returned. "Is there anything I can do to help you prepare?"

"Not that I can think of. Thank you."

Sparky continued to sip her chai, but Anu stayed where she was, eyes averted. Two sips later, Sparky became more aware of Anu's hovering.

Anu cleared her throat, and Sparky looked up to see Anu looking ... above her? Past her? It was some subtle hint that she was failing to get. "Anu, I'm not good with clever hints. What are you trying to tell me?"

"It is simply that the Chief Inspector will be here to pick you up in an hour and a half. I could help you with your hair during that time."

"I hadn't plan to do anything with ... Do I need to do something? I like it down like this. It's easy to work with."

"If I may suggest, the hairstyle you choose sends a message."

Like many women in the States, at least the western ones, Sparky had her hair so long that it went down her back just below her shoulder blades with bangs in the front. The sun had kept it blond, similar to the color it was when she was a child. The cut gave her many options for wearing it: straight down, up in a nice bun, gathered with a clip or leather strand, or with a single braid down her back. Sparky began to understand that Anu might be trying to provide gentle guidance that none of these useful hairstyles would do for tonight.

Sparky uttered a single word query, "Message?"

"Yes, ma'am. Your hair down means you want to be friends or colleagues. Up in a bun suggests an air of confidence, independence, and tidiness with a touch of purity. A simple curl indicates you want to be seen as pretty and fetching."

"Which of those would you suggest?"

"None, actually. I recommend we put your hair up in a fancy curl. The obvious effort means that the evening is important to you. That would be my humble opinion."

Anu averted her eyes again, indicating that she wondered if she had overstepped her post with the proposed hairstyle combined with the implication that tonight was significant. Sparky thought Anu was both thoughtful and generous in her offer and also correct in her assessment. That being said, she didn't look forward to a night of having her hair piled on her head in the manner of a furry mammal napping on her cranium. And the glue-like substances that would be used to keep its airy structure static were not appealing in either their application or employment.

Sparky smiled as pleasantly as she could. "I agree we should do something. Your help would be greatly appreciated."

Anu smiled broadly and led the way upstairs.

At seven-thirty exactly, a tall driver stopped his shiny black cabriolet in front of Jonathan Lord Ashleigh's row house. His jet-black horse whinnied and lightly pawed the paving stones, making a distinct set of horseshoe-on-stone sounds. The cabriolet door swung open, and out stepped Erasmus in his black frock coat, bright blue waistcoat, black cravat, and starched white shirt. When he stepped down to the cobblestones, he donned his top hat and strode up to the door. He clacked the knocker once, and the door swung open. Virat kept himself hidden so as not to block the presentation of Sparky as she stood in the entranceway. She wore a well-fitted, deep purple dress with three-quarter length sleeves, and her hair was arranged in a manner that took Erasmus' breath away. It was elegantly piled in open loops on the crown of her head and held there by purple ribbons with some locks of curled hair hanging loosely down as bouncy blond spirals accompanied by similarly coiled purple ribbons. Sparky stood tall on her higher-than-normal heels, a great achievement for her, which gave her an additional air of sophistication.

Anu approached Sparky from behind and added to Sparky's ensemble a finely made shawl in the pattern of a subtle purple tartan.

"You look fabulous," he said to Sparky, as he picked up her hand to kiss it.

"I could say the same to you," she replied.

The restaurant, if one could call it that, was a collection of five tables in the sitting room of a well-appointed Italian household in the Clerkenwell area of London. There wasn't a menu, per se, but rather a list of what was being served that night from the household's kitchen. The waiter sat Sparky and Erasmus near the front window to show them off to the passersby, as if to say, "See how nicely our clientele are dressed?"

Other patrons filled the rest of the tables. Erasmus thought they were a bit stuffy and rather uninteresting, being there mainly to be seen and eat. He, instead, had planned to enjoy a lively conversation with his dinner companion.

Their conversation tripped along in a light and fun way as they enjoyed their Lambrusco wine while waiting for dinner to arrive at the table. Sparky, in particular, enjoyed the aroma of the wine. "I think I sense a hint of strawberry. Do you?" she asked.

"But of course," he replied. Erasmus was not a foolish man. When your date senses a particular note in the nose of a wine, agree with her. As a woman, her olfactory senses were superior. But in this case, he knew that Lambrusco was well known for that flavor element, which made it a good wine to start the evening meal.

The server delivered their dinner on a warm serving plate and placed it centrally on the table. It included a wonderful collection of fresh vegetables and pork sausages, all seasoned with vinegar, olive oil, basil, and oregano. The vegetables had been quickly sautéed in a small portion of pork lard, except for the tomatoes that were served fresh! Quite a difference from any of the British vegetable preparations, which always involved a good deal of boiling or stewing. The two diners helped themselves to the comestibles.

Between bites, Sparky mused, "I'd love to visit the countryside of the Italian Peninsula. This cuisine is so different than British, French, or even the hodge-podge in the state of California. But I hesitate to go while the Italian nationalists are causing such a fuss with their unification effort."

"I would enjoy that," Erasmus mused.

The conversation rolled along, covering a broad range of topics as they consumed their meal at a leisurely pace. They discussed the unhealthy tightness of current women's fashions, the importance of segmenting teamwork in a way that allows each person to take ownership of their area of responsibility, a silly accident an inventor caused while trying to set up a burglar prevention device using electricity, the strange ailments of the affluent due to rarely washing their bouffant coiffures, the short history of Scotland Yard, including the trials and tribulations of a state-run organization of officers and detectives, the lack of proper airship fields in Australia, and the disagreements by the various university football teams over the inconsistent application of the Cambridge Rules.

When their plates neared emptiness, Erasmus asked, "May I change the subject?" He looked a bit concerned, given the lightness of the exchange. "I have a small issue that has been on my mind that I wanted to discuss with you."

"Of course, Erasmus. What is it?"

"Remember telling your tale of experimenting on yourself to test if licorice root would counter the effects of foxglove?"

"Yes, I do."

"Why experiment on yourself?"

"Well, if I may correct you, you've described the experiment the wrong way around. I had to know the effects of foxglove so that the explanation about dying miners provided by my mother made sense. The licorice root was to revive myself. I tried my best not to poison myself, actually. But to answer your question directly, I didn't want to administer foxglove to anyone else because I might endanger their life. And if I had, I couldn't count on anyone else to accurately describe what they were experiencing. Erasmus, you understood that part already. Why do you ask?"

Erasmus hesitated to answer immediately, fearing that this may be a strange confession. "Hmm. Dr. Pogue has decided to use me to test the effects of a so-called elixir that is being sold in a number of apothecaries. I am not sure I am comfortable playing the role of a laboratory guinea-pig."

"Really!? That's odd. Why you?"

"Because I have a rare reaction to the concoction. It increases my engineering and scientific capabilities."

"To a measurable extent?"

"Oh, my, yes. Just the other day I lead the effort to finish his prosthetic arm. It is now fully functional."

"That's great!" Then Sparky hesitated and made a smirk, adding, "I'm concerned that Dr. Pogue may no longer be experimenting and instead is taking advantage of your new-found abilities. Has he modified the mixture to figure out what's causing or not causing the effect?"

"Not yet, although we have only gone through one test. But I am not really excited about running more experiments."

"Then, as a representative of the medical establishment, I suggest you give him a limited number of trials, and then cut him off. You're not an animal; you're a human being."

"That is sound advice. I shall do that."

"I'd like to see the prosthetic arm. I had promised Dr. Pogue to incorporate embedded cleats to help reduce the complexity of the attachment mechanism. I'd like to see how you addressed that issue."

The waiter leaned over and handed each of them a card.

Sparky smiled. "The dreaded dessert list! This place is fiendish, I tell you."

Erasmus wondered to himself, *"What is a cannoli Siciliani? I know that canna is Latin for 'reed.' Could they possibly be following this lovely meal with a dessert of Sicilian marsh grass?"*

MUNDANITY

BY DR. KATHERINE L. MORSE

"I'm afraid I've eaten so much of the delicious dinner that I cannot possibly eat any dessert, no matter how tempting it might be."

The waiter made a face at Sparky that looked like she had suggested that Bordeaux was superior to Chianti.

Drake chimed in, not wishing to make his date watch him eat dessert alone, "I am quite full as well, although the cannoli pique my interest," but he couldn't really get the idea of marsh grass out of his head.

The waiter sniffed, turned on his heel, and left. He returned a moment later with the check, all without saying a word. Drake and McTrowell looked at each other as if to say, "Well, what was that all about?"

"Edmond, dearest, it's time to come away from the lab. Dinner is ready," Esmeralda called down the stairs.

Drs. Pogue and Young looked up from where they were tinkering with the leather harness for his new mechanical arm. Yin asked him, "Would you like to put the harness on?"

Edmond winced slightly at the thought of more chafing. "Esmeralda, what's for dinner?"

"Beef stew with dumplings."

Pogue replied to Yin, sotto voce, "I don't think that will be necessary," relieved at the thought of a meal he could eat without employing both a knife and a fork. Yin smiled a little sadly at him. It pained her to see him suffering, no matter how brave a face he put on it. He called up to his sister on the landing, "Has Miss Slate arrived yet?"

"Miss Slate?"

"Yes, I had Bingham deliver her an invitation to join us for dinner. I'm keen to hear how her trip to Carlisle with Howgill went."

"Carlisle? Howgill?" Esmeralda fairly choked on the implication.

"I believe they're making excellent progress on their plans for the new mill in Carlisle. Miss Slate has promised to bring her plans for the new loom design. This is a very exciting development!"

Sarah Slate was already standing in the dining room when the Pogue siblings and Yin entered. Esmeralda hung back when she saw Sarah. Oblivious as always to the tension between the women, Edmond strode right up to Sarah and took her hand. "Miss Slate, I'm most anxious to hear about your adventure up north. Did you bring the drawings?"

"Of course!" She happily spread out the roll of drawings she held tucked under her arm. Edmond and Yin huddled around the unfurled paper, but Esmeralda stood stock still in the doorway. As her inquisitive colleagues poured over the details of the plans, Sarah stood up straight, took a deep breath, and turned around.

"Esmeralda, I wanted to tell you how much I enjoyed your costume for the masquerade ball. It was quite ingenious. Did you design it yourself?"

Miss Pogue was struck dumb for an instant. When she recovered from the shock of the warmth of the inquiry, she replied, "Why yes, I did. Thank you. But I had quite a bit of help with the execution."

"Whoever made the dress should employ you. You have a real gift for design."

It took Esmeralda a moment for the enormity of this compliment to sink in. "I should see that dinner makes its way to the table." Her head was buzzing with ideas as she made her way to the kitchen to tell the cook to serve dinner.

Meanwhile, Sarah was mentally sending a small thanks to Charles Howgill. His tutelage on human relationships was already proving to be valuable. She allowed herself the small hope that she would continue to enjoy his instruction and company for a long time to come.

"Dr. McTrowell, should I hail us a cab?"

"No, thank you. After that marvelous dinner, I think a bit of a walk would be a good idea."

"I quite agree. I am pleased to learn that you enjoyed the meal. It seems that you and I have shared quite a bit of excitement, but rarely peace and quiet."

She chuckled as she took his arm. "Truer words were never spoken, my dear Chief Inspector. I shall have to write this in my journal, 'July 8, 1851: Chief Inspector Drake and I had a quiet dinner together.' When I'm an old woman, I'll marvel at the mundanity of the entry."

"Mundanity?" He nearly pouted.

"I didn't mean it like that. I only meant that you and I seem to have one adventure after another with barely enough time to catch our breath. I very much enjoyed catching my breath this evening." She leaned in as if to kiss him, but stopped cold.

"Are you all right, Sparky?"

Under her breath, she said, "Give me a quick kiss and then turn around slowly as if we're going to continue walking down the street. Look to your left as you do so."

By now he knew better than to question her instructions, nor did he wish to decline the invitation of a kiss. Sadly, it would have to be a brief one. He kissed her softly on the lips, lingering just a little longer than necessary. He glanced to his left as he raised his head. She pulled his arm tight to her side and put her head on his shoulder so she was close to his ear. "Do you see those two men across the street loading a crate onto a cart?" He nodded as if she had just whispered a sweet nothing into his ear. "Isn't that Mr. Horace Hedgley and his associate, Mr. Martin. What are they doing in London?"

ONE THING RIGHT

BY DAVID L. DRAKE

The main street of Clerkenwell enjoyed the steady illumination of a dozen or so gas lamps, which might have been fine to throw light on an evening stroll, but was a bit deficient for serious labor. In the darkness between two of the lamps, the sounds of a pair of men laboring with a heavy object could be heard.

The crate was incredibly heavy for the two men to lift. The cool air of the evening helped a little, but both men had still sweated through their jackets and stained their bowlers. The cart springs groaned as they loaded the weight onto its back, and the cart's horse had to take a few steps to maintain the cart's balance. Both men stopped to bend over and catch their breath, bracing their arms on their knees. Between deep breaths, the taller man started a new conversation.

"You know, Mr. Martin, we could simply vanish, leaving this insanity to Monsieur Punaise. Loading black market clockwork parts in the middle of the night. What rubbish! And to think I got an engineering degree … for this! What do you say we simply make good an escape and start over?"

"I've always looked to your business sense, Mr. Hedgley, but I dare say it's going to be hard to run away from our own business. We own it together, although you have the majority share. Monsieur Punaise is a contractor! Should we run away from our fiduciary responsibilities because we have sourced our work to a mad man? If it's our losses you wish to cut, we should simply stop doing business with him."

"He has us over a barrel! If we cut our ties to Monsieur Punaise, we lose access to all of his knowledge and the plans he's proposed. If he's right, we stand to make a great deal of money!"

"While you ponder this momentous decision, let's go fetch the last two crates, so we can get some sleep tonight. The longer we delay, the greater the chance we'll be asked why we're loading crates from the back of a gear maker's warehouse. I only hope the guard will still have the exit door ajar."

The men righted themselves and begrudgingly headed back toward the nearby alleyway.

Across the street, Erasmus and Sparky watched from the shadows. When the men had turned the corner and were out of earshot, Sparky looked quizzically at Erasmus. "From their accents, it makes sense they're here. They sound like educated Londoners. Given their conversation, or what little I could hear, they're caught up in some dubious business. Again!"

Erasmus opened his jacket and glanced at what he had with him. No knife, no cane, and certainly no pistol. Earlier that evening they just did not seem to be the right things to bring on a date. "Neither of us is dressed or equipped to track them. Perhaps we should leave this until tomorrow and since, we know their names, I could …"

Sparky cracked a wry little smile as she interrupted him, "Is my date not a man of action? What should we do?"

Erasmus played along, musing, "I could run over and cling to the bottom of the cart, staying there until they finish loading more of their ill-gotten goods. Figure at least a half-hour of mind-numbing grasping. Then they will take their cart over the roughest of London's roads to hide from the main thoroughfares while I try my best not to lose my grip or bump my head, which would reopen my wound. We cannot have that. It would leave a tell-tale trail of blood. Then they will pull to a stop after twenty miles of my hugging onto a rusty rotating axle in my finest clothes. I would leap out, defeat both of them, some number of contracted henchmen, and perhaps the tall French maniac who probably followed them here from France, using just my bare hands, tired as they be. I would then pull out the one tool I have, my policeman's whistle, and signal for assistance. Tweet! Tweet! Case closed!!"

"Ahh, you have it all backwards, my good Chief Inspector. I will sprint into the alley in these dress boots, in an instant determine where they are and what crimes they're committing and, ignoring the shoulder injury and the lengthiness of my dress, punch and kick them into submission along with any of their accomplices. Then I'll secure their hands and feet by tying them up with their own braces. You will saunter in and arrest them for whatever crimes are obvious from their 'ill-gotten goods,' as you put it and, by one o'clock in the morning, you'll have finished all of the proper paperwork for the arrest. Best first date ever!"

They chuckled to themselves, left the shadows, and headed to the nearest corner to hail a cabriolet. Erasmus thought to himself, *"She got one thing right. Best first date ever."*

Herr Euler

By Dr. Katherine L. Morse

They both laughed so hard they almost fell over. "Chief Inspector Drake, I hadn't imagined you to have such a gift for irony."

"I will take that as a compliment, thank you. And please call me Erasmus."

"Well, Erasmus, I have something back at Lord Ashleigh's residence that I would like to share with you."

He studied her face for a moment, attempting to divine what this "something" could be. "Very well," he replied but somewhat diffidently.

Once Virat had admitted them to the row house and gone to fetch them chai, Erasmus settled himself in a comfortable chair in the sitting room. Sparky went up to her room, collected her notebook, and joined him. She opened to the diagram she had sketched on the train. Drake glanced at it, thought about its possible meaning, and asked, "Hello, what is this?"

"It's a graph, a fascinating field of mathematics. Graph theory is used to describe relationships between things. Herr Leonhard Euler first used it to reason about whether one could cross all seven bridges connecting the island in the Pregel River in Königsberg without crossing any of them twice. For his inquiry, he represented the banks of the river as vertices," she pointed to the circles on the page, "and the bridges as edges," she pointed to the connecting lines. "There have just been too many coincidences for my taste lately, and I was curious to attempt to discover any relationship. I started this exercise this morning on the train."

"Fascinating. This could be a very useful tool for police investigations. Do the arrows indicate the direction of an action?"

"Yes, you've understood the symbology precisely. Do you see how Abusir's interest in the statue of Osiris leads to you, or rather leads me to you, as this graph is from my perspective?"

"Yes."

"I've used a single line to indicate that I think this is merely a coincidence." She paused for an instant and smiled with one corner of her mouth, "but a happy one." Drake smiled back at her. "The question marks indicate relationships I know exist, but whose origins may or may not be relevant to the purpose of my inquiry. For example, I don't know how you and Dr. Pogue became acquainted."

"That is an intriguing tale."

"And one I would delight in hearing. However, this evening I want to draw your attention to the box with the question mark in it. The dotted lines indicate relationships whose intentionality I can't determine. I've added the box to highlight my thesis. I saw Miss Sarah Slate boarding the same train on which I was traveling with a gentleman I didn't recognize. Since they were embarking at Carlisle, which is a mill center, I surmised that he was probably Mr. Charles Howgill, a friend of Esmeralda Pogue's who may be helping Miss Slate with her chameleon fabric."

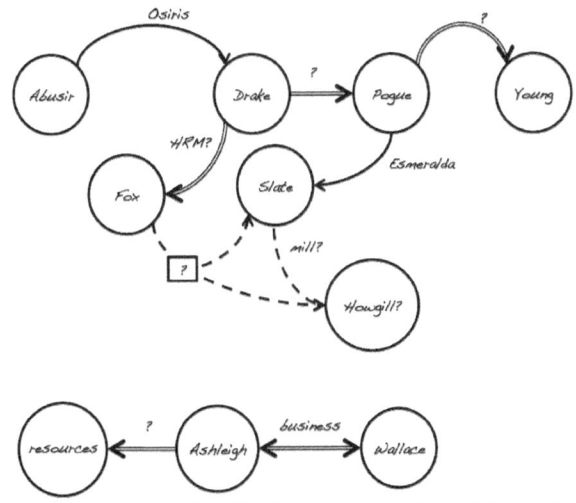

"Is this Sergeant Fox?" Erasmus interjected impatiently.

"Quite right."

"What is his relationship to Miss Slate and Mr. Howgill?"

"That's precisely what I'm wondering. He was tailing them. Why would Sergeant Fox concern himself with the comings and goings of a fabric designer and a mill owner? Certainly he was acting at the behest of someone else."

They were both staring intently at the page when the door opened, and Jonathan Lord Ashleigh entered followed by Virat with the silver tea service. "Good evening, my good friends. What are you about?" He peered over their shoulders as Virat poured steaming cups of chai. He gagged out an uncomfortable little cough.

"Dr. McTrowell was just explaining graph theory to me and illustrating the astounding interconnectedness of our recent acquaintances."

"Erasmus and I were leaving dinner when we spotted Mr. Hedgley and Mr. Martin. I thought I should add them to the graph I started on the train this morning." Lord Ashleigh took a sip of chai from the cup Virat handed him. "Oh, I should add a link between the two of you. And then there is this interesting 'coincidence.'" She pointed at the box connecting Fox to Slate and Howgill. "I spotted him following Miss Pogue's friend, Miss Sarah Slate, and a gentleman friend of hers at the Carlisle train station. I can't imagine what his interest in them might be. Lord Ashleigh, are you quite well?"

"Yes, my dear. I must have just swallowed wrong." Virat and Lord Ashleigh exchanged an anxious look behind the backs of Drake and McTrowell, who were focused on updating the graph.

"I canno' tell ye haw thrilled I am to be letting me mother's auld cottage. It's a wee bit dusty since it has no' had her tidy hand since her passing."

"And ze prize includes ze barn in back?"

"But o' course."

"Excellent!" The bug-eyed twig of a man with a shock of wild, frizzy brown hair handed the landlord two sovereigns, which the latter happily pocketed without question. He handed his new tenant a key.

"Mrs. Haversham will be by tomorrow to see to the cleaning and the marketing."

"Zat weel not be necessary."

"Suit yourself."

Monsieur Punaise watched the landlord walk out the garden gate and down the lane. He immediately exited the back of the cottage and entered the barn. He paced its length and width. He stood in the center, mentally arranging equipment. He paced its length and width again. He proceeded through the back of the barn to the stream running behind it. He was assessing the volume of flow when he heard a cart creaking up the lane. He walked back around to the front of the barn.

"What took you zo long?"

"The guard at the gear maker's warehouse was feeling underpaid. He left before we were finished loading, and it took us half the night to find a way back in. We missed the early train."

"Unload in ze barn. We must get started right away!"

The Three Tests

By David L. Drake

Erasmus and Sparky sat in Lord Ashleigh's sitting room during the uncomfortably quiet minute after discussing the graph. Lord Ashleigh was unusually silent. The couple gave each other a knowing look, and Erasmus announced, "Well, I really must be going. I plan to meet with Dr. Pogue in the morning. Dr. McTrowell, it has been the loveliest of evenings. We must do this again some time."

"Yes, we must. I had a fabulous time. May I see you to the door?"

On the stoop, the pair embraced. Erasmus whispered in his date's ear, "not to spoil the moment, but is it possible that Lord Ashleigh was surprised to see Her Majesty associated with Sergeant Fox in your graph?"

She whispered back, "no, I don't think so. He is in Her Majesty's Aerial Marines. And, yes, you're spoiling this moment. Kiss me and get home safely."

The sun was coming up as three men opened and inspected the last of the crates. Monsieur Punaise stretched and walked outside, feeling the feeble warmth of the morning. He put his hands on his hips and looked around. He liked the size and location of the barn. It had been used to hold hay and grain for years, although it was now empty of both. The dry dust of the previous contents lingered and swirled in the air as the other two men walked out. Monsieur Punaise smiled as he thought of the structure as an excellent laboratory and assembly plant. Just a little cleaning and organizing was all that was needed.

Mr. Hedgley started the early morning conversation. "Monsieur Punaise, why are we starting fresh? The EPACTs seem like a great place from which to begin. We put a good deal of engineering into them, as you know."

"Meester Head-jelly. Zat eez a good question. Ze EPACTs had some fundamental flaws, weech we weel not repeat. Ze new mechanisms weel not be controllable by just anyone zat can make a high-pitched zound. Zey weel be able to repair zemselves, as well as assemble new mechanisms, to some extent. But most importantly, zey weel not be blind."

This short speech took Mr. Hedgley and Mr. Martin by surprise, causing them to stare briefly at Monsieur Punaise. Somehow, in this quaint cottage and barn, the three of them planned to build the most extraordinary machines in creation and release them upon the world.

꠸꠸꠸꠸꠸꠸ ☺☺ ꠵꠵꠵꠵꠵

Erasmus clanked the large doorknocker at Dr. Edmond Pogue's residence. Since Edmond had invited Erasmus to call, he answered the door himself, his classic smile on full display as he looked around the door.

"Jolly good of you to come by. And right on time. Splendid."

As the door swung fully open, Erasmus noticed that Edmond wasn't wearing his prosthetic arm but instead had his left sleeve rolled up just short of the amputation site. He thought it improper to ask so early in the conversation why Edmond wasn't wearing it. Perhaps later.

"So nice to see you again, Dr. Pogue. You seem in fine spirits this morning."

Edmond motioned for Erasmus to walk with him toward his laboratory as they talked, and Erasmus complied with the unspoken request. The door shut, and they made their way down the hall.

"So far it's been a great day. Many things accomplished. But more to the point of your visit, I received your letter. Your request made a good deal of sense, and I accede to your wishes."

"I appreciate your willingness to do so. I simply want to limit the number of times that we perform these experiments. I understand that you have only administered one so far, but I must consider my duties to the Yard. I also do not want to," Erasmus hesitated, "endanger new relationships. I just do not know how these, well, drugs if I may call them that, might affect me."

"Quite understandable. Actually, I asked you here because I want to perform one last experiment. Only one more, and we're done."

"Really? I am relieved to hear that." Erasmus suddenly felt that he might have limited the scientist's ability to fully understand the phenomenon surrounding the green concoction and his baffling reaction. However, it could be that, by limiting the quantity of trials, he would force Edmond's hand in getting to the heart of the matter.

As the pair of men descended the curved staircase to the lab, Erasmus saw Dr. Young keeping a close watch on a complicated arrangement of various shapes of glass beakers and oddly contorted glass tubing coupled by rubber plugs. A familiar-looking green liquid was flowing from receptacle to receptacle, sometimes heated, sometimes chilled, and eventually dripping out of an opened spigot into an ordinary drinking glass. By the time the men reached the laboratory floor, Yin had closed the tap and was looking happily at the resulting fluid, holding it up to the light with two hands, verifying its color and temperature.

Edmond gestured to a chair and asked Erasmus to have a seat. He nervously complied. Yin handed the half-full glass to Edmond, who smiled pleasantly at receiving it.

"Erasmus, this is what I'd like to do. Dr. Young and I have synthesized a stronger version of the blended potion. I would like you to drink the same amount as before, eight ounces. I will then ask you to attempt three tasks. Then I'll make my assessment. Is that acceptable?"

"That sounds reasonable enough." Erasmus tried to sound strong. He was doing his best to hide his feeling of creeping doom. *"Jumping into a fog-filled gully. Running in the woods in darkest night. Taunting an immense sleeping beast with a short stick."* He forced these metaphorical thoughts away as best he could. "I am ready," he declared out loud, hoping he would convince everyone including himself.

Edmond handed the liquid to Erasmus. Erasmus looked at it for a second and then at Edmond, who responded with a "drink up" gesture. Erasmus closed his eyes and complied. The anise-flavored spirit seemed slightly more viscous and aromatic than before. He rolled it around his mouth and swallowed hard. He opened his eyes and noticed that Yin had stepped closer, holding a laboratory notebook and readying her pen for scribbling observational notes.

Dr. Pogue started a chronometer to record event times. While looking at it to make sure it was running correctly, he explained, "I'll give the mixture thirty seconds to take effect. While that's happening, tell us how long you've lived in London?"

"I came here when I was fourteen, so it has been about twenty-one years."

"And you prefer walking to getting rides, do you not?"

"As you know, I do. Good for both the mind and spirit."

"Have another sip and close your eyes." Erasmus obeyed the simple request. Dr. Pogue continued. "Imagine that you're walking from Victoria Park to Grosvenor Square, and you want to take the shortest route, sticking to named streets rather than taking alleys, crossing parks, or traversing green spaces. What route would you take?"

Erasmus felt the second sip drive the potion's effect on him even more than before. He could imagine the entire course in his mind all at once, as if he could fly over it. He even smiled at the prospect of being a homing pigeon dodging buildings as he rapidly flew back and forth between the two locations. With his eyes still closed, Erasmus asked his testers, "Ready?"

"You may begin," Yin replied.

Erasmus started naming the streets as quickly as he could utter them as his imaginary homing pigeon darted over the fabricated urban surroundings. Yin fell in to a pattern of quietly saying, "yes, yes," as she tried to keep up with Erasmus.

"… and then you continue west on Oxford Street until turning south on Duke Street, which leads to Grosvenor Square."

Edmond exclaimed, "Good!" while he showed his chronometer to Yin, who jotted down the time. "That was test one. On to test two. Did you ever read The Parish Boy's Progress?"

"Oh, yes. I read it after I … er … while I was in school. I … could relate to the story. I always thought of it by its other title, Oliver Twist."

"Excellent. Tell me about the second chapter, as much as you can remember."

Erasmus looked off into the distance. He thought back to when he read the book. He had borrowed it from his friend, René, a short time after they escaped the orphanage and were living on the street. Erasmus remembered taking it out of his rucksack and flipping through the pages. The pages came into focus, one by one. Fifty-three chapters, most of them short. Chapter one was just two pages long, but chapter two was seven and a half pages long. Chapter two started with a long title and an interesting first sentence. "Chapter two is entitled 'Treats of Oliver Twist's Growth, Education, and Board.' It begins 'For the next eight or ten months, Oliver was the victim of a systematic course of treachery and deception. …'"

Erasmus continued on, simply reading the page that was in his mind. It wasn't difficult to recall; the words were right there on the pages his young hands held open. He could even continue reading while looking at the accumulated dirt under his thumbnails and thought to himself that he would never handle a book today while coated with that much grime. "'… Occasionally, when there was some more than usually interesting inquest upon a parish child …'"

Erasmus was nearing the end of the first page, when Edmond stopped him. "That will be enough, Chief Inspector. Well, that was delightful! Just delightful! I don't think Dr. Young was planning to write a word-for-word account. Jolly good. Now on to our third test."

Yin set down her notepad and pen and rounded the table to retrieve a large, sturdy wooden ball. Its girth was just enough that it was too large for Erasmus to hug and touch his hands on the far side. Yin placed the ball in an open area of the laboratory on a sizable floor rug and placed a footstool next to the wooden ball.

Dr. Pogue gave Erasmus one of his broad smiles, explaining, "This will be a dexterity test. I'd like you to stand on this ball, balancing by yourself. Have you ever attempted this?"

Erasmus had never attempted such a thing before, although he had spent most of his early childhood standing on the rolling deck of a ship and had done a number of balancing tricks as part of his street performances in his teens. But not this. He shook his head to indicate to Edmond this was not in his bag of tricks.

He stood, removed his jacket, untied and took off his shoes, stripped his feet bare of socks, walked over, and stepped up onto the stool. Yin steadied the ball. Erasmus put one foot on top of the ball and tried to imagine how he was going to get the other foot and his weight up onto the ball. After a half second of consideration, he figured this wasn't something he could puzzle out, but rather he needed to commit and figure it out on the fly. He committed to the step, trying his best to put both feet near the top of the ball.

His step was lively enough, but even with Yin's efforts to steady the sphere, the ball rolled immediately away from Erasmus, taking his feet with it. Erasmus fell with his feet over his head. He tried his best to catch himself with his left arm. In an instant, he was on his back on the floor, his left elbow smarting from its collision with the rug and floor. Erasmus noticed the shape next to him and was amazed that he hadn't hit his head on the stool as he went down. He looked at his testers and was again amazed that they hadn't jumped to his assistance nor had they called off this last trial. *"Well, this is silly,"* he thought. *"There must be a reason they gave me this ridiculous test."*

As Erasmus stood and straightened his waistcoat, he thought hard. *"Have I ever seen anyone perform this skill? Yes, yes, I have. At a street fair in London. A young athletic-looking man performed atop a ball smaller than this one. He was also juggling three brightly-colored pins in various patterns while walking the ball around a collection basket. I only glanced at him because I was there on duty, tracking a thief. How did he move? He kept his feet farther apart, almost shoulder-width, and held his arms up for balance."*

Erasmus closed his eyes and took a second to imagine the man on the ball. He slowed down the actions in his mind, concentrating on each body movement, particularly the performer's shifting of weight from foot to foot. Erasmus reopened his eyes and resolutely ascended the stool again. Yin placed her hands gently on the wooden orb.

Erasmus lightly placed his right foot atop the ball but this time without the plan to put any real weight on it until he had hopped up and was able to place his other foot farther away on the other side of the ball while maintaining a crouching position.

Up he sprang off his left leg, anticipating the ball roll a bit better. His left foot touched the ball momentarily, but the sphere continued in its roll. Erasmus' feet shot out from under him, away from the stool, and this time he landed on his side in a rotating bounce on the hard surface of the ball before falling onto the floor again, this time on his side. His ribs had taken the brunt of the fall on the ball, and they hurt.

Erasmus stood and concentrated. Then he ascended the stool. He tried again with a slight variation and fell hard once more.

Again he tried. And again he fell. He repeated this process twenty-three times until it was clear that his falls and the resultant insults to his frame were starting to affect his performance. He lay on the floor, panting, with perspiration covering his face and dampening his white shirt to the point of clingy translucency.

Erasmus stood and looked at Edmond and Yin. Edmond stood there with his chronometer and the notebook. Yin steadied the ball once again. They appeared unmoved by his lack of progress, his injuries, or his fatigue.

Erasmus addressed the stool, and stepped up.

Edmond took a minor step forward and signaled Erasmus to conclude his efforts. "That will be enough, Erasmus. We can stop now."

"Much appreciated. Sorry to disappoint."

Erasmus looked down at the state of his clothes and himself. He noticed that he had even bruised the little knuckles on the top of his toes on his left foot.

"Edmond," Erasmus continued, "if you happen to find the two buttons I have lost from my waistcoat, I would greatly appreciate their return."

"Of course, my good man."

Erasmus suddenly felt the full extent of his exhaustion and sat down on the stool. "Can we conclude anything from these results? Do you need time to draw your conclusions?"

Edmond smiled. He pulled out a handkerchief and handed it to Erasmus, who started to wipe his face with the welcomely dry material.

"We've learned a great deal. The challenge is how to present it to you. I'm actually a bit hesitant to tell you much at all, other than we need not perform any more experiments, which I'm sure you're glad to hear."

Erasmus didn't like the sound of that, but being ignorant of Dr. Pogue's conclusions seemed worse than knowing. "I believe I am made of stern enough stuff to hear what you have surmised. I dare say that delaying telling me will not improve the situation, if I may be so bold. So, doctor, what do you think is happening between me and this so-called elixir?"

Edmond twisted his face up a bit in thought and committed to telling Erasmus his opinion. "First let me tell you the behavior you're exhibiting. After taking the drink, you have the ability to concentrate all of your thoughts on the task at hand. Not in a super-human way, mind you, but in a manner that far exceeds what most people experience as they use the jangled mess of poorly applied reason and improperly recalled memories in their heads. It's as if the fog of recollection is lifted, and your tempo of analysis is accelerated to the extent that you feel flooded with excellent, well-organized ideas."

"I cannot argue with that. That is what I experience. Is there more?"

"Oh, yes. As we know from your previous episodes, you can intellectually learn new things more quickly, such as the inner-workings of the EPACTs. But as we found out today, you don't physically learn new things faster. You acquire athletic abilities at the same rate as a normal, able-bodied person, even when the toll of failing is high. I'm afraid that you smacked that elbow pretty hard, by the way. It was hard to remain objective while watching you repeatedly fall, but I'm afraid you had to experience failure to fully test my theory."

"I see. But I cannot say I am surprised."

"There is one more thing. Dr. Young, what was in the concoction that you gave the Chief Inspector?"

Yin looked up and to her off to her left into nowhere as she recalled the ingredients. "Oil of green and star anise, tea made from Florence fennel, coriander, juniper, and a touch of nutmeg reduced through simmering. I added simple sugar syrup to balance the bitterness and brought it to room temperature. Finally, I added a few drops of grain alcohol to make the mixture similar in aroma to Green Fantasy. I believe that was everything."

Erasmus furrowed his brow. "Wait. Pardon me. You did not give me a concentrated form of Green Fantasy?"

Edmond smiled and answered, "No, we misled you, I'm afraid. Today we presented you with a slightly thickened form of green anise tea. It shouldn't have had any more effect on you than a weak cup of Earl Gray. Ah, I see you're surprised! Good. And here's what's happening: each and every time you have had one of these reactions to Green Fantasy, you did it all yourself, because you were given permission to act this way. And bravo! You have the power to get into this state all on your own."

"I must disagree, my good doctor. I had never gone into this state of concentration until offered this drink by Mr. Rutherford."

"Think back. When you're under great pressure to act courageously, solve a life-threatening case, stand up to a villain, what's your inner state? How do you feel? Close your eyes and, again, think back."

Erasmus obeyed and let his mind wander over the situations that were the most pressured. In the middle of a broadside attack against a slaving ship. Escaping the orphanage. His first time facing a loaded weapon while empty-handed. Defending the Baroness Lovelace. Facing Professor Farnsworth's rampage. The attack on

Sparky in the Great Exhibition. Crossing swords with Queen Ishild. "I feel calm."

"In fact, you're at your best while in the same situation where most others are acting out of panic. I suggest that you seek out these situations. You abhor the ordinary day-to-day and prefer to be thrust into action. Am I right?"

Erasmus looked at the two scientists. He wondered how he could have gotten to this year of his life without knowing he was living his life specifically to satisfy this inner drive. "I fear you are correct."

Erasmus sat in silence for a moment to absorb this life-changing realization. He had one issue he kept coming back to over and over again. Was this the type of person that Sparky should be burdened with? Would he constantly be putting himself in danger to fulfill some self-destructive inner demon? Or worse, would he end up putting her life in danger as he attempted to accomplish some derring-do? He would have to think about this some more. Perhaps a conversation with James Crocker, the barkeep at Ye Olde Cheshire Cheese, would help air this out. A beer might help the process.

Wishing to change the subject, Erasmus asked, "Edmond, is there an issue with the arm? Would working in the laboratory not be easier if you wore it?"

"To be honest, the leather yoke fits nicely when the arm is not moving, but it chafes when the arm is actuated, particularly when lifting. I've written to Dr. McTrowell about it, and she replied that there are new types of steel being synthesized that can safely be secured to bone. Incredible! She's offered to install some cleats that will allow the prosthetic arm to be fastened to my remaining limb. She may be able to perform the procedure within the week. I look forward to being able to wield both a fork and a knife at the same time without discomfort."

"With your help today, I now have an even better understanding of what discomfort is. Hello! There is one of my waistcoat buttons!" Erasmus then wondered to himself, *"How will I explain to Sparky that I look like a banana that lost a boxing match?"*

CONVENIENT

BY DR. KATHERINE L. MORSE

"Good evening, Chief Inspector Drake. Good evening, Dr. McTrowell. Good lord, you look destroyed!"

"Well, good evening to you too, Lord Ashleigh. You sure know how to flatter a girl."

"I'm terribly sorry. I only meant to express concern. Would you like a cup of chai, or would a glass of port be more appropriate?"

"Tempting though the port sounds, I think a cup of chai would revive me, thank you."

"Did Dr. Pogue's procedure not go well?"

"On the contrary, it was entirely successful. It was just exhausting." Virat appeared with the evening post, which he handed to Ashleigh before pouring Sparky a cup of chai. "Thank you, Virat."

A broad smile blossomed on Lord Ashleigh's face. "A letter from my mother." He opened it before the rest of the mail and scanned it rapidly. "She's coming to London for a visit!" he announced brightly. And then he was crestfallen. "Dr. McTrowell, I'm so sorry. It seems I'm doing nothing but insulting you this evening."

"It's quite all right, Lord Ashleigh. I knew the accommodations were only temporary. And Dr. Pogue has invited me to stay with him while he recovers from the surgery."

"How convenient." But the look on his face was cryptic. Drake and McTrowell exchanged a look that said, "For whom?"

Sparky paused a beat and continued, "He has made it quite plain that hospital rest is not to his liking. Besides, if I keep eating Anu's fabulous cooking, I'll have to buy all new clothes. After Dr. Pogue's convalescence, I should actually find more permanent lodgings." She was addressing Ashleigh, so she didn't see the wistful look on Drake's face, but it wasn't lost on Ashleigh.

McTrowell descended the arc of the staircase briskly. "Good day, Dr. Young. The lab is considerably quieter in Dr. Pogue's absence."

"Yes, Dr. McTrowell."

"Your housekeeper, Mrs. Bingham, got me sorted out in short order, and I've looked in on Dr. Pogue, who seems to be resting well. I take it you've been giving him the bromide as I instructed."

"Yes, Dr. McTrowell."

"Well, then. I'll leave you to your work." She turned to leave when another figure appeared at the top of the stairs. It was none other than Miss Sarah Slate, and she was carrying a cumbersome wrapped parcel.

"Good day, Miss Slate. How nice to see you again. We haven't had a chance to talk since before Carlisle."

"Carlisle?"

"Yes, I was on the train through Carlisle last week when you boarded with a gentleman."

"Ah, yes, Charles."

Sparky turned to exchange a conspiratorial look with Yin, but the industrious Dr. Young had already returned to her task of calibrating a lab instrument.

"Charles?"

"Oh, um, Mr. Charles Howgill."

"As I suspected. And how was your visit to Carlisle with Mr. Charles Howgill?"

"Fabulous!" It was a considerably more animated response than Sparky had expected. Miss Slate held up the parcel. "In fact, I have something for Esmeralda. I think we left things on bad terms, and I owe her for all my amazing good fortune. I wanted to make up with her. Do you know if she is around?" Sparky had been through Carlisle more than a few times and could not fathom what was so marvelous there as to account for Sarah's ebullient mood.

Without looking up from her fine tuning, Yin replied, "Since the masquerade ball at Kensington Palace, Miss Pogue has found her calling designing fancy dresses for Maricela's Trapeze. I believe you may find her there."

"Fabulous! I'll look for her there and maybe something for myself as well. Good day." She dashed back up the stairs. Sparky stood in the middle of the lab, purposeless and flabbergasted. Miss Slate had never mentioned what was in the mysterious package, and then there was the inexplicable change in personality. What on earth would a normally reserved, sensible woman like Sarah Slate want with a dress of the sort that was presumably purveyed at a store called Maricela's Trapeze? And then there was Dr. Young having more of a conversation with her instrument than with her visitors. What an odd pair of women.

When Sarah exited the Pogue residence, she found a hansom cab conveniently parked at the curb. The cabbie hopped down from his perch energetically, even athletically.

"Good day, Miss. Do you need a cab?"

"How convenient. Yes, I do."

"And where should I take you?"

"Do you know a dress shop called Maricela's Trapeze?"

"Yes, I do. It's on Oxford Street. Would you like me to secure that heavy package for you?"

"Yes, that's very kind of you."

His shoulders strained at the ill-fitting cabbie's coat as he took the bundle from her and opened the door of the cab.

Shadwell was a fair piece outside the fashionable part of London, so Sarah had quite a bit of time to plan what she would say. She ran through it several times in her head, but it never came to quite the conclusion she desired.

The cab halted in front of a small shop with a very ornate sign. Half a dozen acrobats attired in Renaissance motley were performing various improbable circus maneuvers and acts of contortion, but the central figure was a woman in the brightest, most garish costume of all. She was flying off a trapeze with her arms open as if to embrace the name of the shop rendered in gold baroque font, **Maricela's Trapeze**. The windows were crammed with dressed mannequins, draped scarves, and dangling masks to rival the attire of the advertising acrobats. Sarah had no doubt that this was where Esmeralda had acquired the dress she had worn to Kensington Palace. She was still gaping at the spectacle when the cabbie hopped down, setting the whole cab to swaying. He whisked open the door. She paid him somewhat absentmindedly, and he returned her package while she still gawked. He was on his way before she collected herself to enter the establishment.

It was only then that she noticed that a corner of the paper wrapping her gift to Esmeralda was torn a bit. How annoying! If he wasn't going to keep her parcel safe, he shouldn't have offered to take responsibility for it. She tried to let her vexation go before entering the shop. Diplomacy wasn't always her strong suit. She preferred directness, but she very much wanted her interaction with Esmeralda to go well. When she felt her plan was firmly set in her mind, she stepped forward and opened the door.

She needn't have worried about how to start the conversation because Esmeralda was just inside the shop, experimentally draping swaths of fabric around a mannequin and cocking her head this way and that as she checked for effect. The tinkling of the bell on the shop door drew her attention.

"Miss Slate, what a surprise! Do you think the cranberry or magenta suits better?"

Sarah couldn't have said which suited better because she was not at all sure which was which. She tested her diplomatic skills. "I'm sure I couldn't possibly offer a more informed opinion than your own."

"Very well, cranberry it is!" Esmeralda draped one of the two pieces of fabric that Sarah would have described as red over the shoulder of the mannequin and tossed the other piece of material that Sarah would also have categorized as red over a nearby chair. "This is so invigorating! What brings you here today? Are you in need of a new frock?"

"Possibly."

"Excellent. What's the occasion? Because it must be a special occasion if you've come to Maricela's Trapeze for the dress."

"Yes, well about that. Rather, I have something for you." She held out the parcel to Esmeralda, who took it with a confused look on her face.

Miss Pogue was even more confused when she opened it. "My dear, I don't think the colors suit you at all, although it has a wonderful texture." She held up a corner of the fabric between herself and Sarah to check her assessment of the shade against Sarah's complexion. Of course, she was right. It would have made poor Miss Slate as attractive as a bucket of wallpaper paste.

"It's not for a dress for me. It's a gift for you." Esmeralda started to open her mouth to explain that it was an even less suitable hue for her when Sarah continued, "It's the fabric we discussed in your brother's hospital room."

Esmeralda stood blinking for a moment, trying to remember the conversation. Sarah could tell the instant that the memory returned because Esmeralda whirled around to face the window. She held the cloth up to the window, turning and flipping it to see it better in the sunlight. She marveled at its shift back and forth between blue and gray. "This is breathtaking! How splendid! But surely you must want it for yourself."

"No, it's a gift to thank you for all the kindness and generosity you've shown me."

"Oh, think nothing of it. How did you get it made so quickly?"

"Well, that is the other matter I've come to discuss with you. As you predicted, Mr. Charles Howgill was very interested in my idea. He has very clever loom designers at his mill in Carlisle, and he set them to work right away building a prototype from my design. This is the first run from the prototype. They are now building a full-scale loom and expect to be able to mill bolts of the fabric within five months."

"Surely you will want to keep this as a memento of this success."

"Um, no, I would rather you have it as a token of my appreciation."

"Miss Slate, you keep using words like kindness, generosity and appreciation and insisting I keep this obviously valuable and personal object. I have the strong sense that there's something you're struggling to tell me. Please stop beating about the bush, my dear."

Sarah could no longer avoid the inevitable. "Mr. Charles Howgill has asked me to marry him, and I have accepted." She felt the ensuing silence crush her as if the roof had fallen in.

"How splendid! You must let me design your wedding dress. It will surely make the society page in the *Times* and be all the rage. All the fashionable young ladies will clamor for an Esmeralda Pogue-designed wedding gown. How very convenient for you that I've taken up this vocation."

Beyond a shadow of a doubt, this was not the response that Sarah had expected. She could only stammer, "Of course."

"I'll get started right away on sketches. Oh, and I must call out for fabrics. Only the best silks and lace will do for you, my dear. Come back tomorrow at tea time, and I promise we'll be off to a shining start!"

Sarah eked out another, "Of course," before she made good her escape. She was standing on the curb in a daze when a cab approached. The same cab with the same cab driver with remarkably broad shoulders.

"Take you somewhere else, Miss?"

She was too absorbed in what had just happened to complain about his mistreatment of the bundle of cloth. "Yes, please. Howgill's Mill on Rotherhithe Lower Road."

"Yes, Miss."

For the entirety of the trip, her head was awhirl with wedding thoughts. Until Esmeralda had set the appointment for tomorrow to discuss the gown, it hadn't really occurred to Sarah that she must plan the entire affair. Growing up in Connecticut, she had always imagined that she would marry one day but that had rarely included much consideration of a wedding, per se. The ones she had attended had been simple affairs at the parish church followed by a party at the home of the bride. It was just sinking in that she was marrying a man of money and position, thousands of miles from home, and she had no mother or sisters to lend a hand. She was on the verge of tears when the answer struck her smartly in the face. She didn't quite have a sister here in London, but she had the next best thing. Surely the only thing Miss Esmeralda Pogue would like nearly as much as designing her wedding dress would be planning a fancy, society wedding. Sarah was in a positively cheerful mood when the cab deposited her at the door of her fiancé's mill. She took no notice of the haste with which the cab departed.

The cab flew down Union Road and Jamaica Road, following the same route as the road changed names. It turned left on the Borough High Street, which proved to be a bad choice because St. George's Circus really was like a circus that afternoon. The normally calm driver was nearly frantic by the time he crossed the Thames at Westminster Bridge. He needed to make one more stop before returning the cab to the bona fide cabbie. There was no avoiding the mess of Charing Cross, but Piccadilly was smooth going. The horse hadn't even come to a full stop when he leapt to the curb and sprinted up the steps of the townhouse two at a time. Fortunately, a servant answered the door almost immediately, and he delivered his message. The servant repeated it to ensure that he had the details correct before closing the door to relay the message. The cab departed at a slightly more relaxed pace.

Jonathan Lord Ashleigh glanced at the sign displaying the shop's opening hours and checked his watch. He was cutting it close, but he would take his chances. He opened the door. The business appeared to be unoccupied. Then he heard a voice from the back, a voice like warm caramel, "I'll be with you in a moment."

He was fixated on his watch when the body that went with the voice emerged from the behind a heavy brocade curtain blocking the rear of the shop, and the figure was just as noteworthy as the voice. She was tall, taller even than he. Statuesque? Curvaceous? However one might describe her, her shape was undeniably female despite her height. She was almost the same shade as Lord Ashleigh, but her features weren't Indian. Perhaps a parent from Tortola? And speaking of color, her ensemble was even more flamboyant than his, and that was saying something. She had been gawked at by the inhabitants of London more times than she could count, but rarely in so appreciative a manner. She let him stare stupidly for a moment longer. "May I help you?"

"Um." He glanced down at his watch so he wasn't staring and attempted to collect himself. "Am I too late?"

She smiled at him, perhaps a pinch wickedly. "It's never too late for such a fine customer. What can I do for you?"

"I need a new waistcoat, but it's for a very special occasion at which I wish to be the center of attention. It must be something truly unique, the likes of which no one has ever seen. A statement if you will. I was hoping for something in blue and gray."

Fresh Blood

By David L. Drake

The day was dragging on and on. Erasmus was studying his twelfth case, going over the charges brought against suspected criminals, verifying the procedures that his inspectors and constables had applied, and looking over the list of evidence. His interest was not piqued by any of it except for the fact that, out of all the cases he had looked at over the past three days, something was missing. But he would think about that later. The grandfather clock in the open floor area chimed quaintly for two-thirty in the afternoon. He looked out through the windows of his office and watched the bustle of the inspectors as they broke from busying themselves with the minutia of their jobs for their afternoon tea. Erasmus sighed and wished he were outside on the streets getting real work done. Yes, yes, Dr. Pogue was right. He'd rather do anything than this boring fact checking and would prefer chasing down some villain.

As if on cue, Bartholomew Horner walked past Erasmus' window and rapped lightly on the door. Erasmus motioned for him to come in.

"Good day, Erasmus! We haven't talked for days. Is all going well?"

"Good day. As well as can be expected."

"Hmm, that's a bit guarded. What's on your mind? How can I help?"

"I truly appreciate my promotion. And I understand your role in helping to make it happen. I just miss the excitement of working outside of the office. On the other hand, do not worry yourself. Consider it a trifling. Matter of fact, just saying it out loud has dissipated my concern."

"Don't worry. I think I can help move some responsibilities around. Sergeant Tate seems to relish the paperwork end of things. Crossing Ts and dotting Is, as it were. Let's get together tomorrow to discuss it. Unfortunately, I need to run off to a meeting with a local merchants' cooperative that feels they need more protection at night. Blaa, blaa, blaa. Everyone wants more support from Scotland Yard. Oh, before I go, this arrived for you. Perhaps it will provide some more interesting opportunities."

Bartholomew pulled a small envelope from his jacket's inside pocket and tossed it on Erasmus' desk. He smiled and left the office.

Once the door was shut, Erasmus thought, *"Well, this is the beginning."* Using his sword-shaped letter opener, he sliced open the top edge of the letter in a single stroke. The thin paper note inside was simple enough:

Meet us at 19 Cheyne Row in Chelsea at 9 p.m. For security reasons, enter without knocking. Please destroy this invitation.

The lack of signature made sense to Erasmus but was still unnerving. Was all this secrecy really needed? He quickly memorized the address. From his top desk drawer, he removed a Congreve, a friction match, which he struck on a scratch board he kept beside it. With a sputter, its flame came to life. He put the diminutive fire to the corners of both the note and the envelope, letting go of the paper as the flame neared his fingers, and permitting the fragile embers to gracefully fall into the empty dust bin. He deposited the ashes into his empty teacup. He carried the teacup nonchalantly to the indoor washroom, wet the ashes, stirred them with his finger, and poured them down the drain. *"That ought to do it,"* he thought. After thoroughly rinsing his cup, he went to join his fellows at teatime.

Erasmus walked through the night carrying his cane rather than rapping it along the cobblestones. He felt this was both stealthier and kept his primary weapon ready for wielding. This area of Chelsea was near enough to the Thames to force Erasmus to wrinkle his nose at the unpleasant odor of the city's river. Sadly, the growth in London's population had overwhelmed the municipality's sanitation capabilities, and the same river that allowed London to flourish had also taken the brunt of the overflow of the city's sewage system. The use of airships had become a welcome mode of transportation to continental Europe and beyond for those with the means to afford it, but for most of the working stiffs, both people and goods was transported on the polluted river. Erasmus couldn't help but think about the planned citywide upgrade of the sewage system and that it couldn't be finished too soon. To Erasmus, the still of the night air made the pungent aroma linger just beyond the point of ignorable. This forced him to look forward to reaching his destination.

The streets of eastern Chelsea were still alive with pedestrians as Erasmus passed through. They mainly kept to themselves, but they were an odd lot. Some were workers who labored on the docks and boats, which was clear from their demeanor and attire. Others were self-satisfied middle class, pretending to have the disposable finances to be able to afford the original art sold in the district. But the majority of them were artists and bohemians with their counterculture faux fashion and outlandish mannerisms. Most likely, they were short of means but still found enough money to keep them in wine and paint supplies. A smattering of the remainder were society's castoffs: pickpockets, urchins, drunks, and the like. This last group was the most vocal and noisy in their comings and goings. But to a person, most of them ignored Erasmus. He walked with purpose and exuded confidence. Although he was dressed nicely, he didn't look to be the type of man who would be carrying items of value. And whatever possessions he was carrying certainly weren't worth tangling with him.

The meeting location was plain enough on the outside. It looked like an ordinary "walk-up," and the second story windows were illuminated. Erasmus climbed the stone perron steps, verified the number on the door was nineteen, opened the door, and walked in. The quality of the environment changed considerably. The stairs leading up to the second floor had a cheerful rug runner, and the dark wood of the handrail and its supports shined with polish. Erasmus shut the outside door. Once sealed away from the street, Erasmus heard a cheerful conversation muffled behind the door at the top of the stairs. He climbed the staircase and opened the door to a large room appointed with overstuffed furniture, which had a blessedly, and at this point welcome, light scent of cigar and pipe smoke.

The seven men in the room had arranged themselves in various unstructured conversation circles, some chatting, others listening to an obviously extended monologue. When Erasmus closed the door, a familiar face turned to him. Sergeant Fox stood and made a beeline for the Chief Inspector, his hand out for shaking. They grasped and shook hands as old friends who had faced danger together and lived to tell about it.

"Chief Inspector, glad you could make it. You're right on time. The others came a bit early so we all could be here for introductions."

"Pleased to see you again, Sergeant. I am glad to see a familiar face associated with this endeavor."

"Let me get things underway formally. I'll take care of the introductions."

The Sergeant turned and put his hands up in a quieting motion. He announced, "Everyone, Chief Inspector Erasmus Drake has arrived. We can get started."

The rest of the room quieted, save one. From a burgundy leather chair in the far corner, a heavily-mustached gentleman huffed his discontent. "Now hold on my young friend, I was finishing my tale of how I singlehandedly sank five battle-ready junks on the Yangtze in the China War! This isn't a tale that can simply be terminated mid-sentence like the prattling of a mindless drug-addled native. This story is as invigorating as it is educational to our compatriots. The end of the account is the best part. What say you, gents? Oh, I'll just finish the bloody yarn!"

At that, he took a deep breath and, despite the concerned look of his so-called audience, he renewed his narrative. "Where was I? Oh, yes. I was swimming upstream in the Yangtze in nothing but a scratchy loincloth with black tar slathered on my face to hide me in the night. Six kegs of black powder floated behind me, also slathered in tar, lashed together and tied to my waist with a cord I'd made out of strips of the kimono taken from the dock guard, whom I had previously dispatched …"

J. B. Fox restarted the call to order, even though both he and the other man were speaking at the same time for half a sentence. "I must interrupt you, Colonel. We're on a schedule, and we must cover some groundwork tonight. Gather round, gentlemen."

Despite some tut-tutting from the Colonel, all the men gave their attention to the Sergeant, including some chair turning and rearrangement to better form a circle. Erasmus hung up his leather cape coat and bowler. J. B. offered the chair next to himself to Erasmus, who took it with a quiet "Thank you." Erasmus wasted no time before setting to the task of observing the gentlemen. All but one was at least slightly older than himself, with the exception being about Sergeant Fox's age. All were dressed as gentlemen, without additional ornamentation that would set them apart from ordinary middle-class Londoners. The Colonel, however, sported a large bushy mustache that was a continuous growth across the bottom of his cheeks all the way to his sideburns, creating a sizable, white, wooly 'W' across his face. It was simultaneously overly masculine and outrageous, making the man distinctively conspicuous in any gathering save an extravagant mustache competition.

J. B. started the meeting. "As the chairman, I want to welcome you all here for our periodic assembly. As you know, we have a new member, Chief Inspector Erasmus L. Drake of Scotland Yard. I will make introductions shortly, but first some important precautions. Although I'm covering this mainly for Erasmus, reiterating it would be good for us all. Our mission here is to serve Her Royal Majesty Queen Victoria in her pursuit of security of the British Empire. Because of our objectives and the particulars of our knowledge and actions, our secretiveness in all of our communications and dealings is of the greatest importance to the success of our overall mission. This location is secure, but outside of it, be exceedingly cautious."

The gentlemen around the circle nodded their heads in agreement. They even went so far as to look around at each other so as to bolster the importance of the Sergeant's words.

J. B. continued, "Our overall team is larger than the eight men here tonight. Many of those not present gather information and report it to us and our superiors. Our duty, the eight of us, is to carry out engagements."

Again, another circle of nods. Erasmus could have let this pass, but thought clarification would help. He spoke up, saying, "Pardon me, but 'engagements?' It sounds as if you are using that word in a unique manner."

"Yes, we are. Engagements actively change situations that are counter to the security and safekeeping of the British Empire and, as of late, our political partners. Our actions are considered military undertakings and are protected as such. As an example, you were involved with our protection of the Burke & Hare, which protected British subjects and secured our political relationships with multiple countries. To put it more succinctly, engagements are dissimilar from passive information gathering in that, when we have successfully completed one of our engagements, things have changed for the better."

The new round of head nods included a good dose of "Here, here" and other acknowledgements. Erasmus was impressed with the concurrence on the point J. B. had made.

"Now for the introductions. You all know of the Chief Inspector. His recent exploits have been covered in the news periodicals, and you all have heard my report on his accomplishments on the Burke & Hare. Erasmus, let me be the first to welcome you. To Erasmus' right is Sir Sidney Fredric Porter, Knight of the Most Excellent Order of the British Empire."

Without hesitation, Sir Porter reflexively uttered quietly, "For God and the Empire."

J. B. continued. "He earned the Order of British India in the Anglo-Afghan War and has continued his role in the British Army. Next to Sir Porter is The Honorable Jacob Lenthall, Chief Judge in Islington. He may not look as spry as the rest of us, but his knowledge of modern firearms, cannons, and explosives has been invaluable. We can thank the British Royal Navy for his training. To his right is Mr. William Fothergill Cooke, one of the inventors of the Cooke-Wheatstone electrical telegraph and one of the founders of the Electric Telegraph Company. He had a distinguished career fighting in the Indian Army, but he now brings with him the latest of technological advancements in the use of electricity and communications. We are lucky to have him here tonight, given all of his duties at the Electric Telegraph Company as of late."

Mr. Cooke animatedly hopped up and shook Erasmus' hand, adding "Pleased to finally meet you. I am personally looking forward to our working together." He sat back down as quickly as he had stood.

"Next to Mr. Cooke is Colonel Howell Michael Spreckler, who fought in the China War. Next is …"

The Colonel sat up straighter, hoping to amplify his description, "I also attended the signing of the Treaty of Nanking! The Empire obtained Hong Kong that day, back in August of '42. We …"

J. B. cut in again. "Next is Captain Herbert Harold Vaughan of the British Royal Navy. His strengths are espionage and covert activities. On his right is Army Sergeant Barrett Wentworth, a soldier decorated for long, faithful, and honorable service. I believe his last assignment was in the War of the Axe, where he fought alongside the Mfengu against the invading Xhosa and later stood fast at Fort Peddie. Now, onto our agenda for tonight."

Erasmus could tell that the introductions for these men were uncharacteristically short given their service to the Empire, but he hoped more details would be revealed over time. He had heard of most of these men before, save Sergeant Wentworth, due to their notoriety and positions.

"Our next assignment will involve some investigation. We have heard from our sources that two known criminals have been seen in the London area. Their names are Mr. Horace Hedgley and Mr. Martin. Mr. Martin's first name has not yet been determined. These men have been known to work with at least one other person whose identity is also not yet known. Their crime was not of a violent nature, per se. They were illegally mining limestone from the quarries near Paris, France. The Parisian authorities were unable to capture them. The issue at stake is that they have access to a controllable army of ambulatory metal contraptions that can act upon commands sent by various means, such as whistling. The clockworks are fast and dangerous. I've seen them myself while in Paris, but from a distance. We have a scientist here in London who has an example of one. Erasmus was directly involved in the capture of it in France. Our concern is this: whatever these men are doing in London is most likely a danger to its citizens. Rather than waiting for disaster to strike, we must investigate and take appropriate action."

A round of questions ensued, and the Chief Inspector had the privilege of answering many of them, including the nature of the EPACTs and details regarding the sighting of Mr. Hedgley and Mr. Martin. He left out the fact that he had been on a date with Sparky. No need to bring his personal life into the spotlight. However, he couldn't help but think back to the graph Sparky had drawn and that it might help determine how the details of sighting Mr. Hedgley and Mr. Martin were passed along to Sergeant Fox.

After giving the assignment, J. B. went on to cover some administrative minutia, such as the next meeting date and providing the date and time of a technical presentation that Mr. Cooke was giving to the public on his "single needle telegraphic patent" that others might want to attend.

Unexpectedly for Erasmus, J. B. subsequently distributed envelopes containing notes of payment for each of the meeting attendees. Erasmus had not negotiated a salary, so this was quite a surprise. No one else opened his, so Erasmus followed suit and stashed his away in his jacket's inside pocket.

Once the meeting adjourned, each attendee broke off to leave. J. B. quietly asked Erasmus to stay behind.

As the men took their leave, one by one, Erasmus shook hands with each, adding some pleasantry. When it was just J. B. and Erasmus, J. B. checked the stairwell to verify they were alone. Then he turned to Erasmus.

"I'll be blunt. Do you remember the story your old friend Tobias Fitzpatrick told? Well, there's more to the story. The last critical assignment we performed as a team was to help King Maximilian with a sensitive assignment. A messenger from the Town of Melköde arrived at his court, returning all the cash the King had offered, refusing to accept his payment or his terms. The messenger's name isn't important to the story. Actually, I don't think I know it. The King requested that the British Empire provide escort to return the messenger and the cash offering and renegotiate the deal. He asked us to help for two reasons: the residents of Melköde were, in a way,

British refugees. They were more our problem than his. The second is that he was trying to appear strong even though he was negotiating multiple times with a town that was known to be full of pirates and thieves. So, he left the task in our hands."

Erasmus nodded his understanding.

J. B. proceeded, "Well, this was before I was added to the team, so I don't have all of the particulars. But three of our team airshipped to Bavaria, took possession of the funds, and started the process of escorting the messenger back to Melköde by horseback. Due to inattentiveness, the group was jumped by thieves who stole the cash and killed the messenger along with one of our team members. Not considering how it would be taken, the remaining two proceeded on to Melköde with the body of the messenger. Ishild Tuttleford didn't believe their story and assumed the King had killed her messenger and kept the funds. Not surprisingly, this made matters worse, not better. The result was that King Maximilian was unhappy with our handling of the simple task, and our superiors brought me onto the team. I orchestrated our presence on the Burke & Hare to make sure we didn't have any additional issues with the residents of Melköde. Our superiors also suggested your involvement in the protection of the Burke & Hare. I'm sorry I couldn't brief you on the entire background at the time. I was also ordered to observe you during the operation. To be honest, we didn't expect to throw you into the hornet's nest, but the good news is that we persevered."

"Well, that is quite a tale. Does it end there, or is there more?"

"I've also been ordered to clean house. When this team was put together, they got the toughest and most knowledgeable chaps known. But for someone to be known, they tended to be older, proven warriors. It's time for fresh blood. That's why you're here."

"I shall take that as a compliment. Does that mean some of these gentlemen will be leaving?"

"That's what our superiors want. Decisions are still pending. This next assignment may make those decisions clearer. Glad you're on the team." J. B. smiled broadly, which seemed like a rare thing. Erasmus thought to himself, *"Excellent! I am back on the street where I belong."*

MATSUMURA SŌKON

BY DR. KATHERINE L. MORSE

McTrowell split the end of the new bandage lengthwise and tied it neatly around Pogue's stump and the protruding cleats. "There you are. The healing is progressing nicely. I'll go to the apothecary tomorrow and get you some salve to rub around the bases of the anchors. It will help with the healing and reduce the itching. I know you don't care for how the bromide makes you feel, but it's very important at this stage that you get plenty of sleep."

"I sleep quite well, actually."

"Yes, I know. Right up to the point where you dream of some improvement to your latest invention, hop out of bed in the middle of the night, and scurry down to your lab."

He looked like a six-year-old who'd been caught pinching tarts by the cook. "How do you know about that?"

"I recognize the syndrome, and my quarters are between your bedchamber and your lab. I swear if it weren't for the sensible offices of Mrs. Bingham, you'd just bunk in the lab." His attempts to prevent a repeat of the tart pinching face failed. She handed him the bromide and a glass of water. "Good night, Dr. Pogue."

She closed the door behind herself and paused in the hall for a moment, focusing past the door to her sleeping quarters toward the stairs down to the lab. She felt an unwelcome ache. As much as she was enjoying the attention of Erasmus and the companionship of Jonathan, she felt a bit adrift without some sort of task or mission ahead of her. She envied Edmond the proximity of his lab and the immediacy of his experiments and tinkering. She entered the suite of rooms Pogue had generously assigned to her. The old factory certainly had the advantage of having an abundance of square footage. She couldn't recall ever having such commodious accommodations, but for all the space, there wasn't anything for her to do with it. It was only seven o'clock, and she was already contemplating going to bed because there wasn't anything else to do but tackle the stack of books on the nightstand she had borrowed from Lord Ashleigh. Ah yes, Lord Ashleigh. If she were still his houseguest, she would just be sitting down to one of Anu's delectable, tongue-scorching creations. The thought made her even more melancholy. She shook her head. She was being ungracious. She had no business begrudging Lord Ashleigh a visit from his beloved mother.

She realized that she had reached another one of those junctures in her life where she needed to take her fate back into her own hands rather than allowing outside forces to set her trajectory. She wandered around her quarters searching her thoughts for some inspiration. That very act suddenly enlightened her. She had so much room precisely because the building was an old factory. She closed her eyes and visualized the outside of the building. Then she oriented and placed the rooms she had seen in the last few days. Dr. Pogue was too disingenuous to be hiding enormous secrets. Even accounting for Esmeralda's pied-à-terre, there must still be huge unused portions of the property. Now, where was her mechanical surgical assistant? Was it still at the Great Exhibition? It seemed unlikely that Wallace would have gone to the trouble to have it removed.

She went to bed with her brain buzzing. She found herself rereading the same page over and over again without its contents penetrating her consciousness. It didn't help that the sun was still up and wouldn't set for a more than an hour. She lay there in the gathering dusk reliving the near-death experience of being trapped in the surgical assistant as Abusir attacked. Not that she ever expected to have another such encounter in her life, but it would certainly make the apparatus easier to operate under general conditions if she added some counter weights that would enable her to manipulate it when it wasn't under power. She had designed it to work on an airship, so she had never considered the circumstance that she might not have power. If one's airship lost its steam engines, one had much more pressing concerns than the inoperability of a surgical machine. As she considered her redesign further, she realized that the surgical assistant could be operated with less power, which would in turn mean that it could use a smaller steam engine. A smaller engine would be safer and could be situated closer to the surgeon. If the steam engine were closer, she could run a line from the boiler to the surgical assistant so she could clean her surgical instruments with steam without removing them from their brackets, even during a procedure! Surely Pogue would see the value of such an enterprise and allow her to set up shop, at least temporarily, in some unoccupied corner of his cavernous dwelling. She was so excited, it was a miracle she managed to get to sleep at all.

The horizon was only faintly pink when she awoke with a start. She hopped right out of bed and wasted little time washing up and getting dressed, all the while having a mental stroll around the building. It seemed the most likely location would be in the basement adjacent to Pogue's lab, where there might still be belt conduits to the boiler room. She couldn't remember any exits from the existing lab. If the basement extended the entire length of the building, as she so fervently hoped, the entrance to the other portion must be the opposite direction, past Pogue's quarters. She turned left out her bedroom door. Her cerebral geometry paid off. There was a door to a staircase at the end of hall but off to the side where she had mistaken it for another bedroom or closet.

She descended one flight of stairs and stopped on the landing. Much to her delight, there was another flight down to the basement. But there was also a door on this level. Of course, this was the ground floor. The kitchen, dining room, what passed for a parlor, and Dr. Pogue's enormous library were all on this floor. But once again, those rooms couldn't possibly fill the entire length and breadth of the building, and they were all at the far end. What else could be on this level? With her imagination and curiosity on overload and nothing but time on her hands, she decided to delay her quest in favor of a little random exploration.

The initial result of her assessment was disappointment. A long hall paralleled the one upstairs with widely spaced, blank doors and no decoration or indication as to the purpose of the rooms hidden behind them. Although there were sconces spaced evenly between the doors, none were lit. The only illumination came from the long, narrow window at the end of the hall next to the door by which she had entered. The light from this window mostly illuminated a swirl of dust motes, and her entrance had stirred up cloud of mustiness. At least she had been correct in her calculation about unoccupied space.

She'd turned back toward the stairwell when she heard sounds down the hall: faint, rhythmic thumps and grunts. She smirked to herself. Perhaps the Pogue residence had more interesting secrets than she had originally imagined. Well, who was she to interrupt someone else's fun? She was preparing to tiptoe back onto the landing when she realized that something was not quite right. Airships and inns had thin walls, so her sample size was sufficiently large to alert her to the fact that the noises coming from behind one of the doors did not correlate with her original assessment.

She turned back around and pointed her tiptoeing feet down the passage. She was nearly to the end when she identified the portal cloaking the mysterious activity. She grasped the knob slowly and began to turn it stealthily. Well, wasn't that interesting? It was well oiled and turned smoothly. She expected that she would not find the other doors down the hall to be so well maintained if she tested them. She peered through the crack. There was considerable light above the door and to the left, but none leaked out through the gap beneath it. She didn't see anything else identifiable, so she opened the door farther. First mystery solved. There was a large, Oriental screen blocking the door from the rest of the room, obviously intended to achieve the effect that had just fooled her; the room itself was well lit, but a casual observer in the hall wouldn't be able to discern this fact. The room was also considerably cleaner than the hall. Although the wood floor was worn, it was obviously recently scrubbed, and the clouds of sneeze-inducing dust were absent.

The thumping and grunting started again. Taking care not to set the floorboards to creaking, she peeked around the edge of the screen. What she saw so astonished her that she certainly would have given herself away if the sources of the sounds had not been so entirely engrossed in their activity. The room was suffused with the early morning light streaming in through large windows that covered the opposite wall. The only furnishings in the room besides the screen behind which she was secreting herself were several large reed mats covering the floor almost to the walls. And who should be occupying this palette of padding but Sergeant Fox and Dr. Young!? To add to the incredulity of the situation, they were both attired in cotton clothing that resembled Indian pajamas and striking at each other with their hands and feet! She knew this activity had been underway for several minutes, at least since she had arrived on this floor, but neither of them seemed to be injured or on the verge of yielding, although both of them were quite sweaty. The bout looked almost choreographed, as if they were dancing rather than dueling. Then, without any obvious signal, they stopped. They stepped back from each other, smacked their right fists into the palms of their left hands, and bowed to each other from the waist, holding eye contact.

She ducked back out of view behind the screen just as she heard J.B. say to Yin, "I wish Sensei Sōkon were here to instruct us through our sparring, but I'm still grateful we can practice together."

Yin replied, "Yes, but you must go before the house awakes." That was Sparky's cue to beat a hasty, but silent, retreat. Her temporary workshop would have to wait for another day. She needed to get back to the graph in her notebook to make more additions. The blasted thing was starting to look like a bird's nest. She wondered to herself, *"Do I have time to make the changes and still catch Erasmus at Ye Olde Cheshire Cheese before he leaves for Scotland Yard?"*

The Unexpected Visit

By David L. Drake

Mr. Haversham was a worrier. He had six houses to rent, but his late mother's old cottage held a special place in his heart. He had hoped to have a young family rent it and be there for a spell. But it had stood empty for far too long, so he had to let it go to the odd gentleman who answered his ad in the local weekly and his two friends. Despite the income and the handsome deposit, it just didn't sit right with him. He knew the three men would use the place for some temporary business work, probably commercial or industrial. Either way, it would tarnish the memories and reduce the quaintness of the place. Mr. Haversham's worrying drove him to walk the two miles to the cottage to check in on the men and see that his fears were unwarranted.

"Prob'bly wasting me time," he said out loud to himself as he kicked a stone out of the road in frustration. "They don' wan' me both'ring them." But he continued on his trek, worrying.

He made his way up the well-worn path leading to the cottage. From the far side of the cottage came the unmistakable sound of a clattering steam engine, and he could see in the distance the blue-gray haze of steam engine exhaust wafting its way up into the pastoral sky. He shook his head to himself as he passed through the wooden gate.

"Hello!" he shouted was he walked up the stone steps toward the house. "Anyone home?"

He rapped uselessly on the door. After a short wait, he decided that if anyone were there, they must be near the commotion behind the cottage. He trundled around the corner and was dismayed by the scene. The barn windows were lit up like an iron foundry, and the din of manufacturing filled the air, hissing and banging with an occasional buzz of a saw. As he walked toward the barn, he even saw some sparks fly out of the main doors. Well, this wasn't how he wanted this dear cottage and its land used!

Between Mr. Haversham and the barn stood a sturdy, old well his father had made from natural stone. It had an old-fashioned hand crank with a weighted pail that worked perfectly when lowered. Mr. Haversham recalled that the water in the well was sweeter than that from the creek, and he wondered if this temporary factory was going to foul the soil, ruining the well. Mr. Haversham's ire rose. With each step, he started rehearsing what he was going to say to these "gentlemen."

Suddenly, a dark figure ran out of the barn, moving at an amazing speed. Mr. Haversham stopped dead in his tracks, frozen. The basic shape looked like a muscular dog with long legs. But instead of a full head, it had a tube resembling a snout. It ran full tilt to the well and screeched to a stop. It reared up, making Mr. Haversham gasp in fear, still frozen in place. The monstrosity poked the bucket, which went flying down into the well with a splash, and then latched on to the hand crank and turned it so quickly that it looked like a blur to the landlord.

"Lord help me ..."

When the bucket reappeared, the dog-like brute stopped its cranking and stuck its snout into the bucket. It made a ghastly sucking noise, draining the bucket of its contents and storing it, well, who knows where? In its body? It used its snout to nudge the bucket back onto the ledge of the well. It immediately dropped back down to all fours, twisted, and sprinted back toward the barn.

Mr. Haversham screamed in fright. It didn't last long since he likewise turned in place and sprinted back out of the gate and down the path as fast has his feet could carry him.

A Farthing for Your Thoughts

By Dr. Katherine L. Morse

Drake was wiping the last of the shaving soap off the square corner of his jaw when he heard a knock on his door. Ah, that would be his breakfast right on time. The day was likely to be frightfully busy, so he'd asked James to send up some victuals once he had finished his morning regimen with the dressmaker's dummies. He knew old Crocker could hear him when there was no one in the pub, so the timing wasn't that miraculous. He whipped open the door with one hand and fetched a farthing out of his pocket with the other to tip the pub boy.

"Um," Sparky murmured.

"Oh, it is you. You are not whom I was expecting."

She looked between the farthing in his outstretched hand, his bare chest, and his face. "Clearly."

"I was expecting the pub boy with my breakfast."

"Ah, that would explain why you thought it appropriate to answer the door half naked."

"Oh, dear." He made as if to cover his torso with his hands, then, recognizing the futility of the endeavor, handed her the farthing and dashed across the room to retrieve a shirt from the wardrobe. He commented over his shoulder, "Technically, I am only about a third naked."

She stood in the doorway wondering about the origins, because clearly there were multiple, of the scars on his chest and back. She heard a creak on the stairs behind her. A boy about ten years of age stood a few steps below her holding a rough tray of food and wearing a look of indecision on his face. She held up the farthing. "I'll trade you." He nodded and reached up to make the exchange before scampering back down the way he'd come. No point in arguing with an odd lady so long as there was a fair wage paid.

She flipped the door closed behind her with her foot and placed the tray on the table, by which time Drake had managed to cover himself and the map of scars. Almost all of the ones on his chest had been on the left side, either thin and clean or puncture wounds, probably inflicted by a narrow, bladed weapon. Well, no mystery there. But there were a few messier ones on his back. She filed that away for a future investigation. Curious as she might be about the stories that went along with the old injuries, they were indeed old, and she had newer and more urgent matters on her mind.

"My dear Dr. McTrowell, what brings you here so early in the morning?" He leaned forward and kissed her on the cheek. It felt a touch bold to him, but then she had come to his room uninvited, and there was no one to see the deed. And he hoped in might divert her attention from his flat. He had always found it quite workable, but since meeting Sparky, he worried that it might be too drab for the tastes of such a well-traveled woman.

His whiskers were still damp, but his cheek was pleasantly smooth against hers where he'd just shaved. She was delightfully distracted for a moment. "I'm terribly sorry for barging in like this, but I've just seen something so remarkable that I had to speak to you in private where I could be absolutely certain we wouldn't be overheard."

"Considering the things you and I have seen over the last two months, this must be truly incredible. Toast? Tea?"

"No, thank you. Oh, yes please. I'm so enervated I hadn't realized that I'm famished." He found another mug and proceeded to smear a healthy dollop of marmalade on a piece of toast while she rummaged in her Gladstone bag for her notebook and pen. She flipped open the book to the page with the graph. She waved her finger over the nest of arcs and nodes. "Do you remember how I suspected that this amount of connection couldn't be a coincidence?"

"Of course."

"This is what I just saw at Dr. Pogue's residence, obviously intentionally concealed." She drew a sweeping, double-lined, double-headed arrow between Fox and Young.

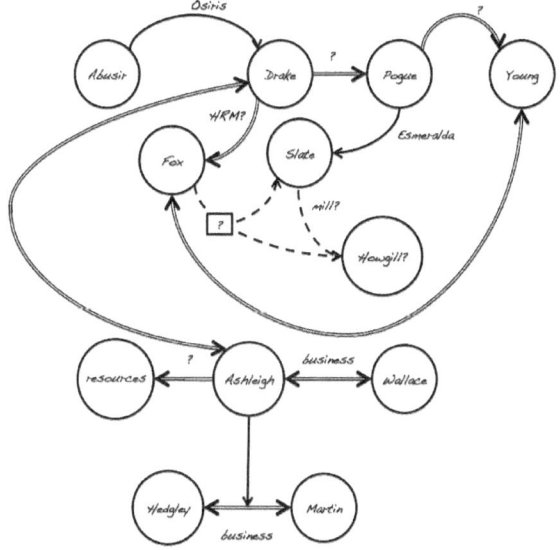

"Good lord," he sputtered. "They were fighting?!"

"They weren't *having* a fight. They were sparring, striking at each other with their bare hands and feet. It was somewhat ritualistic, but I'm quite sure the technique would be highly effective against an antagonistic opponent."

"And they were hidden?"

"Yes. I heard them when I was up early exploring the unused parts of the building. They had obviously taken great pains to hide both their location and their activity."

"Did they see you?"

"No, I was quite careful."

Drake realized he'd been clenching his fist as if he expected to have to strike someone at any instant. He thought about his meeting with Fox and the others. As much as Fox had revealed, he had clearly concealed even more. Drake sat down in the chair next to McTrowell and took a sip of tea, giving himself a moment to think. He reached over and gently closed her journal, willing it never to open to that page again.

"I want you to promise me something and understand that I am deadly serious."

"What could be so grave?"

"You must promise me that you will draw no more lines on this graph, and you will never show it to another soul?"

"It's just a few lines on a page."

"Promise me!" She started. He'd never raised his voice at her before. "I am sorry. I am not angry with you. But there are things from which I cannot protect you."

"I've been protecting myself just fine for quite some time, thank you very much." She hadn't meant for it to sound peevish, but honestly, she felt more than a bit that way.

"This is not the wild West where you can just punch someone in the nose and escape into the wilderness on a horse. This is the British Empire, and you are not Her Majesty's subject. Crown law is not on your side."

A painful silence stretched between them as she examined his face while considering what he had just said ... and not said. He felt as if his ribs were tightening like an iron maiden around his heart and lungs.

"Chief Inspector Drake, when we first met not so long ago, I was drawn to your honesty and forthrightness. For all the talk of honor in your British Empire, I find there is too little for my way of thinking. Yesterday I realized that I'm about to embark on a new chapter in my life. I had hoped you would be a part of it, a significant part. However, something has changed recently. Something that has put me at risk. Something that you know about. And yet something that you fail to share with me despite your professions of concern for my safety. Whatever it is, you value it more than you value me. Good day and goodbye, Chief Inspector."

She swept the notebook and pen into her Gladstone bag and stormed out the door, slamming it behind her. She hoped his attention had been drawn to the pantomime of anger so he didn't notice the tears forming in her eyes. She was practically choking as she stumbled past the barman sweeping the walk in front of the pub.

Drake wished his ribs would just close the rest of the way, stopping the pain in his chest. Fool! He hadn't even gotten out of the chair to try to stop her. This was not the man he was. Without realizing he was speaking to himself out loud, he muttered, "Well, Drake, you have really cocked this up."

CROSSING POULTRY

BY DAVID L. DRAKE

Standing alone in his flat, Erasmus was beside himself. He thought he'd conveyed the proper level of concern to Sparky that she was edging into a dangerous area with her graph. He also remembered the warnings he'd received at the meeting about not revealing anything to anyone. But at what cost? He had to talk to her.

Erasmus realized that he didn't even have a waistcoat on. He grabbed one and slipped his arms into it as he scampered down the steps. He stopped at the bottom, looking out of the glass in the large doors to see if he might have caught her in time.

Erasmus walked through the door, working on his waistcoat buttons. James Crocker, the barman, looked up from his sweeping. "You're probably too late, my good friend. And what, pray tell, did you say or do to make that pretty thing cry?"

"Cry? I did such a thing?"

"She was crestfallen."

"Oh, my. When she left, she was displeased with me to the point of never wanting to see me again. That was the Dr. Sparky McTrowell of whom I have spoken frequently."

"That was her? Well, don't just stand here yapping at me, you fool! She went that way down the street!" James' right arm pointed eastward.

Despite that Erasmus had not finished buttoning his waistcoat, he sprinted up Fleet Street to see if he could get a glimpse of his forlorn lady friend. It took a full block before he saw her boarding a hansom cab. Erasmus spun in place to look down the street for a similar vehicle. There one was with a lively chestnut horse and no passengers. Erasmus practically jumped out in the road to hail it and hopped up on its side before it could stop.

"Follow that cab!" he shouted, pointing to the one Sparky was in, which was now nearly a block and a half away.

The driver seemed up to the challenge. Giving a quick "Yes, Sir!" reply, and flicking his reins hard, he urged the horse to a gallop.

The clatter of horseshoes and iron-rimmed wheels filled the street. Pedestrians and slower-moving traffic dodged for the curb, panic in their eyes. Erasmus' driver snapped the reins again, this time adding a whistle, and the steed put its all into the chase.

Sparky's driver was an older gentleman and was slightly uncomfortable giving a lady a ride without a gentleman accompanying her. He was startled by the commotion behind them. "Sorry, milady," he croaked out as he started to pull the hansom over toward the curb. Sparky leaned over and looked back to see what the kerfuffle was. It was Erasmus! He was pointing at Sparky's hansom and looked earnest. Quietly to herself she said, "Well, he wants to chase after me, does he?" Then to the driver, she offered, "Driver! That hansom is chasing us! Do your best to keep ahead. There's a pretty tip for your efforts."

The driver, Jacob, acted without hesitation and shouted for his horse, Davy, to take to a gallop. Jacob had been a hansom driver for the twelve years since he had given up the business of making shoe lasts. He thought he had seen everything in this business, but taking part in a street chase was not in his nature nor to his liking. Unlike some drivers, he owned his own hansom, and any damage to it would come out of his own pocket. But he had been so used to following instructions that he committed himself to keeping ahead of their pursuer.

The two cabs charged across Farringdon Street, sending horses rearing and women screaming. Fleet Street turned into Ludgate Hill & Street. Jacob reined Davy left at the fork onto St. Paul's Street. A small clutch of parishioners gathered on the sidewalk outside of St. Paul's Church wearing mad "well, I never" faces and shaking their fists at the racing hansoms as they sped past.

Without yielding, both carts joined the traffic on Cheapside. Red-faced drivers shouted for them to slow their vehicles, but slow them they did not. Cheapside turned into Poultry and narrowed considerably.

A large cart carrying crates upon crates of potatoes was transitioning from Princes Street to Lombard Street, its single driver a fourteen-year-old boy delivering his father's crop to a nearby market.

The cart was full length across Poultry as it crossed the thoroughfare, blocking all traffic.

Sparky grabbed for the wrought iron arm rests. Jacob gasped and pulled up hard on the reins. Davy had been trained by show riders who fell on hard times before having to sell their beloved horse; he showed off one of his last remembered tricks: an all-four-legs fifteen-foot sliding stop. The hansom bounced around a bit, but both rider and driver hung on.

The chestnut horse did a quick jump to the left to avoid the back of the lead hansom, skidding clumsily to a halt. The second hansom leaned far to the right, then rocked quickly to the left, and stopped next to Sparky's cab. The driver was still clutching the reins even though he was down on his knees.

Sparky was furious. She pointed at Erasmus and said, "You … you … nearly caused an accident!"

"I just wanted to catch up with you to explain myself."

"Is 'goodbye' difficult to understand?"

"I need your help."

Sparky felt her heart soften. It was her fault she had asked the driver to stay ahead. Perhaps she should hear Erasmus' side of things. "I'm listening."

"I will explain the dangers. I need you. Please come back."

"Oh. I see." Sparky slid down off her seat and crossed to Erasmus' hansom, where he offered his hand to help her up to the seat.

"I am truly sorry for my outburst this morning. I … I want you to be a significant part of my life, too."

"Oh. I see," Sparky echoed, but more softly this time, adding, "so how can I help you?"

"I ran out of my flat without a thing in my pockets. Could you help me by covering my hansom fare?"

C. LLEWELLYN MCTROWELL

BY DR. KATHERINE L. MORSE

"Just hold your trews on! I'm not as spry as I used to be," the lady hollered as she made her way from the kitchen to the front door, wiping the flour from her hands onto her apron. She looked the visitor on her stoop up and down. His face was fortified with the expression that boys on the verge of manhood wear when they're attempting to be serious and authoritative beyond their years. "Good day, young sir. What can I do for you?"

"I have an important message for Mr. McTrowell."

"Oh dearie, you're a wee tad too late. Mr. McTrowell has been dead and gone more than ten years now."

The serious expression dropped off the face of the messenger to be replaced by one of confusion and despair. He sensed that he was about to fail in his mission. "Why weren't we notified?" He flapped his arms in panic, revealing the missive he had obviously been intent upon delivering. It was wrapped in a green ribbon fastened with sealing wax. The sealing wax bore an insignia that Miss Catherine McTrowell hadn't seen in quite some time, but recognized immediately. The young man was too absorbed in his own distress to notice Miss McTrowell do a double take.

"Ah, I'm terribly sorry. I thought you were referring to my late father. You meant my nephew. He has been in London of late. I'll be happy to see that he receives the letter." She began reaching for the message in that calm, stealthy way that one uses when trying not so spook a mouse. Unfortunately, the mouse on the doorstep was a little too clever for this ploy. He pulled his hands back against his chest.

"I'm to deliver the message to him personally." He was certainly faithful in the execution of his duties.

"Yes, dearie, I completely understand. But I'm thinking it's important that he get that message right quick, and I don't think you're supposed to be walking all the way to London." She began reaching again, more deliberately. She managed to grasp a corner. She had to give a sharp tug to get him to release it, but he gave way rather than allow the pristine letter to be torn. "I'll take this to the station and have it posted to her'im right away."

He stood stock still as if he expected her to head straight out to the station that instant. "Dearie, I can't very well go out in my apron without my head covered. I'll just fetch my coat and hat. You run along now." She made a small shooing motion with her fingertips. He wavered in indecision for a moment before heading back down the steps.

She closed the door behind herself and leaned back against it, letting out her breath in one go as she slumped forward. She paused in that position, waiting for her heart to stop pounding. That had been much too close for comfort! She stepped into the parlor and sneaked a peak out between the lace curtains. Her young visitor was just rounding the corner at the end of the street. There was no time to lose. She whipped off her apron and hung it on the coat rack by the door, exchanging it for her coat and bonnet. She snatched up the letter and her purse off the console table in the foyer and dashed out the door, heading east toward the train station.

Virat handed the day's post to Lord Ashleigh after putting it in the order he felt was most appropriate, as always. Jonathan glanced at the addressee of the plain envelope on top and raised an eyebrow at Virat. At times, Virat was very obvious in his subtlety. Ashleigh walked to the window and held the envelope up to the light. He could make out the green ribbon inside, and he could feel the dollop of sealing wax but nothing more. He didn't dare open the outside envelope for fear that his tampering would be noticed.

Virat was still lingering by the door to the sitting room. Ashleigh handed the envelope back to him. "Please forward this to Dr. McTrowell at Dr. Pogue's residence. And no need to hurry back." Virat merely nodded his head ever so slightly and departed. *"Well,"* thought the young viscount, *"this is about to get interesting."*

Lord Ashleigh had finished reading the rest of the letters and his newspaper and had moved to his writing desk to answer some correspondence when Virat returned a couple of hours later.

"What news?"

"I delivered the letter into Dr. McTrowell's hands," Virat reported. "She opened the outside envelope. The inside envelope was addressed to C. Llewellyn McTrowell and bore a seal."

"What did the seal look like?"

"A circle in the center over a saltire with rays between the arms of the saltire. There was something in the center of the circle and lettering around the edge, but I couldn't see it well enough to identify either."

"And then?"

"Dr. McTrowell appeared very agitated. She thanked me and left the room. I waited on the street out of sight for three quarters of an hour. She came out wearing her traveling clothes and carrying a small bag. She hailed a cab that took her to the airship port where she went into the office of Western & Transatlantic. I couldn't follow her without being seen, but I waited another half an hour, during which she didn't leave. There is only one more airship flight tonight. It goes to Edinburgh at ten o'clock."

Lord Ashleigh snapped open his pocket watch and looked at the time. "I hate to ask this, old friend, but please go tell Anu to hold dinner. I'll have another message for you to deliver this evening, and it must go right away." He reached for a fresh sheet of monogrammed parchment from his writing box, pushing aside the missive he had been composing. It took him only a couple of minutes to scribble the critical details and seal the letter. Virat had returned from the kitchen and was waiting when he finished. "Deliver this to Prince Albert, and no one else."

The overnight flight to Edinburgh was lightly occupied. Since the flight already had a pilot and co-pilot, Sparky was seated with the passengers. Most of them were slumbering, or at least attempting to do so, and paid her no attention. She mentally inventoried the contents of her bag, hoping her aunt would have the items she still needed before tomorrow evening. This business of not having all her belongings in one place was becoming more than simply a bother. She made a mental note to start looking for a more permanent residence when she returned to London, assuming that the next day didn't result in her needing to flee this island nation in haste.

She hadn't really had enough time to alert her Auntie Catherine to her impending arrival, not that such a notification would have been advisable under the circumstances. One could never be sure who was watching which avenues of communication. Besides, her aunt would almost certainly be expecting her, or she wouldn't have forwarded the letter. Despite her promise, she hadn't expected to be seeing her aunt again so soon.

As she had expected, there were no night trains to Stirling. She checked the times for the morning trains at the station and then found a small inn just off Princes Street. It wasn't very fancy, but it was clean, and she only needed a place to sleep for the night. By catching the first train, she was at her aunt's front door by half past nine the next morning. The door opened even before she reached the stoop.

"Come inside quickly, dearie, before someone sees you." Sparky didn't need to be told twice. "Tea?"

"Yes, please. How did you know I was coming? Did you read the summons?"

"No, I didn't have to. I've been keeping an eye out the window ten minutes after every train from Glasgow or Edinburgh since yesterday morning. I knew there was trouble as soon as I saw that damned seal, pardon my language, dearie. Your grandfather was a hard-headed fool for cooking up this charade. It's no wonder your father came out the way he did." She handed Sparky a hot cup of tea and one of those heavenly cream scones.

"Well, what's done is done. I have to be up at the castle in time for afternoon tea. Do you still have any of grandfather's old shirts and tartan trews?"

"I think there might still be some in a trunk in the attic. Lucky for you I didn't feel like climbing up that rickety old ladder, or I'd have long since given them over to the church. They'll need some taking in and taking up. Go climb up there and see what you can find. I'll fetch my sewing basket."

Sparky was sneezing ferociously from the dust by the time she found what she needed and brought it back to the kitchen. Her aunt had poured her another cup of tea, which was a welcome relief for the itch in her throat.

"Well, go ahead and put them on," her aunt prodded her. Sparky took off her corduroy skirt and blouse and replaced them with the shirt and trews. She held out her arms in a way that made her look like a baggy scarecrow. "I haven't time for a proper tailoring, but a few stitches here and there and a coat to cover up the rest. Do try to find a dark corner though, just to be on the safe side." Auntie Catherine started tucking and pinning up the shirt.

"What about my hair? Maybe I should cut it off."

Her aunt looked like she would faint. "Oh, dearie, not that! I'll tie it back loosely and braid the end. We'll tuck the braid inside the collar of the shirt. If anyone says anything, you can just tell them it's the fashion in the Americas." Sparky liked that answer considerably better than facing the prospect of drastic barbering.

When she looked at the finished result in the mirror, she was once again impressed by her aunt's unusual, but practical, set of skills.

Sparky stood nervously by the front door at a quarter to two. "Wish me luck."

"I have great faith in you, dearie." Catherine McTrowell kissed her niece on the forehead and opened the door for her.

Sparky turned left to walk north to the castle, keeping her head down and walking at a measured pace, neither too fast nor too slow, so as to avoid drawing attention to herself. She reached for the summons from the inside pocket of her coat as she approached the south gate of the castle. She proffered it to the steward stationed there. She said simply, "I'm expected."

"Indeed you are," he responded brusquely. She had expected to be directed to the Chapel Royal. Instead, two members of the Black Watch appeared from just inside the gate. Without a word, each one took her firmly by an arm and steered her into the casemate on the west side of the castle. They only released her arms once they had closed the door firmly behind themselves. They stationed themselves between her and the door.

Sitting in a chair that was incongruously ornate for the setting, which was not unlike a cellar despite its being above ground, was the reason for the security to which she had just been subjected.

"Your Majesty. I'm at a loss for words."

"That is just as well as we have many words for you. We are unaccustomed to being duped by our subjects and look even less kindly upon being duped by those who are not even our subjects. There was a time not long past when we could have dispensed with such traitors without the slightest interference. While you have not been entirely secretive in your movements this last day, the only person who knows your whereabouts and intentions precisely is your maiden aunt. She is hardly in a position to provide a meaningful defense, particularly as she is a co-conspirator."

Sparky felt the room getting colder and her knees preparing to give way. She glanced around to try to collect her bearings. She focused on the young man who was standing by Queen Victoria's side. He was so still that, if not for his breathing, he might have been a mannequin ... and looked remarkably like her. He was only slightly taller and broader in the shoulders, but he had the same hair and eye color as she. He could have been her twin brother or a first cousin. And he was wearing remarkably similar clothes, although his were considerably newer and better tailored.

The Queen continued, "We would never have acquiesced to admitting your grandfather's half American 'grandson' into the Order of the Thistle, except that we were grateful for his faithful service and sympathetic to his disappointment in his only son." Sparky had to smile in agreement with the last statement. "While we are grateful for your service in the recent unpleasant business in Bavaria, there are still rules. Women are not permitted to be members of the Order of the Thistle. Charles Llewellyn McTrowell was acceptable. Czarina Llewellyn McTrowell is not."

A hopeful flush of relief washed over Sparky. The Queen was only going to eject her from the Order. She wasn't going to cut off her head! She had always found the Order a little stuffy anyway, and she had only acceded to her grandfather's wish because it made the old man feel a bit better about her father's failings. "I understand, Your Majesty."

"No, Dr. McTrowell, you do not. As you are generally an observant individual, you have almost certainly noticed this young man." She gestured over her shoulder without taking her gaze off Sparky. "His garb is entirely intentional. You must now make a choice. As you are not our subject, we cannot command you. However, as sovereign, we can deport you and prohibit you from ever returning. We can separate you permanently from persons for whom you care deeply. Do you take our meaning clearly?"

Sparky's brief warm happiness drained back out of her. "Yes, Your Majesty."

"Our agent will approach you shortly. You will do precisely and entirely as he directs. If you agree, you may proceed to the Chapel Royal and the meeting as you planned. If you do not agree, 'Charles' here will take your place at the meeting. The Black Watch guards behind you will shackle you and carry you bodily from this room. Your feet will never touch the soil of our land again. Choose wisely, Dr. McTrowell."

Sparky wanted to simultaneously cry and shout. This must be what Drake was so worried about protecting her from. And now she was right in the middle of it. Correction. They were right in the middle of it! She couldn't imagine anything more dangerous than what they had already been through together, and they would continue to be in together. "I choose to stay, Your Majesty."

"An excellent choice, Dr. McTrowell." The Queen rose from the chair and the Black Watch guards opened the door for her. "And for heaven's sake, change clothes with 'Charles.' You look as if you have been living in an attic for a decade."

EMPTY HAND

BY DAVID L. DRAKE

It was well past eleven o'clock when Sparky exited the Chapel Royal through a gauntlet of hardy handshakes and "So pleased to meet you" speeches. She was practically hoarse from using her lowest octave to croak out "Just call me C. L." and "So glad we finally met" and all of the associated social niceties that one exchanges with complete strangers.

Through all of the smiles and nods, her inner voice recited, *"Why did I follow through with this insane idea? Becoming a knight? In a society that doesn't permit women or foreigners? And, on top of all that, displeasing a monarch who now wants favors?"* As she hurried away to return to her aunt's home, she thought back over the ritualistic protocols and formalities she had just endured for three hours: the wearing of vestments and accoutrements, the call and answer chanting, and the standing and kneeling. Was this really what she wanted?

The walk back allowed Sparky to introspectively reassess her situation. She experienced the odd feeling of not belonging in any place. Did she really want to be tied to this island and its people? She loved the west coast of America, her birthplace, but she was too worldly now to live there. She wanted to see more of the world, but she was making ties in Great Britain that might make her globe-trotting ways more difficult. She welcomed the site of her aunt's front door as it came into view and the opportunity to talk this over with a friendly ear.

As Sparky walked up to the house, Auntie Catherine flung the door open and hugged her tight, tears welling up in her eyes.

"Oh, Czarina! You're still in one piece! I was so worried!"

"What happened?"

"Two of Her Majesty's guards showed up after you left, hammering on the door as if to knock it down. They scared me so! I let them in, of course. They said that they knew about our ruse and that I shouldn't breathe a word of it to anyone! What have we done?"

"It's all right. They just wanted to frighten you into keeping quiet. It's all been worked out." Just inside her door they held each other for a while until Sparky's aunt regained her composure. *"Perhaps,"* Sparky thought, *"this isn't the best time to be discussing my problems."*

Erasmus drummed his fingers as he sat at his table in Ye Olde Cheshire Cheese. He didn't care for waiting. He was just killing time for both his beer and his dining companion, J. B. Fox. J. B. had agreed to meet Erasmus for dinner, and Erasmus was early. But that didn't make his standing by any better.

A lad in an apron rushed over with a newly drawn beer and plunked it down in front of Erasmus, causing its foamy head to cascade over the sides of the mug. After a quick nod of gratitude and a finger wipe to clear the drinking side of the mug, Erasmus raised the vessel and took a swig of the brew. Ahh, it tasted good. When he returned the mug to the table, J. B. was sitting next to him, as if he had been there all along. Erasmus smiled and started the conversation. "I see you have developed cat feet. Quite stealthy!"

Erasmus extended his hand for shaking, which the Royal Aerial Marine met heartily. "Good to see you again. I got your message that you wanted to talk. What's on your mind, Erasmus? Oh, mind if I order? I'm famished. What's good?"

"The mutton and potato dish is superb. They have lighter fare, soups and chicken and the like, but you cannot go wrong with Crocker's mutton. The reason I wanted to talk was to make sure I handled something correctly. Should we talk upstairs in my flat?"

"No need. We won't get into anything too sensitive, I believe."

Erasmus nodded his understanding. "As you know, Dr. McTrowell and I have spent some time together socially. A couple days ago she showed me a diagram, a graphical representation of relationships, if you will. Because of the names that appeared on it, I asked her to destroy it."

"This may come as a surprise, but I know of the drawing. You're right. It shouldn't be floating about. Did she follow your advice?"

"Her initial reaction was to dislike being ordered about. Particularly since she did not know why. In retrospect, I should not have been surprised at the reaction. I finally convinced her to memorize what she wanted from the diagram and then we disposed of it accordingly together."

"I take it this occurred after your two-cab race through town?"

"Why, yes. Word does get around, I see."

"It wasn't subtle, my good man. But don't worry about it. Affairs of the heart lead us to do and say strange things."

"… Of the heart, you say? Oh, pish posh. I shall not quibble with you over such things. You are probably right."

They ordered dinner and continued their conversation about small matters over mouthfuls of mutton and potatoes smothered in gravy. Erasmus was anxious to get to his real question. As they laid their flatware to rest on their plates, Erasmus found his opening. "J. B., Sparky indicated that she saw something interesting while lodging at Dr. Pogue's. She told me this wild story that she saw you and Dr. Young doing some kind of stylized fighting movements. I was not aware that you two even knew each other."

J. B. hesitated for a few seconds, which was very uncharacteristic of him. Erasmus perceived the hesitation and waited patiently. J. B. narrowed his eyes. "I wasn't aware that she had seen us." J. B. took another couple of seconds of thought before continuing, "I've changed my mind; this conversation should be moved upstairs."

Wordlessly, the two men rose, paid for their meals, and proceeded up the side stairs. Erasmus unlocked his door and let in his guest.

"Nice place. It could use some more light and, well, have you thought about a rug?" J. B. flashed an uncharacteristically wry smile.

Erasmus played along, "Perhaps that is why Sparky ran out of here. An astounding lack of rug."

"Actually, it's a very nice practice area. I now see why all dress mannequins look fearful when you pass by a ladies' frock shop." Again, the wry smile.

"To the matter at hand, tell me about Yin Young. Oh, where are my manners? Chair?"

"Thank you. May I add, if you ever expect company, especially a particular doctor, perhaps buy another chair?" With Erasmus seated on the bed and J. B. in a chair nearby, J. B. started his story. "Yes, I do know Yin. I've known her for a very long time, actually. It all started back in 1841, when I was performing an auxiliary activity during the China War. I was investigating a Chinese officer who had fled to one of the Ryukyu Islands in the East China Sea. I was assigned to look for the high-ranking defector on the island the Japanese call Okinawa. I was there for eight months, doing my best not to draw attention to myself. I learned the local language as best I could, and I sought out locales where I could practice my military hand-to-hand training. I was directed to seek out a tall, thin man, who was quite a bit older than me, but tough as nails, to put it nicely. I'll never forget his name: Matsumura Sōkon. He taught a number of styles, as he put it in his native tongue, which included fighting with swords and specialized weapons that were variations on farm implements. But his specialty was a weapon-less style he called empty-hand, or ka-ra-te. I'll show it to you some time. Soon, in fact. Don't let the name fool you. The style uses practically every surface to both strike and block: hands, elbows, shins, knees, feet, and heels. They train to strike hard and move rapidly."

J. B. paused for a second, realizing that he needed to get back to the topic at hand. "I was in my early twenties and quite fit, or so I thought. Matsumura Sōkon let me train under him, but because of my inabilities, I was only allowed to train with the children under his tutelage, the eight- to ten-year-olds. To add to the insult, in the beginning, these children could easily punch and kick me at will. They had learned to jump as high as my chest and strike at me with their fists or spinning kicks which I could not parry or retreat from. But I swallowed my pride, and I learned. One of the most useful lessons he taught was the practice of forms or, as he called them, shapes. In the native language, ka-ta. These were ritualized movements defined by critically important actions and their timings. I was able to memorize these. One of the most promising students was a thirteen-year-old named Yin Young. At that age, she was her full height and incredibly fast.

"At the end of eight months, I was able to corner the high-ranking renegade officer and deliver him to my Marine superiors. I was making preparations to leave the island when I was approached by Yin's family. They had no means to support her and were being forced to sell her into the labor trades for cash. They begged me to take her with me back to Great Britain and let her teach karate in the West. I relayed her story to my superiors knowing that it would never be approved. In a few days, I received word back that contradicted my expectations; Her Majesty wanted me to escort the child here to London. What I didn't know was that the only teaching she would be permitted was to a small, special company of Royal Aerial Marines. I was able to train with her during that time. What we found during that five-year experiment is that the karate fighting style made little sense to the Marines brought up as Marquis of Queensbury pugilists. The order came down to transfer Yin to undercover intelligence while she also attended engineering school. As you can tell, she received an offer to work for Dr. Pogue, who is unaware of her assignment under the Royal Aerial Marines. I continue to train with her. In secret, of course. Which is what Dr. McTrowell observed. I hope that clears things up, Erasmus."

"Yes, it does. But what should I tell Sparky?"

"Tell her … you need a new rug, and that she should help you pick one out. She should then forget what she saw."

"I doubt that. Oh, and one last question. How did you learn about Sparky's diagram?"

J. B. wiggled his eyebrows in an "I know something and you don't" manner. "All in good time, my friend. All in good time."

The Misfortune of the Mislaid Missive

By Dr. Katherine L. Morse

"Will you be havin' another, Tavis?"

"Just keep 'em coming, Angus. There's new gettin' tha sight ou of me 'ead."

Ferguson's Public House had been in Angus' family for seven generations, and Angus himself had learned the art of listening at his father's elbow while perfecting his glass-washing skills. Angus could wash, rinse, and dry a pint glass without ever taking his eye off a patron. And he could put three glasses back on the shelf with one hand while tapping a fresh pint with the other. He topped up a fourth pint for his old friend and faithful customer, Tavis Haversham. It wasn't like Tavis to drink more than two at a go. He was one of those fellows who would make a big show of drinking with his lads on a Friday night, but he paced himself. The only time Angus had seen him drink as many as three was the morning after Mrs. Haversham had given birth to their first healthy child. She'd already miscarried one, and the birth had been a long, hard one. Haversham was a solid sort and liked others to think him a proper, stoic Scot, but Angus knew that the only thing Tavis had feared more than the loss of his child was the loss of his beloved Moira. Whatever Haversham had seen at his mother's cottage had frightened him even more than that.

"It's a wee tad unclear to me, Tavis, about this dog on fire that you saw."

"It waren't no dog, Angus! It waren't even alive! It ware like a hellhound bitch whelped a steam locomotive! Those three are mad, but that Frenchman is maddest 'o the lot." Tavis looked like he was going to cry. He dropped his head into his hands and trembled. Well now Angus had seen and heard it all. As unclear as the situation was, it was clear he would get no more useful information out of his shaken friend tonight. He leaned over and said to his own son, "Neill, run and fetch Mrs. Haversham."

Tavis made no move to pick his head up from the bar. It seemed the combination of shock and hops was too much for him. None of the other customers were sitting at the bar. Angus reached up under the counter and retrieved a small, nondescript leather pouch. He extracted a single sheet of paper with a few lines of printing while keeping an eye on all of his customers to ensure that none of them saw his actions. He lashed the thong back around the bone button and tucked the folio back into its hidey hole. Pulling the stubby pencil from behind his ear, he scribbled a few words on the form. He folded it in half, in quarters, and finally into eighths. He slipped the folded paper into the pocket of his bar apron and returned the pencil to its perch over his ear. He was nonchalantly swabbing the bar when Neill returned with Moira Haversham in tow.

She took one look at her husband, shook her head, and tsk tsked. "What does he owe you, Angus?"

"No need to give it a care, Moira. He's had a terrible fright. Do you need a hand?"

"Oh, no thank you, Angus. You're a good friend. Tavis, darling, let's get you to bed."

No sooner had Moira Haversham shouldered her intoxicated husband out the door than Ferguson pulled the paper from his pocket and handed it to his son. "Send this to our friend in London." Young Neill Ferguson grasped the proffered message tightly in his fist and dashed out the door toward the train station. He so loved these commissions, not least because they came so rarely.

"Mr. Westley, do you have today's reports?"

"Yes, Colonel Spreckler."

"Anything worth a look?"

"There is this one, sir. It's rather odd."

Spreckler read the scant words hastily written on the report form and subsequently smudged by the sweat of a small hand and the long ride wedged into an envelope in an overstuffed mailbag. No more than five seconds passed before he harrumphed and tossed it back at the clerk who flapped about a bit to catch it. "Nothing but the ranting of a drunken Scot. But then I'm being redundant." He laughed at his own, crass joke.

Mr. Westley did not laugh with him. Instead he wrote the date and the letters "HMS" on the blank, back side of the page, and filed it in the front of an already overstuffed file drawer. Colonel Howell Michael Spreckler strode to the sideboard, poured himself a generous brandy, and deposited himself in his favorite red wing chair. He picked up his newspaper and began reading, not giving the missive another thought.

"Well, this is unexpected."

"What is it, dear Miss Slate?"

"Oh, Charles, I wish you would call me Sarah, even when we're here working."

"I would rather call you Mrs. Howgill." He beamed at his fiancée sitting on the opposite side of the partners' desk he had just had made and delivered to his London mill.

She returned his smile. "That will come soon enough. Miss Pogue is making excellent progress on my gown and the preparations. She is such a salvation. I know I could not have managed all the details without her. As I was saying," she held up the piece of paper she had been examining that had initiated their exchange. "We have just received an order for ten bolts of our color-changing fabric."

"One thousand yards? That is unexpected. Who has ordered it?"

"An export company."

"How very odd."

"Dr. McTrowell?"

"Yes, Mrs. Bingham?"

"You have a visitor, Chief Inspector Drake. Shall I set up some tea?"

"Yes, please."

As Erasmus entered the sitting room, Sparky quipped, "Chief Inspector, will you join me for something as prosaic as a cup of tea, or should we set the building on fire, then dash about smashing windows and throwing the occupants to safety before the whole structure explodes?"

"Dr. McTrowell, one need not be a chief inspector to detect that you are still angry about the incident with the cabs. However, such sarcasm does not become you. It is a poor use of your wit."

"Yes, you're quite right. I've had rather a bad turn since I last saw you, and it's left me in a foul humor."

"Would you care to tell me about it?"

"Thank you, but I'm not quite ready to discuss it." Mrs. Bingham returned with the tea tray, which she deposited on the table. A quick glance at the pair made her decide to check back later to see if they needed anything else. Now was not the time. "What brings you here today?"

"I have a question for you. Or perhaps it is more of a request."

"Yes?"

"Sparky, would you help me purchase a rug?"

THE FRONTIER MEDICAL WOMAN

BY DAVID L. DRAKE

The sitting room at Dr. Pogue's residence was a comfy setting. The overstuffed chairs and couches made a neat ring around a wooden table. A score of fringed pillows had taken up residence on the sitting surfaces. The embroidered cloth on all of the furniture was of rich colors: burgundies, deep blues and teals, with intricate gold patterns. This splash of impressive decorum was a direct result of Esmeralda's influence on Edmond's furnishings.

The wooden table was thick and heavy and didn't quite fit the Victorian décor. It had been handed down through the Pogue lineage and had originally been a worktable in the Scottish Crookston Castle located about five miles southwest of Glasgow. Edmond and Esmeralda had ancestors who had worked in the castle back in the first half of the eighteenth century. The lore surrounding the table was that one of the table legs was damaged in the bombardment of cannonballs from the famous cannon Mons Meg when it was used to attack the castle in 1489. The table had been left unused in storage for two hundred and fifty years until it was repaired to a working state by Edmond's great, great, great grandfather. Upon this table he had performed many of his smaller workman's tasks, including machinery repair, leather tooling, and toy construction. The table was passed down to his family upon his death as one of many tokens of gratitude by the castle's owner, William Graham, 2nd Duke of Montrose.

The table had been shortened to make it a suitable height for drinks and flower vases, but instead Edmond had a dozen or so current scientific periodicals scattered about on it. It held a few copies of the Scientific American newsletter, a periodical that Edmond had been collecting from its inception in 1845. There were also a couple of copies of The Lancet, the weekly medical journal and a dog-eared copy of Flora, which looked heavily thumbed through, despite its being written in German.

Yin had chosen the carpet under the table. It was a colorful carved silk depiction of scenes along a twisting Yangtze River. The rug was primarily blue, with bright yellow, red, and cream images of traditional Chinese field and river laborers in iconic poses performing their tasks. Yin had bought the rug locally in the Shadwell district. The irony of how she had been brought to London by a Royal Aerial Marine who was involved in the China War fought over the Yangtze River was not lost on her. In an odd way, the carpet was a reminder of how she had been rescued.

Sparky settled into one of the chairs, and Erasmus took a central spot on the couch. Erasmus had just started into his tea, hoping to get an answer to his question regarding getting Sparky's help selecting his rug. His indirect request wasn't lost on her at all.

She squirmed a tad at the question, and then replied, "I am … not the type of woman to help you select your furnishings. I …"

"I did not ask to get your refined sense of decoration. I asked because I want you to be …"

Mrs. Bingham stepped into the room and cleared her throat. "Doctor, you wanted me to let you know when it was quarter past eleven."

"Oh, thank you! I must be going. Erasmus, can we continue this conversation soon?"

"That would be fine. However, may I ask where you are going?"

"Certainly. Just last week I received a very welcome request from the British Medical Association asking me to demonstrate my mechanical surgical assistant to an assembly of physicians. I need to be at the Great Exhibition at one o'clock."

"May I join you?"

Sparky was taken aback by the request. Exhibits of surgical procedures were not normally for the untrained spectator. Erasmus was not one to avoid unpleasantness, but she wasn't sure this was his cup of tea, as it were. "Are you sure? It may get …"

"Technical?"

"No, a better word would be 'grisly,' although I haven't thought of surgery in that way for quite a while. Are you still game for tagging along?"

"Yes. We have more to discuss, and I would like to take advantage of our travel time. In addition, I am fascinated and curious to hear what you will present to your colleagues."

Sparky excused herself to collect her things for the demonstration and walked swiftly off toward her temporary bedroom. Erasmus just had time to gather his cape coat, bowler, and cane before Sparky returned. She had on her leather duster and was carrying her Gladstone bag, which looked rather full. "Let's go!" she offered with a smile.

A cab was waiting for them. The two hopped in without a single word regarding racing or nearly running over pedestrians. Once the cab was off, Erasmus restarted the conversation. "I wanted to ask you to help me investigate something."

"I don't understand. Don't you have all of Scotland Yard to help with that?"

"No, not in the traditional sense. Since we have a few minutes, I shall explain. Something has been bothering me for the past few weeks. I have been reviewing reported crimes and the associated investigations, and I have been getting a nagging feeling that something is … not quite right. And then, I figured it out this morning. It is what I have not seen." Erasmus stopped to adjust the curl on the left-hand side of his moustache, adding a scrunched up pensive look on his face.

"Go on," Sparky urged.

"At the end of our date, which was wonderful by the way, we saw Mr. Hedgley and Mr. Martin engaged in some nefarious activity on the main street of Clerkenwell. I did not report it since I was not sure what crime was being committed. I assumed that whomever was being robbed, if that was in fact what was happening, would report the malfeasance. But it was never reported. There is no crime to investigate. So I was hoping to get your help in doing some undercover work to figure out what actually happened. Are you up for a bit of role-playing?"

Sparky's flashed a wry smile, and pronounced, "Well, this sounds more like the man I've come to know."

"I am not trying to get you involved in another grand chase."

"Oh. I'm not fooled. A rose by any other name, to quote one of your countrymen. Of course I'm interested. Let's try to steer clear of oversized metal insects this time!" Sparky looked quickly out the window and called to the driver, "This is fine, thank you. We'll walk from here."

The two of them hopped out and joined the crowd waiting to enter the large glass and metal building housing the exhibit. It took another half hour to get inside and find the location of the exhibit. A young man in medical garb approached them once they were inside the building. "Hello! Hello! I'm Dr. Durham. I'll assist you in preparing for your presentation."

Sparky was happy to see a guide. How nice they had provided an assistant. "I'm Dr. McTrowell, and this is Chief Inspector Erasmus Drake of Scotland Yard. He is joining me today to observe. Is there somewhere I can get into my surgical gown?"

"Oh, we have a room waiting. Please follow me, both of you." Dr. Durham led Sparky and Erasmus to a side door that opened on a hallway hidden from the publicly accessible exhibit rooms. Sparky was shown a room where she could prepare, and Dr. Durham led Erasmus out to join the audience of doctors.

It only took a few minutes for Sparky to get her gown on and make sure her tools were ready. Gladstone bag in hand, Sparky reemerged from her room. Young Dr. Durham was in the hallway, waiting patiently. "Right this way," he directed, "the representatives are ready to see you."

The walk down the hallway was short, but Sparky had enough time to ask, "Was there much interest? I was hoping we would get a least a dozen …"

As Dr. Durham swung open the door, he looked back at the wide-eyed adventuress. "No, we have closer to four-hundred and fifty medical practitioners. Practically all of the association is here …"

Sparky walked out onto a stage. It was lit by an open skylight that shone sunlight brightly off her polished mechanical marvel. In front of her was raised auditorium seating, containing row upon row of doctors: some balding and bespectacled, others fresh from medical university with quick eyes and unruly hair. Way up in the back sat Erasmus, smiling proudly at Sparky for being the center of attention.

Others also sat along in the back row. Reporters from the local newspapers? Perhaps. And article writers for medical journals, most likely.

Dr. Durham stepped to the front of the stage. "Welcome, gentleman of the British Medical Association, to this most amazing demonstration! Here at the Great Exhibition of the Works of Industry of All Nations, we have a rare sight indeed. The frontier medical woman of the State of California of America, the high-speed racing airship pilot, and inventor of the unexpected, Dr. "Sparky" C. L. McTrowell, will demonstrate her one-of-a-kind 'mechanical surgical assistant.' Please give her a warm welcome!"

The applause were warm indeed. It went up like a thunderclap and lasted long enough for Sparky to enter center stage and nod her appreciation two or three times. "Thank you! Thank you! Today you will see an apparatus I designed and built specifically for aiding a single doctor performing full surgery in the confines of an aloft airship." She went on to point out the mechanical uses of the four armatures, the foot pedals, and the hand controls. "Today, we will demonstrate the removal of the gall bladder from …" Dr. Durham pushed a wheeled stretcher onto the stage. Under the white sheet draping the gurney lay the familiar shape of a human body. "… this forty-five-year-old male cadaver."

She removed the sheet. With the exception of a tidy undergarment, the audience's eyes fell upon the full, pallid body of a medium-build laborer laid placidly on the bed. Sparky proceeded to strap into her apparatus as the whine of the mid-sized steam engine in the next room came up to a serviceable speed, feeding the rotating linkage that attached to the back of the mechanical surgical assistant.

Sparky's gently lifted up the entire remains and placed it back down lightly, demonstrating how controlled strength was possible.

Erasmus looked on with both awe and curiosity. It was fascinating to see Sparky in her element. And then Erasmus looked at the crowd. On the edge of their seats, they were. He only had one thought for that second. He was proud.

The Disease of Kings

By Dr. Katherine L. Morse

"Ah, good morning, Mrs. Wallace."

"Good morning, Mr. Littleton."

"Will Mr. Wallace be arriving shortly?"

"No, his highness will be spending the day in bed."

"His highness?"

"He fancies that being stricken with 'the disease of kings' makes him royalty." She all but sniffed her disdain at her husband's vanity.

"Um, well there is this one bill of lading." He held out the sheet of paper tentatively. "It requires Mr. Wallace's signature, and it has no recipient. This is highly irregular. I was hoping Mr. Wallace would know what to do with it."

Mrs. Wallace took the bill from Littleton's hand and scanned it. It was as he said; it required Reginald's signature and lacked a destination or recipient. The contents were identified as 350 pounds of clockwork gears. Why on earth would her husband be engaged in such commerce? And who could possibly need that much clock hardware?

"Mr. Littleton, where is this crate?"

"No need for you to worry yourself about this, Mrs. Wallace. I'm sure Mr. Wallace will take care of it when he returns."

"Yes, Mr. Littleton, that is precisely what concerns me. Where is the crate?"

Mr. Wallace might have been the loud, demanding sort, but it was his bride whom Littleton actually feared. "It's in warehouse number seven."

Keeping a firm grasp on the document, Annabelle Wallace promptly made her way around behind the office building to the row of warehouses in back. The clerk at the desk just inside the door of number seven did a double take when he saw her. Although he had never been introduced to her, he had seen her a few times from a distance in the company of her husband. He had never expected to see her in the musty environs of his work place. He hopped up from his chair clumsily, setting it to clattering and nearly knocking it over. "Good morning, ma'am. What can I do for you, ma'am?"

She held out the bill of lading so he could see it, but maintained a firm hold on it to make it clear that she had no intention of relinquishing it. "I need to see the contents of this shipment."

"Yes, ma'am, Mrs. Wallace. Right away, ma'am." He scrambled back behind his desk and flipped frantically through his ledger looking for the corresponding record. In his nervousness, he passed the correct entry twice before seeing it on the third pass. He grabbed for the pry bar on the shelf behind his desk, knocking it to the floor rather than getting a grip on it. He was sweating and trembling by the time he retrieved it. He took a ragged breath and cleared his throat. "This way, ma'am."

The clerk had his first piece of luck when they reached the right row and section. The offending crate was on the ground. He wouldn't have enjoyed the repercussions of making his employer's wife wait in the dark, dusty depths of the warehouse while he fetched some air stevedores to bring it down from the racks. Through sheer determination, he managed to pry the top loose without embarrassing himself further by dropping the iron bar again. He lifted the lid off to the side so Mrs. Wallace could inspect the shipment.

Despite the dimness of the light filtering through the dirty windows close to the ceiling, Annabelle Wallace could tell immediately that the contents did not consist of clockwork gears, although some might have been used in the construction of some unidentifiable device. It was obviously disassembled, and she tried to put the pieces together in her mind, but none of the things she could assemble in her mind from the components she could see made any sense. Seconds stretched into minutes as she stared into the incomprehensible mess of wood shavings and dull, black, metal parts. She needed to have a solid plan before she took her next step. The poor clerk looked as if he would faint from anxiety waiting for her to make up her mind.

She reached into the crate and retrieved a smallish part that appeared the most complex to her. She looked at it from many angles, but additional perspective did nothing to increase clarity. Satisfied that she had done everything she could in this venue, she turned to the clerk. "Reseal the container. Let no one open it or move it. Is that clear?"

"Yes, ma'am!"

Despite her husband's grumbling, Mrs. Wallace insisted on a light dinner of broth, fish, fruit for dessert, and no wine. He was already in a truly foul mood when she broached the subject of the mysterious shipment. "Reginald, Mr. Littleton brought to my attention a container requiring your signature with no destination on the bill of lading."

"No doubt some sort of fool clerical error. I'll see to it when I return to work."

"I thought it highly irregular, so I went to inspect it myself."

A sense of foreboding began to infiltrate Mr. Wallace's physical discomfort. "Humph," he grunted noncommittally.

"The bill listed the contents as clockwork gears, but it seemed to me that it was some type of machine much larger than a clock." She pretended to return her attention to her dish of fruit, but she kept a close eye on her husband's face.

"I hardly think you can claim expertise with all manner of machinery. It was probably parts for a large clock … perhaps for a town square." Suddenly, the compote in front of him was more appetizing than usual.

She didn't press him further. She had been married to Reginald Wallace more than long enough to know when he was lying to her. She wouldn't get any more useful information out of him.

Despite the light dinner, Wallace did not sleep well and was still in no condition to return to work the next day. His wife spent the entire carriage ride to the airship port tapping her foot against the carpetbag secreting the pilfered part and considering how to solve its mystery. She needed someone who could discern its function and whom she could trust to be honest with her.

"Good morning, Mrs. Wallace. Is Mr. Wallace still recovering?"

"Yes, Mr. Littleton. Do you know how I might get a message to Dr. McTrowell?"

CLOCKWORK PUZZLE

BY DAVID L. DRAKE

The hansom ride from the Great Exhibition back to Dr. Pogue's residence passed quickly. During the trip, Sparky was excited and quite talkative about the positive reception she'd received for her demonstration of the mechanical surgical assistant.

"Did you see their reaction when I used the outer arms to hold the forceps while making two simultaneous tool changes with the inner arms? I don't think they were expecting the assistant to give the surgeon that many useful hands. And I think there were five different medical journal reporters there. This may get a great deal of attention in the press."

Erasmus smiled at her enthusiasm and nodded his agreement. He was new to seeing surgical operations, so he tried his best to inquire about the procedure without sounding naive. "Is there much difference between operating on cadavers rather than living patients?"

"Well, there is the simple matter of worrying less about the outcome. But seriously, the organs of the dead are either desiccated or turgid. The inter-organ tissues are considerably viscous and less elastic. So the entire procedure is more difficult. But the attending doctors understood that, knowing that a living patient would have been easier to work with for the physical part of the process. My early surgical training involved working with the departed, so I'm quite comfortable working with the differences."

The sign for Shadwell appeared at the bend, and Sparky pursed her lips in the sudden realization that she had allowed the conversation to be all about her and her presentation. She turned it into a grin and took Erasmus' arm.

"Tell me about our upcoming adventure. Do I need to be in disguise? It's been fairly warm these summer nights. I hope it's acceptable not to wear a great many layers."

"A disguise? My first reaction was 'no,' but given your medical and piloting avocations, not to mention inventing, I am wondering if a plain dress is actually a disguise. … I am sorry, that was ungentlemanly of me. What I was hoping was that we would look like an unintimidating couple. So I guess it is a bit of a ruse."

Erasmus tried to read Sparky's reaction to determine how his quips were being taken, hoping to stay away from being perceived as teasing and instead as rather clever. But the look on her face wasn't giving him a pleasant reassurance. His guess was that she both understood how she was different from others but was fiercely proud of the fact. Light jabs at that differentiation were not very welcome. A change in tack was in order. "I have a very general plan. We visit a number of the shops looking like a couple. We may even visit nearby residents if needed, looking to see why two secretive men covertly hauling extremely heavy crates of something in the middle of the night was not reported. We find out whatever we can, looking particularly for some indication as to where we might find Mr. Hedgley and Mr. Martin."

Sparky's eyes lit up at this more matter-of-fact approach, and Erasmus was pleased with her reaction. Apparently she liked banter, but not at her expense. This was a lesson worth remembering, and he tucked that away in the back of his mind.

Without a look of concern, Sparky asked, "Should we be prepared for attack? Other than my fists, I'm not sure what I'd bring."

"I do not think you will need anything. We will just walk around in Clerkenwell near the 'restaurant.' We should not have any tussles. And I do have my cane if it comes to a minor show of force."

The hansom drew to a stop in front of Dr. Pogue's residence. The couple paid their driver and entered the heavy front door. Mrs. Bingham met them in the hall. "Dr. McTrowell, a letter arrived for you. It was hand-delivered, rather than by post." She presented the letter on a small wooden tray. Sparky thanked Mrs. Bingham and picked it up, examining both sides. The letter was plain enough. It had a written address on the front, but the printed address on the flap was for the London office of Western & Transatlantic Airship Lines.

Sparky deftly tapped the contents to one end of the envelope and neatly tore the opposing end off. "This must be my upcoming flight schedule. I was expecting this." She blew lightly into the torn end, puffing out the paper container, providing easy access to the missive it contained. She flipped the single piece of paper open. "Hmm, this is strange. Erasmus, let me read it to you."

My Dear Doctor McTrowell,
I have need of your assistance regarding the contents of a package that we have received. Due to your knowledge of machinery and associated apparatus, I would appreciate your help in this matter. Please see me tomorrow morning so I can take the appropriate action.
Regards,
Mrs. Reginald Wallace

Sparky wrinkled her nose a bit. "This is a very odd request. First off, it came from the missus rather than Reginald. Why would she be that concerned over the contents of a shipping crate? And, I must say, it's a polite enough letter, but it pretty much demands I go to the airship port tomorrow morning to peer inside a box of what are probably bits of some machine. This isn't my idea of a way to start the day. I'm sure there's quite a bit more to this story. Oh, look at the time! We'd better change and get over to Clerkenwell if we want to visit open shops."

The cab dropped the pair off near the Italian restaurant on Main Street, Clerkenwell. Erasmus had borrowed a lightweight jacket and jaunty bow tie from Dr. Pogue's closet, softening his appearance. It didn't fit Erasmus' shoulders, as he knew it wouldn't when he picked it out. Sparky wore a simple summer dress with three-quarter length sleeves with just a band of ruffled lace. Her stride didn't quite match the demure dress, but instead she projected an engaging self-assuredness. It was, no doubt, a result of her successful presentation to the medical community that day.

As they walked, Erasmus looked across the businesses on the side of the street opposite the restaurant. The storefronts offered a hodge-podge of curios and notions. "Although we overheard some of

Mr. Hedgley's and Mr. Martin's conversation, it has long enough that I do not recall much of it."

"Perhaps it's time for you to use your secret powers! Do you have the jelly babies that Dr. Pogue gave you?"

"Them? That was some of the most outlandish balderdash I have ever heard. He said that if I eat one of the anise-flavored jelly babies he provided, they will allow me to enter that heightened state again. Something about our olfactory senses causing the best recall. I do, in fact, have a few in my pocket here. I keep them in a waxed paper bag to keep them fresh, but I am sure that they have become a tad chewy. Do you really think I should give this a try?"

"There's not much drawback, unless the jelly babies have turned."

Erasmus fished the bag out of his pocket and, unfolding the top, peered inside. The five gumdrop-shaped treats were starting to adhere to each other. He reached in and plucked one from the bunch. After replacing the bag into his pocket, he held the aromatic morsel up to his nose and instinctively closed his eyes. To Erasmus, it was pungent to excess, as if his whole world were immediately focused on this compact gelatinous blob. The image of Yin preparing them and handing the bag to Erasmus while Dr. Pogue explained their use came back to him.

Erasmus popped the jelly baby into his mouth, and he was instantly back on the street on the night of their date. But this time he was watching the scene from the other side of the street, standing next to the cart being loaded. He could see Sparky and himself tucked into the shadows, just their shoes visible in the gaslight.

He turned to the two men, sweaty and tired, and listened to their conversation. The critical parts were that they didn't want to continue their workings with Mr. P ... a French name he couldn't quite make out and that Mr. Hedgley had an engineering degree. The crates contained black market clockwork parts from a gear maker's warehouse.

Erasmus opened his eyes and blinked a couple of times. "Well, this will be much easier now." He explained his 'vision' to Sparky, and pointed to the clock maker and watch repair sign hanging over the doorway of an unassuming shop just on the other side of an alley.

"Thank you!" she replied.

"For ... which part of that?"

"Using your secret powers, of course. Please gain more of them." She waved her hand in a circular motion as if to indicate that such things were fairly easy to obtain. "They'll save us a good deal of time during these adventures!"

They started walking toward the shop, and Erasmus added, "Grand idea. I shall see what I can do. Any preferences for my next batch? Flying? Heal the sick?"

"I can do those things myself. But if you could create out of thin air a hot cup of chai and a chocolate caramel candy on the side, that would be splendid!"

The two chuckled to themselves as they entered the shop. It was a cramped little space with a small area to stand and a tight counter over which to do business. A glass display under the counter showed some conventional pocket watches and mantle clocks. The first thing that caught Erasmus' eye was that all of the displayed timepieces showed different times and weren't running. The remainder of the shop appeared to be open storage for parts, some in pressboard boxes kept haphazardly on dusty shelves, and elsewhere just stacks of clock bodies and frames. A couple of gutted grandfather clocks also stood near the back, one without even hands on its sun-faded face.

The sound of activity emanated from behind a row of shelves. Perhaps packing or searching, it was difficult to tell. Erasmus took the lead.

"Good day," Erasmus called out. The rustling stopped for a few seconds. "Good day there. Could you give us a minute, please?"

A man with a workman's apron approached the counter, with a look of "Why are you here?" on his face. "What can I do for you?" he asked, but it didn't feel as though he wanted an answer.

"My ... fiancée is looking for a new ladies watch. Could we see what you have?"

"So sorry, but we don't carry new watches. Good day."

It was clear to Erasmus this man didn't want his business. Very odd.

Sparky jumped in to see if she could make more progress. "Actually, I have a watch, but I'm having trouble with the setting lever. Could you take a look at it for me?"

The man was clearly hesitant. He paused for a second, not looking away, but rather studying the two visitors to his shop.

"Unfortunately, I'm in the middle of a task at present, and I won't be able to …"

The door came flying open and a rough looking street urchin rushed in, pockets bulging. Like a child, he didn't pay any mind to his surroundings as he blurted out, "Mr. Palmer, look what I've got!" Then he noticed the pair of interlopers. "Pardon me! I'll … just … wait over here." He slunk back into a corner, giving Erasmus the impression that he didn't feel welcome nor did he want to retreat back to the street.

Erasmus took the opportunity to speak up. "Well, thank you, sir, for your time." He put out his arm for Sparky to take and proceeded out of the door.

As soon as they were out of earshot, Sparky asked, "Was that what I think it is?"

"Yes! How perceptive. Mr. Palmer is taking in stolen watches and clocks, disassembling them, reassembling them, and selling them to others as used timepieces. But he does not sell them directly; he is instead selling them to legitimate stores. A classic black-market dealer. The bad news is that he will not tell us anything about the theft the other night for fear of exposing his own criminal enterprise."

"That makes sense. Thank you, jelly babies."

"Hmm, charming. But here is what we do know. Mr. Hedgley and Mr. Martin hauled enough clockwork parts out of there to fill three heavy creates. Whatever they are constructing is either a single big object or there are a great many of them. That would require a sizeable shop for the manufacture and storage of their final product. There are only a few places in London that could secretly house that level of production. On the other hand, they may be working outside of London, which would make finding them all the harder. If they were building something along the lines of the EPACTs, then there should be some sighting of their activity. We also have one more fact, the Frenchman, Mr. P."

"So, what are our next steps?"

"In reverse order: thirdly, set my Scotland Yard dogs on Mr. Palmer. He needs to be caught red-handed. Second, look for recently leased or purchased factories or warehouses where the products being created or stored have not been made public. First, and most important, figure out where we can have dinner together to discuss this clockwork puzzle."

"Let me add one thing to your list. If these three men came from France to London, they most likely came by water or air. If they gave their real names, we could track them down by the passenger manifests. It would take some looking, but it hasn't been that long. Since I have access to people at the Western & Transatlantic Airship Lines, I could start there. I plan to be at their offices tomorrow, looking at the contents of a crate. I can get this search started."

"Excellent! Now to search for food. Are you game for Italian? We could just get the dessert, and see how the waiter reacts!"

IRREFUTABLE EVIDENCE

BY DR. KATHERINE L. MORSE

Sparky chuckled. "You're not always funny, Erasmus, but you are always witty. I rather miss Anu's cooking and Virat's chai. Might I persuade you to go for a curry?"

"As you wish, my good doctor." He touched the brim of his bowler and winked at her.

She regretted her choice slightly when she awoke the next morning with her insides still burning. However, it had been gloriously spicy and flavorful. She would have to ask Mrs. Bingham to provide her with a glass of milk for breakfast. She wasn't looking forward to her audience with Mrs. Wallace and was tempted to dawdle over breakfast, but she was equally anxious to get a look at the recent passenger manifests. Nothing would do but to get moving.

"Good morning, Littleton."

He didn't look entirely well and she was about to inquire after his health when she heard a commanding female voice from Wallace's office. "Mr. Littleton, has Dr. McTrowell arrived?"

With a more than usually harried look on his face, Littleton nodded toward the half open office door. "She's been here since seven o'clock and asking for you every ten minutes since then."

Sparky popped open her pocket watch. It was nine o'clock. No wonder Littleton looked so worn. "I'll go right in. I have a request with which I need your assistance. May I have a look at the passenger manifests from Paris since May 28th?"

"I'll pull them from the files for you. You'd best get in there." He nodded toward the door again.

"Good morning, Mrs. Wallace. I confess that your summons intrigues me. How may I be of assistance?"

Annabelle Wallace walked around behind Sparky and closed the office door. "A crate arrived with this bill of lading." Without further exposition, she handed the slip of paper to McTrowell.

The fact that it listed Carlisle as its point of origin made Sparky a tad anxious. Not being acquainted with the finer points of the shipping business, the signature requirement didn't pique her interest. But when she read, "Contents: 350 lbs. clockwork gears," her throat tightened. She did her best to conceal her trepidation from her employer's wife. "I see. And what is it that concerns you?"

"The irregularities in the bill of lading caught my attention, so I went to the warehouse and had the crate opened. It contains several pieces of machinery whose purpose I could not divine. I thought your mechanical expertise might help me solve this mystery and put my mind at rest." She opened her carpetbag and proffered the small component she had extracted the day before.

Sparky was nearly overcome by a wave of nausea at the sight. It couldn't be! She turned it over in her hands and examined it from multiple angles. It was a jointed appendage that was indubitably anthropomorphic. No, there was no mistaking the styling and handiwork! She fairly shrieked, "Which warehouse?"

"I beg your pardon, Dr. McTrowell!"

"Which warehouse? Where is the crate?" She waved the offending item at Mrs. Wallace.

"Number seven."

McTrowell flung open the office door and dashed to Littleton's desk. It was stacked with ledgers.

"Ah, Dr. McTrowell. I have the passenger manifests you requested."

"Thank you, Littleton, but no need. I found the piece of information I needed. Send a carter and two air stevedores to warehouse number seven immediately."

Mrs. Wallace hustled to keep up with McTrowell as she ran down the line of warehouses. She caught up as Sparky was trying to explain to the warehouse clerk what she wanted. "It's down this way," Mrs. Wallace gasped, "if you'll follow me." The clerk had the good sense to follow the two women with his trusty iron pry bar. He reopened the crate without being asked.

Sparky rummaged around in the straw packing, extracting the pieces she could reach easily. She examined each carefully and made some cursory attempts to fit them together. Having no success with that approach, she closed her eyes and tried to visualize the pieces floating together. This approach resulted in similarly unsatisfactory results. She put the perplexing puzzle pieces back into the crate, including the one with which Mrs. Wallace had started this misadventure. She was still scowling into the crate when their attention was drawn by rattling and coarse voices at the front of the warehouse. She whistled sharply. "We're back here."

Two weather-worn air stevedores, each of them twice Sparky's size, lumbered into the depths of the warehouse to join the party of three encircling the crate. One of them exchanged "don't I know you glances?" with Sparky, but she was too preoccupied with the mysterious shipment to give it a second thought. "Please load this crate on the cart."

"Dr. McTrowell, I requested your presence this morning to determine the contents of the crate. This is not license for you to spirit it away. The shipment was intended for my husband, and I must insist that it remain here until he returns to disposition it."

"Mrs. Wallace, I can understand your position under the circumstances. However, I'm quite certain that this is now a matter for Scotland Yard, and your husband will have to resolve ownership of this shipment with them. For all our sakes, I hope that his involvement is circumstantial and not intentional."

The clerk suddenly remembered some urgent paperwork requiring his immediate attention at his desk. Annabelle Wallace was uncharacteristically nonplussed. The stevedores, on the other hand, smirked at each other as they loaded the crate onto the waiting cart.

The carter asked, "Where shall I deliver it ma'am?"

"I'll provide directions as you drive," McTrowell replied. "I have no intention of letting that box out of my sight."

"As you wish, ma'am."

Except to give directions, they sat in silence all the way to Shadwell. Once they reached Pogue's residence, Sparky realized she had failed to plan for getting the extremely cumbersome package inside. She was considering whether to begin unpacking it piece by piece when she spied Yin returning from some morning errand. "Good morning, Dr. Young. I have a delivery for Dr. Pogue. I'm wondering how to get it down to his laboratory."

Revealing no indication that such a request was the least bit out of the ordinary, Yin replied, "Drive around to the side of the building. I'll meet you there."

Although Sparky was a bit surprised, she knew to take Dr. Young at her word. She got back on the cart and rode around the corner of the building. There they encountered an enormous door with equal width horizontal metal panels filling a space the size of the entire ground floor of a row house. She and the carter waited in continuing silence for a few more minutes before they heard the coughing and sputtering of a steam engine firing up on the other side of the door. The machinations of the engine smoothed out over the course of a few more minutes and were followed by unidentifiable creaking and whining, also inside. One of these noises finally resolved into the groaning of hinges within the door itself. A moment later, it shuddered into motion, rolling up into the building. Once it was completely retracted, Yin stepped out from behind the wall. "Please back the cart in."

Ordinarily that would have sounded like an outrageous request, but the interior space was twice as deep and at least three times as high as the cart. Sparky couldn't quite be sure about the second measurement because the interior was dark except for the ambient light from outside and a small, utilitarian gaslight on the wall just inside that illuminated some kind of control panel. That must have been where Yin had been standing to operate the door. Sparky had the sense that the building was bigger on the inside than the outside.

When the cart was in the building, but the horse still in the alley, Yin held up her hand to signal to the carter that he should halt. She returned the control panel and grasped two levers, one of which she pulled gradually toward herself. Sparky heard the steam engine chug along more arduously out of sight, accompanied by more creaking and whining from the dark recesses of the ceiling cavern. Sparky stared up into the gloom. Something pointed and metal began to emerge from the darkness just as Yin began smoothly pulling on the second lever with her left hand.

The nature of the apparatus revealed itself in the daylight. Yin was lowering an enormous claw with her right hand and opening it with her left hand. She gradually returned the right lever to the neutral position as the crane approached the crate, slowing its descent to a smooth halt. Yin simultaneously reversed the direction of the lever in her left hand, closing the tangs around the body of the container. She notched the lever into one of the many side catches in the lever's track, locking the claw's grip into the wood with a slight crunch.

Without removing her right hand, she gave the claw and crate a quick visual inspection before throwing an arced slide on the panel from one end to the other in one smooth gesture. With her attention on the ceiling, Sparky hadn't noticed that the floor wasn't the same all the way to the back. As the hidden engine complained even more strenuously, a seam opened in the floor in the back half of the room. Light sprayed up from the room below. Sparky checked her position relative to the opening before peering into the widening gap in the floor. She was looking straight down into Pogue's lab as if it were the cargo hold of a ship! The cargo doors came to a halt with a thud.

"Dr. McTrowell, please step back." Sparky had been so engrossed in the operation of the crane that she had forgotten she was interfering with Dr. Young's work. She moved back toward the horse, which the carter was doing an excellent job of keeping calm. Yin pushed the original lever away from her just enough to lift the wooden box off the cart before returning the control to its neutral position and switching hands so her right hand was free. She used her dominant hand to grasp a fourth control on the panel, a lever that appeared to move freely in two dimensions. With minute adjustments in both directions, she maneuvered the crate expertly to center it over the opening in the floor, moving slowly enough to prevent it from swaying.

McTrowell observed the operation with admiration and fascination. Dr. Young had obviously operated this machinery many times to be so expert. At the same time, Sparky visualized the gears, pulleys, and belts that must be hidden above them to make the operation feasible. Yin lowered the crate into the opening, backing off the lever until the crate settled onto the floor of the laboratory with a soft thump.

Sparky paid the carter and sent him on his way while Yin retracted the crane into the ceiling and closed the cargo doors. "Dr. Young, I count on your good sense and powers of persuasion to convince Dr. Pogue not to open that crate until I return with Chief Inspector Drake. I don't wish to sound overly dramatic, but we don't have enough EPACT parts left to build him a second arm if he should decide to meddle with the contents."

Yin's face displayed the first real emotion that Sparky had ever seen on it, and it was true anguish. Sparky was anxious to change the subject. "I'll return with the Chief Inspector just as soon as possible." She pointed toward the darkness above them. "This device is a remarkably effective achievement."

"Thank you."

Sparky made a mental note to herself to engage Dr. Young at a later time about her design for the two-dimensional control. If it were made significantly smaller, it could simplify the mechanical surgical assistant and make it more compact. It could also allow the surgeon to move patients on and off the surgical table without assistance. She snapped out of her reverie. She needed to find Drake now. She could worry about redesigns later. She nodded to Yin and exited through the side of the building. She heard the metal door rolling back down behind her as she headed for the road to flag down a cab.

She chided herself for her shortsightedness all the way to Whitehall Place. While riding back on the cart wouldn't have been as comfortable, it would have been a lot faster. It had taken her fifteen minutes to find a cab as they tended to be rare in Shadwell. She shouldn't have been so hasty in dismissing the carter. It was nearing the lunch hour by the time she reached Scotland Yard. She hoped Erasmus hadn't already departed for his noon meal.

"May I help you ma'am?"

"I'm here to see Chief Inspector Drake."

The sergeant at the desk looked her up and down. *"I'll bet you are,"* he thought to himself. That Chief Inspector Drake always got the odd ones. He jerked his head over his left shoulder. "All the way to the back. Name's on the door."

"Thank you." She swept past him, the tails of her leather duster flying behind her as her boot heels clicked on the floor in rapid succession. She could see Erasmus at his desk, the crown of his head barely visible over the top of the morning's edition of the *Times*. She opened the door without knocking. In her agitation, she unintentionally slammed the door behind herself, drawing the attention of everyone in the room outside the door. Drake dropped the paper in surprise.

"Sparky, your demonstration yesterday is reported on page two of the *Times*." He pointed to a spot in the middle of the page that she couldn't actually read from the other side of his desk.

"Hmm, yes. I need to talk to you."

Drake could tell there was something on her mind. "Would you like to join me for some lunch?"

"There isn't time for that." The two of them were oblivious to the elbowing and postulating transpiring outside his office. In the absence of their dialog, speculation was running rampant about the nature of the obviously tense conversation between the newly minted

Chief Inspector and the outrageous American airship pilot with whom he had been keeping company of late. "You need to come to Pogue's with me. I have irrefutable evidence that Monsieur P. is in England."

UNWRAPPING THE SCARY PRESENT

BY DAVID L. DRAKE

The entire group was present. Sparky and Erasmus had arrived at the Pogue residence just a few minutes before, and Yin had retrieved Edmond from a nearby pub where he had downed a quick noontime meal. The crate sat in the middle of the laboratory floor, its top off, with a bit of the straw packing on the floor nearby. The four of them stood around the crate, making a plan.

Dr. Pogue cocked his head slightly and stated the obvious, "Let's avoid what happened last time." Without looking at it, he held up the mechanical section of his left arm to emphasize his point. "May I suggest that we create a controlled environment from which we can escape if something goes awry."

Yin offered, "We could use a winch to haul all of the parts up away from us quickly by attaching a line to each part."

Edmond shook his head. "Too risky. This thing could climb, cut the winch lines, or worse, there may be multiple mechanical entities in here that would make it hard to corral them all."

Yin continued, "We have the makings of a cage, left over from the work that you did on hardening the railings around Her Majesty's garden. It wouldn't take long to create an enclosure with a single exit."

Sparky nodded approval. "I see. We could tie a line around whoever is working on the parts to pull them to safety if needed. Once they're out of the cage, the door can be slammed shut and locked. That may be rather harsh, but it might save their life."

Erasmus offered his observation, "Do you have enough grating to cover the top of this cage? And the bottom, now that I think about it."

Edmond thought for a second, and then answered, "No, but we could build it into a smaller room, so the cage is fastened to the floor and ceiling." He gasped at his own moment of realization. "Oh, yes! Delightful! There's another benefit if we use one of the rooms off the lower hallway. The cold water conduit for the building's steam engine runs through there. We can tap off of it to make it possible to flood of the room. The device in the crate is metal. So, if needed, we can flood the room, leaving the contraption on the floor while the person working on it can swim to the top of the water, escaping danger."

Yin reacted, but so subtly that only Erasmus noticed. To him, it looked like Edmond had said something that disturbed her. Perhaps Edmond wasn't aware that she and Fox were using the room on the lower hallway for sparring, and she was hoping he wouldn't find out about it. His first thought was that he wasn't concerned about the outcome. It wasn't his job to either help Edmond find out or to help Yin prevent it. But then he remembered that Sergeant Fox was involved, and if he and Yin thought it should be kept secret, then it would be best if it stayed that way. Now how could he get either Yin or Sparky to reveal which of the rooms it was so he could help with the ruse? "Yin, why don't you and I go to select the best room for the task while Sparky and Edmond figure out a way to transport the crate and fence segments?"

Yin nodded her head, "Yes, that's a good plan. Doctor and Doctor, please excuse us."

Yin and Erasmus wound their way around a few worktables in the laboratory and made their way to a heavy wooden door in the back, which Erasmus hadn't noticed before. Judging by its position, it led to a basement level under the retired mill. Yin lead the way and yanked the door open, signaling Erasmus to enter.

Erasmus stepped into a stone hallway with a series of doors on each of its sides. It was lit by a few small gaslights that just barely kept the hallway from being dim. The hallway was clean, but smelled musty. "I am constantly amazed by the number of rooms in this place. What are these used for?"

"These were originally grain storage and milling rooms. On the right side, there's a shaft running through all of the rooms near the ceiling that's attached to the main steam engine in the room at the end. Originally it was belting for grain grinding, sack making, and other machinery. We occasionally use the rooms for such machinery, but the laboratory has stayed the primary location for most our work and experimentation. The rooms on the left are used for storage of a great number of odds and ends. The second door there has the hardened wrought iron garden fencing."

Erasmus grabbed the ring on the door and gave it a yank. Locked. Or stuck. He looked at Yin, who was already fishing a ring of keys out of her pocket.

"Dr. Pogue keeps doors locked in his own place?"

Yin smiled as she fit the key within the lock. "We work on things that require discretion. Some for Scotland Yard. Some for universities. There are others, too."

She turned the key and swung the door open. Erasmus was greeted by a slightly unkempt room of parts and pieces that one might expect in a laboratory that performed a wide range of scientific inquiries. It was even mustier than the hallway. Shelves lined the three doorless walls, all containing baskets and wooden boxes of mechanical parts, pots, oversized and specialty tools, beakers, and hoses. The floor was covered with black wrought iron fence grating, wooden table parts, and a couple of handcarts.

While getting the handcarts and loading the gratings, Yin worked her way through a soliloquy describing how the room was storage for solid objects, as opposed to nearby rooms with chemicals, soils, and specialized vessels for those substances, while other rooms contained delicate optical instruments for microscopy and astronomy. She also suggested that the room across the hall would be perfect for setting up the cage. The room housed an industrial force pump that, in its day, had been used to pump any unwanted water out of the building. Its floor was the lowest in the mill, even lower than the floor of the laboratory. It was also relatively empty and had overhead water pipes with spigots. Unfortunately, it had a stone ramp from its hallway door down to its floor, so moving the garden fence into the room was going to take a bit of muscle.

All the while, Erasmus wanted to ask her about the room for sparring. But he had to stop himself for one simple reason. He wasn't sure that Yin knew about his new relationship with Sergeant Fox. It might be the case that J. B. was gathering information on Yin and Edmond, and Erasmus would be tipping his hand to even reveal that he knew about the encounter. Erasmus was good at keeping secrets. What he had to curb was his curiosity, and that was a challenge. The best way for him to learn more was to approach J. B. So he needed to tuck his curiosity into a musty storage room in the back of his mind.

After about six handcart trips between the storage room on the right and a workroom on the left, they'd moved enough wrought iron to build a cage. During the trips, Erasmus noticed that the workroom not only had the steam engine shaft running from apertures in the walls, but it also had two pipelines with tap points. That would provide the flooding Edmond recommended. At the end of the ferrying, Sparky and Edmond joined them.

Sparky looked at the two of them and noticed their fatigue. Her heart went out to Erasmus. "My dear man, I cheated you out of your noontime meal. Would you like to join me in some sustenance?"

"Yes, I would. But I don't want to abandon the construction effort to Doctors Pogue and Young."

"Oh, pish-posh!" Edmond exclaimed. "This is what we do. Run along, you two. There are a number of establishments that should suit you nearby. I recommend a new place over on Gravel Lane called the White Swan and Cuckoo. Great food. Just opened last year."

After considering their options, Sparky and Erasmus headed out to find the White Swan and Cuckoo.

When they returned, contentedly full of lunch, both Sparky and Erasmus were impressed by the progress. Pogue and Young had fastened the grating together using various bolting systems so it extended floor to ceiling within the room in an area that did not contain the shaft or pipelines. The grates were anchored to both the floor and ceiling by chisels fastened to the grating and wedged in between stones. The combination of all the sturdy points of contact made it a solid cage. They had left two exits: a door of sorts that hinged on three chains, and a window, if one could call it that, opposite the door and hinged in a similar manner. There was room to walk around the entire closure, and Erasmus took that walk to inspect the workmanship.

A carpet covered the floor inside the cage. They had set up a workbench and placed the crate in a corner. Two pipes ran along the ceiling and terminated about waist height with red-painted crank shut-off valves on the ends.

Edmond was standing in the cage placing tools on the bench. He had a chain linked around his waist that trailed off outside of the cage through the door. Edmond noticed Erasmus' inspection and wry grin and asked, "Why the smile, may I ask?"

"You may have been too busy to notice the little leaves and flowers on the garden fence contrasting with the oversized hammer and spanner on the bench and the chain around you. I enjoy juxtaposed dissimilarity. While at the same time, and please do not think of me as being unkind, but I could not help but think of you as a scientist in a scientist cage. Like a bird might be."

This raised similar smiles from Sparky and Edmond, but Yin seemed unmoved by the observation. Sparky thought to herself that Erasmus' wit was growing on her. She let her gaze rest on him for a few seconds, before entering the cage to help lay out the parts.

Yin spoke up uncharacteristically. "May I suggest a plan? I would offer that Dr. Pogue and I unpack and inspect the parts. Dr. McTrowell, if you would be willing, please mind the chain for Dr. Pogue, and haul him out if needed. Chief Inspector, if you would, please man the water spigots."

Sparky was not really happy with the assignment, and though she tried her best not to show it, failed. "I'm not sure that's the most efficient approach. I'm an inventor. If I help with the reconstruction, the three of us should be able to get the work done more quickly."

Yin smiled, but only to show she wasn't hurt by Sparky's response. "You're correct, Doctor, that it would be more efficient. But I'm afraid that speed isn't our primary concern. It's safety. I'm offering that Dr. Pogue and I put ourselves in the greatest danger. The water pipes, both the distilled cold water for the boiler and the Thames water, are under enough pressure that the spigots are difficult enough to turn that the Chief Inspector should have that job. We're counting on your quick hands on the chain."

Sparky didn't like the idea of standing about while others got their hands on the hardware. But she saw that Yin was right. "Fair enough. But Yin, you don't have a chain. How will you escape if an issue arises?"

"With Edmond's mechanical arm, he will not be able to swim. One cannot whistle under water. I'm a strong swimmer and can make my way through the window if needed. Lastly, you should use all your strength to get Dr. Pogue to safety. You wouldn't be able to pull both of us out in time." Sparky begrudgingly nodded agreement.

Everyone manned their stations and began work. Erasmus stood on the window side of the cage within an arm's reach of the two spigots. Sparky stood near the door, the chain resting on her foot so she would have quick access to it.

Two hours passed. Edmond and Yin had pulled most of the parts from the crate and laid them out all over the cage on every horizontal surface. Packing straw and thin strips of curled wood lay strewn everywhere, even some of it hanging outside of the cage. A few of the parts were already assembled, particularly those components with complex gearwork, tubes, or a series of lenses. The pair in the cage extracted and examined each piece before showing it to Erasmus and Sparky. The components sparked lively discussions. What was the function of the component? How did it fit into the chassis? Why were the connections made in the way they were? There were almost no screws or bolts. The metal chassis resembled armor or the outer shell of a wasp. This was not the slick polished brass of the EPACTs but rather rough iron with interior fastener knobs.

Edmond removed the final piece, another rugged iron leg, the sixth of its kind in the crate. It, like the others, resembled the shape of a mountain lion's rear thigh. Edmond looked deeply into the crate to make sure they had removed every tiny piece. "Hulloooo! Delightful! Seriously delightful!"

He hopped up a tad, landing with his waist on the rim of the open crate, and readied his left arm. He breathed out a series of quick little toothy whistles that were too quiet for anyone else to hear, but they clearly instructed his arm to reach to the bottom of the crate and retrieve something. He sprang back down to the floor, clutching a single piece of paper in his metallic fingers. Practically sing-songing the word, he held the paper high, "Instructions!"

Erasmus and Sparky grabbed the gratings and held their faces close to get a better look. Edmond spread the slightly wrinkled paper on the workbench and smoothed it out with his right hand. Yin craned her neck over his left shoulder.

Edmond's voice took on the air of a discoverer, as if he had just stumbled upon previously unknown hieroglyphics carved in the side of an ancient tomb. "It's handwritten in French. 'Assembly for Dragon's Tooth Style 5.' It then goes on to list eighteen steps. That's odd. There are more than eighteen pieces here. Is it possible that we're missing the rest of the instructions?"

Each of the four had an opinion, and they all tried to get them into the conversation in sputtering anticipation. French? Dragon's Tooth? Style 5? Should we construct it? Misinformation, perhaps? But Edmond held up his hand to stop the chatter. "Let's carefully follow what we have, and see where that takes us. Wait, wait, what's this?"

He flipped the paper over. "There are another five steps. And it's signed! By Misters Hedgley and Martin; no first names. It also has another name. Monsieur Punaise! Delightful!"

Sparky chimed in. "That's the mysterious Monsieur P!" Eyes closed, she did a bit of a dance with her arms but then soberly followed that with, "it's interesting there's not a fourth name. What did Lord Ashleigh say his name was? Oh, yes, a Mr. Grossman. Maybe he was just involved with the limestone theft near Paris."

Edmond held his hand up again. "Enough sleuthing. We can discuss that later. On to the assembly!"

Edmond had no difficulty reading the French directions, which he did out loud in French. The instructions used simple verbs and not many of them. There were a few rough drawings with numbered parts and arrows, but they mainly detailed how parts connected rather than providing an overall drawing of the finished construction. Most of the initial work was connecting internal parts. Some were clearly the power transmission components; others were timing and sensing constructs. It seemed like they were only a quarter of the way into the effort as they neared the end of the instructions.

Edmond scratched his head using his right hand, of course, as he tried to puzzle out why the directions were so partial. The internal parts were all connected. They included a good number of tubes and other parts loosely held together, but the external structure was still lying about the floor and bench. The final step said to open a door in the side of the empty spherical chamber and toss in a handful of wood blocks and chips. He followed the instructions to the letter, including shutting the door and latching it. "Well, that's all we have." He instinctively looked into the crate to see if there were one more thing he should have done or followed.

Yin pointed at the parts and gasped, "Edmond!" The shock of hearing her use his first name was what surprised Erasmus and Sparky first. They looked at each other with a "what was that about?" look.

It was clear to Yin that shutting the door of the spherical chamber set off a chain reaction. The system hissed, and the chamber grew hot. Dr. Pogue stepped toward the workbench, reaching for the chamber's hatch, but it was already too hot to handle. He pulled his hand away. "I must have caused a striker to ignite the wood!" He stepped back to give himself a buffer of safety.

Hot air filled the black rubber hoses, and the collection of parts sprouted inflated elastic legs. But after inflating for a few seconds, they bent and became jointed. The wobbly automaton righted itself on the workbench. Erasmus jumped to the spigots, and Sparky grabbed the chain from the floor. The object teetered on the bench for a few more seconds, like a surly balloon animal. "Hold steady." Edmond cautioned. "Let's see if this is the end of it."

Four people held their breath with their eyes glued to the six-tube-legged beast. As suddenly as it started, a gust of air issued from a number of small vents. It crouched and swung its compound optical assemblage around as if it were surveying the environment. Each of them jumped back as if a bear were trying to sniff them.

Instead, the creature rolled its right side into one of the exoskeleton enclosures, snapping the armor into place. It immediately rolled back up onto its tube-end feet and flipped over another enclosure piece, rolling its left side into it with a snap. It now looked like a bizarre armored dachshund from hell, hissing as it waddled on its six black rubber conduit limbs. It jumped off the workbench, landing just right to force a front rubber leg into an armature assembly.

It then jammed the other front tube onto another armature, allowing it to tip up into its newly acquired crutches.

Yin yelled to Edmond, "Leave! Now!"

WATER WATER EVERYWHERE

BY DR. KATHERINE L. MORSE

One more perfectly executed hop and the creature blocked Pogue's exit from the cage, standing on his chain. Not knowing whether it could "hear" or not, Sparky raised her fingers to whistle at it to attract its attention. And then she realized that doing so might have disastrous, unintended consequences, given the signaling for Pogue's arm.

Yin yelled at Drake with an intensity that startled both him and McTrowell, "Open the valves!" Looking at the situation with Pogue and the creature, Drake hesitated. Yin hollered even louder, "Now!" Drake cranked the valve handles as fast as his wrists would rotate.

Oblivious to the water rushing in, the metal beast began tearing up the rug and workbench in the cage without budging off the chain. Stunned by this activity, Sparky froze. What could it possibly be doing? She lost precious seconds in this reverie before she remembered that it was her responsibility to extract Pogue. She grabbed the chain at her feet and tried to haul him out. The shoulder she had injured dragging Drake over the railing of the Burke & Hare screamed in agony. An image of the packing slip for the crate flashed through her head. The monstrosity cutting off Pogue's escape route weighed nearly 350 pounds! Letting the chain get wet wasn't helping either. It was all she could do not to break a finger as her hands slipped on the links and in between them. As much as she adored her red, four-button leather gloves and would have hated to ruin them, she wished she had them at that moment. At least they would have provided more traction, maybe enough to pull Dragon's Tooth Style 5 off balance.

Yin had begun crawling up the far side of the cage toward the window. Despite the constraints of her cumbersome dress that was further weighed down by its soaked hem, she was making good progress. She was clear of the water and just a couple of handholds from the window when she looked back. The creature was undeterred by the water that was already up to its "knees." It was bending some of the metal scrap on the workbench. It was assembling something rather than just destroying the contents of the cage! It had formed the wood from the workbench and the metal strips into a crude barrel-like form. It swiveled its head around as if it were searching for something. It pointed itself at Pogue. To the horror of all four of them, it fixed its attention on his left arm. Not one of them needed to guess what that meant.

Drake yelled over the sound of rushing water, "Dr. Young, I have to turn off the water or Dr. Pogue will drown!"

"No!" If Sparky didn't know better, she would have thought that Yin sounded hysterical. Despite everything Sparky had recently discovered about her scientific colleague, she was completely unprepared for what Yin did next.

While hanging onto the side of the cage with her left hand, Yin grasped the piping at the collar of her dress with her right hand. With one swift, deft pull, she yanked it up and away from her body. It wasn't piping; it was a cord. Sparky had mistaken the tiny metal adornments down the front of the bodice and the inside of both sleeves as mere decoration. Given the supreme practicality of Dr. Young, McTrowell should have known better. They were tiny swing clasps. The dress burst open like a chrysalis to reveal a lighter version of the pajama-like ensemble Sparky had seen Yin wearing while sparring with Sergeant Fox.

Yin sprang lightly to the floor of the cage. The water was nearly up to her hips. Despite that encumbrance, she hopped up onto the remains of the workbench and executed a handspring, vaulting herself over Pogue's head and landing on the back of the beast. She wrapped her legs around its neck and began striking it with the sides of her flat, rigid hands. It acted mildly perturbed by this assault, but slogged inexorably through the rising tide toward Pogue, or to be more precise, his left arm that he was trying to keep above the water line. Yin wrapped her legs around her opponent's neck, grasped the head with her hands and the full length of her forearms, and twisted viciously. The head spun off the neck and disappeared into the swirling water. And then something truly unusual happened; Yin smiled.

Sensing that the danger had passed, Drake reached down into the water to crank the valves closed. One of them moved fairly easily, albeit somewhat impeded from being submerged, and he closed it snugly. The water was rising only half as fast, but it was still climbing. For all his strength, he couldn't get the other handle to budge. "It is jammed! I cannot close it!"

Sparky finally abandoned the completely hopeless task of pulling on the chain. There was so much water in the room that she no longer had any leverage against the floor, and the headless hulk was still standing on the chain. She grabbed the cage and attempted to drag herself around to Drake, but she was fighting the current and her freshly inflamed shoulder. The water was inching up Pogue's chest and it was clear she wouldn't make it to Drake in time.

Yin's smile vanished. She took a deep breath and dove into the murky maelstrom. Drake and McTrowell held their breath. Sparky began counting anxiously. Perhaps Yin had trained as a pearl diver in addition to her other interesting pursuits. Sparky and Erasmus looked back and forth at each other and Edmond desperately. How could they have so misjudged the danger of the situation? The water had crept up to his chin when he suddenly bobbed up. A second later, Yin surfaced next to him, grabbed him under his left arm, and began swimming for the door of the cage. Drake swam for the ramp, reaching it just before McTrowell who was still struggling with her wounded right arm. He dragged her up above the water line.

Fortunately, the room's original intended use worked in their favor. There was still a grating a couple of feet below the door that had originally been for the force pump's discharge pipe. Once the water reached that level, it began flowing out of the room and down some drain toward the Thames. The two of them waded back into the water up to their knees to help Yin haul Edmond to safety. The four of them collapsed in a heap at the top of the ramp, gasping for breath. Although Pogue was clearly out of danger, Yin continued to clutch him tightly in her arms. She appeared to be shivering from the cold. The water was running off her hair and down her face. At least that's what Sparky chose to believe.

Surveying the lake in his basement and showing no concern from his brush with almost certain death mere moments before, Pogue wondered aloud, "Do you suppose that force pump still works?"

SECRET POWERS

BY DAVID L. DRAKE

Mr. Reginald Wallace looked uncharacteristically powerless as he entered the Western & Transatlantic Airship Lines' London Terminal on crutches. He was unfamiliar with operating such supports, and hc labored with the timing and balance needed to make the confident-looking strides one traditionally needs to run such a business. His gout-swollen foot was trussed up to prevent any possible chance that it would touch the floor to prevent the incredible, shooting pains that would result.

Reginald made his way through the wide main corridor toward the reception desk where Mr. Littleton was working. Between the racket the crutches were making on the floor and Mr. Wallace's strained breathing, Mr. Littleton looked up from his books before the lame man had made it to the counter. Mr. Littleton jumped to his feet, clearly concerned for his employer's welfare. "Mr. Wallace, how may I assist you?"

"Please retrieve my wife. I need to speak to her." Mr. Wallace's tone was uncharacteristically somber.

"Understood, sir. Can I have a porter fetch a wheeled-chair for you?"

"Priorities, Mr. Littleton. Fetch my wife." He was more curt than usual, and that was saying something.

"Yes, sir!" Mr. Littleton kicked up his heels and ran to the back office.

In a few moments, Mrs. Wallace strode out toward the reception desk, Mr. Littleton following closely behind. She cleared her throat in an authoritative way before addressing her husband. "You should not be up and about, dear. Would you like me to arrange for a cab to pick you up?"

"Thank you for the concern, but no. I wanted to attend to a particular shipment that may not have gone out. You mentioned it the other night. A crate of clockwork parts. I'd like to help get them shipped to their destination."

"I'm aware of the crate. I'm afraid that is out of the question. One of your pilots, Dr. McTrowell, had it transported elsewhere."

"That doesn't make sense. Why would she do that? And why did you allow her to do that? ... My dear." Reginald was not practiced in the art of hiding his displeasure, and he failed to do so. But he also realized that, to get through the process of retrieving the crate and getting it shipped off, he would need his wife's cooperation.

"She absconded with it. She insisted that Scotland Yard would have an interest in it. I don't know where the crate is now, but she suggested you should take up the matter of ownership with them. Would you like me to arrange a cab for Whitehall Place?"

Reginald's eye twitched. He had no immediate response for his wife. He broke off his stare at her and looked at Mr. Littleton, who instinctively looked away and took a small, awkward step back. Reginald looked around at his terminal. What a mess had he gotten himself into? *"Wait,"* he thought to himself, *"the Chief Inspector! Drake's his name. I'll see him and clear all of this up. But first, I need to write a letter saying the shipment will be delayed."* He did his best to feign confidence and answered his wife, "Such effort for a trifling. A cab to Scotland Yard would be excellent, although I typically wouldn't go to such lengths for a single crate. First, a sheet of letterhead and an envelope, Littleton. I need to clear up a minor matter."

Mr. Littleton immediately went to fulfill his employer's request. Reginald looked at his wife, who was seething inside, and he knew it. "Don't worry my dear, I'll get back to the mend as soon as I address these trifling issues. You know how I can't stand to be away from my work."

She cocked her head slightly and narrowed her eyes. That's all it took to clearly convey to Reginald that she knew he was up to something, and he was going to have to do some fancy dancing to avoid problems with the Yard. Then Mrs. Wallace smiled politely. "Wonderful. Let me arrange your cab. And be careful with the foot, dear."

It took a few minutes for the four in the flooded room to catch their breath. Yin, still dressed in her sparring clothes, responded to Dr. Pogue's question about the force pump. "Yes, it still works. I'll set up the belt to the drive shaft." She pointed overhead to the shaft that ran near the ceiling. Without hesitation, she dove back under with water to retrieve the belt stored in the stone pit with the force pump. Edmond crawled his way up the ramp toward the door, struggling to get out of the rising water. He stood, trying to get any remaining water out of his mechanical left arm. After a number of shakes, he gave up and forced it through a ninety-degree rotation, releasing it from his arm so he could tip it up more easily. More than a cup of water poured out. Edmond reattached his arm and waited to help Yin when she resurfaced.

Erasmus signaled to Sparky, saying, "Let us see if we can get that water shut off."

Sparky wearily nodded, adding, "I can only do so much with this shoulder. But I'll do my best."

Erasmus and Sparky swam against the incoming water to get to the uncooperative spigot. It was now well below the waterline. It took repeated diving and considerable underwater struggling with the valve. They had to execute more than a few synchronized bobs up to get air before they made progress. Once freed, the faucet closed. By the time the two had swum back to the ramp, Yin had already climbed up a set of ladder-like stones and, with Edmond feeding the belt up to her, configured the drive train belt around the drive shaft. She dove back underwater to attach the belt to the pump and draw its laces tight. Edmond volunteered to go connect the shaft to the running house steam engine. He disappeared out the door, still shaking moisture off his metal fingers.

When Yin resurfaced, the three looked over the flooded mess the room had become. The water was now chin-deep. It was scummy with the dust of the room and mixed with the packing straw and splintered wood from what had been a worktable. Some lubrication oil from the force pump had also mixed in, giving the water a truly disgusting sheen in various spots. Sparky mentioned how lucky it was that the gas lamps were high on the walls, and that it would have been a bigger misadventure if they had been extinguished, leaving them in the dark and underwater.

The drive shaft above came to life, slowly at first, and then increasing in speed, as Edmond was obviously easing its clutch into place in the mechanical room. After the initial slippage, the belt grabbed tight and the three, who smiled at the progress, heard the muffled sound of the force pump doing its duty underwater. They also heard a secondary gurgling as the force pump drove the water up a drainpipe, out of the room, and toward the Thames. Edmond returned to the room, pleased with the sounds of the working pump.

Erasmus suddenly realized the wetness of his clothes and how cold he was becoming. He reached into his pockets to clear them. Out of his left front pocket he pulled what had been a white, waxed paper sack, now stained gray. He opened it to find three sad-looking, anise-flavored jelly babies, stuck together in a gooey clump. Erasmus remarked to Edmond, "Hmmpf, I shall have to ask you to make more of these."

Edmond smiled. "Don't worry, my good man. You can just buy more of them at my favorite sweets shop. Morgan's Tobacconist and Quality Confections at 22 Cleveland Street. It's a distance from here, I know, but I'm particular. Oh, don't look at me that way! There isn't anything miraculous about them other than being thick with the anise oil that invokes that unique state in you. It's a reaction similar to the smells of mother's cooking conjuring clear memories from one's childhood. Only … more extreme." He wagged his head a bit as if this were all a simple notion.

The four of them wrung out their sleeves as the water slowly receded from the soggy room. Yin went and fetched some tea to warm everyone up. By the time they had emptied their cups, the room was back down to standing puddles.

Edmond left to disengage the drive shaft, stopping the flapping of the rotating belt and silencing the force pump. They ended up standing around the cage, looking at the metallic body, the separated head, and the incredible mess it had made. Edmond squatted down to take a better look at the head. "*What an odd set of perception units it has,*" he thought. He pointed with his left arm just inside the cage to the place under the optical lenses. "What could that be? A single nostril?"

Just then, they heard the faintest whistle, just a bit of air passing over a metal lip. Edmond's mechanical arm sprang to life, grabbing the bars of the cage. It gave a wrenching twist, and through its own motion, unclipped itself from Edmond's stump, separating the mechanical from the living flesh. Edmond gasped at the loss, and the others followed suit.

Still commanded by the Dragon's Tooth head, the arm swung itself inside the cage, and wormed its way over to the torso, reached inside the shoulder joint and popped off the front left leg. The arm then forced itself backwards into the stump, where it appeared to attach itself, creating a new complex limb. Without hesitation, it grabbed the automaton's head and snapped it back onto its neck with a small twist, rejoining the beast into a single automaton again.

All of these actions happened quickly, far faster than any of the humans in the room could have reacted to. Everyone was stunned as the contraption rose back up on its five remaining legs and went back to feverish work disassembling the workbench and carpet.

Yin jumped at the cage door, wanting to get into it and rip off its head again. Edmond, minus a left arm, stepped back in amazement, looking at the scientific marvel. Sparky looked around for a weapon.

Erasmus, still holding the wax bag, instinctively reached inside the small sack, ripped out the gummy contents, and popped it into his mouth. It was initially a disgusting watery goop flavor, but once bitten, the strong anise flavor filled his senses. "Wait," he said. His brain filled with clarity.

Sparky turned to him. "Pardon me? Are you serious?"

"Wait," he repeated. "Listen to me." All three stopped and paid attention to his incredibly calm voice.

"First: there were instructions in the crate, which means the shipment was to someone who was buying or using the Dragon's Tooth. They were unfamiliar enough with it that they needed clear instructions to use the contents of the crate.

"Second: there was no additional information beyond the limited instructions. The recipients must have received an earlier message or package since they knew what to expect once this Dragon's Tooth came to life.

"Third: because of this, the Dragon's Tooth was not sent to destroy the recipient, but rather it was a demonstration of its capability. Since it is building or constructing something, and is interested in mechanical hardware, the most likely explanation is that the previous shipment contained a different Dragon's Tooth. This one is trying to demonstrate its ability to reconfigure the previous Dragon's Tooth. Let us watch this Dragon's Tooth Style 5 until it finishes its demonstration, and see what it constructs."

The three others stared at Erasmus for a few seconds, trying to transition from panic to observation. They turned and watched the beast go about its mysterious task. Erasmus' first impression was how eerily the contraption was immediately taking advantage of its additional arm to speed its progress.

Over the next forty-five minutes, the automaton continued, including tossing additional wood blocks into its burner. Edmond rattled along with his observations as Yin transcribed them in a notebook she had fetched from the laboratory. Edmond observed that its vision, if one could call it that, was actually very spotty; it could distinguish between light and dark objects but not much more. It did a great deal of feeling around and had to try things multiple times to get them right. When it finished, it had constructed a very poor imitation of itself with three wooden legs, one of its own metal legs, and a body woven together out of carpet and straw. It did a final search throughout the cage, laid down, and became completely still.

At this, Edmond turned to Erasmus, exclaiming, "This is all delightful! The next round of jelly babies is on me."

Erasmus smiled. "Fine with me. I think I am ready for some dry clothes."

You Know How to Whistle, Don't You?

By Dr. Katherine L. Morse

"Aren't we forgetting something?" Sparky asked, pointing at the Dragon's Tooth Style 5 slumbering on its ill-gotten left front leg. They exchanged exhausted looks. None of them was fooled by its seemingly quiescent state or relished the idea of tangling with it again when it inevitably awoke. They all stared blankly at their opponent. A couple of minutes passed during which Pogue gazed wistfully and longingly at the stump of his left arm.

Sparky suddenly brightened up. "I've got an idea, but it's a little mad." The other three looked at her as if to say, "Mad, as compared to what we've just come through?"

"Dr. Pogue, how much do you suppose the arm weighs?"

"Eleven pounds. Dr. McTrowell, what do you have in mind?"

"So long as it can't find any new materials, it seems to remain in some sort of waiting state. And, it can't see very well. I propose we go back to your laboratory and assemble a non-functional replacement. We'll bring it back here under wraps. The Dragon's Tooth is resting close enough to the edge of the cage that Dr. Young and I can unfasten the limb if we work quickly. Once we've released your arm, you'll whistle for it. Dr. Young and I will attach the replacement once yours has crawled free."

Yes, mad was clearly an accurate adjective. But as none of them had a better plan, they agreed it was worth trying. "But first, perhaps some dry clothes," Sparky suggested

Erasmus deposited a small peck on Sparky's cheek. "Dr. McTrowell, you seem to have things well in hand." The expression on his face suggested he wasn't being entirely truthful. "Just promise me you will not open that cage again. I need to go and report our discovery to the authorities." He attempted to twirl his sodden moustache back up and into shape, but it was hopeless. He squelched out of the room, leaving his equally soggy compatriots to execute the slightly daft plan.

Crocker knew better than to ask too many questions when Drake slogged into Ye Olde Cheshire Cheese and asked the barkeep to send up a ploughman's. Drake looked as if he'd been caught in a sudden downpour without an umbrella, except for the fact that it was a clear summer day, and his bowler was dry. Upstairs, Drake devoured the thick, chewy sandwich while hanging up his wet clothes and putting his moustache to rights. Saving people from drowning was hungry work.

It was after dinner by the time he reached Cheyne Street. He really hoped Fox was still about because he didn't want to have to wait another day to report what they had discovered. He needn't have worried. Some of the other fellows were spread around the room, drinking brandies and smoking cigars, but Fox was stationed at a small desk with a pile of newspapers at his left elbow and another pile discarded on the floor to his right. He had his left hand perched on top of the stack with his index finger tracking the text of a small article while his right hand, holding a pen, hovered over a notebook on the desk. He looked up as Drake entered. Although he tried to make the action look casual, he closed the notebook before Drake quite reached the desk. Drake took in the situation at a glance. The newspaper on the top of the stack was in a Germanic language, but not German. Dutch? The one on the top of the discard pile was Italian. There were no dictionaries on the desk. He filed away his observations for later.

"Sergeant Fox, I have come on the matter of Mr. Martin and Mr. Hedgley. They are almost certainly in Carlisle. Dr. McTrowell serendipitously intercepted a crate shipped from there containing a dastardly mechanical contraption that can only be the work of their co-conspirator, Monsieur Punaise. We also have good reason to believe that this is neither the first such shipment nor the only type of device they are producing. This would certainly explain their black-market deal to obtain clockwork gears. They must have some sort of factory."

"Chief Inspector, I don't doubt your facts or your deductive powers, but it's highly unlikely they could have built such a factory without revealing themselves."

"I agree, but the facts remain. I would gladly show you the device to confirm what I have reported."

"That won't be necessary, at least not this evening. There's another possible explanation. Westley, have we had any reports recently from Carlisle?"

"Carlisle, you say? Hmm, that does sound familiar." Westley pondered for another moment before turning to the filing cabinet. He rifled through a couple of crumpled, askew slips of paper before pausing. "Here's one from yesterday morning." He handed it to Fox, who read it rapidly while Drake peered around the substantial bulk of his shoulder.

Fox looked at Drake. "Does this description sound like what you intercepted?"

"It is not Style 5, but it might be 3 or 4."

"Excuse me?"

"I shall explain later. This is certainly what we are seeking."

Fox turned the sheet of paper over and read the initials, HMS. His expression grew dangerously dark. He scanned the faces in the room, not finding the one he wanted. Drake was a little relieved. He really didn't want to have to arrest the Sergeant for murder this evening, which would surely have been the outcome if Fox's intended target had been in the room.

"I'll deal with him later," Fox growled. "You and I need to get to Carlisle immediately. Meet me at Euston Station tomorrow morning for the first train. Oh, and perhaps you should bring Dr. McTrowell as well. We may need her unique skills."

"I know I cannot convince the three of you to stop for a proper meal, so I brought some tea and scones. I've put on a pot of oxtail soup for when you drop from exhaustion." Mrs. Bingham left the laboratory without waiting for the response that she knew would not be forthcoming.

Poor Pogue, having only one good arm, was mostly reduced to directing traffic in his own laboratory while Sparky and Yin scavenged for likely-sized pieces for the decoy limb. They had to keep reminding each other that it didn't need to be functional, only the size, shape, and weight of the real arm. And, of course, it had to match the cleats. It was more like art than science or engineering, which was a challenge for all three of them. They made a final check that it fit the fasteners on Pogue's stump and he confirmed that the weight was right before they wrapped it in a bit of tarp to carry it down the hall. Sparky stuffed the spanners and screwdrivers she'd been using into the loops of her tool belt. She swept the remaining couple of handfuls of nuts and bolts into the pouch on her belt for good measure in case they had to make some modifications in a hurry. They polished off their tea and scones to fortify themselves and headed out the laboratory's side door with their swaddled package.

Sparky put her ear to the door they had bolted for good measure. "I don't hear any sounds of movement. Perhaps you two should stand back while I make sure." Yin put out her arm and swept Pogue behind her in the direction of the laboratory as she stepped away from the door. Sparky unbolted the door and opened it slowly, although quietly was out of the question given the recent elevated dampness.

The gaslights were turned down, but there was enough light for Sparky to see that nothing was moving below on the basement floor. She opened the door the rest of the way and motioned for Young and Pogue to follow her. They didn't exactly tiptoe down the ramp, but they approached slowly and quietly. They stopped near the edge of the cage closest to the Dragon's Tooth. Yin placed the wrapped decoy limb gently on the floor next to the cage and began to unwrap it stealthily. The creature hissed, chugged, and lurched to its feet. McTrowell and Pogue froze. Although Yin had changed into dry clothes, she had not returned to a dress. She was wearing a pair of her "pajamas," a "gi," as she had explained to Pogue and McTrowell. This one was black rather than white. Without hesitation, she sprang between Pogue and the cage, striking a fighting pose.

Sparky admired the foresight of Yin's choice, but didn't take her eyes off the occupant of the cage. She held her breath, preparing to run if necessary. The monster made two circuits around the cage, searching for parts. Finding nothing usable, it resumed its previous resting posture with its full weight pinning the gleaming brass arm to the floor.

Sparky let out her breath slowly. "I think it's designed to wake up periodically to perform whatever tasks might be at hand. I would rather not wait to find out how often it does so. Dr. Pogue, would you please take your place around the corner of the cage. Dr. Young, you're with me. I don't know if it will wake up if we jostle it, so let's not find out." She pulled the screwdrivers and spanners out of her belt and placed them on the floor next to the edge of the cage. She and Yin laid down, head to head, next to the cage, and reached in with all four of their arms. They loosened the clamps on Pogue's appropriated arm. Sparky finished unwrapping the decoy, threaded it carefully through the grating in the cage, and handed it down to Yin who placed it on the floor inside the cage right next to the Dragon's Tooth. She resumed her position adjacent to Yin and asked quietly, "Are we all ready?" Pogue and Young nodded. "Dr. Pogue, please summon the arm." Pogue whistled softly, but nothing happened. "I fear you'll need to whistle louder." Sparky could feel the sweat trickling across her forehead and into her ear. Her arms were cramping and her shoulder was screaming as she stretched to insert the false limb. Pogue whistled louder. The mechanical arm made a fist, causing it to lurch toward him, bumping the replacement slightly out of alignment and nudging the Dragon's Tooth. It started to hiss. Sparky and Yin knew they couldn't wait for the chugging to start. They forced their faces against the cage, scrambling to lock the replacement limb in place. The two of them barely managed to pull their arms back out and roll away as the beast stumbled to its feet. Pogue snatched up the inching arm with his right hand and fished it out of the cage.

Sparky pointed at the door and yelled at Pogue, "Go!" She didn't have to tell him twice. He sprinted up the ramp. The beast stamped around the cage furiously, thumping the inferior limb on the floor in a way that almost suggested frustration. It turned on Sparky and Yin, and then looked down. The spanners and screwdrivers! If it got ahold of them, there was not telling what damage it would do. It banged on the cage, trying to get to the tools. She didn't dare to reach for them. Then she remembered the nuts and bolts in her pouch. She grabbed a handful and threw them through the grating like she was feeding chickens. The Dragon's Tooth whirled around and began snatching them up. With its attention diverted, she and Yin retrieved the tools and retreated in Pogue's wake, slamming and bolting the door behind them.

Sparky flattened herself against the door, trying to listen inside the room through her gasping breath and the pounding in her ears. The room fell silent after a couple of minutes. She waited a bit longer to ascertain that nothing else would happen. "Did Mrs. Bingham say something about oxtail soup?"

A Late Visit to Scotland Yard

By David L. Drake

Mrs. Wallace turned to Mr. Littleton. Her eyes were tight and menacing, but somehow conveyed that it wasn't Mr. Littleton who was vexing her. "Now that Mr. Wallace has left, I would like you to hand me his letter." She held out her open hand, and wiggled her fingers with a "give it here" gesture. He hesitated with a false sense of propriety and loyalty. "Now, Mr. Littleton, ... please." He sheepishly deposited the letter into the beckoning hand. "Thank you, my good man," she replied. He imagined that she would rip it open right there in front of him and be shocked at whatever contents it contained. But that waking nightmare didn't come to life. Instead, she made an unexpected request, "Fetch me a cab to take me to Scotland Yard."

Without thinking, Mr. Littleton asked, "Are you going to join Mr. Wallace there?"

"Normally I don't disclose such things, but I strongly doubt my husband is going there directly. I believe that I'll arrive in advance of him. But that is neither here nor there. A cab, if you please."

Mr. Littleton looked at his counter, and chose the button labeled "Transport Request" to hold down for a few seconds. "It should be here shortly, Mrs. Wallace."

She nodded to him as she placed the letter into her handbag, turned confidently, and strode toward the front of the terminal to get her ride.

Mrs. Bingham gave the soupspoon a last lap around the oxtail soup, scooped up a bit of the broth, and gave it a sip. She pursed her lips and looked off in the distance with satisfaction at the flavor. Sparky, Yin, and Edmond sat at the wooden kitchen table normally used for food preparation and casual dining. To a person, they looked only slightly refreshed by their clean up and fresh clothes and were looking at the cook in anticipation. With two kitchen towels for insulation, she picked up the pot with both hands, carefully turned, and placed it on the trivet in the center of the table. She promptly filled their bowls, and the hungry eaters dug in.

Mrs. Bingham smiled at the enthusiasm. "Glad to see you enjoying my soup, but I have not seen three such hungry mouths at this table in as long as I can remember."

Dr. Pogue was willing to take the time to respond. "We've worked up a great appetite, Mrs. Bingham. I assure you this hot soup is exactly what we need." He looked around the table. "I think another round is needed, please. And do we have more of that rustic bread?"

The diners continued on in silence for a while. The warmth of the soup made Sparky almost nod off at the table. "Oh! Please excuse me. I've exhausted myself. I'm going to lie down, if that's acceptable."

Dr. Pogue cheerfully replied, "Why of course!"

Sparky quietly left the kitchen and trundled off to her room to get some early sleep. Mrs. Bingham gathered up the pots and cooking utensils, excused herself, and left for the scullery.

Dr. Pogue looked at Yin, who was slowly enjoying her meal. He noticed her black, straight, unwoven hair, still damp from her bath. He admired her cream-colored kimono, decorated with small white birds, either flying or roosting in crooked black trees with pink flowers. She looked up from her bowl with kind eyes. Why hadn't he noticed her eyes before?

In a voice lowered but steady, he said "You saved me. At least twice."

She set down her spoon. "Yes. I … I …"

He slid his right hand slowly over toward her, stopping short of touching her. She gave him a quick smile but lowered her gaze to hide it. She moved her hand over to his and took it. Her petite hand on top of his countered the specifics of who saved whom. They sat at the table, quietly soaking in the intimate moment until they heard the clanking of Mrs. Bingham returning with the clean kettle full of utensils. Yin reluctantly removed her hand. Their gaze continued to stay locked, and Mrs. Bingham noticed. "Well, I had a full day. I'll be off to bed, if you don't have anything else for me, Dr. Pogue."

Hearing his name brought Edmond back to reality, if only a bit. "Oh, yes, of course. See you tomorrow, Mrs. Bingham." Yin smiled at his awkward recovery.

Just as Mrs. Bingham was about to leave the kitchen, the deep thud of a heavy doorknocker filled the air. Mrs. Bingham whipped off her apron and scurried to answer the door. From the kitchen, Yin and Edmond could hear the housekeeper exchange pleasantries with the visitor and then shut the door. The sounds of two voices approached. Edmond took the opportunity to look deep into Yin's eyes once more. Mrs. Bingham cleared her throat and announced, "Chief Inspector Drake has arrived."

The pair turned to look at their guest. Erasmus was dressed in black pants, a white pressed shirt, and a blue waistcoat. He carried his frock coat over the same arm that held both his black bowler and cane. Edmond studied him for a split second. "Erasmus, you have that look about you. You're on a serious mission."

"I am sorry to interrupt your evening, but I need to make sure that Sparky can join me early tomorrow. We have a journey to take. Is she about?"

"She turned in for the night. What kind of journey?"

"I am afraid I cannot say. Official business and all that." Erasmus noticed that Yin was paying particular attention to him. *"Odd,"* he thought. "Do you mind if I stop by her room? Which one is it?"

"Not at all, but I warn you that she's exhausted from today's hijinks." Edmond began to give convoluted directions for finding her room.

Mrs. Bingham cleared her throat to interrupt politely. "Chief Inspector, allow me to show you the way."

"That would be grand. Lead on."

Edmond turned to Yin. "How very interesting. Erasmus doesn't look the least bit tired from today's battle with the Dragon's Tooth. He looks like he's starting a brand-new day."

When Mrs. Bingham and Erasmus arrived at Sparky's door, it was closed, without any sound of activity from within. Mrs. Bingham gave a polite knock and asked in a quiet voice, "Dearie? You have a visitor." There was a very slight sound from inside the room, and then it stopped. She knocked again.

The door opened a crack, and Sparky's petite face appeared, squinting from the light in the hallway. "Who? … Oh, Erasmus. I was asleep. Can you come back tomorrow?"

"Actually, that is why I am here. Sergeant Fox and I would like you to join us for an assignment tomorrow. Can you do that?"

Her sleepy voice contradicted her words. "Of course. Of course. Where?"

"Meet us at the Euston train station first thing in the morning. We will be headed north. Be ready for … anything."

Sparky woke up a bit at that. She paused while taking the time to comprehend the weight of Erasmus' request. "Understood. I'm going to go back to sleep now. See you in the morning."

"Good night, Sparky."

Erasmus rejoined the cab he'd left waiting for him. He nimbly hopped up and directed the driver to take him to Scotland Yard. He wanted to go there to tidy up any remaining tasks he could perform in an hour and delegate the rest. As the horse broke into a trot, Erasmus tugged his beard a bit as he thought about which set of weapons he wanted with him tomorrow. They were traveling by train, which meant they could take a rifle if he could secret it away in a case. He could also bring one for Sparky. A frontier woman has experience with one, surely. But the issue was that they were probably going to have to carry everything that they brought, like a foot soldier would. That meant their entire arsenal would have to be light enough to maneuver. But it was the three of them, J. B., Sparky, and himself, going up to find and perhaps arrest three people, Mr. Martin, Mr. Hedgley, and Mr. Punaise. They shouldn't need too much firepower.

When Erasmus arrived at the Yard, it was just a few minutes before nine o'clock. Compared to the daytime population, there were very few staff present. Despite the hour, a well-dressed woman was waiting, seated outside his office door. "Good evening, ma'am. Can I help you in some way?"

Mrs. Wallace stood, and addressed him confidently, "I certainly hope so. I'm Mrs. Annabelle Wallace, wife of Mr. Reginald Wallace, the owner of the Western & Transatlantic Airship Lines. I'm waiting for Chief Inspector Erasmus Drake. It's my understanding that he was aboard our Burke & Hare racing airship during the international airship regatta last month. Do you know where I can find him? I've been waiting for quite some time." Her words flowed without a single intake of breath, and they sounded very rehearsed.

Erasmus correctly guessed that she had been mentally practicing that introduction for the entire time she'd been waiting, and it was critical to her that she appear important to everyone she encountered. *"Good for her,"* he thought. "I am the Chief Inspector. My apologies for your wait. How can I help you?"

"I assume you are familiar with Dr. McTrowell. She was the pilot of the Burke & Hare during the regatta. Today, she took a crate from our warehouse, saying that she was delivering it to Scotland Yard for analysis. No one here is aware of this, so I waited for you."

"Ahh, you are correct, ma'am." Erasmus knew he needed to provide some information to Mrs. Wallace, but not too much. "Dr. McTrowell did deliver the crate to one of our technical analysts, who has determined that its contents are of great interest to the Yard. I assume that there will be some paperwork we will need to provide to your company regarding this acquisition."

"Was it 'acquired' because it was dangerous or because it was evidence of a crime?"

"That is a very interesting question. May I inquire why you are asking?"

"Because of my husband. He was concerned about the crate and wrote this letter regarding it."

Mrs. Wallace produced the letter from her purse, and handed it to Erasmus. It was addressed to Mr. Punaise! It also gave his address in Carlisle. This would make the next day's mission all the more straightforward. "Mrs. Wallace, this letter is unopened, and I do not have the authority to go through private mail."

Mrs. Wallace took the letter out of the Chief Inspector's hand. "Allow me to help with that." She deftly ripped one of the shorter sides off the envelope and handed the contents to him without even looking at it.

Erasmus found this odd, but he didn't want to seem surprised by her willingness to help him in his investigation. He opened the letter and read it silently. "Yes, this will help us a great deal. Thank you."

Mrs. Wallace smiled a polite smile. She dipped her head as if to leave, but, as if in afterthought replied, "I do hope I've been of service. Please have the paperwork regarding the crate delivered tomorrow. Thank you, Chief Inspector." She turned and left.

Erasmus looked at the quickly written letter one more time. *"Well,"* he thought, *"this changes everything."*

A CLANDESTINE TRYST

BY DR. KATHERINE L. MORSE

"Good morning, Sergeant Fox. It's amazing how often I see you coincidentally, particularly in and on trains. Where are you going this morning?" Sparky meant for her slight smile to be ironic, suggesting that she didn't think the situation the least bit coincidental.

The subtlety of her facial expression was lost on him, not least because he had expected she would know they were traveling together. "Carlisle."

"You see, there is that coincidence again." Apparently, the Sergeant wasn't an adherent to the school of irony.

"You're going to Carlisle as well."

She pretended not to notice the lack of rising intonation at the end of his sentence, and treated his statement as a question. "I can't be sure, but it's the most likely conclusion. Ah, and here is the man who can confirm my deduction."

"Good morning, Sparky, Sergeant Fox."

"Good morning, Chief Inspector," the Royal Aerial Marine replied. "I have booked us a private compartment so we can arrange our final plans."

Sparky turned those words over in her head, "arrange our final plans." She hoped this conversation included telling her what the devil was happening. For the time being she had to content herself with following her companions onto the train and into the private compartment booked by Fox. They sat in complete silence while the rest of the passengers boarded. Once the train was underway, she started to open her mouth to ask questions, but Fox silenced her immediately by just raising a finger. She continued to sit and fume, wondering at this extreme caution. Only a few moments passed before there was a knock on the door. Fox slid it open to reveal a middle-aged woman in an apron pushing a tea cart. The usual discussions of drinks, sugar, and cream transpired efficiently in just a couple of minutes before the tea cart moved on down the passageway. Fox looked up and down the hall before closing and locking the door.

"Drake, you haven't briefed Dr. McTrowell on our mission."

"I was accompanied the last time I saw her, so I was unable to give her any instructions beyond the request to meet us this morning at the station. Additionally, another very valuable piece of information came into my possession last night." He withdrew the letter provided by Mrs. Wallace from the inside pocket of his coat. He showed Sparky the address and then opened it for her to read. Her eyebrows shot up. Drake passed it to Fox who was sitting opposite them. His reaction was almost as pronounced as Sparky's, which was saying something considering his more reserved nature.

"This will make our work today easier, but it complicates the whole business quite a bit. How did you come by this letter, Chief Inspector?"

"Indirectly through Sparky's intervention. When she had the crate sent to me, she piqued Mrs. Wallace's curiosity about the business arrangement. Mrs. Wallace intercepted the letter from her husband and brought it to me last night."

Fox made a mental note that Drake had taken to referring to Dr. McTrowell by her nickname with considerable regularity. "I'm sorry to have to ask this, Dr. McTrowell, but did you have any prior knowledge of this business relationship?"

"No. I had no idea about it until Mrs. Wallace asked for my assistance with the crate."

"Very good."

Sparky wondered what Fox found very good about that answer. More than anything she wanted to ask Sergeant Fox what his true mission was because there always seemed to be more afoot with the young Royal Aerial Marine than there ought to be. However, she doubted he would give her a full and honest answer, even if this were the right time.

"We have the element of surprise on our side," the Sergeant continued. "However, we should be cautious. It would be best if we could capture Punaise, Hedgley, and Martin without the locals noticing. I think the three of us are up to that task."

"And what about their manufacturing facilities?"

"No need to worry about that, Dr. McTrowell. Local resources will take care of that after we have captured the enemy."

Sparky was suddenly carried back to her first few interactions with Jonathan Lord Ashleigh in which he had used that same word in such a mysterious and oblique way.

Fox continued, "We will leave the train separately. I have to go one place before we proceed to our destination. I had not anticipated that Chief Inspector Drake would provide the extremely valuable location information, so I made an appointment to collect local intelligence. You two should stay out of sight in case any of our targets are about the village. Our advantage will be ruined if you're recognized."

They finalized the remaining details of their plan to regroup once they arrived, after which there wasn't much more to discuss until they arrived at the cottage and surveilled the situation and the locations of their targets. Sparky wondered if Drake had taken the time to acquire more jelly babies because he seemed quite alert considering their exertions the day before. She, on the other hand, was still completely exhausted. She tried to make some notes in her pocket journal, but dozed off almost immediately. Even a second cup of tea when the cart came by again wasn't enough to revive her. She slept almost the entire way.

Fox was up and out of the compartment even before they reached the Carlisle station. Erasmus shook Sparky lightly to wake her. He pointed to the left, "I will go this way. You should exit from the other end of the car. I will see you in 15 minutes." The train ground to a halt. He dropped a kiss onto her cheek and ducked out the door. She was still a little foggy, but she smiled to herself before heading the opposite direction down the passageway.

Looking neither right nor left, she exited the train as if she were traveling alone. But she also took care to keep the brim of her hat tipped down to hide her face. She searched her memory. Yes, she was wearing different attire, including headwear, than she had been all the times the trio of troublemakers might have seen her. Hoping that she was striking just the right balance between nonchalance and purposefulness, she took her time making her way around to the far side of the west water tower, out of sight of the comings and goings at the train station. Drake was already there.

Without saying a word, he started down Warwick Road. She waited a minute by her pocket watch and followed. As she approached the intersection with St. Aidan's Road, she nearly caught up with him. He was standing at the crossroad consulting the time on his own pocket watch. She hadn't quite reached him when he flicked his eyes left surreptitiously. Without actually making eye contact, he snapped his watch closed and marched northeast on St. Aidan's. As soon as she was close enough to the corner to keep an eye on his progress, she stopped and made as if she were retying her boot. She raised her eyes to peer from under the brim of her hat just in time to see him duck into the bushes along the road. No one else was about. She followed again, pretending to be looking at the birds and flowers, but really just making sure that she wasn't seen when she joined him in his leafy concealment.

"How long do you think we'll need to wait for Sergeant Fox?" she whispered.

"I should think not more than half an hour," he replied sotto voce. "We will need to keep quiet."

"You make this sound like a clandestine tryst." She smiled a rather wicked little smile the likes of which Erasmus had not yet seen on her face. Despite the welcomeness of the attention, it did make him blush slightly.

When Fox approached, he was walking so silently that Drake didn't notice him until he had passed. Or at least that's how Drake excused his inattentiveness in his own mind. Drake gave a short, high-pitched trill like a chaffinch. Fox turned and shouldered his way into their hidey hole. It was now too crowded for comfort.

Without preamble, Fox reported, "my local resource confirms the story in the report. He considers his source to be highly reliable and corroborated the address of the cottage. Punaise hasn't been seen around the village, but Martin and Hedgley haven't been able to stay away from the Dog and Duck Pub."

Sparky thought to herself, *"There's that word 'resource' again."*

"They've been careful enough not to reveal any details, but they seem to be unhappy with their relationship with Punaise. It also seems that the Frenchman may be truly mad. I think it best to revise our plans slightly. Dr. McTrowell, you'll be responsible for apprehending Martin. Drake, you will take Hedgley. Punaise may be dangerous, so I'll take him. Is everyone clear?"

Sparky nodded, but she couldn't help thinking that she wasn't clear on the reason she was here instead of someone more … qualified. They repeated the stealthy leap-frog the last few hundred yards up the road to the dirt cart path that led to the cottage. As they crept up behind the trees, they discovered their quietude was almost completely unnecessary. The air rang with the sounds of metallic industry. They skirted the perimeter of the property in a counter-clockwise direction, avoiding the cottage and the open yard around the well. They approached the barn from the stream side embankment.

They crawled up the slope and peered over the edge. Sparks flew out of the open barn door from which a glow emanated. They could even feel a little of the heat on their faces from their blind several yards away. But what instantly captured all their attention was arrayed in regimental lines, filling the space between the well and the cottage: several dozen Dragon's Teeth of multiple designs. Fox signaled them urgently back down to the stream. He didn't bother to retrace his steps around the property, but just waded straight across the stream until they were well out of sight. "We're going to need a bigger force."

FOR THE WANT OF A WARM PUB

BY DAVID L. DRAKE

The unkempt brush on the far side of the stream was difficult to maneuver through, but it did provide exceptional coverage for hiding Sergeant Fox, Dr. McTrowell, and Chief Inspector Drake. After they broke through the thickest part of the greenery near the stream, the land opened to a field of tall grasses. The three gathered around. Not one of them mentioned the fact they were now soaked from the waist down, nor that their armaments were now just additional weight to carry given their inferiority to the metal army amassed nearby.

J. B. slipped effortlessly into his commanding voice; a tad deeper and resonant, but delivered with a piercing gaze. This time his eyes were fixed on Erasmus. "I've made my assessment of the situation, but I want to hear from you first." Sparky temporarily held her tongue. Being left out of this initial conversation wasn't to her liking, so she did her best to wait for the conversation to come to her.

Erasmus' response was immediate, his constable's training showing through. "There were thirty-six Dragon's Teeth; six rows of six. I counted five different types, none of them matching the one we assembled at Dr. Pogue's laboratory. The majority had multiple shoulder-mounted barrels. Some had large heads and bodies and long snouts. I am not sure what those are for. The third type had bladed appendages. The fourth type had wheels and looked like a lorry for hauling. The final type was shorter and blockier. My guess is they are mobile mortars, perhaps planting their pointed tip tail and aiming their heads at their targets. My conclusion is that they are building an ambulatory army."

"Hmm. Interesting assessment. Dr. McTrowell, what's your assessment?"

Sparky furrowed her brow and pursed her lips before speaking the truth that was plain to her. "If these machines are operational, and I assume they are, we're essentially outmanned and outgunned. We should leave and reassess."

"Do you think they would attack us if we approached unarmed?"

Sparky replied the fastest. "Yes!"

Erasmus followed suit with, "Absolutely."

Sparky explained her affirmative answer. "Erasmus and I were in a very similar situation in Paris, walking unarmed into the warehouse storing EPACTs. Monsieur Punaise set his metal bugs on us without hesitation. If it weren't for the fast work of Erasmus and Jonathan Lord Ashleigh, the EPACTs would have destroyed more of me than the hem of my dress."

The Sergeant looked thoughtful for a second, and nodded his agreement. "Excellent evaluation of the situation. I believe the best thing we can do is to get back and gather a force that can handle this situation. Given the contents of Reginald Wallace's letter, we can't allow them to continue any longer."

Monsieur Punaise put his hands on his hips in indignation and stared at the sorrowful Mr. Martin, who looked back with sad eyes. "Do we have to destroy them?"

"Meester Mar-teen. Zeeze are not pets!"

"It's not that," Martin whined. "We've worked so hard to build them and get them working. I just don't want to have them … damaged."

"Zey are just a product. Zey need testing. Prepare to start zem up."

Mr. Martin reluctantly slouched off to the control panel near the door. Monsieur Punaise walked over to Mr. Hedgley, who was verifying that the four Type 5s were ready. "Are zey ready?"

"Yes. I just need to finish filling their fuel boxes."

Monsieur Punaise walked back to Mr. Martin. "Start zee test." Mr. Martin's finger hesitated over the brass control button on the console. "Now, Meester Mar-teen!"

ॐ൲ॐ൲ॐ൲ 👥 ଓଓଓଓଓ

"J. B., I have another observation," Erasmus added to the conversation. "All thirty-six Dragon's Teeth have the same finish, even though they are made of unfinished iron. Not one of them has any rust on them. That means they were manufactured within a short period of time, even perhaps within the same day, and recently. Monsieur Punaise may be using the yard as a staging ground. There may be more of these machines stored elsewhere. We need to take that into account if we come back with a larger ..."

The sound of all thirty-six Dragon's Teeth starting up drowned out Erasmus' statement. All three instantly went into a crouch to prepare to run, duck, or fight. J. B. reacted by sprinting the few steps back to the hedge to peer through at the activity on the other side of the stream. The thirty-six Dragon's Teeth were all flexing their legs to prepare for movement. Sparky and Erasmus joined him in looking through the greenery.

Just as with their legs, the Dragon's Teeth shifted their barrels and spun their buzz saws in hideous synchronization. J. B. quietly commanded, "Move!" He backpedaled into the field, and with Sparky and Erasmus on his heels, ran away from the imminent danger.

Three of the rows turned on the other three rows and, at the same time, opened fire on each other. Saws took off legs, bullets rang out, denting bodies and disabling joints; the din was staggering.

The unceasing sound coaxed J. B., Sparky, and Erasmus to switch from a fast trot to a sprint. They were across the field faster than they would have expected. They had no idea that the volley wasn't meant for them. They stopped at the far edge of the field, hands on knees, doubled over, gasping for breath. After a short recovery, they realized they were standing on the dirt road leading back to town. "Everyone whole?" Erasmus asked. J. B. and Sparky nodded. "Let us go."

The melee lasted only a minute. Bent and broken metal parts littered the lawn. The grass was scorched from hot fuel boxes blown open by close-range mortar rounds. Mr. Martin started to walk toward the wreckage. "Stop," Monsieur Punaise warned, freezing Mr. Martin in his tracks. "Unexploded ordnance." Monsieur Punaise pulled a spyglass from his work belt and snapped it to its full length. "Two units left operational. A Type 2 and a Type 4."

Mr. Hedgley added, "That's about 95% of units disabled."

Monsieur Punaise cracked an uncharacteristic smile. "Zend in ze repair units."

Mr. Hedgley pushed another brass button on the console. Four Dragon's Teeth ran out of the barn and onto the field of devastation.

It took less than a quarter of a mile for the sloppy, squishing noises from their boots to go from annoying to funny to maddening. The three of them stopped, sat on a log, poured a small amount of muddy water out of their boots, and wrung out their socks as best they could. It didn't help much. Every step toward town contributed to a moist aspirated syncopation that belayed the importance of the trip.

The distraction made Erasmus wish, "I just want a warm pub, an open fire, and dry socks."

HMA BRITANNIA

BY DR. KATHERINE L. MORSE

"I know just the place," replied Fox, leading the way. The three abandoned any pretense of stealth. Not only did they expect that their three targets were back at the cottage, but they were too discomfited by the fully clothed wading expedition. At least Drake and McTrowell were. They struggled to keep up with the Sergeant, who was trained for such privation.

When they entered Ferguson's Public House, the barman greeted them civilly, but with no indication that he knew any of them. "What can I get you?"

Fox turned to his soggy compatriots and pointed toward the hearth, "I'll fetch us some food while you two dry out." He didn't need to ask them twice; they made straight for the two well-worn, but comfortable-looking chairs nearest the fire. Once she had removed her sodden boots and had the soles of her feet pointed at the fire, Sparky looked over her shoulder at Fox standing at the bar. How long could it take to order food? She might have thought he and the barman were old friends from the length of their conversation, despite the barman's attempt to appear nonchalant as he wiped down the bar. Just as well. It would give her an opportunity to have a few choice words with Drake.

"Chief Inspector," Drake winced at the formality of the form of address she chose. "I agreed to accompany you today with the expectation that some explanation for your recent secrecy would be forthcoming. Quite to the contrary, it seems that there's even more I don't know. While I am not, in general, inclined to delve into all your secrets, this secrecy put me in grave danger today. Either you will explain yourself, or I will return to London on the next train, and that will be the last you see of me."

Drake swallowed hard. He felt like an insect on a pin. He was sworn to secrecy about his business with Fox, but she had a point about putting her in danger. And he couldn't bear the thought that today's misadventure might be the last time he would see her. He cleared his throat and began to choose his words carefully when he heard the barkeeper say in an overly loud voice, "Good afternoon, Tavis. Pint o' stout?"

Erasmus and Sparky turned in surprise, only to hear Fox reply in an equally loud voice, "Right, then, a ploughman's, two lamb pasties, and three pints of ale." He slapped his hand on the bar in an amicable signal that their business was complete and moved to join his companions near the fire. Drake looked at Fox plaintively like a cornered animal. McTrowell opened her mouth to demand an explanation from Fox, hoping he would be more forthcoming than Drake. Before she could utter a word, Fox held a finger up to his lips to silence her. He pretended to be unlacing his boots, but she could tell from the way he cocked his head that he was listening to the conversation at the bar.

The barkeeper continued in a raised voice, "How are things at your mum's cottage? Any more strange goings on?"

The new patron followed his lead and very helpfully spoke loudly enough that the trio by the fire could hear the conversation if they stayed silent. "A'll tell yew Angus, thas noothing strenger on heaven end earth than whas happnin' at tha' cottage. A'll be glad to be shut o tha lot!" He took a stiff draught of his pint of oatmeal stout to emphasize his point.

"I do hope for your sake that will be soon." Angus started pulling pints of ale as if they were discussing the weather or the crops.

"Na soon enough! I was daft to have tha Frenchman let by the week. Thank the laird he and his lot are shoovin off by the end of the week."

Fox and Ferguson made meaningful eye contact. "Well, Tavis, you certainly are having a rough patch. How about another pint for all your troubles?"

Fox reached into his rucksack and withdrew a compact leather envelope from which he extracted a printed form on a piece of paper and a pencil. He scribbled rapidly for about a minute while Sparky and Erasmus observed, perplexed. When he finished, he folded the sheet in quarters and returned the pencil to its rightful place before stowing the envelope back in his bag. The threesome sat in silence, drying their feet and waiting for their food while Fox held the mysterious message firmly in his hand.

A boy of about ten years appeared from the kitchen with a large wooden tray half full of food. He stopped at the bar where his father added the three pints to the tray. Despite the weight of the tray, the boy managed to deliver it smoothly to the party by the fire. While he was unloading the tray onto the low table between the chairs, Fox extracted a shilling from his pocket and folded the paper twice more until it was in sixteenths. Once the lad had finished delivering the bowls and mugs, Fox pressed the shilling and the paper into his hand. Evidently without any interest in either, the boy put both in his pocket and said, "Thank you, sir." He disappeared back to the kitchen with his empty tray.

Erasmus looked at Sparky with an expression he hoped she understood to mean that he had no more idea what was going on than she did. As hungry as they were, they turned immediately to their food and didn't see young Neill Ferguson fly out the door like the place was on fire. They wolfed down their food, keeping an eye on their watches. It didn't need to be said that none of them wanted to be stuck for the night. Sparky tested her boots. They were mostly dry, but they were going to need some serious attention with saddle soap after the train ride. She pulled them back on and laced them up. She asked Fox, "Was the whole meal only a shilling."

He replied bluntly, "It's been taken care of," and walked out the door without checking to see whether she and Drake were following. He turned left toward the train station. Sparky sprinted to get ahead of Fox, no mean feat considering the state of her boots.

"Stop right there! I'm owed an explanation and unless I get one, I'm not getting on that train. I've more than half a mind to get on the next train going the opposite direction to visit my Auntie Catherine in Stirling and leave you two to your mysterious mission."

"Dr. McTrowell, allow me to remind you of your promise to Her Majesty at the meeting of the Order of the Thistle when you were in Stirling the last time."

That stopped Sparky cold. How did he know about that? "How do you know about that?" No answer. "Are you Her Majesty's 'agent?'"

"Not directly. However, I am his agent, and he will make himself known soon enough. We must return to London immediately. Your skills are required. The security of the Empire depends on all of us." And then he made that same annoying, self-assured maneuver of heading to the train station and expecting them to follow. This time, Drake shrugged at her to make it perfectly clear that he was just as baffled as she was.

Once they were settled in their private compartment for the trip back to London, Fox said to them, "We'll meet tomorrow morning at Wellington Arch at eight o'clock. Plan to be away for a few days. Dr. McTrowell, you'll require your flying kit. I suggest you both get as much sleep as possible, as there may little time for such luxuries for the next few days." And he proceeded to do just that. Drake just shook his head.

As annoying as she found Fox's military attitude, she had no reason to believe he was being untruthful. She strongly suspected she was going to regret getting involved in this. But she had cast her lot during that fateful meeting with Queen Victoria in the casement of Stirling Castle. She removed her boots and leaned back into the upholstered corner of her seat to do her best to nod off for the long trip back.

శ౦ఴ౦ఴ౦ఴ ⚙ ಌಙಌಙಌಙ

Sparky presented herself, as ordered, at precisely eight o'clock the next morning at the arch between Hyde Park and Buckingham Palace Gardens. She was dressed in her aviator's cap, goggles, and leather duster, her tool belt loaded up with various navigational aids. Her Gladstone bag contained a few clean articles of clothing and her physician's field kit. She was just removing her four-button gloves to tuck them in her belt when Drake and Fox rounded the corner of the monument. Fox had his weathered rucksack over his shoulder, and Drake was toting a leather satchel. Fox jerked his head in the direction of the palace. Well, in for a penny, in for a pound.

They walked into the grove at the edge of the grounds. They weren't more than a few yards in when two more Royal Aerial Marines materialized from behind a couple of trees. They saluted Sergeant Fox and disappeared back to their posts. The three walked a few dozen more yards before they came to a tall flat-board fence painted in trompe-l'œil to look like more of the grove. Fox rapped a complex tattoo on the fence, and a section swung inward to admit them. It was a gate with no handle on the outside. That meant that someone was always on guard inside the disguised fence's perimeter, which also meant that someone wanted to keep secret whatever was hidden inside.

And it was dazzling, quite literally. "What is that!?" Sparky blurted.

"Dr. McTrowell, I would expect you to recognize an airship." Sarcasm from Sergeant Fox, now she'd had two stunning surprises already this morning. The craft's enormous size and the scores of propellers took her aback. It was undoubtedly the airship one would build if cost were no object. But there was an additional wonder. "Yes, but never one that … color."

"This is Her Majesty's Airship Britannia. It's being refitted for our mission. It used to be green on the top and black on the bottom." She raised her eyebrows. "Although no one is allowed to fly over Buckingham Palace, the green was meant to camouflage it against the trees."

"Why go to all that trouble and then paint it black on the bottom? It would look like a giant beetle against the sky."

"Not at night." He waited for that idea to sink in. "Its very existence is a secret. Until now, it has only ever flown in the dark. How do you think Her Majesty met you in Stirling and returned without anyone noticing her absence?"

Sparky made a mental note to herself never to try to put one over on the Queen again. That one, she was clever. As they were talking and walking, they had approached the airship enough for Sparky to get a closer look at the envelope. It seemed to be changing color as her perspective changed. An idea dawned on her. And then a recent memory tickled at her brain. "You've been to Carlisle quite a bit of late, haven't you?"

"Yes, I have."

Drake interrupted. "Would one of you please explain what you are talking about?"

Sparky offered, "Do you remember when I told you that I saw the Sergeant follow Miss Sarah Slate and Mr. Charles Howgill onto a train in Carlisle?"

"Yes, you drew it on your graph."

She pointed straight up at the dazzling fabric of the envelope. "This is what he was pursuing. This is the fabric Miss Slate designed and Mr. Howgill built a mill to produce." She turned back to Fox. "Is there more of this fabric, or is this all of it?"

"There is more of it. And we have all of it."

"Of course, you do. And who is 'we' in that sentence?"

"This will be made clear shortly."

It was all Sparky could do not to stamp her feet like a five-year-old who'd been told she couldn't have another boiled sweet because one was plenty, thank you. Erasmus thought he might have to throw his cape coat to put out the fire. The situation was rescued by a female voice calling from the direction of the aft section of HMA Britannia.

"Dr. McTrowell is that you? I thought I recognized your coat." And who should come walking toward them but none other than Miss Sarah Slate!? "Chief Inspector Drake, good day."

Sparky tried to calm herself so as not to subject Sarah to her ire. "Have you been hired to help with this ..." she waved her arm a little futilely to indicate the giant sky chameleon looming over them.

"Yes, isn't it exciting? We're just laying on the last strips at the back. Come see!"

Before following Miss Slate, Sparky fixed Drake and Fox with a deadly look that clearly conveyed, "It seems everyone knows what's going on except me ... including the other American."

Sarah, absorbed in her work and oblivious to the non-verbal exchange, continued walking and talking. "Charles and I were very surprised when we received such a large order for my color-changing fabric. But the purchaser paid in full in advance, so we made the full run. It was all very mysterious because they asked for it to be completely covered before it left the mill, and it was collected in a closed lorry after the mill closed for the day. I was making wedding plans, and I didn't think anything else of it until about two weeks ago when I was called 'here.' Well, it's more complicated than that. It's all very mysterious."

Sparky thought to herself, *"I'm having that feeling quite a lot lately."*

"They were having difficulty getting the fabric to lay flat without wrinkles and the seams to match invisibly." By then they had reached the rear section of the ship and were standing under a warren of scaffolding where crews were working rapidly to cover the remainder of the envelope. Sparky could just see the last bit where the top was still green and the bottom still black.

"Why do the seams have to match?"

"So, it will invisible during the day," Sarah replied, as if it were as obvious as the sky above them.

"Invisible?!"

"Well, I exaggerated a bit. The color shifting fabric makes it look like the sky. It works particularly well against the grim English sky."

"Why does it need to fly during the day?"

"They won't tell me that. I think it has something to do with the reason you and Chief Inspector Drake are here." Sparky felt a tiny bit better. She wasn't they only one left in the dark.

Sensing that it might be safe again to approach, Fox joined them. "Dr. McTrowell, you're needed on the bridge."

With her attention no longer focused on the envelope as she retraced her steps down the length of the ship, she took the time to inspect the gondola. It was remarkably stark and plain for a ship expressly designed to convey Her Imperial Majesty, the Queen-Empress. But then, it was meant to be functional. No doubt the interior was elegantly appointed. Just as they approached the gangway, an apparatus attached to the hull caught Sparky's eye. It was mounted on a swiveling mechanism, and it looked somewhat like a gun, but it had large perforations in the side of the barrel that would have made it useless for firing bullets. Nor was there anywhere to load bullets, just a tube leading back to a large tank. She had seen this device before. She closed her eyes and tried to place it in its previous surroundings. Pogue's lab!

"Where did you get this? Is Pogue here?" She looked around frantically, but she already knew the answer. He had just arisen and was still eating breakfast when she left his home that morning. Unless he had some transportation device that defied the laws of physics, he couldn't be here. Was she the last person to know everything?

"We 'acquired' it. Dr. Pogue is not here and has not ever been," Fox replied in his increasingly annoying enigmatic fashion.

Well, that was a bit of a relief. On the scale of her recently acquired friends, she knew quite a bit less than Drake, a little less than Miss Slate, but more than Dr. Pogue. At least Jonathan Lord Ashleigh didn't know any of it.

"What is it?" She asked Fox, pointing accusatorially at the ventilated barrel attached to the tank.

"Are you familiar with Professor Edmund Davy of the Royal Dublin Society?"

"I have read his work lightly. Chemistry is not my field."

"He discovered a new carburet of hydrogen. He proposed its use for lighting. Dr. Pogue has been experimenting with other uses."

"Airships and gaseous hydrocarbons, what could possibly go wrong?" Sparky quipped.

Polished and Prepped

By David L. Drake

J. B. and Sparky had just gotten to the front edge of the gangplank when two Royal Aerial Marines in full regimental dress reds and carrying ceremonial spears marched toward them. J. B. explained quietly to Sparky, "They are just formally escorting us aboard. Must maintain appearances and all that." Stopping just in front of them, both Marines performed a perfect turn and led them across the gangplank. Once onboard, the Marines retook their posts, and J. B. led the way to the bridge.

Erasmus was already there, hunched over the charts for the Carlisle area, obviously formulating his concept for the correct aerial position to approach the cottage and barn. At the helm stood a tall mustachioed Marine in full Aerial Pilot uniform. He was requesting the status of the aft engines through one of three gleaming brass voicepipes arrayed in front of him.

J. B. and Sparky joined Erasmus, who pointed on the map to the field on the far side of the stream from the barn, "I have been told we have a full squad of sixteen Marines on board. I wanted to get a feeling for the best place to deploy. This is the best location for such a large craft, but then we will have the same issue of wading across the stream. Well, maybe we could deploy over here, behind the cottage …"

"Dr. McTrowell?" A young Marine stood at attention in the doorway. Sparky, Erasmus, and J. B. all turned and noticed the youthful military man. "Chief Inspector Drake, Sergeant Fox, may I escort the three of you to the Royal Hall?" It was one of those orders disguised as a polite question.

J. B. gave the obligatory affirmative response, "Yes, of course. Lead the way."

The Marine set a quick, steady pace with which Erasmus and J. B. had no issue keeping up. But Sparky had to push her normal pace a bit. She silently hoped it wasn't a long walk. It reminded her of a fellow she once knew, who insisted on being one step ahead of her wherever they went. But that had been a long time ago.

HMA Britannia was unlike any airship she had been on before. It had two wide hallways on each edge of the main deck, promenades if you will. They were led in the aft direction on the port side of the craft. On their right were large windows. Despite being covered by the camouflaging material, one could still easily see out. Arrayed along the interior left side of the promenade was a series of beautifully varnished doors with gleaming brass fittings. Between the doors hung portraits of royalty and distinguished military men. Sparky caught herself glancing at the incredibly rendered artwork as they hurried to their destination.

At midship, the young Marine turned left and headed down another wide hallway toward the heart of the deck. The trio followed. In front of them, another two Marines stood guarding an elaborately decorated double door. The guards opened the doors in a well-timed maneuver as the party approached, allowing them to enter without breaking their stride. They marched up to the middle of the Royal Hall, where their escort halted, turned, gave J. B. a snappy salute, and marched back out of the double doors. The doors closed.

Both Sparky and Erasmus could not help but gasp. The room was expansive for one on an airship. Sparky guessed that it was two decks high, an unimaginable luxury for a flying craft. The wallpaper was a deep royal blue with a raised, flocked pattern of golden lilies encircling crowns. The carpet was a grand burgundy red with hashes of gold and blue. In front of them on a carpeted dais stood a velvet-covered chair, also in burgundy and gold. Other than the chair, the room was devoid of furniture, as if it were for assemblage. But with a few touches, it could be used for a great number of things, including parties.

The door opened again, and the same young Marine entered. Sparky gasped. He was escorting Dr. Yin Young! She was dressed for battle as a Marine but with her outfit tailored for a woman. Sparky thought it both flattering and functional. The Marine turned and headed out the way he had come in. Yin broke the silence. "Welcome aboard Her Majesty's Airship Britannia, Dr. McTrowell and Chief Inspector. I hope you find it comfortable."

Erasmus smiled and replied, "How could we not? It is an awe-inspiring wonderment. Did you have a hand in its preparation?"

"Only some of its recently-installed artillery. But I have traveled on her as a sentinel and scout."

"Well, your skills will be appreciated for this …"

A pair of side doors opened, and another two Marines stepped in, announcing "Her Majesty, the Queen!"

Queen Victoria entered the room; the atmosphere changed immediately. Quiet. Serious. Reverent. She walked directly to the dais and her chair. The two Marines backed out of the room with a bow, closing the doors behind them.

She stepped up onto the dais and, without ceremony, sat. She looked across the team assembled in front of her for a second and fixed her gaze on J. B. "Sergeant Fox, your telegram from Carlisle was both timely and informative. The timetable for outfitting our Britannia was accelerated to meet your request. You are to lead this mission; the squad aboard is yours to command. You may begin your mission after we disembark. Please remember our ultimate goal. The Empire is counting on you not to deviate from our objective. Good luck and Godspeed."

Sergeant Fox executed a formal bow, adding a quiet, "Yes, Your Majesty."

Queen Victoria's eyes then fixed on Erasmus. "Chief Inspector Drake, we understand congratulations are in order. Sergeant Fox reports that you, with help from your associates, were the first to locate and report the whereabouts and circumstances of Monsieur Punaise and his confederates. While others at Her Majesty's Eyes and Ears have failed in this mission, you have persevered." She flashed a cursory smile, but Erasmus knew that it was a formality, a type of royal punctuation affirming things had gone the way she wanted as opposed to her being exuberantly pleased. *"So that is what she calls our band of agents,"* he thought, *"Her Majesty's Eyes and Ears. How fitting."* Imitating Sergeant Fox, he bowed low and quietly responded, "Yes, your Majesty."

The Queen turned to Sparky, who couldn't help but think, *"I've seen a great deal of this monarch lately!"* The Queen cocked her head slightly before addressing the American, as if she were still studying some new type of creature. "Dr. McTrowell, you have proven yourself a skilled airship pilot when under duress. You would make an excellent pilot for this mission."

"May I ask a question?" Sparky's voice forced a crack into the formality of the gathering. The men's eyebrows rose in surprise. Their spines stiffened. This wasn't the person to have a give-and-take conversation with. The Queen moved her hand in a small gesture beckoning Sparky to proceed. "When can I find out what's going on?"

"Sergeant Fox will brief you on the mission as you are underway."

"Do I have a choice about participating?"

The Queen smiled in a way that hinted at a smirk. "We have the best of brokered circumstances. The Empire can provide something you want; you can provide something the Empire wants. Is there even a need to quibble over terms? We think not." Without waiting for a reply from the stunned flight surgeon, the Queen rose, turned, left the dais, and walked toward the side doors. The doors opened precisely at the right time, and the Queen was gone.

Once the side doors closed, Erasmus and Sparky had just enough time to look at each other in amazement before the doors behind them reopened, and the two Marines stationed there approached to escort them out of the Royal Hall.

Sergeant Fox had his command voice ready. "Dr. McTrowell, before you return to the bridge, there's something I wish to show you. Chief Inspector and Dr. Young, I want to confer with you on the bridge when we get underway. You both, as well as Dr. McTrowell, have first-hand experience dealing with these 'Dragon's Teeth.' I'll want to put that knowledge to use in our plan of attack."

Their walk brought the team to the promenade where a gentleman in a dark gray redingote was standing, waiting for them. For Erasmus, his fancy attire stood out from the buttoned-down garments of the British military. The man's upstanding shirt collar was far higher than the current fashion in London with the texture of fine linen. He wore his pure white neckcloth tied in what the dandies on High Street would call 'regency style,' where the body of the bow was full and puffy. His vertical striped cream waistcoat sported wide lapels. Who could this possibly be?

The flamboyant man took a relaxed step forward. "Chief Inspector Drake. Allow me to introduce myself. I am Jean Chemiserouge, your counterpart from France."

Erasmus extended his hand, adding "Pleased to meet you." Monsieur Chemiserouge took Erasmus' hand in the lightest of grasps, three fingertips across two fingers at best. After the initial touch, the hold was broken, superficial and fleeting. Erasmus had to resist the temptation to request another handshake, one that had meaning. Instead, he pressed forward in the conversation. "My counterpart, you say? May I ask if you can extrapolate? Oh, and your English is impeccable."

"Thank you. I fear my schooling is showing. As for my role, I have been invited by the Empire to be the French emissary. Upon his apprehension, I am to deal with Monsieur Puniase's deportation. Let us hope that we are successful."

"Will you be aiding us in the arrest?"

Monsieur Chemiserouge yanked his head back a small theatrical amount. "Oh my, no. I will leave that to you and your company. I will be escorting, nothing more."

"Fair enough. Please excuse us, for we need to make our final preparations. Good day, sir."

J. B. turned to Erasmus and continued his instructions. "Erasmus, please follow me and Sparky. I want you to know about this, too. It will only be a few minutes."

The three of them walked further to the aft of the airship. After a couple of moments, J. B. approached a door with a brass plaque above it spelling out **"Infirmary."** J. B. turned the knob and, holding the door open, offered Sparky and Erasmus entrance.

Inside, Sparky let out a happy squeak as if seeing an old friend unexpectedly. There in the middle of the room sat her mechanical surgical assistant, polished and prepped for use. A shaft issuing from an opening in the wall was connected to the base, which was already spinning at operational speed, although there was no annoying engine sound. The power plant must be farther away than she was used to.

Erasmus smiled at her joy. Maybe she would see a bright side of this brokered abduction.

She turned and, without a hint of irony, said, "Okay. Now I'm ready to enlist in your operation."

The three left and headed back toward the bridge. Erasmus thought to himself, *"Well, for her, and her alone, I know what makes this woman happy."*

STEALTH AND THE LACK THEREOF

BY DR. KATHERINE L. MORSE

Sparky spent the flight north observing HMA Britannia's pilot, Captain Cox. One didn't need Drake's deductive skills to determine that he was not pleased with the idea of being relegated to back up once the actual mission was engaged. She stayed out of his way and spent the time profitably assessing his touch on the controls. She wouldn't have the luxury of learning their feel; one mistake could be fatal to herself and the others on board.

When Captain Cox wasn't actively piloting the ship, Sparky distracted herself by watching the countryside pass below. At one point, they passed over a small clutch of grazing cows. Although Britannia was a relatively quiet airship, she wasn't entirely silent. The cows perked up a bit when they heard the approach. One actually looked skyward as the shadow of the envelope passed over it like a fast-moving cloud. Admittedly, cows aren't the brightest of creatures, but Sparky struggled to stifle a giggle when this particular bovine free-thinker looked at the sky, looked back at the shadow sweeping over it, squinted back up at the sky, then gave up and went back to grazing. Captain Cox was not amused.

Once they got close to Carlisle, Sparky went aft to join the company for Fox's final briefing. "Wings will jump from the starboard platform; sails from the port. We don't want any tangles." Sails? Sparky recognized the extendable wing apparatus worn by two of the fire teams and Fox. They were identical to the one he had employed so effectively during the Bavarian Airship Regatta. But the mention of sails confounded her. The other two fire teams, as well as Drake and Young, were wearing some kind of rucksacks attached to their torsos by harnesses with multiple, snug straps.

"Dr. McTrowell, once we jump, you will keep Britannia at the ready to extract us, but out of range."

She didn't like the sound of any of this! Since Drake was wearing one of the rucksacks, he was obviously going to be "jumping." "Out of range of what?"

"Mortars."

"And what would that range be?"

"Judging from the length of the barrel that we saw, I'd say 2,000 horizontal yards."

Two thousand yards? That was more than a mile! Even taking into account the advantage of altitude, how was she supposed to return in time to save them if they got into serious trouble? "And how am I to 'extract' you without a mooring tower?"

"Private Jones," he indicated a boy who didn't look old enough to shave, "will operate the platform hoist. Gunner Hepburn," who looked old enough to shave, but not old enough to hold his drink, "will cover our egress with the flame cannon."

Flame cannons and platform hoists. She was pretty sure she'd considered the perils of the former before boarding. The dangers of the latter would, no doubt, reveal themselves in time. She barely managed to squeeze out a, "Very well," before retreating to the bridge.

She was just recognizing the Carlisle train station when she heard Sergeant Fox's command over the voice pipe, "Dr. McTrowell, please bring us in from the south at a speed of five knots and an altitude of 1,000 yards."

McTrowell reached to take the controls from Captain Cox. The look on his face suggested he would rather have bitten her hands off at the wrist than let her have the controls. She briefly reconsidered the value of her membership in the Order of the Thistle. As she ought to have expected, HMA Britannia was the smoothest handling airship she had ever had the fortune to steer. The gentlest touch sent her on a new course with grace and precision. She was indeed the finest that unlimited money could buy. Sparky shook herself out of her reverie to focus on her critical task in this mission. She was retracing their route along St. Aidan's Road. Had that only been yesterday?

The Dragon's Teeth were right where they'd been the day before, neatly standing in rows in the yard. As soon as she'd cleared the barn, she climbed and banked starboard. She gasped at the tableau that revealed itself. The winged fire squads had deployed like a flock of pelicans flying in V formation along the top of a cresting wave. The "sails" looked like dandelion seeds snowing down to the ground. Once Sparky recovered from the visual poetry of the sight, she realized the apparatus was very similar to the one that Lord Ashleigh had improvised out of the silk throws in his cabin aboard the Burke & Hare. Somebody hadn't wasted any time converting the prototype into a useful military tool. The sails obscured their passengers, so she couldn't tell which one was Drake. But they all landed safely, a few by bumping along their backsides once or twice before coming to a halt and extricating themselves from the harnesses. She set a circular holding pattern just "out of range" as ordered by Sergeant Fox.

The Marines formed up at the edge of the yard. Sparky switched between chewing her lower lip and her cuticles as she watched. Because the Marines were all wearing uniforms, she could tell easily that Drake wasn't among them, just Yin in her black pajamas. She must have shed the uniform in favor of her less restrictive gi pajamas. But where was Drake? Nothing moved on the ground, which did nothing to steady Sparky's pounding heart. Her two previous encounters with Monsieur Punaise's pernicious mechanical minions only strengthened her certainty that something horrific was about to ensue, and she would be returning the helm to Captain Cox while she strapped into the mechanical surgical assistant. *"Please, not Erasmus,"* she fretted. She didn't know if her hands would be steady enough to do what would be necessary.

She was snapped out of her ominous ruminations by movement on the ground. The Marines had deployed themselves into two semi-circular flanking lines. Those armed with the latest Enfield Pattern 1851 rifles alternated with others wielding good old-fashioned fire axes. Rather than attacking the Dragon's Teeth, the Marines were cautiously circling the neat ranks, one flank toward the cottage and one toward the barn.

Drake gave himself one last pat down to ensure nothing on his person would make the slightest unexpected noise. He'd learned his lesson in Paris about Punaise's creations. They might be as nearsighted as a wild pig, but their hearing was as keen as a hare's. He hadn't shinnied through a tight spot like the hole cut in the side of the barn for the drainpipe since his childhood days untangling rigging. After wriggling through the opening, he slid silently around the pipe and settled into a hay-filled corner, waiting for his eyes to adjust to the darker interior. It didn't take long because this particular barn was nowhere near as dark as the ones he'd explored during his summers at the country estate of Edwin Llewellyn. This one was lit up like the factory it truly was.

He counted six stations, each connected to the overhead belt system leading to an enormous steam engine from which the drainpipe issued. At least he needn't worry about making noise. There was already plenty of that to cover him. But there were no human workers in the factory. Parked next to each station was a Dragon's Tooth of the same design as the one they had battled in Pogue's basement. All six were rapidly and efficiently assembling another Dragon's Tooth, one of each design, including another assembler. The enormity of the situation nearly knocked the breath out of Drake. That's how Punaise had assembled so many so quickly. He was bootstrapping his production!

In addition to the belts, each station was connected to a central, raised station by a narrow, winding chute. And there, on the central platform, was the man himself, gleefully observing his destructive enterprise in action. Drake wracked his brains. How were they going to capture Punaise while he was surrounded by his armored army? Drake feared the only recourse might be to just blow up the entire structure with the inventor inside. As much as Drake loathed the man's amoral actions, he thought killing him was an extreme solution. He was mentally cataloging every access route to the control center when he heard a tremendous racket in the yard.

The two formations of Marines had nearly reached the cottage and the barn when the Dragon's Teeth sprang to life. The soldiers and cutters fanned out, attacking both lines of Marines at once. Fortunately, the Dragon's Teeth soldiers were slow to slew their guns around, so only a couple of Marines were wounded rather than slaughtered. Unfortunately, return fire bounced benignly off their iron skins.

Fox bellowed, "Axes and stay low!" The Marines bearing rifles dropped them and unslung their own axes.

The battle attracted Punaise's attention as well. He swung around to face the open door of the barn. Drake watched an expression of rage cross the face of his adversary to be replaced almost immediately by one of ecstatic madness. Punaise began working frantically, although Drake couldn't quite make out everything he was doing. He turned his back to Drake and began moving his hands over a control panel. After only a moment of this task, he bent down to retrieve something from below the control panel that he placed at a workstation next to the control panel. His next action was more physical and repetitive, some sort of part task. Six times he moved something from one side of the table to the other, pausing in the middle to operate a large lever that looked like a press. Drake had a clearer view of the final step of the process. Punaise held six shiny disks in his left hand. He rolled each edgewise into one of the six chutes leading to the six assembly stations.

The Marines were having considerably more success with the axes. Their superior maneuverability allowed them to duck in between the lines of soldiers and cutters, severing their barrels and blades, or just hacking some into much smaller parts. Although the Dragon's Teeth were still mobile, without their armaments they just chugged helplessly in circles. A few began to slow down and wheeze hotly. Fox assessed the situation. "Fire squads one and two, keep these things contained. Fire squad three, search the cottage and barn for our human targets. Fire squad four, field dress the wounded and signal for Britannia. Yin, you're with me."

Just as the Marines began to regroup, the snouted and wheeled Dragon's Teeth fired up. The Marines dropped to the ground and readied their axes. The snouted machines headed to the well, the wheeled ones toward a woodpile near the cottage. "Hold your positions, men!" Fox barked.

Having read the initial intelligence report, Fox wasn't completely surprised by the actions of the Dragon's Teeth at the well. They filled up with water and made for their overheating brethren, refilling their empty boilers. Their water bearing duties completed, they returned to their original stations. The lorries loaded their cargo bins with wood and replenished the sluggish Dragon's Teeth before reforming near the water bearers. Although some of the fighting machines were now more active, they were still unarmed. "Stand down!"

Inside the barn, Drake heard the battle wind down. Maybe this wouldn't be as hard as he feared. One of the disks rolled to a halt at the assembly station nearest him, sliding neatly into a slot in the side of the assembler. The assembler froze instantly. Drake's stomach dropped. He remembered seeing a smaller version of the disk in Pogue's basement. This wasn't going to be as hard as he had originally imagined; it was going to be much harder.

The assembler detached itself from its station and made for the barn door simultaneously with the other five. Drake was torn. Without the assemblers to defend him, Punaise was vulnerable. But the Marines were even more vulnerable. They had no idea what was coming at them! When Punaise turned to watch the exodus, Drake scrambled back out the way he'd entered.

When the assemblers exited the barn, the Marines were more prepared than they had been for the water bearers and refuelers. These new contraptions were unarmed, so the Marines let them inside the perimeter so they could be guarded.

Drake sprinted around from the back of the barn, "Stop them!" Too late! The assemblers had already succeeded in reconstructing three soldiers and two cutters from the parts of eight damaged and destroyed ones.

Hearing the alarm in Drake's voice, Fox sprang up from where he and Yin had been selectively collecting parts. "Fall back! Fall back!" He shouted. The Marines dispersed, sprinting for the cover of the trees. By the time the company reached St. Aidan's Road, fire squad four had succeeded in signaling Britannia, which was hovering a hundred feet off the ground. Fox reached above his head and opened and closed his fist twice. To Drake's surprise, a section of the gondola's hull detached itself and appeared to drift down toward them. The section halted a couple of feet off the ground, bobbing and swaying on the cables at its corners as McTrowell worked to keep Britannia on station. Without prompting, fire squad four loaded the wounded onto the platform.

"Regroup on Warwick Road. Drake, you're with us." Fox and Young hoisted two heavy, canvas-wrapped bundles onto the platform before hopping aboard themselves. Drake joined them without further prompting.

Despite having just jumped out of this same airship with little more than a bedsheet to support his descent, the swaying of the platform made him a little queasy. He searched for a handhold. The cable at the nearest corner was greasy and too close to the edge for his comfort. There was a row of fasteners or grommets around the perimeter just inside the cables, but they barely qualified as fingerholds.

"What is the purpose of this … apparatus?"

"Her Majesty employs it to disembark when she travels at night and doesn't want to attract attention at a mooring tower."

"You lower the sovereign of the realm on this contraption in the dark!?"

"It has a guard rail and a safety harness when she's aboard."

McTrowell surveyed the state of the approaching boarding party. "Captain Cox, Britannia is yours."

"As it should be."

Sparky took one look at the returning party. "Let's get the wounded into the infirmary. And take that monstrosity there, too. We can dissect it on the surgical bed, although I'd rather imagined that I would be using that more for its intended purpose. Keep the pieces far apart, and yell at the first sign that one of the pieces so much as twitches." The young Marines gave Sparky a very queer look, but they were well trained to follow orders, and so they did.

Once in the infirmary, she glanced inside the tarp before turning her attention to the casualties. What she saw made her gasp, "This changes everything!"

GREEN GRASS, BROWN WELL

BY DAVID L. DRAKE

The woods were cool and shady compared to the warmth of the open area near the barn. Despite the pleasant setting, a drip of sweat ran down Mr. Martin's face as he toiled in his leather overalls. He was bent down over a Dragon's Tooth, overseeing the tightening of a nut on a radial saw. Mr. Hedgley stood by and hovered a pencil above his clipboard, waiting to check off verification of the last of the metal contraptions. As Mr. Martin labored, Mr. Hedgley let his mind wander, taking in the cool calmness of the woods as the nearby stream gurgled and imagining a more serene life than that of their hectic and quirky business.

Mr. Martin twisted his head around and declared with confidence, "The assemblers did an absolutely wonderful job of putting these back together. I never thought it was possible. With the exception of a few loose nuts, they are as good as when they left the barn. Do you want to perform any additional testing? Cut down a few trees?"

Mr. Hedgley looked across the rows of Dragon's Teeth stretching throughout the shaded grove. He had grown tired of testing and re-testing. "No, I don't think that's necessary."

Mr. Martin twisted and sat on the loose leaves carpeting the ground. "I wonder if we should have used linear saws rather than radial. Linear would have been harder to transport, but would make it possible to cut down larger trees."

"Hmmph." Mr. Hedgley showed his indifference.

"I've got a question. Why did Monsieur Punaise name them 'Dragon's Teeth?' It just doesn't seem to fit their form or function."

"Ahh, my engineer friend. You haven't done your classics homework. Didn't you read about Jason's quest for the Golden Fleece? The myth arises from a canonical Phoenician legend. One of their princes, Cadmus, killed a sacred dragon. The goddess Athena told the prince to sow the teeth on the ground and a warrior would grow from each. He used these men to help build the citadel of Thebes. The hero, Jason, also got some of the teeth, sowed them, but then had to defeat the warriors that appeared by himself. Monsieur Punaise was captivated with contraptions that repaired other contractions. Something springing forth from the scraps of the perished. Cute, huh?"

"Interesting, but overly cerebral. Cute in a morbid way, if such a thing exists."

A series of rifle reports echoed through the glen, stopping the progress of their labors. Mr. Hedgley looked at Mr. Martin quizzically. "Why would Monsieur Punaise be testing the soldiers again?"

The sound changed, and the distant clanging of metal on metal joined the cacophony. Mr. Hedgley spun in place, adding "What the …?" He sprinted to the edge of the trees overlooking the cottage mill, Mr. Martin right behind him. The battle was already underway below. Uniformed Marines were swinging axes, knocking heads and arms off the metal brutes.

"We must get down there!" Mr. Martin cried out.

"Ahh, my brave friend, not us but rather our machines. What could we mortals do that our goddess' Dragon's Teeth could not do better?" He smiled at his own cleverness. "How many can we send down there?"

Mr. Martin stopped panicking and started mentally counting, including helpful head bobs as he performed his tally. "Fifty … no, sixty cutters, twenty wagons, and forty mortars. But the mortars have no ammunition. The cutters aren't as fast as the soldiers, but for hand-to-hand they're much more deadly. Should I signal them to head in?

Wait ... what am I saying?! Those are the Royal Aerial Marines! Our own countrymen are down there!"

They both looked again at the battle. Mr. Hedgley wrinkled his brow. "Why are the Marines doing that?" He emphasized his question by pointing at the maneuvers on the field.

Some of the Marines had broken off and run toward the buildings. "Wait ... They're trying to get to the barn. And the cottage. They must be after Monsieur Punaise. Well, I say let them have him!"

Mr. Martin quickly agreed by exclaiming, "You will get no argument from me!" They shared grim smiles at the opportunity to free themselves from Monsieur Punaise.

Mr. Hedgley peered more closely at the scene below. "How did they get here? Where did the Marines come from?" They both looked around, searching for signs of troop movement across the fields or the road. Then an oddly square hole opened in the gray sky out of which a platform lowered.

Mr. Martin saw the strange phenomenon first. "My stars! There's a giant airship right there!" He pointed wildly across a wide swath of the sky over the field.

"I don't see it ... oh, yes! There it is! It looks like it's covered in mirrors and reflects the sky itself. It's practically invisible! How did they do that?"

Sparky knew her priorities. She stepped swiftly into the surgical assistant, strapped in, and took on her first patient's bullet removal. Erasmus sprinted into the infirmary. "Sorry for the delay, I had to brief J. B. on the situation in the barn. What did you find out ... oh my!"

Sparky glanced up briefly from her medical work. "Oh, I forgot that it has been a while since you last observed me doing this type of work, and that was with cadavers. Even doing our best, surgery is ... messy work. We can thank Dr. Crawford Long for the use of this misted ether." She pointed her eyes quickly at the crooked hose above the patient. "Without it, this young man would ... well, let me just say this entire process would hurt a great deal more." She dropped the spherical bullet she had removed from the young Marine's upper thigh into a metal dish with a clank and immediately started cleaning and closing the wound. Within a few seconds she had secured a neat row of sutures and moved her attention to the same patient's arm wound. All the while, the surgical assistant provided multiple metal helping hands. A suction tool kept the bleeding from obscuring her work. Two arms with forceps held wounds closed both before and after Sparky's handiwork, and a parabolic-mirrored gaslight provided an intense illumination on her area of interest. It might have been this illumination that startled Erasmus, Sparky thought. It's one thing to see a wounded man but quite another to visually highlight the ragged damage.

A few feet away, another surgeon worked his trade on another wounded Marine. Erasmus noticed that, despite their age, they were a tough lot. Within a minute, Sparky dropped another shot into the metal bowl and finished closing up her first patient. The third and last of the injured Marines walked on his own over to her table and sat down. He had a rough laceration on his shoulder. He was doing his best to staunch the bleeding with his hand, but it needed immediate attention.

Sparky asked in an authoritative voice, "Can you sit as still as possible for me? It would be best if we don't lay you down. Turn your head to the right, away from the wound, bite down on this towel, and I'll work as quickly as possible. It may help to shut your eyes." With the towel in place and his head turned, four metal arms descended on the shoulder. The work was fast and meticulous. Clamping. Cleaning. Unclamping, Suction. Cleaning. Interior sutures. Suction. Exterior sutures. Dressing. Bandaging. The patient moved nary a twinge and, with the exception of a very quiet groan and a single tear, he showed not a sign of suffering.

"Get yourself outfitted with a sling. I want that arm immobilized so the stitches hold and the muscle heals." The patient looked at Sparky and mumbled something. Sparky continued, "You can spit that towel in here." She pointed to the bucket on the floor filled with other bloodstained cloths.

He followed her advice. "Thank you, ma'am," he said and slid off the table.

Sparky wiped off her hands and turned to Erasmus, who had just turned his attention to the metal pieces under the tarp. "You came in to ask a question. What was it?"

Without looking up from the scraps, Erasmus replied, "Did you get to take a look at this?"

"Just a quick glance, but that's all I needed. Did you notice the disk?"

"Yes. And we both know what this means. They are just like the platters that control the EPACTs. I saw how the disks are delivered: Monsieur Punaise has a conveyor system to deliver a master disk to the assemblers. The assemblers duplicate them and courier them to the other working units. It creates a chain of command. The only question is: what were Monsieur Punaise's latest orders?"

J. B. burst through the door of the infirmary and tossed another of the rucksacks to Erasmus. "Chief Inspector, here's your sail. Let's go!" Without waiting to even see if Erasmus caught the pack, J. B. turned, ran to the railing, opening his wing apparatus as he sprinted, and leapt overboard.

Erasmus turned to Sparky. "I shall be returning to the fray it seems. Keep a light on for me." He sprinted through the door and, as it swung back and forth, Sparky watched Erasmus strap into the sail and follow Fox. All she could think was, *"I hope we're high enough for that thing to work."* She turned and headed to the sink on the wall to give her hands a good scrubbing before returning to the bridge.

Erasmus stretched out his arms and legs as far as he could as soon as he cleared the railing. Looking down, it was obvious that HMA Britannia had returned to an altitude of 1,000 feet. He counted to three as previously instructed and pulled hard on the cord that attached to the back of the pack. The tug broke the thread that held the cord in check, unleashing the contents of the knapsack. The sail had the feel of a "work in progress." It did slow his fall, but it was still a heart-stopping, unbridled, out-of-control descent. Erasmus knew he would land wherever the fates determined. He would have to make the best of it. If the winds were favorable, the landing would have a bit of a horizontal aspect so that running could be combined with the impact. That didn't appear to be the case this time. He was spiraling down, his legs pointing slightly to the outside of his helical drop.

Erasmus saw the well appear and disappear from his estimated impact point. All that stone and wood was an unappealing location to come down. He bent his knees and prepared for the corkscrewing earth that was rushing up at him. Green grass. Brown well. Green grass. Brown well. Gree … His legs blasted up into his body with a force that he couldn't stop. Erasmus took two rapid, squat-legged steps forward and was hit in the gut by the stone hardness of the well, knocking out his breath and sending his Colt Pocket 1849 revolver out of his jacket, over the gaping mouth of the well, and sliding across the grass on the far side. A previously quiescent Dragon's Tooth wagon deftly scooped up the pistol with a front appendage and nonchalantly placed it into its bed. *"Well,"* he thought, *"as soon as I can breathe again, I need to wrestle my weapon back from that automated lorry."*

Following J. B.'s orders, the Royal Aerial Marines fell back and regrouped by St. Aidan's Road. While the Marines waited and watched, the assemblers completed rebuilding most of the Dragon's Teeth the Marines had damaged with axes. The wagons stocked the repaired contraptions with fuel and ammunition; the water bearers refreshed their boilers; the assemblers delivered new disks. It was as if a brand-new set of adversaries were ready for another assault. And Erasmus had dropped into the middle of the pack.

Erasmus rubbed his sore abdomen and took slow deep breaths to recover from the impact. He was amazed that his legs and knees had withstood the landing, but he was sure that by tomorrow he might have a different opinion. He looked at the waiting Dragon's Teeth that encircled him. Would they attack if not provoked? He skirted the well, taking a few slow steps toward the gun-stealing wagon. When he was within a few feet, it reacted by turning its head and pointing its sensors directly at him.

"It cannot see well. Maybe if I look innocuous," he postulated. He slowly crouched down on all fours and crawled mechanically toward the wagon. It didn't react! When he was within a couple of feet, Erasmus stopped and extended his left arm. The Dragon's Tooth reached back with a fore appendage, deftly grabbed the pistol, and placed it into Erasmus' open hand. *"Stupendous!"* he thought, *"but I will never convince the Marines to crawl around like this. Now how do I retreat?"*

He slowly slipped the revolver back inside his jacket. Reversing his all-fours crawl, he backpedaled methodically to the well. Then he heard the charge. The Marines poured in from the road, axes raised and primed for battle. Erasmus stood to make himself visible. At the same time, the thirty or so Dragon's Teeth all turned their heads toward the onslaught. And then they ran. All thirty of them. In every direction except for the direction of the approaching Marines. They scattered outward. In doing so, one of the mortars got a hind leg tangled in Erasmus' sail cloth. Unlike an animal, it simply carried on running. The Chief Inspector was jerked off his feet, landing on the grass, and was dragged thirty-five yards before he could release his knapsack.

Erasmus jumped to his feet and surveyed the situation, trying to determine the best way he could help. Twenty or so Marines were now in the center of the lawn wielding axes. Their rifles from their first assault lay scattered around them. The retreated Dragon's Teeth stood watching from the periphery.

As if on cue, all sixteen soldier Dragon's Teeth broke into a full sprint, rushing the Marines. Each picked a trajectory that allowed it to pass by the pack and keep running. The Marines' instincts were to stay close, guarding one another. At the closest point to the Marines, the soldier Dragon's Teeth all fired their rifles in unison. Sixteen bullets ripped into the crowd of uniformed men. Screams rang out, and six men fell. The mechanical soldiers ran back to the periphery and turned to make another pass.

Marines jumped over their fallen toward their rifles. Others scattered to avoid being pinned down again. Erasmus knew that both axes and rifles were poor defenses against this new attack. "To the woods! Run!!"

The Marines had no time to react. Although the Marines had spread out, the Dragon's Teeth executed their next pass with mechanical efficiency, the running metal soldiers firing their rifles in unison at their human counterparts. More men fell, but Erasmus couldn't tell how many. "Run! Run!"

Bodies lay strewn across the battlefield grass, discarded rifles and axes scattered about, uniformed men running for cover, and gunpowder smoke lethargically dissipating. Erasmus said out loud to himself, "I can't help here!" He looked to the barn and thought of the man inside controlling these killing machines.

He sprinted to the open barn door. Just inside, Erasmus stopped to squint and adjust his eyes to the indoors. He stumbled in to find Monsieur Punaise, hoping to put a stop to this. That's when he heard raised voices. Rather than rush in, he thought it best to keep his presence a secret. He crept forward and discovered a most interesting scene.

J. B. was on the floor level with a rifle pointed at Monsieur Punaise up on his raised platform. J. B. was livid. "Shut them down! Now!"

"Or what?" Monsieur Punaise laughingly replied. "You will zhoot me? Zat will not stop my little soldiers!"

Erasmus slowly pulled his revolver and looked about. Spanners. Tools. A controller panel. Blank disks. Iron parts. He thought, *"We are stopping this right now!"* just as another round of rifle reports echoed from outside.

Danger Plus Opportunity

By Dr. Katherine L. Morse

Sparky watched the battle unfold in helpless horror. She had to do something to stop it! She had to do something to retrieve the wounded! "Captain Cox, we're going in low to evacuate casualties."

"Are you mad? Those monstrosities will fire on Britannia!"

"They're only firing small rounds and they can't aim very high. The worst they'll do is put a few holes in the gondola." She didn't bother to mention the mortars; hopefully they wouldn't be able to "see" the airship. The way Cox flapped his lips and grasped his chest, one would have thought she had suggested allowing the enemy to fire on Her Majesty in the flesh. "Or perhaps you would prefer to tell Her Majesty that you think her gunwales more dear than her Aerial Marines." Although it was a wholly inappropriate time for humor, it occurred to Sparky that her comment might be interpreted as somewhat bawdy. No matter. Duty called.

On their next pass over the battlefield, she throttled back the engines and eased the ship lower. She shouted into the voicepipe,

"Prepare the hoist!" She turned to Cox, "Do your best to hold her on station while we board the wounded." She couldn't tell if the look of deep offense on his face was because he interpreted her order to mean that she thought him incapable of the task or because it sounded like she didn't trust him to follow her orders.

No sooner had she relinquished the controls than she was reminded that hope was not a plan. The mortars began rotating on station. What were they doing? As Britannia approached, the activity of the mortars stopped mimicking the motion described by the biologist, Robert Brown, and took on an intentional aspect. They were orienting toward the approaching airship. How could that be? There was no way they could see it with their limited vision. The shadow! Britannia cast a shadow as it approached from the west. As they locked onto their target, they planted their spiked backsides into the ground.

"Pull up!" Captain Cox only looked at her grumpily. "Pull up, damn you!" She practically knocked him to the ground to grab the controls. The mortars fired in quick, synchronized succession. The first couple missed, but the third one grazed the airship before Sparky pulled her out of range.

"I trust you will be explaining the condition of the gunwales to Her Majesty," Cox sniped.

Sparky had half a mind to knock him to the floor again. She grabbed the voicepipe again, "Dr. Young, meet me in engineering!" She turned back to the pilot. "Captain Cox, I'm sure I don't need to tell you to keep the ship out of range of those mortars." She departed the bridge before he could answer because she was sure she didn't want to hear it.

Sparky stopped in the infirmary first. She pulled back the tarp and rummaged recklessly through the scraps, finding only three of the punched disks that she took to engineering. She examined the disks carefully as she walked. They were all made from the same template with a finely etched radial grid pattern. Within each cell of the grid were four dots, also marked faintly, which formed a trapezoid that was wider toward the outside of the disk. Some combination of the four was punched out in each of the cells. She did some quick arithmetic in her head. Each cell could indicate one of sixteen possible combinations, assuming the location in the cell mattered. And she was pretty sure it did because she found all sixteen combinations on at least one of the disks. Perhaps the radial tracks conveyed one type of order and the sequence in the track indicated the specific order. Or maybe it was the other way around. She would have loved to spend the time to consider all the ways such a device could be used to encode information, but she had a more urgent and less elegant requirement at the moment.

She nearly ran into Yin as she entered engineering because she was holding the stack of disks up to the light and rotating them to determine if they were all the same or different. They were different. "Dr. Young, we need to duplicate as many of these as possible, and quickly."

Yin took one of the disks from her and examined the punched holes. "How do you know which holes to make?"

"Any holes will do, so long as they fit the pattern." She pointed to the dots indicating where the holes should align.

"I understand."

"I'm going back to the bridge. It may get a bit bumpy."

"I understand," Yin repeated.

As Sparky hustled back to the bridge, she thought about how lucky Dr. Pogue was to have such a brilliant and competent colleague. Two together were mightier than two alone. "Captain Cox, I have another, safer plan."

The look on his face said, "Oh, I can hardly wait."

"Circle directly over the ring of mortars at an altitude of 1,000 feet. If my calculations and our recent experience are accurate, that will put us just out of range. I will draw their fire, but it's critical that you hold Britannia on station … just out of range." She probably didn't need to remind Cox to stay out of range given that such an order was closely aligned with his natural proclivities. She just hoped the man had more nerve than he'd shown so far because, if he flinched, her plan would all be for not.

She left the bridge once again. This time she headed amidships to locate Gunner Hepburn's station. As the flame cannon had been a recent retrofit, its controls had been squeezed into some repurposed space. Judging by the cabinets with their brackets and latches, it had been a china pantry. Probably just as well that the royal porcelain had been removed under the circumstances. "Gunner Hepburn, I'm Dr. Sparky McTrowell, temporarily in command of this vessel."

"Yes, ma'am."

"How much fuel do you have for that weapon?"

"Ma'am?"

"How long can you fire that cannon?"

"Five minutes steady, ma'am, but it does tend to overheat, ma'am."

She did more arithmetic in her head. "That should do it. When I give the order, I want you to fire bursts, thirty seconds on, thirty seconds off until I tell you to stop."

"Yes, ma'am."

She marched back to engineering. Yin had the entire engineering crew busily hammering scrap metal flat and cutting it into disks. She was meticulously punching the control holes herself. A couple dozen were complete. "Dr. McTrowell, wouldn't it be better to punch no holes? The machines would stop moving."

"If they are not moving, they can be repaired. Is crisis not danger plus opportunity?" Yin nodded in agreement and understanding. "Four more should be enough." She took a fresh disk from a crewmember, picked up a yawl, and began punching holes. With some professional chagrin she noted that Yin's punches were cleaner than hers. No matter. Duty called. They finished the last few.

Sparky led Yin to Private Jones' station at the controls of the platform hoist. Sparky had to admit to herself that she admired how thoroughly connected the communications on Britannia were. Everywhere there was a crew station, there was a voice pipe. She grabbed the one at hand. "Captain Cox, are we on station?"

"Aye aye."

"Gunner Hepburn, are you ready?"

"Yes, ma'am."

"Dr. Young, aim for the soldiers and the cutters." Yin just nodded.

Sparky pulled out her pocket watch and waited for the second hand to come around to the top of the minute. "Now, Mr. Hepburn." She kept an eye on the watch while listening carefully. After two bursts of the flame cannon, she heard the mortars start to fire again. She heard the shells whistle past the ship, or maybe she just imagined she could hear it from inside the gondola. She held her breath. If her calculations were wrong, it would all be over in less than three minutes, one way or another. She nodded to Yin to get on the platform. At the end of the third burst, she signaled Private Jones to lower the platform holding Yin. She ran to the edge of platform hole, poked her head out, and scanned the circle of mortars. She hopped back up and grabbed the voice pipe. "One more burst, Mr. Hepburn." She sprinted back to the descending platform and jumped down next to Young, who handed her a stack of the disks. With their backs to each other, they began hurling the disks down toward the battlefield, spinning as they went, aiming at the soldiers and cutters. Sparky had another of her inappropriate thoughts, thinking back to Drake's story about the flying contraption and the baby coincident with the Annual Symposium of the Occidental Inventors' Society.

Sparky shook herself out of her reminiscing to survey the effects of the ploy with the flame cannon. She felt herself rather clever at that moment. The bright bursts from the flame cannon had drawn the fire of the mortars. By circling just above their formation, HMA Britannia had tricked them into doing what no human would have done, firing on their own troops. The mortars were reduced to a smoldering ring of shrapnel. And there was still a minute and a half of firing time left in the flame cannon.

When she and Yin had dispensed the last of the disks, she signaled for Jones to hoist them back up. Although the platform gave her an excellent vantage point on the melee, it left them dangerously exposed. "Yin, please stay here and be prepared to help with the wounded."

Sparky headed back to the bridge yet again. She couldn't help thinking that she was sorely looking forward to a hot bath at the end of this expedition, assuming she survived it. She pulled out her spyglass and surveyed the state of the Dragon's Teeth. The assemblers regrouped and began trolling the mechanical carnage. As she had hoped, they discovered the counterfeit disks on the field and began inserting them into the nearest operating automatons. At first nothing seemed to happen. And then the Dragon's Teeth with new disks froze.

Well, that was something of an improvement, but not quite the desired result.

Finally, the malformed instructions took hold, and sheer bedlam broke out. They ran into each other. A couple of the cutters began sawing up everything in reach, including water bearers and soldiers. One of the assemblers began disassembling and reassembling itself with its parts in the wrong places. Some of the soldiers ripped off their own barrels. One of the water bearers dumped itself into the well, blocking that as a water supply. The lorries all drove in random directions, running over all their compatriots. Sparky allowed herself the luxury of a small smile. "Captain Cox, I think it's time to start cleaning up this mess."

Swords to Plowshares

By David L. Drake

Sergeant J. B. Fox looked through the sights of his gun. As an expert marksman, he had the choice of aiming at his target's torso, the recommended military target, or his head, the decisive shot for the kill, but with a lower probability of success. Monsieur Punaise was backlit by the sunlight coming in the expanse of the barn's front door, and J. B. was aiming straight into the center of the lit halo of frizzy hair that defined the perimeter of Monsieur Punaise's head.

"Shut them all down!" he barked emphatically.

Erasmus took a small step to improve his angle on the mad inventor. He carefully raised his pistol, hoping to keep his location concealed. While keeping his rifle pointed at Monsieur Punaise, Sergeant J. B. Fox flashed his eyes over to Erasmus. Whatever J. B. was thinking, he didn't give it away.

J. B. continued his monologue, "We have you cornered, Monsieur Punaise. And, yes, we will shoot you."

At that, Erasmus cocked his Colt Pocket 1849, an unfortunately loud but requisite precursor to firing the pistol. Now it was Monsieur Punaise who glanced at Erasmus, but it wasn't fear that he exhibited. Instead, he cackled with glee.

"You are not going to zhoot me! O' you would 'ave already!"

J. B. flashed a second glance at Erasmus, but this time he subtly but quickly nodded his head in agreement that he wasn't going to shoot Monsieur Punaise. Erasmus knotted his face into a momentary grimace indicating he understood the situation was about to get a great deal tougher. J. B. had planned, or better put, was ordered to bring Monsieur Punaise back alive. That was an easier plan when they had hoped to have a dozen Aerial Marines helping out. But those men were now dealing with the worst of it outside the barn. Inside, it was just the two of them and a madman obsessed with power.

"You zee?! No zhooting! Ah have zomezing better zan guns! Now you zee!"

Monsieur Punaise's face scrunched up and he whistled the loudest note, or was it a pair of notes, Erasmus had ever heard from a single person. Then thump, thump, thump! A heavy running sound echoed from the recesses of the barn. Six assemblers sprinted into the light, racing toward J. B. and Erasmus. The pair dropped their guns, knowing they would be useless, and made their initial, instinctive evasive jumps to the side. The metal brutes turned in sync with the dodges and prepared to attack. In the background, Monsieur Punaise howled with laughter.

Mr. Hedgley and Mr. Martin poked their faces out of the woods on the hill just enough to watch the melee below. "Look at that," Mr. Martin stammered out while pointing at the Dragon's Teeth running about. "How did they learn to do that maneuver?"

"Clearly Monsieur Punaise had some tricks up his sleeve. That looks like a Roman army tactic. Maybe. Just a bit? Or like those American savages attacking from horseback?"

"How can you be ... intellectual about this? Our countrymen are down there!!"

"Mr. Martin, look at the airship! It's firing a massive torch!"

They both stared wide-eyed as the flame lit up the sky, its heat making the air shimmer and dance. Thrice it fired.

Then the ring of mortars below fired at the light and heat, arching their explosive loads up and over, curving through their peak, rushing downward to land in simultaneous detonations on the Dragon's Teeth on the far side of the circle. The parabolic trails of smoke were beautifully symmetric. The ring of devastation was impressively accurate.

The noise of the blasts caused both men to cry out and cover their ears a split second too late. They glanced at each other and retreated back into the woods. They looked at the mechanical army awaiting their orders. Mr. Hedgley placed his hand seriously on Mr. Martin's shoulder. "My good friend. How do you feel about the agriculture business?"

"I see what you mean. We can turn these into planters, plows, and weeders. Swords into plowshares, right?"

"Yes, yes, Mr. Martin. When things calm down below, we still have a half year's lease on this property. By winter we can have all of the Dragon's Teeth refurbished and prepared for spring. Make sense?"

"More sense that anything we've done in the last year. It's time we got to know the townsfolk, too. I'm ready to settle down."

"Well, the first thing is for us not to be detected. Let's go for a walk."

Erasmus ducked the first swipe of a great metal arm, but the kick from the rear leg of the second Dragon's Tooth caught him square in the stomach, skittering him across the hay-covered floor. He stood up next to the controller panel. He needed a weapon! Any weapon. He grabbed at the bench and came up with a long spanner. A Dragon's Tooth leapt at him, front legs stretched out to do damage. He swung the tool at its head, hoping to disable a sensor or two.

The spanner banged heavily on the side of its head, denting the iron, and shooting a reverberating pain into Erasmus' left hand. *"A spanner is just not made for striking,"* he thought.

The legs defensively shot out to disarm the Chief Inspector. The ferocity of the attack gouged his hand, struck his chest, and ripped his clothes, the corners of the square feet scratching trails across his skin. Erasmus went down again. He could hear J. B. struggling with a similarly one-sided fight. Monsieur Punaise had switched to a high-pitched giggle.

It was only the briefest of moments while Erasmus' backside bounced off the ground for the second time, that he thought, *"I cannot win through strength or perseverance. Think! Think!"* And then he remembered ...

Erasmus jumped to his feet. Three Dragon's Teeth pounced at him as the same scene unfolded for Sergeant Fox. Erasmus took a deep breath and whistled a loud hail for a cabriolet. All six front left limbs of the Dragon's Teeth shot up and knocked their own heads clean off. The contraptions landed clumsily, staggered a bit, teetering to keep their balance, and then fell over, lifeless.

J. B. sprang up to his feet. Erasmus got his first good look at the Sergeant since the attack. His hands and face were bloodied, but not visibly damaged. His uniform was ruined from what looked like claw marks from grappling with metal machines. In one motion, he leapt up and grabbed the flooring of the platform where Monsieur Punaise stood, swung up, and landed impressively on his feet. He deftly pulled irons from the inside of his coat and screwed them onto the yelping and grimacing Monsieur Punaise.

Erasmus surveyed the damage he had wrought. He suddenly remembered the battle out on the grounds. He scooped up his pistol, and shouted to J. B., "I am headed out to help ..."

He never finished the sentence, as multiple mortar rounds went off all at once. Erasmus staggered back, temporarily blinded by the flash and deafened by the blast. J. B. looked up in time to see Erasmus run out into the dust and smoke.

A TALE OF TWO ARMORS

BY DR. KATHERINE L. MORSE

"Mr. Hepburn, please remain at the ready," McTrowell ordered. "Dr. Young and I are going down on the platform hoist to retrieve casualties. I think the battle is won, but things are still moving about a bit too much for my taste."

"Aye, aye, ma'am," echoed from the voicepipe.

"Mr. Jones, lower away."

Just as the hoist began to budge, Jean Chemiserouge bustled into the hoist's bay, making his presence known for the first time since the day's frenetic activities ensued. He was practically flapping his hands like a dodo as he hopped down the few inches to the platform.

"Monsieur Chemiserouge, what are you doing?!"

"I am prepared to execute my mission to capture Monsieur Punaise." McTrowell started to reply but thought better of it. As if Her Majesty would let the wild-haired troublemaker out of her jurisdiction. As if Chemiserouge were actually "capturing" the villain after so many brave Marines had given their lives. The fop had probably been sitting in his cabin fretting about his café au lait spilling during maneuvers. Harumph!

"The situation on the ground is not entirely secure. Either help us evacuate the casualties or stay out of the way and don't do anything … dangerous." She'd wanted to say "stupid."

Private Jones stopped the platform just a few inches off the ground. Captain Cox was doing a world-class job of holding HMA Britannia steady and level. She shouldn't have been surprised at their mutual skills. It was this well-coordinated choreography they used to deliver their sovereign as gently as if she were a baby bird.

The uninjured and ambulatory Marines were already lining up with the wounded when McTrowell and Young touched down. The Marines began efficiently laying their brothers in arms side-by-side on the platform. They had already performed the grim task of battlefield triage; the casualties they brought first looked the most injured that were likely to survive. Their actions were so well coordinated that she stepped back to allow them to proceed without interference. She took a moment to scan the devastation.

Chemiserouge was observing a partially disabled soldier Dragon's Tooth at close range. It was whirring and agitating on the spot. It was clearly jammed, but still struggling through its inability to solve the problem. "This doesn't belong here." He smiled at his own cleverness. And with that, he pulled out the offending gear.

Sparky almost gagged as her heart leapt into her throat. There was no time to shout a warning. The automaton swung smoothly into action, slewing its barrel around. It fired point blank into

Chemiserouge's chest. The trajectory of the barrel continued its arc toward the platform. Sparky, Yin, and all the Marines were in range.

"Hepburn!" Sparky shrieked straight up in the air. Her voice must have bounced around the platform hoist's bay and reverberated down the voicepipe because she felt the heat of the cannon's flame come on over her head, even through the leather of her flight cap. She ducked a bit and flipped up the collar of her duster to protect herself from the intense blue heat. When the conflagration ended, the machine was an unrecognizable slag heap of cinders. And Monsieur Chemiserogue's body was also considerably worse for the encounter.

Private Jones called down, "Gunner Hepburn says to tell you that the cannon's fuel is expended."

"Indeed." Sparky turned to Yin, and said in a voice she hoped none of the Aerial Marines would hear, "I doubt we can save them all, but we must do our best."

"It's not so bad as it seems," Young replied.

Although McTrowell realized Young had probably seen more than a lifetime's worth of violence and carnage, she still thought the response inappropriately callous.

She tried to focus on the gruesome task ahead of her. "Gentlemen, we'll take this group up. You and you," she pointed to the two nearest, uninjured Marines, "will ride with us to transport the wounded to the infirmary. The rest of you round up the remaining casualties. We'll send the hoist back down." She stood on one corner of the platform and held onto the cable. The Marines and Yin followed suit. "Mr. Jones, bring us up!"

Sparky sprinted ahead to the infirmary to strap herself into the mechanical surgical assistant. Her invention was getting considerably more use than she had ever anticipated. She really must discuss patenting it with Jonathan Lord Ashleigh when the current excitement passed. The thought of her friend gave her pause. She wondered what he had been doing while she and Drake had been pursuing Punaise with Fox.

Her pleasant intellectual diversion was interrupted by the delivery of casualties. She pointed to the three tables and the wounded to indicate how to arrange them. "Corporal, I'm out of ether. Bring Her Majesty's best brandy."

"Yes, ma'am."

"Private, start cutting away their jackets around the bullet holes. I'll remove the remnants of cloth when I extract the bullets."

"No," Yin interjected.

"Dr. Young, how dare you countermand me? While I respect your skills as an engineer, you are not a physician. Time is of the essence."

"No, look." Yin hastily unbuttoned the jacket of the Marine on Sparky's operating table. A bloodstain wicked out from a remarkably clean indentation in his shirt. The aforementioned undergarment didn't make sense to Sparky. It was soft, smooth, and the color of undyed silk, as if it were a fine lady's unmentionable. But it appeared to be holding the shape of ripples, as if from a pebble dropped in a puddle.

The corporal trotted back into the room holding a cut crystal decanter large enough to use as an anchor, sloshing its amber contents. Sparky nodded at the patient on the table in front of her. The corporal poured the liquid slowly into his comrade's mouth until the fellow couldn't swallow any more. Without prompting, the corporal wadded up his leather gauntlet, stuck it in the wounded man's mouth, and took his hand firmly while still managing to stand out of the way.

Yin waited patiently, "be ready."

Sparky wasn't sure what she needed to be ready for because she was already prepared to operate. Yin grasped the edges of the ripples and pulled away from the wound in opposite directions. The fabric stretched taut and then popped the single shot into the air like a champagne cork. Yin pulled the garment up under the man's chin to reveal a chest wound in dangerous proximity to his heart, but which appeared to have only penetrated his pectoral muscle. Sparky's head swam with questions that, unfortunately, would have to wait until later. She had three men to sew up immediately and at least two more on the way.

By the end of it all, she was really thankful for the mechanical surgical assistant. Her hands were shaking from exhaustion to the point where she couldn't have finished without it. There was a surprisingly neat row of crystal decanters on the floor against the wall of the infirmary, placed there by the corporal when he emptied one into a patient and had to fetch another. And her impromptu loblolly boy's glove was ruined from the gnawing of his wounded brothers. The young corporal reached out to steady her as she unstrapped from the mechanical surgical assistant.

"Corporal …?"

"Bennett, ma'am."

"Corporal Bennett, is there any more in the Queen's stores?"

"No, ma'am."

"Just as well. They needed it more than I did. Thank you for your able assistance."

"Yes, ma'am." He saluted smartly, turned crisply on his heel, and departed with the purposefulness of someone who knew exactly what to do next. She envied him that. She could stay and clean up the operating theater or go lend her services to cleaning up the theater of battle. No doubt Her Majesty had an army of stewards and maids to keep her airship spotless. McTrowell decided she would be of more use on the ground.

As she stepped onto the platform once again, she reflected that she and Private Jones were practically becoming friends. She would need to invite him over for a cup of tea, if only she had an actual domicile. She added that to her growing mental list of tasks to undertake upon her return to London.

When she arrived on terra firma, she found Dr. Young waiting for the return trip. There were several piles of machine parts at hand, although calling them neatly sorted might have been going too far. At least there was some sensible order to them. Closest to the platform's footprint were two shapes draped in canvas, two shapes that bore the unmistakable outline of bodies. McTrowell pulled up the top corner of one. A neck shot. The, as yet unexplained, undergarment couldn't have stopped it.

Dr. Young peered over her shoulder and said, "Collar."

Sparky just screwed her face up in perplexity. She peeled back the second tarp. She had to remove it two thirds of the way to discover the cause of death, exsanguination from a brutal saw cut to the femoral artery. She replaced the cover and turned to Yin.

"I think an explanation is in order."

"We must add a collar. As a government official's."

224

"I beg your pardon."

"I believe you call them mandarin."

"I have no idea what you're talking about."

Yin gestured to the first body. "We should add a collar to the armor. The type on high government officials' uniforms."

Sparky blinked once. Twice. Yin had that blank, factual, engineer expression on her face. Sparky blinked for the third time. She reminded herself to think like an engineer, not like a physician who had just lost two patients that she was sure she could have saved if she'd only just gotten to them in time. If only she'd foreseen the mortar attack on the first pass. She squinted at Yin to focus both her vision and her attention. "A high, straight collar might have stopped the shot that killed this Marine," she concluded, pointing at the first tarp.

"Yes."

"Yes, I agree. Now, would you kindly explain why the arm and leg wounds I treated today are much worse than the chest wounds that should have killed those three men?"

"Miss Slate is very talented and useful." Sparky made her "that is not an explanation, and you know it" face. Dr. Young continued, "Genghis Khan and his Golden Horde wore silk armor. Your English ancestors wore chain mail. Miss Slate thought that shirts woven of both would be highly protective."

"I didn't see any chain mail."

"Miss Slate is very talented and useful."

It was clear to Sparky that she wasn't going to get any more information without going to the source. She turned her attention to the remains of Monsieur Chemisrouge. Yin handed her another sheet of canvas without comment. As McTrowell wrapped his crispy carcass in the heavy cloth, she wondered to herself, *"What is it with me and Frenchmen coming to unsavory ends?"*

THE INVERTED MARIONETTE

BY DAVID L. DRAKE

Dirt and debris continued raining down. The air was thick with smoke and atomized soot and redolent with the stench of gunpowder sulfur and burnt grass. It burned Erasmus' throat to breathe as he ran across the yard, so he placed his handkerchief over his nose and mouth with his right hand as he kept his pistol at the ready out in front of him. Soldiers moaned in the unseeable distance. He moved toward the sound, hopping over the twisted chucks of metal that used to be operational automatons. Small orange flames licked outward from their broken interiors, issuing black, greasy smoke.

Once past the line of metal destruction, Erasmus saw the wounded on the field. If any of the Marines had been ambulatory before, they had been knocked to the ground by the detonations. Erasmus looked around for any further threats to the men and noticed the perfectly circular blast ring around the Marines. Then he caught an odd motion out of the corner of his eye. He spun on it and led his gaze with his pistol. Where was it? He took a few steps toward the well. Still nothing obvious. He completed the walk to the well and slowly checked behind the waist-high stone structure. Again nothing. Then his peripheral vision saw it again, beyond the ring of smoldering debris, over near the cottage. He continued his cautious march. He exited the burning ring, stepping between two piles of mangled metal. The smoke was clearing now. He replaced his handkerchief into his pocket and steadied his pistol hand with his now free right hand. The movement flashed again in the window of the cottage, and Erasmus instinctively took a series of quick side steps to get a better angle on the cottage door.

Circling in, he placed his hand on the cottage door latch. His strong but steady squeeze silently unlatched the door. He opened it just a crack, planning to glance in. If there were imminent danger, Erasmus figured he could throw his weight back to jerk it closed again. Instead, through the gap he saw only the tranquil scene of a well-maintained country house without a person in sight. At least that was the case for the two-foot vertical slice of living room he could see through the crack.

He opened the door slowly and evenly with the aim of not squeaking the hinges, a maneuver which worked better than he thought possible. He slipped inside. The contrast between the battlefield outside and the tranquil interior of the house was jarring for

Erasmus. He had the feeling that he should have wiped his feet before entering. The cotton curtains were clean, well pressed, and perfectly tied back. The coordinated, colored cushions on the circle of chairs and couch were recently dusted and fluffed. And the fireplace was devoid of soot and ashes, with a clean set of logs and tinder set for lighting. The room smelled faintly of freshly-brewed coffee and baked bread. Erasmus' initial thought was that, for a cottage shared by three men working on a fabrication business, the domicile was eerily neat and tidy.

The first noise he heard was a small splash in a room to his left. Actually, it sounded like a plate being submerged into soapy water, as if someone were washing dishes just around the corner. Through the connecting doorway, he saw what was surely a kitchen table, set with three places. Erasmus took a few stealthy steps into the room to get a better angle on the doorway, with his pistol held out ready for trouble. Erasmus thought it might be one or both of Monsieur Punaise's helpers, Mr. Hedgley or Mr. Martin. Or perhaps a hired housekeeper. But what didn't add up was that no one with a lick of sense would be calmly doing housework while full-fledged combat raged outside.

Erasmus raised up his pistol momentarily, took a decisive side step into the doorway, re-lowered his weapon, and aimed at the sink area from which the sounds of domestic industry were emanating. There stood a five-foot, slight, almost delicate, wooden contraption, puttering at the sink. Erasmus stood for a few moments, intrigued, as it took the top plate off a short stack of dirty dishes from its right, placed it into a sink full of soapy water, rubbed the surfaces, transferred it to another sink full of rinsing water, agitated it, and placed the resulting clean plate in a drying rack to its left. The body and arms of the mechanism were made of some dark hardwood, perhaps cherry or rosewood, which looked to be oiled or shellacked for water-tightness. A metal box acted as its footer, on top of which a small steam engine purred, delivering power through a spinning metal shaft that stood vertically and ran downward into the heart of the metal box. Upwards through small guide loops in the box ran a series of metal cables to the various moving parts above, operating the contraption like an inverted marionette. It seemed quite oblivious to

Erasmus' presence, which was a relief to him and a pleasant change from the metal menaces without. Erasmus was mesmerized by the operation of its hands, the fingers working in unison, and their fine smooth motion during the dishwashing operation. *"No need to interrupt this,"* he thought.

He turned and walked through the rest of the house, finding nothing of great interest except an uncluttered, orderly residence. He was primarily looking for any potential dangers but found none. However, there a stack of books and notes on a bed stand in one of the bedrooms. He would revisit it later if he had the time.

Upon his return to the kitchen, Erasmus witnessed the amazingly smooth transition from washing to drying. The contraption reached for any remaining dishes to wash and, feeling none, unstoppered the sinks. While the basins drained, the dishwasher pushed with one arm against the edge of the counter and spun itself ninety degrees on its metal box foot. Then, bending at the waist, it reached down with its wooden hands and placed them on the floor. It proceeded to scoot itself forward about half a foot and then repeated the process for another half a foot. It righted itself again, pushed with the other hand against the counter, and turned itself back to face the stack of wet dishes. It deftly picked a cloth towel off a nearby rack and proceeded to dry the dishes in a similar manner as washing, transferring the dishes from a wet stack on its right to a dry stack on its left. After all the autonomous gadgetry that Erasmus had seen of late, this seemed so useful, domestic, and tame. He silently nodded his approval.

Erasmus returned to the stack of books and notes in the bedroom. He took the time to uncock his pistol and return it to his interior jacket pocket, which freed up both his hands. He went through the stack, one item at a time. The books were a hodgepodge of engineering books, mechanic's tables, British history, and adventure fiction. Buried under them was a sizeable leather portfolio of notes. Erasmus untied its leather thong and opened its well-worn cover.

The Wallace residence was a sprawling affair for a residence within London. It was, of course, much smaller than their country home, a multi-floored, many-roomed, stone-walled, labyrinth of a domicile. In their London home, the rooms were spacious, well-appointed, and showed the taste and refinement that Reginald's wife, Annabelle, applied to her decorating.

Reginald's study acted as his sanctum; a dark-wooded lair with two upholstered chairs, a dark, hardwood desk, and his own fireplace. Two of the walls were filled bookcases. It smelled faintly of good tobacco, brandy, and new leather. Despite these appointments, it was not cramped.

Reginald sat in his chair, a fine wool blanket over his lap, a glass of brandy in his hand, and his unshod, gout-inflamed foot propped up on an ottoman. He was deep in thought, but it was more of an unproductive brooding than beneficial analysis. A light rap on the door started him out of his moping.

"Come in, come in," he mumbled.

The door swung open, and the Wallaces' housemaid stepped carefully into the opening, keeping her hand on the doorknob. She looked very agitated to the point of slight panic.

"Mr. Wallace, three men are here to see you. But they are very …," she stammered and looked back over her shoulder to see if they were in ear shot. A man's hand thumped on the door, and the housekeeper lost her grip on the doorknob.

"Out of the way, young lady," boomed a voice from behind her. She retreated sheepishly back into the hall, and a bushy mustachioed man stepped forward, refilling the doorway. "Reginald Wallace, you need to come with us!"

Reginald sat up a bit straighter and gave the stranger a quick once over. His formal military uniform was out of date by fifteen years or so. And his face looked very familiar.

"Colonel Howell Michael Spreckler? By jove, man, you haven't changed a wink since I saw your face on the China War Victory broadsheets! You look fit and dapper."

Wallace's cheeriness threw the Colonel off his game. "Well, thank you. I'm astounded that you remember me."

"Of course, of course! Just give me a private minute to put the shoe on my swollen foot and retrieve my crutches and jacket. I'll be with you gentleman shortly." Reginald politely signaled with his finger to close the door as he slowly scooted.

The Colonel looked back over his shoulder at his two companions, Sir Sidney Fredric Porter and Sergeant Barrett Wentworth and gave them an inquisitive "is that acceptable to you" look. They nodded in agreement. "Thank you, Mr. Wallace. We'll be right here." Colonel Spreckler quietly closed the door.

The three men knew their mission. Word had come down from the top of Her Majesty's Eyes and Ears that chances were not to be taken, and they needed to bring Reginald Wallace "to the Tower," the Tower of London, of course, and hold him there for questioning. Reginald's letter to Monsieur Punaise proved he was in league with the Frenchman. The three war veterans were the right men for the job.

The three men stood patiently as they heard shuffling behind the closed door. Then a quiet click. And then silence. They waited about ten more seconds. Still nothing. The Colonel reopened the door to a now unoccupied room. "Where the hell is he?!" the Colonel bellowed. "Get that housemaid back here."

The young lady appeared quickly on her own. "How may I help you, sir?"

"How did Mr. Wallace leave this room?!"

She apologetically pointed to the rear of the room. "Sir, do you see that small door? The one painted to match the wall. That's the servants' entrance. He may have …"

The three men all raced to the half-width door, the Colonel getting there first, flinging it open, and then doing his best to charge down the tight wooden spiral staircase. At the base he found two doors, one clearly leading back toward the house, most likely to a kitchen or washing room. The Colonel threw the other door open to the sight of a busy London street. He stumbled out onto the sidewalk looking for any trace of Mr. Wallace. Instead, he only saw various vehicles, including at least a half dozen cabriolets proceeding away from the spot where he stood. Sir Porter and Sergeant Wentworth breathlessly joined him, all three looking about to see where the lame man had disappeared.

The Colonel finally shrugged in resignation and flatly stated, "I guess we should return to headquarters to determine what to do next."

Her Majesty's Eyes and Ears' headquarters at 19 Cheyne Row in Chelsea was not as collegial as usual. The six members not assigned to the HMA Britannia were all there, having arrived just minutes before.

The Honorable Jacob Lenthall spoke first. "Does anyone know why we were summoned? I have a ruling I need to make this afternoon."

The Colonel reviewed the situation, "We ran into a bit of a spot apprehending Mr. Wallace. Temporary setback. We'll have him in no time. I alerted the brass just so they know."

The door swung open, and the Chief of Her Majesty's Eyes and Ears entered. The men immediately found their seats. The Chief cleared his throat and declared, "Gentleman, I received a mission report regarding the attempted apprehension of Mr. Wallace. A man who, I might add, is made lame by gout and walks with a cane. Sir Sidney Fredric Porter, Sergeant Barrett Wentworth, and Colonel Howell Michael Spreckler, you are all relieved of duty. Collect your things and leave."

The surprised men sat in silence for a short moment. They weren't used to being talked to in such a terse manner and certainly not used to being dismissed. The Chief continued, "Now, gentleman."

The three men rose and walked away without a word. Everyone at the meeting knew this was just short of a miracle for the Colonel.

The Chief proceeded, "The rest of you three will go to the offices of Western & Transatlantic Airship Lines and seize control of the business. Ensure no crates of Dragon's Teeth are shipped out of Britain."

"I'm afraid I have a ruling I need to make this afternoon," Magistrate Lenthall restated.

"You're also dismissed. Collect your things and leave."

The magistrate was aghast, but he rose and walked out as well. The remaining two men, Mr. Cooke and Captain Vaughan, nodded their approval. Mr. Cooke responded, "Sir, we're on our way." The two stood and left.

Alone in the room, the Chief said quietly to himself, "Well, I was ordered to clean house, and I did." He pivoted smoothly toward the door and departed.

Starting from the top of the leather portfolio, Erasmus found a collection of letters between Monsieur Punaise and Reginald Wallace, complete with details of Reginald's negotiations with various nations for the sale of Dragon's Teeth. "Ah ha!" he said quietly. Most of Reginald's reports back to Monsieur Punaise indicated that the officials he had talked to were either disinclined to pay the high price Punaise was demanding or had a concern with unleashing mechanisms that weren't completely controllable. In response, Monsieur Punaise urged Reginald to press on with negotiating with additional nations.

Under these letters was a draft fifteen-page document, complete with maps, hand drawn diagrams, and proposed timetables. This discovery caused Erasmus to gasp out loud. Monsieur Punaise had written a treatise on how to cripple the British Empire through a series of attacks using Dragon's Teeth. Erasmus thumbed through it quickly and concluded that it was well researched to the extent that, if delivered into the wrong hands, it would have made an excellent blueprint for global control of the Empire's territories. In the first few pages, it noted that Britain had dominance of the world's seas through the strength of its Royal Navy. It pointed out, quite correctly, that the British Empire was in the process of eliminating ocean-going piracy and slavery and was instituting a forced peace on the oceans by acting as the world's maritime police force.

But Britain did not control the air or land. The airways were the domain of commercial airship lines, which were not beholden to any nation but rather to the laws of commerce. It flatly stated that Western & Transatlantic Airship Lines could be the dominant air power if it wanted to use its vessels for both transport and armed combat. It went on to state that land wars were currently dominated by another empire: Russia. The document listed the victories Russia had recently achieved under the rule of Tsar Nicholas. The text concluded that, if Russia were interested in Dragon's Teeth, she could dominate Asia, move across Eastern Europe, and Britain would not be able to stop them.

The single-page letter underneath was handwritten in Russian, which Erasmus could not read to save his life. But he knew that Sparky could. The portfolio was all the evidence needed to explain Monsieur Punaise's treasonous motivation. He secured the portfolio with its leather thong and tucked it under his arm.

Returning again to the kitchen, he watched the wooden helper placing dry dishes into a cabinet, one by one. Erasmus glanced at the scene outside of the window over the sink. HMA Britannia had descended near the ground, and its loading platform was lowered. Royal Aerial Marines were running about, completing the last steps of their mission and securing the scene. But what caught Erasmus' eye the most was Sergeant J. B. Fox leading Monsieur Punaise, who was wearing manacles on his wrists, to the lowered platform.

Erasmus leaned over and pushed a small lever on the puttering steam engine. It quickly came to graceful stop. The arms of the wooden assistant slowly drooped to its sides. Erasmus embraced it around its waist with his free arm, picking it up.

"Spoils of war, and all that!" he thought as he trundled off to reboard the awaiting airship.

BUNDLES OF STICKS

BY DR. KATHERINE L. MORSE

"What's that?"

"I'll explain once we get on board and are underway back to London. What is that?"

"I'll explain once we get on board, and underway back to London." Sparky thought that was a fair and completely vacuous conversational exchange. She waited until Drake had piled his bundle of sticks onto the platform hoist. "Could you lend a hand with this?"

Drake thought the canvas parcel Sparky had indicated felt like a bundle of sticks, but it smelt like the time he'd tried to make Lancashire hotpot and then let his attention drift to the details of a particularly interesting case. It was the fateful cooking attempt that nearly burnt up his flat and burnt down Ye Olde Cheshire Cheese. And, thus, it was the genesis of the arrangement by which James Crocker delivered Erasmus' meals at a reduced rate.

They moved their two parcels off the hoist and to the infirmary in exhausted silence once Private Jones had used the lift to bring them back into the belly of Britannia. McTrowell was only too happy to leave the final clean-up to Dr. Young and the Aerial Marines. She would look in on the wounded en route to London. The components of the Dragon's Teeth would be better examined in the commodious and well-equipped environs of Pogue's laboratory.

"Now then, what is in this bundle?" Drake enquired.

"The remains of Monsieur Jean Chemiserouge."

"The remains?! What happened?"

"He hadn't the sense of a goose when it came to the Dragon's Teeth," McTrowell replied dejectedly.

"He does not weigh much more than a goose. I would have expected him to be heavier."

"He used to be."

Drake took ahold of a corner of the makeshift shroud. "May I?"

"I wouldn't," Sparky grimaced sourly. Erasmus nodded in terse agreement and dropped the flap of fabric. Wishing to move on quickly, Sparky pointed at Erasmus' spoils. "What do you have there?"

"It is another of Punaise's automata."

"And you brought it here?!" She jumped behind the operating table in a defensive posture and cast about for a weapon.

"It is a housemaid, and it can barely move. It is harmless."

Sparky wasn't sure she was willing to take that assertion at face value. "What does it do?"

"I saw it wash and dry dishes. The cottage was neat as a pin, so I think it must be able to perform other chores. I cannot imagine that Hedgley and Martin are such fine housekeepers. And I am sure that Punaise cannot be bothered to concern himself with anything except his inventions. Oh my, have you seen Misters Hedgley and Martin?"

"No. They weren't among the wounded or dead. And Sergeant Fox only captured Monsieur Punaise."

"I wonder if we have seen the last of those two miscreants."

They stood there with the thread of the conversation lost, just staring at each other. The hum of the airship grew louder, and HMA Britannia began to rise. "Well, that's the end of that," Sparky commented off handedly.

"I am not so certain," Drake retorted, reaching inside his jacket.

The visitor cleared his throat loudly in the direction of Littleton. Littleton scowled at him a tad peevishly before turning his attention to the warehouse foreman who had just entered with a sheaf of paperwork. "The customs office wants to inspect these three shipments," Littleton said as he rifled through the stack and handed three of the bills of lading back to the foreman, "so move them to the back of warehouse five."

"Yessir." The foreman departed, but not before fixing the other visitor with a dark look for his tacit refusal to move out of the way.

The visitor coughed softly into his gloved hand, forcing Littleton to look up from the ledger and acknowledge his presence. "Perhaps you should wait until your m ... employer arrives."

"I assure you that you do not want me to arrange for my employer to arrive on the premises." Littleton smiled archly, mostly for his own amusement.

"Your employer, however, will be most interested in my arrival. Would you please inform Mr. Wallace that I'm here?"

Littleton didn't offer the courtesy of asking the visitor's name before replying, "Mr. Wallace has taken ill."

"Are you charged with the operation of Western & Transatlantic Airship Lines in his absence?"

"No." The visitor raised his eyebrows, indicating that Littleton should also answer the implied question. "Mrs. Wallace is … seeing to matters."

"And where might I find Mrs. Wallace?"

Littleton jerked his head toward the door through which the foreman had just left, "Warehouses."

Without further exchange, the visitor turned to the door and opened it with his dove-gray gloved hand in one flowing movement. It snicked closed softly just behind the disappearing tails of his paisley frock coat.

McTrowell emitted a heavy, groaning sigh of exasperation. Would this infernal intrigue never end? Drake produced a folded letter. "I can only read the numbers, so I know how much, but not what of." He handed the paper to her.

Once she unfolded it, she understood his cryptic comment. She scanned it quickly. Her eyes froze half way down the page, and she gasped.

11 июля 1851

Уважаемые господа,

Мы предлагаем грузовые перевозки между Лондоном и Санкт-Петербурге на борту Румянцева. Он имеет грузоподъемность 5 дербицов. Индивидуальные ящики не может быть, чем 3 аршина на стороне. Благодарю вас за дела с воздушного флота России и Транссибирской.

"What is it?" Drake asked anxiously.

"It's a planning specification."

"Why is that surprising?"

"It's not."

"What are they planning?"

"How to ship the Dragon's Teeth in an airship of the Russian & Trans-Siberian Air Fleet," Sparky explained.

"If it is not surprising, why did you gasp?"

"The shipping specification is for the Rumyantsev."

DIRECTLY AND SOBERLY

BY DAVID L. DRAKE

"My dear Sparky, please do not leave me in suspense. I honestly cannot read Russian. I do not even know the vowels from the consonants. This is a planning document for what activity? And what is the Rumyantsev?"

Sparky beamed and held the paper up as if it were a demonstration prop, going so far as to point at it with her other hand. Erasmus was sure she thought her demeanor indicated she was about to impart some invaluable and singular knowledge unto the Chief Inspector, but he also detected a touch of "I know something you do not." He still found it endearing, but he was also sure that she wouldn't have appreciated his take on her enthusiasm.

She began her impromptu presentation. "This letter you found is an ordinary enough document … if you worked in the airship cargo delivery business. It's from the Russia & Trans-Siberian Air Fleet, one of the airship lines that has an office at the London Airship Port. It's mainly a cargo business, hauling imports and exports between London and St. Petersburg. They do some passenger business, but …"

"The letter, my dear. What does it say?"

Sparky cast a momentary glare, a "you interrupted my lecture" face. But it disappeared as fast as it had appeared, and she continued, quoting, "The eleventh of July. Dear sir, we offer cargo service between London and St. Petersburg aboard the Rumyantsev. It has a … what's this in English? … lift capacity … of 5 berkovets. Individual crates cannot be larger than 2 arshins on a side. Thank you for doing business with Russia & Trans-Siberian Air Fleet. It ends there, unsigned, meaning it is their standard letter for their cargo specifications: total weight and unit size."

"The Rumyantsev is a cargo airship. I see. Why was that so exciting?"

Sparky perked up at the opportunity to tell this part of the story. "Well, it has to do with …"

One of the Royal Aerial Marine physicians politely interrupted Sparky and Erasmus to inform them that an early dinner was being provided on the upper deck and suitable attire was requested. Erasmus smiled at Sparky. "Must maintain appearances, and all that," he restated from much earlier in the day. "We should continue this after dinner, privately for security reasons."

She smiled back, silently reflecting her thankfulness that the battle had come to an end. He continued. "I will join you upstairs as soon as I am presentable."

The brig on the HMA Britannia wasn't as posh as the other chambers, although it did have a nice hardwood floor. Monsieur Punaise sat on an overturned pail, his hands still manacled behind his back. The vertical metal bars separating him from his jailer had a door, also made of bars, and a hefty lock. The bars divided the room into two halves, one for those incarcerated and the other for the jailer. Just outside the miniature prison, Sergeant Fox signaled the brig steward, a Marine in his early twenties, to step into the short hallway that led to the promenade for a private conversation. The Sergeant kept his voice low, but it was just as commanding as it was on the field of battle. "I want you to watch him despite the fact that he's locked up. We want him delivered to Her Majesty whole and unharmed, per her orders. Any questions?"

"No, sir," the young Marine replied quietly.

As the two were talking, the prisoner leaned his head back and hunched his shoulders, pressing the top of his trapezius into the back of his skull. There was a subtle ratcheting sound, then a distinctive click, and Monsieur Punaise relaxed his shoulders. A pair of spidery metal legs inched their way out of the mass of hair on the back of his head, crawling slowly down his neck. At the success of this maneuver, Monsieur Punaise chuckled quietly.

A spacious room on the upper deck had been appropriated as a mess hall for the tired and hungry Marines. To a man, each had taken the time to clean up, but the assembly still had a weary look about them and conversation was subdued.

As Sparky and Erasmus entered, they noticed more visible bandages on heads and hands than they would have liked. They found an empty pair of seats facing each other at a shared table. Sparky started the conversation this time. "I haven't seen J. B. for a while. I thought he'd be up here with the men. I hope all's well."

"I am sure that he is just making sure that Monsieur Punaise is properly secured. He is the major prize, if you will, for the campaign. I have some more documents of his that I found. I want to share them with you after dinner. Quite enlightening."

Sparky made an understated nod to agree with the offer, but then followed it with an "I want to change the subject" pursing of her lips. She looked down at her hands for a moment to collect her thoughts. "Erasmus, I have something I want to talk to you about." She looked back up into his eyes. He looked at her gently, but didn't interrupt her. She proceeded, "I know that Her Majesty wanted me here, and I believe I've helped in a number of ways. But, …" She broke off for a pause, took a truncated breath, and sat up a bit straighter. "… I don't want to become a full-time battle nurse for the Crown. It's not the life I want or need right now. And when this is over, I'm thinking of repositioning myself so I'm not consigned to this fate. The reason I'm telling you this is that it may affect … us. I hope you understand."

"I am glad to hear that. This is not the life for you. Nor me, really. Let us discuss this …" He broke off as a young Marine served them two plates with glazed chicken, broiled potatoes, and mixed vegetables. Erasmus resumed, "… let us discuss this after dinner. It is important. However, I am famished. And this smells wonderful." They both eagerly tucked into their meal.

The small, penny-sized clockwork slowly made its way down the back of Monsieur Punaise's shirt, eight claw-tipped legs grabbing and releasing the cloth in a plodding, syncopated manner. When it reached the base of his spine, he took the mechanism into his hands and blindly manipulated a few small buttons and releases on its body to form its legs into the outline of a skeleton key. It took a few tries to reshape it, but he was able to create a variation that fit into the lock on his manacles. He deftly turned it and quietly released his hands as the young guard returned.

They sat and looked at each other for a few minutes as Monsieur Punaise kept his hands behind himself, pretending to be restrained. He then coughed quietly. Took a deep breath, and coughed twice, spasmodically. "Zorry. Ah must 'ave breathed in zome smoke, yes? My lungs, zey burn. Quite dry."

The unemotional Marine sat, still watching the prisoner. He was quite aware of his assignment.

Monsieur Punaise coughed again. Still nothing from his stern-looking sentry. No offering of water, no concerned looks, no sympathy. Monsieur Punaise realized that he needed to take the ruse to the next level. Without a hint of wincing, Monsieur Punaise bit the inside of his cheek. He drew a few drops of blood and positioned them at the corner of his lips. He let the blood drip out of his lips in a single crimson dribble, rolled his eyes up into his head, fitfully coughed a last time, and slumped over in a masterful performance.

The young Marine jumped up and ran out of the brig, through the hallway, and onto the promenade. "Medic!" he yelled, desperate to make sure his charge was not at risk. As soon as he was outside the room, Monsieur Punaise jumped up, makeshift key in hand, and started working on the jail door lock. A few quick tries and the lock clicked open. Monsieur Punaise didn't hesitate a wink. He cast his manacles aside, flung the door open, and sprinted out through the hallway in a strange, gangly loping that looked awkward but propelled him just the same. He threw a bony shoulder into the Marine and darted down the promenade looking for any way to escape. He instinctively headed aft for no other reason than the walkway in front of him appeared to be unoccupied. Over the railing to his right, he could see the open expanse of sky and feel the cool breeze, although he had no idea how high the airship was.

The downed Marine blew his warning whistle as loud as he could, following it with a hearty yell, "Escape! Escape!"

The entirety of the mess hall rose to their feet at the sound of the distant distress signal. All of the Marines ran to the closest exit to get to the deck below.

Sergeant Fox had been in the infirmary conferring with one of the doctors when the whistled alarm grabbed his attention. He turned without apology or explanation and sprinted to the promenade, his sidearm drawn and ready.

The opportunity Monsieur Punaise had hoped for presented itself. Near one of the storage room doors lay a stack of aerial wing backpacks, awaiting cleaning, folding, and storage. He jumped at one and threw it on his back while grabbing at any of the controls. One side snapped into place, but the other was bound up. It didn't matter; he figured he would work it out, even in the air, if needed.

Taking a few steps back to get a good running start, he looked out at the darkened blue of the evening sky.

"Stop!" J. B. bellowed as he slowed his run. The drawn and leveled revolver made the escapee hesitate again. "It's over a thousand feet to the ground below." Monsieur Punaise responded by pulling the now-untangled cord and popping the final wing into place.

Three other Marines with rifles ran onto the scene. J. B. continued; his voice was clear and unwavering, hoping to calm the inventor. "I will give you a choice, Monsieur Punaise. One of four things is going to happen. You will attempt a launch overboard, making the same mistakes every Royal Aerial Marine makes when they first try using the gliding wings, and fall to your death. Or you could miraculously sidestep six weeks of grueling and painful training and actually glide for a while up here in these winds, in which case we will follow you with HMA Britannia and shoot at you like a pigeon. As an aside, this option is more sporting for us than for you. Or you could hesitantly stand there thinking about what to do next, as you are doing now, and my Marines, who are excellent marksmen, will shoot at your knees until even the thought of leaping is no longer possible. Or you could surrender directly and soberly, allowing us to confine you in a civil manner. What say you of your fate?"

Monsieur Punaise's eyes darted between J. B. and the edge of the railing. By now most of the Marines, Sparky, and Erasmus had all arrived on the scene. Monsieur Punaise's eyes narrowed to slits. "I do not wan' to be 'ung az a *terroriste*." He made an instinctual quick pout and a shrug, a Frenchman's way of signaling that his decision was clear, but not to his liking.

Without needing an order, a dozen or so Marines took a knee and leveled their rifles at Monsieur Punaise's legs. The Sergeant provided his final justification, "The Royal Aerial Marines have gone through great pains to ensure that you are brought to London intact. Consider Her Majesty's reasons for requesting that. Bluntly, I don't think she is just planning to hang a healthy man."

The unarmed man resigned himself to his fate. Letting go of the control cords, he put his hands up in defeat. "Oui, oui. I weel return to zee 'olding cell." He slipped his shoulders out of the backpack.

As they returned to dinner, Sparky and Erasmus could hear J. B. ordering a doubling of the guard on the prisoner. Erasmus slipped his arm around Sparky's waist. She looked up and smiled at him. He responded, "We could use a few days of quiet, do you not think?"

L'ÉPROUVEUSE

BY DR. KATHERINE L. MORSE

Sparky watched Drake struggle with his utensils. "May I offer my assistance?"

"I am fine, thank you. After all the excitement of the day, it is helping me to eat more slowly."

Sparky took Erasmus' bandaged hand and turned it over, examining it critically. "Will you allow me to rewrap this after dinner?"

"Yes, if it will put your mind at ease." He soldiered through his meal before letting her lead him to the infirmary for the repair.

Sparky was taken aback by the sight of Fox sitting shirtless on an operating table in the surgery. Somehow, she had always imagined that some portion of the breadth of his shoulders was actually his uniform, but right in front of her was irrefutable evidence to the contrary. She was unsurprised to observe that his torso was decorated with several scars. She'd patched up enough soldiers and air crewman to recognize the results of the hazards of those professions. Fox's constellation was only remarkable from the perspective of the variety of the size, shape, and age of its constituents. And judging by the sloppiness of the hand of the alleged Marine surgeon at work on him, his newest acquisition would dwarf several of the earlier marks. It was probably the same hack who had given Drake the mummy wrapping on his left hand.

Sparky realized she was gawking. Just as propriety compelled her to look away, she glimpsed an incongruity. Hanging around his neck on a patinaed leather cord was a small object bearing a remarkable resemblance to a locket, albeit a dented one that showed as much wear as the supporting thong. She turned to face Erasmus, whose expression showed no indication that he had taken note of the keepsake.

The physician completed his ministrations, and Fox nodded in a perfunctory fashion to indicate that he should leave. Sparky fetched a fresh roll of linen while the physician took his leave, and Fox donned his shirt.

"Despite the casualties, I think the mission was a success," the Sergeant offered.

Having dealt directly with the casualties, McTrowell had a different opinion. "And what mission was that, may I ask?"

"The mission to ... stop Punaise."

"If the mission were truly to 'stop' Punaise as you say, burning down the barn with him and his production plant in it would have been considerably faster and almost assuredly could have been accomplished with no casualties at all. A thorough tactical engagement with the flame cannons would have sufficed. With all due respect, Sergeant Fox, I don't think you've been entirely honest with us. Why are we hauling a pile of mechanical parts, two dead Marines, and a charred French diplomat?!" There was an instant of stunned silence while Drake and Fox recovered from the ferocity of McTrowell's diatribe.

"Dr. McTrowell, Chief Inspector, I owe you an apology. You're correct that our mission wasn't simply to stop Punaise. Unfortunately, I'm not authorized to disclose more at this time. All your questions will be answered on our return to London."

Sparky was not mollified and continued to scowl at Fox. She yanked the loose wrapping off Drake's hand, causing him to wince. The uncomfortable silence in the room stretched out, punctuated only by the snipping of the surgical scissors as Sparky cut a fresh length of linen and the subsequent clank as she dropped the cutting instrument onto the metal table. Erasmus sucked in his breath as she began cinching up the new bandage a pinch too tightly. Feeling the need to rescue the situation, not to mention his hand, he cleared his throat at a theatrical volume. "Dr. McTrowell and I have an important piece of intelligence."

"Yes?" Fox replied promptly, thankful for the interruption.

Drake nodded at McTrowell, calculating that engaging her directly in the conversation would cool her temper. She shot him an "I know what you're up to" look, but took the bait anyway. "Drake found a shipping specification in the cottage for a cargo ship of the Russian & Trans-Siberian Air Fleet. It explains the lack of a shipping address on the crate Mrs. Wallace discovered. The shipment didn't need an address because Wallace only needed to move it across the airship port to the offices of Russian & Trans-Siberian."

Drake continued, "Wallace must have a contact in the office who attaches a new bill of lading for the final destination. This intermediary probably also pays him."

Sparky interrupted, "If Reginald Wallace hadn't been afflicted with gout, and his wife hadn't intercepted that bill of lading, there would have been no trace of his crime."

Drake picked up the thread again, "If one of us were to pose as an air stevedore," here he looked significantly at Fox, "and deliver the crate to Russian & Trans-Siberian, perhaps with the assistance of a Russian-speaking employee of Western & Transatlantic posing as Wallace's agent," here he shifted his significant look to Sparky, "we could apprehend the buyer's agent."

Sparky interjected, "Why wouldn't you just arrest the buyer?"

"In a clandestine enterprise such as this one, it is far too dangerous for the buyer and seller to have direct contact. There is too much risk that they will be seen together, raising questions. The buyer is almost certainly in St. Petersburg. I think we will also find that Mr. Wallace paid an air stevedore to keep silent about moving the first shipment across the airship port. We should also be on the lookout for such an individual who has been uncharacteristically profligate or drunken of late."

Fox seemed simultaneously highly interested in this information and extremely anxious to take his leave. "Thank you for this valuable information. I'll make arrangements to set this plan in motion as soon as we land." And he was gone.

Erasmus flexed his fingers, checking the bandage's tightness. His ploy of getting Sparky talking had succeeded; he still had his circulation. He gazed woefully at the neat formation of depleted crystal decanters. "Do you suppose Her Majesty has some hidden port stores?"

Sparky smiled fondly at him and chuckled, "I believe some reconnaissance is in order."

They didn't have to trouble themselves with extensive searching. Apparently Corporal Bennett knew his battlefield anesthesia because he had eschewed the port for stronger, less sweet liquors. Sparky handled the uncorking, sparing Erasmus' injured hand the stress while he held the glasses. After she recorked the bottle, he held both glasses close to himself. "I believe you owe me a story."

"I do?"

"I am familiar with the name Rumyantsev, especially the family's significance in Russian military and political history. I do not find it a particularly shocking name for a Russian airship." He waited, hoping she would take his meaning. She didn't. "And yet you do." She squirmed. He extended his right hand with the glass of port in it. "Would you care to explain?" He smiled in a manner he hoped was charming and endearing, the curled tips of his moustache contributing to the effect.

"Oh, very well." She plopped down into a comfortable chair, taking care not to splash any of the precious, ruby libation. Drake settled into the matching seat across from her. "As is, unfortunately, so often the case, history records the exploits of the men. And while they're all very important, they aren't always the most interesting stories. Unlike the Pecos Incident, I have no proof that the following story is true. It's only a matter of family legend, but with enough facts to be plausible."

"As are all fictions." He raised his glass to her.

She returned the salute. "Indeed. Countess Praskovya Aleksandrovna Bruce, a Rumyantsev by birth, was less well known than her male relatives but, in my opinion, was just as important to the smooth functioning of the Russian empire. She was a lady-in-waiting and confidant of Empress Catherine the Great. She was l'éprouveuse to Catherine, the tester of lovers. When a fine young man caught the eye of the Empress and Autocrat of All the Russias, it was Praskovya Aleksandrovna's job to test whether the potential paramour's 'skills' were up to Catherine's standards."

Erasmus, while fascinated by the tale, shifted uncomfortably in his seat. "I have heard stories about the Empress' tastes."

Sparky responded peevishly, "Mostly lies perpetrated by men who are afraid of women with healthy appetites. The truth is, she died of a stroke. And, allow me to point out, she sent her former lovers on their way with money and titles to live happily ever after rather than rewarding their loyalty with imprisonment and decapitation as was apparently the custom in your country." She took a sip of her port and exhaled through her nose loudly in annoyance.

Erasmus considered the wisdom of raising Sparky's ire multiple times in one day. He felt it best to return the conversation to safer ground. "You make an excellent point. Please continue with your story." He made a promise to himself not to run the risk of interrupting again.

"The countess overstepped her assigned duties by having an affair with one of Catherine's lovers, Ivan Rimskii-Korsakov. Countess Bruce and Rimskii-Korsakov were ejected from the court for their transgression and lived in Moscow for a short period of time before she returned to her husband. Everything I've told you to this point is a matter of historical fact. Family legend begins with an illegitimate daughter born to the lovers while they were in exile. Neither lover could risk being publicly ostracized for the child's existence, so she was given to a widowed Welsh merchant who raised her as his own daughter. Once grown, she married another Welshman, named Llewellyn, and gave birth to my mother, Elizabeth. My mother was told this fanciful story of her origins when she was a child, although she never entirely believed it. Nonetheless, she named her own daughter Czarina as a sly reference to the Russian empress whose disfavor supposedly set the course for her life. She told me the same story when I was a child. I think she meant to teach me that I was special and that my father's absence wasn't a reflection on me." She took another sip of her port, sighing a little wistfully this time. She stared into her glass, fighting back the urge to cry at the remembered pain. She straightened up. "I learned Russian so I could address a member of my great grandmother's family should I ever meet one."

"Your mother was right."

"You have some proof that my mother and I are descended from the countess?"

"Sadly, no. But I have ample proof that you are special." He stood slightly, leaned across, and kissed her on the cheek.

No sooner had HMA Britannia bumped to a halt in the camouflaged park alongside Buckingham Palace than a Royal Aerial Marine in night kit dropped the crew gangplank and sprinted, invisible, into the night.

The richly attired young man did not deign to address Littleton as he entered the offices of Western & Transatlantic Airship Lines just after opening time. Remembering the uncivil reception he had experienced on his previous visit to the offices, the visitor turned directly to the door of the president's office and rapped twice lightly.

"Enter, please." Annabelle Wallace had aged visibly in the last week, and the return of this particular visitor did nothing to relax the growing creases in her visage. "What can I do for you today, sir?"

"Chief Inspector Drake and Dr. McTrowell will present themselves shortly in the company of another gentleman. They will require some supplies, including a bill of lading, a crate of the size of the one that was seized, a cart, and 350 pounds of scrap metal."

"That is a rather tall order."

"Her Majesty greatly appreciates your cooperation in this matter."

PLAYED

By David L. Drake

Erasmus woke with a start. He looked quickly around his flat over Ye Olde Cheshire Cheese, feeling that the previous day had been long ago and other-worldly. It was hard to believe he was back in the safety of his one-room home. He instinctively felt the bandages on his chest and hand and looked at the inverted marionette lying in the corner of the room. Yes, it had all happened. He anxiously grabbed his pocket watch to check the time.

He knew he needed to get over to the London Airship Port as quickly as he could to aid in the ongoing mission. But first, he really needed to freshen up and dress himself with a proper set of businesslike clothes. He knew Sparky was performing the same drill at Dr. Pogue's. He wondered if it was too competitive for him to want to get there first, as ungentlemanly a thought as that was. "Perhaps I should have placed a friendly wager with the good doctor," he mused out loud. "On the other hand, we have already raced cabriolets though London. Maybe it is too soon to repeat that legal transgression."

After a wash, a shave, and the selection of primarily black attire, Erasmus trotted out of the door and down the stairs, cane and black bowler in hand. He quickly hailed a hansom, plopped his bowler on his head, and adjusted his revolver and shackles as he slipped into the hansom's seat. "airship port, on the double!" he called out. With a crack of the driver's whip, they were off down Fleet Street.

Mrs. Bingham wiped her hands on her apron and turned to the kitchen table, where a sleepy Dr. Pogue and a tired Dr. Young sat nibbling at their aromatic breakfast, a dish recently introduced to London from India called kedgeree. Edmond had requested the special meal for Yin's return. It was a bit of a stretch for Mrs. Bingham's culinary capabilities. The mixture of flaked smoked fish, rice, hard-boiled eggs, curry powder, and cream was not her usual hearty English fare of eggs, sausage, tomatoes, and rustic bread. She was fairly happy with how it had turned out, but the proof would be if it were completely consumed. She took a few seconds to watch over the two to see if that were the case, but their lethargy was getting in the way of their eating.

Edmond, ignoring his cook's presence, said to Yin, "I was worried about you." Their gazes locked.

Mrs. Bingham was no fool. "Well, I hope you like your fancy meal, doctors. I'm going to go clean … somewhere else. Let me know what you thought of it … sometime later." She untied and dropped her apron on the counter and scurried off.

Mrs. Wallace's office was getting crowded. The young gentleman had been there all morning. Members of Her Majesty's Eyes and Ears, Mr. Cooke and Captain Vaughan, had also arrived, followed by Sergeant Fox. Annabelle tried to maintain her best professional composure while her world was possibly falling apart. She tried to comprehend what would happen to her husband's business if things went as badly as she thought they might. She had tried to do the right thing by approaching Chief Inspector Drake three days before with the letter her husband had written. What in the world could have happened to warrant this tremendous, sudden interruption at the Western & Transatlantic Airship Lines' front office?

A soft rap on the door was followed by the entry of the clerk from warehouse number seven. Despite his managerial role at the warehouse, he was clearly uncomfortable talking in front of an audience and looked a bit sheepish as he delivered the news of his progress.

"Ma'am. We've completed your request. A crate has been assembled with 350 pounds of scrap airship parts. Most of them are castoffs, so they're not of great value. A bill of lading has been made, as requested. All of this is waiting in warehouse number seven."

Annabelle looked seriously at the young man in charge. "How do you wish to proceed?" Her voice wavered only a little bit. She was sure that no one noticed.

"I want this to be a civil matter rather than a military one. I'll let Chief Inspector Drake direct this part of the operation when he arrives." The young man smoothly tugged on a gold watch chain, and an exquisite gold pocket watch popped from the pocket of his gray-blue waistcoat and into his hand, the impact pressing the cover release. He peered down only for an instant at the timepiece. "He should be arriving immediately." Snap. The watch was back in place as quickly as it had appeared.

The driver of Erasmus' hansom had urged his steed to break into a gallop for the final few yards to the wide walkway entrance that led to the London Airship Port. As usual, there were a number of conveyances lining the street, either dropping off passengers or picking them up. It had turned into one of the busiest London streets since the airship port had opened. A space at the curb had opened up, and Erasmus' driver set his sights on it.

As the hansom charged forward, a shiny black cabriolet cut them off and slid effortlessly into the spot, forcing the hansom to pull up short. Erasmus had to grab the railing on the dashboard to keep from landing on the horse's rump. He stood, adjusted his cockeyed bowler, and spotted Dr. McTrowell's familiar pilot's headgear on the passenger exiting the obstructing vehicle. Erasmus squinted and tried his best to swallow his annoyance. "Dr. McTrowell, I presume," He called out enthusiastically.

She turned around and grinned at him. With a point of a finger of her still gloved hand, she called back, "I beat you here!" She added a sly wink.

He graciously bowed, showing his acceptance of her triumph in their previously unstated competition. He hopped down, paid his driver, and joined her on the walkway.

"I am here in an official capacity, so I will not be offering my arm, my dear Sparky."

"That's quite all right. I'm looking forward to finishing this 'mission,' as Sergeant Fox refers to it."

After winding their way there, Erasmus knocked on the office door. One of the Aerial Marines inside opened it. Erasmus allowed Sparky to enter first, and then he stepped inside. He first noticed that Sparky was frozen, unsure what to do. Erasmus quickly looked around the crowded room. "What are you doing here?" he asked the well-dressed young man.

After a momentary pause, the young man replied, "Everyone except Chief Inspector Drake and Dr. McTrowell, please leave us. We'll regroup in a few minutes."

Mrs. Wallace flashed a look of surprise at being ordered out of the office since she was treating it as her own. But she just as quickly acquiesced. With a bit of maneuvering, the office's inhabitants executed the order. The three remaining turned to each other when the door clicked shut.

Erasmus couldn't help exclaiming, "Lord Ashleigh, how did you get invited to this? Do you know who is in charge?"

Lord Ashleigh flashed his usual upbeat smile. "Of course! I am."

Sparky made her scrunched up "I don't understand" face.

"Not to question your capabilities, but how could that be? You are leading these military men and their agents?"

"Here's the short version of the story." He took a deep breath. His eyes flashed as he animatedly continued, "Her Majesty and my mother negotiated a mutually advantageous arrangement. For our safe harbor, we promised my support of Her Majesty's Eyes and Ears. Like most, I started as a supporting agent, concentrating on infiltration. Unlike most agents, I displayed the ability to blend in, even when I stood out. I earned my stripes on a couple of high-profile intelligence gathering missions and was promoted to oversee the organizational side of things. A few months ago, I was asked to bring in new recruits and dismiss those who were holding back progress. I started by bringing in Sergeant Fox and Dr. Young. As for cleaning house, I completed that task yesterday."

Erasmus was astonished, but was taking it all in. "So, it was you who 'selected' me?"

"Oh, yes. And others like Sparky."

"I was recruited?!?" she exclaimed.

Lord Ashleigh grinned compassionately, and she calmed down a tad. He proceeded, "I received word from Her Majesty that a Dr. McTrowell was arriving, and I should evaluate her for a position. She indicated you might be willing to discuss terms, as it were. Apparently, your reputation preceded you."

"Was that why you were at the Inventor's Symposium? You were evaluating me?!"

"Yes, my dear. Her Majesty knew of you somehow."

"How did you know I was going there? I didn't even notify University College."

A wry smile crept across Lord Ashleigh's face. "I cannot reveal my sources or techniques. That would take all of the sport out of it." He paused as if remembering back to previous conversations before adding, "I guess you can now appreciate what I meant in our first few discussions about my 'resources' and how they were assisting me."

Sparky nodded her understanding. Her mind drifted to her private interaction with the British Monarch at the recent convocation of the Order of the Thistle. She felt like she had been boxed in. Played. But she also remembered her promise to herself to represent her family, no matter what it took. Her final nod was to herself. This monarch also plays to win. She recognized and respected that.

Erasmus had also put some pieces of the puzzle together. "So you arranged for me to ride on the Burke & Hare. You had me take that trip as a test of my abilities, while you had us believe that you were just another passenger. Huh. Did you also set up my meeting Sparky?"

"No! That was your own doing. Although I can see my influence with the gift of the scarf appearing as a calculated ploy, but it wasn't. I just thought you'd make a wonderful couple and thought I'd lend a hand. As a friend."

Erasmus peered at Lord Ashleigh for a second. Was that the truth?

Lord Ashleigh felt his searing gaze. "I swear it." He extended his hand for shaking to the Chief Inspector. Erasmus acquiesced and took his hand and shook it heartily.

Lord Ashleigh then turned to Sparky. "To you I apologize for the required deception." He took up her hand and kissed it repentantly. She softened her shoulders and shrugged. And then to everyone's surprise, she quickly hugged Lord Ashleigh in a way that said, "I understand."

Without losing a beat, Lord Ashleigh proclaimed, "Let's go finish this operation!" The three invited the rest of the team back into the office to iron out the details of their plan.

The rest of the operation went like clockwork. Sparky borrowed a cap and coat from the clerk in warehouse number seven. In his workman's disguise, Sergeant Fox looked entirely the part of an air stevedore. Erasmus carefully shadowed the two as they delivered the counterfeit crate to the Russian & Trans-Siberian Air Fleet shipping department. Sparky approached the shipping clerk and asked, in her best Russian, to verify that she hadn't made a mistake in the bill of lading since it didn't have a recipient. Although he looked skeptical at the arrival of the crate without Reginald Wallace accompanying it, he took her grasp of the mother tongue as proof that Mr. Wallace had personally selected her. The clerk directed her to the shipping manager, Maxim Petrovich Medvedev, who assured her that the crate was going to him and him alone.

As a prearranged signal, Sparky gave Erasmus a thumbs up behind her back, and he swooped in to arrest Mr. Medvedev. Erasmus handed him over to a local constable, ordering him to escort the prisoner back to the Yard, question him, and attempt to get details on the intended recipient in St. Petersburg.

Meanwhile, Lord Ashleigh revisited Mrs. Wallace in her office. She fidgeted uncomfortably in her chair, trying to hide her concern. Jonathan sat down in her guest chair, every move showing his seriousness about the upcoming conversation.

"You've got the man you were after. Is there anything else I can help you with?" She had asked the question, but was hoping that her business with Her Majesty's Eyes and Ears had come to a close.

"There is the small matter of your husband, whom we need to apprehend."

"And you are hoping that I will help you?"

"I'm an agent of Her Majesty. In that role, I do what's best for the Crown and Empire. I realize that, if Reginald Wallace is apprehended, tried, and found guilty, Western & Transatlantic Airship Lines is a company in limbo. Current law doesn't allow it to be operated, much less owned, by a woman. But if operations were halted, even for more than a few days, it would greatly reduce the influx of visitors, cargo, and related commerce into London. That isn't good for, well, anyone. But we do need to deal with your husband's actions. So, let us see if we can negotiate a mutually agreeable resolution."

Mrs. Wallace nodded reluctantly.

The conversation continued for a few minutes, quietly, behind her closed office door. Sparky, J. B., Mr. Cooke, and Captain Vaughan waited patiently without. The Chief Inspector rushed to rejoin the waiting team. J. B. made a quick thumb point indicating Jonathan was still in the office.

Suddenly the door swung open.

Sergeant Fox asked, "Do we know where he is?"

Lord Ashleigh responded powerfully, "Yes, we do! Everyone, follow me!"

WHERE'S WALLACE?

BY DR. KATHERINE L. MORSE

"Euston Station, please, Virat." Lord Ashleigh, Drake, McTrowell, and Fox clambered into the coach. It had seemed much more commodious to Sparky when she had first ridden in it from Bloomsbury to Berkeley Square. She was grateful that Ashleigh had left Mr. Cooke and Captain Vaughan behind to oversee matters at the

Western & Transatlantic offices. She feared that their inclusion in the next phase of their mission would have resulted in someone having to sit on the floor of the coach or ride on top as baggage.

"Lord Ashleigh, you have yet to tell us where we are going," Drake reminded him.

"Aylesbury, where the Wallaces have a country home. I suspected that might be his first destination, but I wanted to confirm my surmise to avoid wasting time dashing off in the wrong direction."

Sparky interjected, "Given the circumstances, we could have commandeered an airship and gotten there in less than the two hours this will take, assuming the train schedule is even favorable."

"True, but I wish to have the element of surprise on our side. An airship landing in the rose garden lacks stealth." Sparky didn't reply, but she scowled at the implication that she lacked the aerial skills to land on something as large as the back lawn of an English country manor.

Drake, having learned to read McTrowell's expressions, felt it prudent to move the conversation along. "Lord Ashleigh, I believe the three of us are entirely up to the task of capturing Wallace, particularly considering his current state of medical incapacitation. If you will give us directions to his house, we can apprehend him and return him to London."

"Of this I am quite sure. However, Her Majesty is in need of more than just Mr. Wallace. We cannot be certain whether Mr. Medvedev knows the name of Mr. Wallace's Russian co-conspirator. We can be certain that he'll want something in exchange for that information if he has it. Her Majesty is not in the mood to grant such a boon. Nor is she inclined to negotiate with the traitor, Wallace. Her Majesty will dictate her own terms."

Sparky swallowed hard. Although treason was no longer a capital offense, Wallace would be attainted; all his property would be forfeit to the Crown. That would certainly complicate her personal employment situation. She snapped out of her reverie when she realized Lord Ashleigh was still talking.

"As Reginald and I are engaged in a cooperative business endeavor, and he has no reason to believe that I was involved in the discovery and seizure of the Dragon's Teeth. I can present myself at his home on the pretense of discussing business. I may trick him into revealing the specifics of this other venture on the grounds that I might wish to invest in it as well. Failing that, the good Chief Inspector may arrest him and cart him off to the Tower." Sparky didn't like the sound of that either.

The mismatched attire of their party drew several stares as they stood on the platform for half an hour at Euston, waiting for the next train. They avoided conversation as they were already the subject of unwanted attention and didn't want to reveal their plans. That would have to wait until they were seated in a private cabin on the train. *"Preferably with some tea and a light snack,"* Sparky thought to herself. She had to admit that one of the perquisites of this "employment" was the excellent accommodations.

Once they'd settled into their compartment, Lord Ashleigh withdrew a folded sheet of paper from the inside pocket of his velvet frock coat that proved to be a sketch of the Wallaces' country estate, no doubt provided by Mrs. Wallace. McTrowell listened quietly as her three companions laid out the details of the plan, including locations for their concealment, timing, and signals. She was absorbed in the dreadful realization that she was the only one of the company whose life would change as the result of today's actions. She decided not to raise her concerns until the plan was complete. "Lord Ashleigh, I don't see that I'm necessary to this operation. Perhaps I should remain in town when we reach Aylesbury."

"Dr. McTrowell, please recall your agreement with Her Majesty. As I said before, she will dictate her own terms." If Sparky had had any lingering doubts about whether Lord Ashleigh was the "agent" to whom Victoria had referred, they had been dispelled.

Drake was dumbstruck at the reference to an agreement between Sparky and Queen Victoria. He was sorely disappointed that Sparky hadn't confided in him that she had been consorting with his own monarch to the extent that they had reached an "agreement." He was of half a mind to pop over to the City of Washington and have a chat with Millard Fillmore.

McTrowell took a moment to collect her thoughts. "What will happen to Western & Transatlantic Airship Lines if Wallace is convicted of treason?"

"If he were tried and convicted of treason, Her Majesty could seize the Airship Lines and dispose of it as she sees fit." Sparky felt like the roof of the train might collapse on her head. "However, such a course of action is not in Her Majesty's best interests. The publicity of such an affair, particularly as it involves a Russian party or parties, might undermine the British position with respect to the 'Eastern Question.'"

"If she's not going to try him for treason, why are we going to arrest him if he reveals his co-conspirator?"

"Her Majesty has an interesting strategy. Western & Transatlantic Airship Lines will henceforth be administered by Mrs. Annabelle Wallace. Members of Her Majesty's Eyes and Ears will receive transportation to any destination in execution of their official duties, discreetly and free of charge. Reginald Wallace will be arrested for some minor infraction, smuggling or evasion of export tariffs. A little time in jail will serve to reinforce the inadvisability of protesting or revealing this arrangement."

Drake blurted out, "That is beastly clever."

"Yes, well I wish I could take credit for it, but Her Majesty has quite the head for intrigue and subtle manipulation."

"Amen to that!" Sparky thought to herself.

Lord Ashleigh hired a carriage at the station in Aylesbury, and they headed immediately out of town. Drake, McTrowell, and Fox disembarked just before they entered the lane so they could circle around the house and take up their assigned positions. Ashleigh paid the cabbie quadruple the fare with instructions to approach the house slowly, drop him at the entrance, drive back to the bottom of the lane, and wait there.

"I don't want to be involved in no dodgy business," the cabbie worried.

"This is not 'dodgy business.' It is Her Majesty's business, and she requires your cooperation and discretion."

"Right you are, guvnor."

Lord Ashleigh exited the carriage gracefully, then stood in the drive admiring the scenery and breathing deeply of the clean, country air. He hoped he was conveying the impression of a gentleman of leisure, without a pressing care in his head. As he approached the massive double doors, a liveried manservant smoothly opened the left one.

"Good day, sir."

"Good day to you. Is Mr. Reginald Wallace at home?"

"Who shall I say is calling, sir?"

Ashleigh produced an engraved calling card that he proffered to the butler. "Viscount Jonathan Lord Ashleigh. I've come to see Mr. Wallace on a business matter."

"Please come in, sir. I will see if Mr. Wallace is available." After Lord Ashleigh entered the foyer, and the butler closed the door behind him, the butler quickly closed the door to a large drawing room just to the right of the entrance but not before Jonathan noticed that the room was dominated by several partially-filled crates and in a state of disarray suggesting hasty packing. It was as he suspected. Wallace was preparing to flee with whatever items of value he could collect in a hurry. He listened to the receding footsteps of the butler. When he was sure the servant was far enough away that he couldn't return for a moment or two, Ashleigh dashed around, opening as many doors as he could reach quickly and stealing a peek inside. It was the same in other rooms. The furniture was still in the dining room, but the walls bore the telltale outlines of recently removed paintings. The china, silver, and crystal were all laid out on the massive walnut dining table that was ringed by more open crates. He hurried back to his position in the foyer and assumed an air of bored indifference when he heard the butler returning.

"This way, sir." The butler led him to Wallace's study. Wallace was slumped in a worn, leather wingback chair, with his foot elevated on the matching tuffet. The study was in a comparable state of disassembly to the rest of the house.

"Ashleigh, please pardon me for not getting up." He pointed at his swollen, shoeless foot. "Annabelle has us in the midst of an enormous renovation," he lied, waving dismissively at the packing materials and piles of books. "What brings you way out here?"

"I felt the need for some fresh air. I thought to take the opportunity to apprise you of the progress I've made in negotiations with my brother concerning the land in Talkad for our airship port. He's a shrewd and ruthless negotiator. He must have inherited that trait from his mother." He laughed deeply and loudly, although it sounded hollow to him. "I believe he has come to understand the value of this venture to you and me and is demanding additional concessions." He studied Wallace's face. Normally he would have expected Wallace to blow up, but he only appeared withdrawn and distracted. "He has invited the two of us to visit him in Talkad at our earliest possible convenience to discuss extending our routes to the continent, particularly to Eastern Europe, as he thinks that market is underserved." Wallace perked up a bit.

Jonathan continued, "Unfortunately, for delicate political and family reasons, I should avoid putting myself in my brother's custody. Nor do I have any business connections in Eastern Europe. As you have considerably more experience and business acumen than I, I was hoping you might have something to offer my brother and consent to negotiate with him. I believe he will be impressed by your considerable success, and we will achieve a better result under your leadership." He knew he was spreading on the flattery very thickly, but it had the desired effect; Wallace was now paying keen attention. "Do you know someone in a position to offer my brother an opportunity of this type?"

"I may."

"He's particularly interested in Eastern Europe, as I believe he wishes to establish additional connections farther east. My brother is the sort of man who will pay dearly for something he truly desires." Lord Ashleigh hoped he wasn't overplaying his hand.

"Dearly, you say?"

"Yes. In fact, in a recent letter, he sent along a drawing of a lavish residence he is planning to build near the airship port for the port manager." Now he was sure he had overdone it. He stood up nonchalantly and strolled toward the window.

"And who will this port manager be? Has he already accepted the job? Would your brother consider a foreign applicant, of course only if he were exceptionally qualified?"

Lord Ashleigh was thankful he had arisen to face the window because Wallace couldn't see the smile broadening on his face. "He was quite clear that he is still searching for just the right man. I think he used the words 'exceptionally qualified.'" He waited a moment for his words to sink in. "He would need some proof of these qualifications. Sadly, he does not trust his younger brother's judgment. Perhaps an actual demonstration of exceptional qualifications would convince him. A personal introduction to a like-minded businessman who can further his ambitions?"

Wallace took the bait. "I am already engaged in a business venture with the president of the Russian & Trans-Siberian Air Fleet, Prince Konstantin Medvedev."

There was another piece of the mystery solved. The shipping manager must be a family member. That would explain why he was entrusted with forwarding the crates. "A new airship route?"

"Perhaps." Wallace was returning to his previously evasive behavior.

Sensing that he wouldn't get any more information using subterfuge, the young viscount stretched his arm out in a large sweeping circle and brought his hand to his face, as if he were stroking his beard in an extremely exaggerated gesture. "I'm sure my brother will be quite interested." Now he was just stalling.

He heard two pairs of feet approaching rapidly down the hall. Chief Inspector Drake strode purposefully into the room, brandishing a pair of restraints. "Mr. Reginald Wallace, by order of Her Majesty, Queen Victoria, you are under arrest for the crime of ..." He looked up at Ashleigh for guidance.

"Smuggling."

"Yes, smuggling."

Ashleigh continued, "Now Mr. Wallace, you will explain yourself. Unless you wish to be tried for treason, you will explain why you were selling machines of war to a Russian prince."

Having seen Drake enter the house, Fox had followed and entered the room just as Drake shackled Wallace.

"No one was supposed to get hurt," Wallace pleaded.

Fox exploded. "No one was supposed to get hurt?! I have two dead men! I ought to kill you with my bare hands."

Ashleigh placed a calming hand on the Royal Aerial Marine's shoulder. "Sergeant, as much as I share your sentiments, Her Majesty needs Mr. Wallace alive. What were you saying, Mr. Wallace?"

"Prince Medvedev would use the Dragon's Teeth to attack a few freight trains. I would sell more to Her Majesty's government. A bloodless ground war. Prince Medvedev and I would supply both sides."

Sparky strolled into the room, "If travelers thought it was unsafe to travel on the ground, they would travel more by air. Both Wallace and Medvedev would profit additionally."

"Brilliantly despicable," Ashleigh commented, but the look on his face reflected nothing but utter disgust. "Chief Inspector, take this man to the Tower."

KEEP QUIET AND PLAY THROUGH

BY DAVID L. DRAKE

The scene at the Wallace's country house would have been a bit comical if it hadn't been so seriously important. Once Reginald was in wrist irons, he had a great deal of difficulty walking. Out of shackles, he still moved slowly, complete with huffing and puffing and under-his-breath muttering about his aching foot. He kept his arms out to his sides like a drunken steeple-jack, and he performed a hop-step rather than placing any more than the slightest weight on his gout-ridden, sock-covered appendage. His butler offered a cane, which Sergeant Fox examined for weapons, poisons, or tricks of any sort. It didn't have any, but the Sergeant was still hesitant to give even a wooden stick to their prisoner, seeing as he could do some damage if he hit someone with it. It took a full ten minutes to even get Reginald to the front door.

J. B. lost his limited patience. Directed at no one in particular, he asked out loud, "May I just toss him over my shoulder? It would speed all of this up!" Reginald looked at him in horror at the possibility.

Sparky, showing more restraint, saw this as a medical problem, so she spoke up. "Mr. Wallace, how did get around before we showed up? We are here to arrest you, not torture you."

"My dear Dr. McTrowell, in the rush here, I left my crutches behind. I had a cabriolet take me everywhere when in the out-of-doors. Otherwise, this is as fast as I go."

J. B. disagreed. "Not anymore!" He deftly put a shoulder into Reginald's stomach and hefted the rich troublemaker up. Reginald grunted loudly while his legs dangled uselessly in front of J. B. "Let us hope that the coachman followed your instructions, Lord Ashleigh, to hide around the corner of the road, or Mr. Wallace here," and he slapped his butt for emphasis, "will have a long journey into town on his belly!"

As the Sergeant strode down the driveway, the other three laughed and followed. Behind them they could hear Reginald's bewildered manservant, hesitant to call to his master but unwilling to silently stand by while Reginald was literally hauled away.

The trip back to the train station in Aylesbury was crowded, even with the Chief Inspector joining the driver on the back of the coach. Given his treatment in his driveway, Reginald was more willing to try walking normally from the coach to the train. The train ride back was a quiet affair, with the four compatriots playing nursemaid to Reginald while he did his best not to draw attention to himself, despite his foot being propped up on the seat in front of him.

The steam locomotive hissed as it came to a gradual stop in Euston Station. Billows of water vapor puffed around the engine accompanied by a low-throated whoosh. The troupe and their prisoner were the first to step off the frontmost passenger car and were immediately greeted by a uniformed Royal Aerial Marine.

"Sergeant Fox," the young man started.

"Yes?"

"I am here to deliver this," and he presented an envelope to J. B., "and to offer my assistance in any way."

"No assistance is required at this time, Cadet."

Erasmus cleared his throat to get purchase in the conversation. "If I may suggest, perhaps the cadet can summon a constable to escort Mr. Wallace to the Tower. Given the hour, a strategic meeting over dinner might be in order."

J. B. nodded his agreement, adding a quiet, "quite right," and readdressed the Marine. "The Chief Inspector is correct. Fetch a reliable officer, return here, and the two of you can escort this man to the Tower of London. They will be expecting him. You'll need a conveyance." J. B. pointed to the large gray wool sock covering Mr. Wallace's foot. "He's lame, but don't assume he won't try to escape."

"Yes, sir."

Next to a back table in Ye Olde Cheshire Cheese, Erasmus held a chair out for Sparky as she sat; J.B. and Lord Ashleigh stood, as gentleman do, waiting for the lady of the group to be seated comfortably. The eatery's ambient noise was a good cover for their planned conversation.

Once seated, Erasmus set the tone. "J. B., Sparky has the interest and the ability to aid us, but has felt disregarded in the details of our mission." Sparky looked at J. B. both to express agreement with Erasmus' statement and for an explanation.

Lord Ashleigh intervened. "That was my doing, and for that I am truly regretful. To be honest, Dr. McTrowell, you were still being evaluated for suitability to assist Her Majesty's Eyes and Ears, even on this mission. I had taken the tactic of ordering my team to provide you as little information as possible but still have you involved, as ordered by Her Majesty."

J. B. interjected, "On that point, I'd like to read you the letter I received. Well, the important part, buried between the pleasantries. '... The quick and satisfactory capture of Monsieur Punaise and the discovery of evidence at Western & Transatlantic Airship Lines pleases us. As for the latter, we expect Dr. McTrowell will play an important role in guiding Mrs. Annabelle Wallace in the sustained operation of the company, given its established role in the transportation of our subjects and goods within and without our Empire.' It is signed by His Royal Highness Prince Albert. Doctor, it seems you're on the minds of the royals, in a good way, I might add."

Sparky smiled at the good news, although Erasmus sensed a touch of skepticism. *"Good for her,"* he thought to himself, *"one must not let these things go to one's head."*

Sparky calmed her gentleman diners with, "Thank you for informing me about the true nature of the assignment and what's transpired. I'm sure I'll have many more questions later."

One of the tap boys in a green waistcoat delivered their food and drinks, which they consumed while quietly discussing the role of Her Majesty's Eyes and Ears, its members and their roles, and the import of their duty. By the time the tap boy clunked down their warm, sweet puddings, everyone around the table was smiling and nodding, looking forward to their next mission.

Sergeant Fox and Lord Ashleigh drained the last drops of port from their glasses, excused themselves, and took their leave. Sparky and Erasmus sat, looking at each other and enjoying the satisfaction of a completed task, full bellies, and an evening without plans. That lasted about thirty seconds until Erasmus realized he had better figure out what his next step would be.

"Sparky, the evening is rather young. Would you be willing to look at the automated housekeeper that I acquired? I want to see if I can get it restarted."

"I assume it is up in your flat? Can I … trust you?"

"Trust me. I am a Chief Inspector with Scotland Yard," he quipped with a wink and a tip of his simulated hat.

"Does that work on all of the London lasses?"

"It is my first time using that turn of phrase. What do you think? Effective?"

"Well, you're still single, so you be the judge."

Erasmus jokingly mimed that his heart was crushed while Sparky snickered at his silliness. He hopped to his feet and lent her his hand to aid her in standing. While she hung on to his fingers, he led her to his flat.

They unwrapped the delicate automaton, standing it on its foot box. A brass oval water tank was secreted inside the metal box. They refilled it with water and put Erasmus' best pieces of coal in the firebox below it. It took a while to get it started and the water up to pressure. By the time the small steam engine on the box turned over, they had bumped into each other a few times, and both rubbed their own tired backs from all of the bending over.

The housekeeper came to life, reaching about for dishes. Finding none, its arms drooped to its sides, and it turned off its own engine.

Erasmus scratched his head. "There must be a way to set which task it performs and to create new tasks." He looked around his apartment, knowing he would not find anything to help in this endeavor.

Sparky stretched her arms and twisted her back a bit, adding, "You don't have any tools here, do you? How about a worktable?"

"I have a few cleaning tools for my revolver; that is all. Downstairs, James may have a few carpentry tools, but he tends to hire handymen as he needs them. Do not look at me like that."

Sparky sighed. "This work would be a lot easier if we could move this to Dr. Pogue's, but then we'd have to move it back here to test it, because Mrs. Bingham wouldn't like this imperfect imitation of her. It would be a lot easier if we could do this in one place."

"What are you ... asking?"

"Oh, I've just been thinking lately that I need to find a more permanent place to stay in London."

Erasmus was both ecstatic and taken aback by where the conversation was leading, even though Sparky was being earnest, rather than flirty or acting entrapped by the recent events. He thought, *"So, this is one of those moments where I could open my mouth to clarify what we are discussing and get in hot water. Best to keep quiet and play through. If I only had a jelly baby to save me."* He chuckled to himself, and decided to change the subject. "What a day! I think we have gotten as far with this as we can. Can I get you a cab?"

Put a Ring on It

By Dr. Katherine L. Morse

Mrs. Bingham cleared her throat meaningfully. When she got no response, she resorted to shoving the plate of hot food through the small gap between Edmond and Yin. "Breakfast, dearies," she chirped loudly. Startled out of their affectionate gazing, they sat up straight at the kitchen table. Mrs. Bingham seized the opportunity to slide in the second plate, although she wondered to herself why she bothered. She was fairly certain that the pair would have been just as happy to eat from the same plate. She made a mental note to speak with Miss Esmeralda. Perhaps Dr. Pogue's more-worldly younger sister could instruct her brother in the proper way to proceed. Just staring at his colleague was not going to produce the desired outcome; Yin was not one of his experiments.

The housekeeper turned to face the approaching footsteps. "Good morning, Dr. McTrowell. It's so nice to have company for breakfast."

Sparky glanced at Pogue and Young, and then furrowed her brow quizzically at Mrs. Bingham's comment. What had the housekeeper meant by that? Had she overstayed her welcome? She opted to proceed as if everything were perfectly normal, "Good morning, Mrs. Bingham. Breakfast smells delicious, as usual."

"I'll set you up a plate."

The love-struck inventor finally noticed the presence of his houseguest. "Dr. McTrowell, what news?"

"Mr. Wallace has seen the error of his ways. Today I undertake to educate Mrs. Wallace on the operation of an airship business. I'm not certain what I thought I would be doing at this point in my life, but I'm sure it's not this. Her Majesty is certainly an impressively persuasive individual." Her last comment made Edmond visibly uncomfortable. Sparky wondered if she had insulted his sovereign. She had meant it as more of a grudging compliment. She was grateful for the interruption of Mrs. Bingham's delivery of her breakfast. She tucked in. She hadn't realized how much the exertion of the last few days had given her a ferocious appetite.

After a few bites, she tried to change the subject, "So what did I miss while I was in Aylesbury yesterday?" This question made Pogue so uncomfortable that he squirmed in his chair like a schoolboy caught with a frog in his desk. She was wracking her brains for a safer subject when Drake strolled into the kitchen. She smiled in silent plea. Surely, he would have something clever and engaging to say, thus rescuing her from her current discomfiture.

Mrs. Bingham rolled her eyes and shook her head. "Just happened to be in the neighborhood, did you Chief Inspector?" Before he could fabricate a convincing answer, she continued, "How would you like your eggs?"

"Scrambled, thank you. Mr. Bingham just admitted me on his way out. He asked me to inform you that he would fix the loose stair tread upon his return." Mrs. Bingham set another place at Sparky's left elbow. She knew there was no point expecting him to sit anywhere else.

"Drs. Pogue and Young, have you had an opportunity to inspect the Dragon's Teeth remnants?" Drake asked. Pogue's face lit up like a schoolboy who had just discovered tin soldiers under the Christmas tree. Sparky breathed a sigh of relief.

"Why yes, and what a delightful investigation this is going to be! The designs are brilliant!" He seemed to have completely overlooked the fact that the mechanisms were demonstrably effective killing machines, such was his scientific enthusiasm for the technology. "What will you do with them when your investigations are complete?" Pogue's schoolboy look returned, the first lovelorn one. Yin stared intently at the last scraps of her meal.

Mrs. Bingham deposited Drake's breakfast in front of him and wiped her hands briskly on her apron. "Oh, for heaven's sake! Do you lot really imagine that anything that happens in this house can be kept a secret? You might as well tell them." She fluttered her dishcloth in the direction of Drake and McTrowell.

"Sensible as always, Mrs. Bingham," Pogue replied with chagrin. "Yin brought me a message from the Queen yesterday. It was about this Eyes and Ears business. Her Majesty has 'offered' me the position of quartermaster. As you say, Dr. McTrowell, she is very persuasive. The work will be keenly interesting, but this will significantly curtail my publications."

"Well," continued Drake cheerfully, "at least we will all be in this together. 'All for one and one for all,' as Dumas wrote."

"Indeed," Sparky chimed in. She was just grateful to have discovered that she wasn't personally the source of the tension in the room.

The foursome finished their breakfast in between animated discussions about the designs of the Dragon's Teeth and potential, less-menacing applications of Monsieur Punaise's handiwork.

Sparky stood up, "I should get to the airship port. Delaying will not improve the task before me."

Drake popped out of his chair, "I shall accompany you there." He paused for a beat, thinking, *"I need to interview a few more witnesses."* Mrs. Bingham covered her mouth with the dishcloth to stifle a giggle.

"I'll fetch my kit and meet you in the foyer," Sparky replied.

Pogue stood up as well. "Dr. Young, I think we should begin the day's work." Yin nodded and rose to join the two men. The three of them were standing in the foyer waiting for Sparky when the door echoed with the sound of the knocker. Edmond opened the door to find Miss Sarah Slate standing on the landing.

"Good morning, Miss Slate. Please come in. What brings you here this morning?"

She stepped inside and proffered a fine quality, ivory, linen envelope with Dr. Pogue's name written on the front in calligraphy. "I came to deliver these." She waved a small stack still in her other hand. "I'm sorry, Chief Inspector Drake. If I had realized you would be here, I would have brought yours. I posted it to Scotland Yard."

"Thank you, Miss Slate. I shall be on the lookout for it."

Sparky entered the foyer, Gladstone bag and brown leather topper in hand. "Good morning, Miss Slate."

"Good morning, Dr. McTrowell." Sarah handed Sparky's invitation to her, who accepted it with a smile. "Is Miss Pogue at home?"

Pogue looked up from his intent deconstruction of the envelope. "She left early for the shop, something about working on a very important wedding dress, one 'fit for a queen.'" He winked at Sarah who smiled back.

"I had also hoped to discuss some business with her?"

"Business?" Sparky asked.

"Yes, Charles, Mr. Howgill, and I are printing her fabric designs."

Yin interjected, "You may tell them the rest."

Sarah stood frozen on the spot with uncertainty. Yin nodded at her. Sarah looked around before continuing, "We are printing the fabrics as I said. We are also producing other materials based on my own designs. The fabric business allows me to come to see Dr. Pogue and Dr. Young without raising suspicion."

"The silk armor!" Sparky blurted out. "It saved the lives of several of the Aerial Marines!"

"I'm pleased to hear it worked so well. Are we all employed by Lord Ashleigh? Oh no, was I not supposed to say that?"

Drake chuckled, "Yes, we are, so you are safe. But you should keep that between us in the future. Were you also responsible for the sails?"

"Yes. Lord Ashleigh gave me the original design, which I have improved. It may still require refinement."

Drake rubbed his abdomen, remembering his rude encounter with the edge of the well in Carlisle. "I may have some suggestions for you."

"I would be grateful."

"Dr. McTrowell and I must get to the airship port, but I will make some notes for a conversation in the near future. Good day, Miss Slate." He tipped his bowler to her and held the door for Sparky.

They spent the cab ride to the airship port discussing the automated housekeeper. They hatched fantastical plans to make it perform serialized tasks, wheel itself about, and 'discover' its own environs. Their ideas got wilder the longer they rode. They were fairly rolling with laughter by the time they reached the port. He gave her a hand down from the cab, but protested when she reached into her bag to pay the cabbie.

"Chief Inspector," she retorted, "I am a woman with her own means. If you insist on paying for everything, we'll only ever have half as much fun as we could."

He had to admit she was right. "I bow to the wisdom of your argument, my good doctor." He executed a flamboyant bow before capturing her right hand and kissing it. "I hope to see you later."

"I'll look forward to that." She returned his gesture with a mock curtsey and a quick peck on the cheek.

Unfortunately, a later meeting wasn't to happen that day. By the time he finished his interviews and made his way to the offices of Western & Transatlantic, Littleton informed him that McTrowell was out on the field educating Mrs. Wallace on the finer points of airship flight safety inspections.

Drake returned to Scotland Yard feeling a little low. He was intercepted on his way to his desk by Sergeant Parseval, as usual. "This was delivered with the morning post, sir." The envelope was identical to the ones Miss Slate had delivered to Pogue and Sparky that very morning with the exception that this one had his name on it. He extracted a razor sharp, sword-shaped letter opener from his desk drawer and expertly slit the top flap. The enclosed invitation was as elegant as the envelope led him to expect. He held it firmly in his hands, staring at the words. They didn't really penetrate his brains but just swam in front of his eyes. He ran his fingertips over the engraved lettering. It was supposed to be a joyous occasion, but his heart ached. He returned the invitation to the envelope and tucked it in the desk drawer along with the letter opener.

The rest of his day was thoroughly ordinary. He wrote notes, listened to reports on minor investigations, and handed out assignments to the sergeants and inspectors. It dragged on interminably. A couple of times he looked at his pocket watch and thought it had stopped.

Even the thought of an entire evening free to practice with the dressmaker's dummies didn't lighten his mood as he walked back toward Ye Olde Cheshire Cheese. Without a case occupying his mind, he spent most of the time observing the comings and goings of other pedestrians and gazing into the windows of the shops closing up for the night. When he was only a few blocks from home, a particular shop caught his eye. The sign read, "Attenborough Jewellers."

FEELS LIKE HOME

BY DAVID L. DRAKE

Erasmus sat at his office desk, pen in hand, looking at the calendar that he kept in the front of his personal journal. He made a tiny jab of his pen toward each date as he counted. Quietly he said to himself, "… five, six, seven, …," in tempo with each motion he made. "Today is Tuesday the 26th of August, so it is eight days until the Slate-Howgill wedding on the 3rd of September. Let me see, I will take my black jacket and top hat in for a cleaning on Thursday …"

Sergeant Tate Parseval's face appeared in Erasmus' door window and knocked lightly a couple of times. Erasmus waved him in.

"G' Morning, Chief Inspector. We're having an 'all hands on deck' assembly, and I was hoping that you would have the time to attend. Shouldn't be more than fifteen, maybe twenty, minutes."

"Of course, of course. Be glad to." Erasmus replaced his pen into its silver holder and rose to join the Sergeant.

The assembly room was a fairly large room for the men to gather for announcements or, as was the case for the Chartist demonstrations in April 1848, for mustering. Unlike businessmen and their love of chairs and tables, long-winded rants, and braggadocio-filled speeches that they lovingly called 'meetings,' this functional room has a single raised podium and a furniture-barren space for standing. About twenty people were in attendance, mostly Scotland Yard office workers joined by about eight constables, offering their time before starting their rounds. The congregation produced the usual din of small talk that filled the room as they waited for the real business to start. Just as the Sergeant and Chief Inspector entered, the discussion settled down, and Bartholomew Horner took the podium.

"Gentleman, I won't keep you long from your duties, but I do have a few announcements you will find of interest." The men gave their full attention to Bartholomew. "As you know, Chief Inspector Erasmus Drake has been on hiatus for a couple of months. As we indicated before, he's been requested by the Crown to aid in a number of activities outside of London. As such, we haven't had the opportunity to provide him with this," and Bartholomew hefted a wooden plaque onto the podium, "for his role in capturing the robber in the Countess Ada Lovelace jewelry heist. Thank you, Erasmus."

A polite round of applause broke out, and Erasmus made his way to the podium to receive his plaque. Bartholomew knew he wasn't one for speeches, so he handed Erasmus the plaque and gave him a sincere handshake. Erasmus made his way back to his spot in the gathering, garnering a few pats on his back on the way.

Bartholomew continued. "It has also come to my attention that the Chief Inspector may be called out for more of these external activities, so I have asked Sergeant Tate Parseval to run the daily roster and oversee the processing sheets. For that reason, I have decided to promote the Sergeant to Assistant Inspector." The men gave another round of polite applause. The Sergeant smiled broadly and nodded. Erasmus shook his hand. Erasmus was completely aware that Bartholomew was giving him the freedom to continue his support of Her Majesty's Eyes and Ears without affecting the Yard's effectiveness. He also knew there wasn't an official rank of Assistant Inspector, and that it was a temporary measure to keep the Sergeant motivated while he assumed more of the duties. Erasmus recalled a quote of Napoleon Bonaparte's, "A soldier will fight long and hard for a bit of colored ribbon," and realized that Bartholomew must have known the quote as well.

"And to finish, I also want to add that this epidemic of Green Fantasy abuse is on the decline. A bit short-lived, thank goodness. However, issues with laudanum misuse are still prevalent. Today, as with all days, be careful and sharp-eyed." There was clearly relief in the faces in the crowd over the news regarding Green Fantasy.

Since they had seen so little of Erasmus over the past few weeks, a few of the constables wanted to have a bit of a chitchat with him. The conversations were short and lighthearted. Everyone eventually filtered out of the assembly room, and Erasmus found himself walking back to his office with Tate.

"You know, Sergeant, or should I say Assistant Inspector, you have been doing my tasks as Chief Inspector longer than I have."

"I enjoy the work, actually. I take pleasure in doing the final paperwork, making sure all has been done correctly. Quite satisfying."

Erasmus couldn't help but think it was sensational that people like Tate existed since the idea of putting the finishing ink and paper touches on the deeds of the lads working in the streets seemed like pure drudgery to him. "I am so glad to hear that. I am afraid I need to leave again. Official business and all that. Grab the notices on my desk if you would like; they are yours to complete." With that, Erasmus entered his office, grabbed his cane, bowler, and cape coat, and headed out.

Just outside of the guard posts at the Tower of London, Drake met with Sergeant Fox. After a few pleasantries, including a mention of the upcoming Slate-Howgill wedding, they turned their attention to gaining entry to the fortress. The guards admitted them without incident. J. B. knew his way around the grounds well and led the way. He was able to skirt a number of construction sites and avoided the associated noise and dust. After a labyrinthine climb up one of the towers, they joined the Head Warden.

"Glad you could meet me, boys. I wanted to show you my handiwork." After handshakes and polite greetings, the Head Warden pointed through a stone window to a stone-walled room below. Erasmus and J. B. got up on their toes to look down on the site below.

It was a fully equipped laboratory for both chemical work as well as light manufacturing. Two men in lab coats were toiling inside. Erasmus recognized both of them, Monsieur Punaise and Professor Farnsworth. They both looked less manic. Professor Farnsworth looked better fed and in control of his faculties.

The Head Warden smiled at his work. "They are as happy as can be. Her Majesty herself has given them some tasks. I'm not sure what they are building, but for two prisoners, they are eager to rise and work long hours."

Erasmus asked, "But if you do not know what they are working on, who does?"

"Well, that's odd that you're asking that, Chief Inspector. Based on your reports, we hired a young man to oversee their progress. A Mr. Alistair Bennington Rutherford, son of the Baron Rutherford of Oxford. It appears to be a perfect fit."

"Oh," Erasmus said quietly, "just perfect."

Erasmus climbed the steps up to his flat. He had that feeling that he hadn't done enough that day but was still exhausted. The exuberant sound of Ye Olde Cheshire Cheese's clients was normally a stimulant, but it wasn't doing the trick that night.

He tried the door and found it unlocked. He knocked with a light "tap, tap," and walked in. Sparky was sitting in the middle of the floor next to the inverted marionette, spanners, screwdrivers, and other tools scattered about, and she was peering at the indentations in a metal disk. She took one look at Erasmus, unknowingly showing off the sizable grease stain she must have unintentionally gotten when she scratched her cheek. She gave a happy squeak, jumped up in place, and ran to him, planting a well-placed kiss on him. When she withdrew, her happy face changed to surprise. "Oh my, I must have grease on my face, because now you do, too. Welcome home. I want to tell you about everything that's happened!"

Erasmus was able to work a nod into the conversation as he hung up his cape coat and deposited his cane and bowler in their proper places.

Sparky continued without taking time for a breath, "I figured out how the disk sensors work! It's so simple! There's a circular track for each joint. As the disk rotates, the finger ticks into the indentations, triggering the joint. There's even a code for joints that have multiple motions." She held a disk right up to his face. "See how this track has three indentations in close succession here," she pointed to a cluster of dimples, "but only two here?" She pointed to another batch further along the track. "The simpler joints are encoded on the smaller, inner rings, and the more complex ones are on the outer rings. The innermost ring contains the instructions for moving to the correct location to perform the task. It's the trickiest because it depends on the geometry of the working space. This line," she indicated a faint scratch across the radius of the disk not deep enough to be detected by sensors, "is the start and end of the iteration. It's not unlike the repetition facility your Countess Lovelace described in her paper of 1843."

She continued excitedly, "I was also able to get a crude serializer working so the operation task disks will cycle through! That means we can leave her here working when we're gone, and it will cycle through each of her tasks. There's also a disk that represents a dormant state. That means she can wait for hours between tasks. She can also fetch her own fuel and water if you're willing to keep a pile of tinder in one of the corners. And I've gotten my dress for the wedding! I also made friends with Mr. Crocker downstairs. What a wonderful man. Dinner will be brought up at eight. I thought you might like to change and help me test the serializer."

Erasmus was overwhelmed by her enthusiasm and was ready to start what seemed like a new day. "That is wonderful, my dear. Would you rather go out for dinner? There are a number of places right across Fleet Street."

"Actually, I'd rather get her up and working. We can eat and tinker."

"You keep saying 'her.' Have you given it a name?"

"I've been thinking of Rosy. Is that acceptable?"

Erasmus pretended to think for a second, but knew that whatever she wanted to name the automated helper was fine with him. *"Finally,"* he thought, *"I have come to a place I know well, but this time it feels like home."*

E. LLEWELLYN

BY DR. KATHERINE L. MORSE

Erasmus couldn't help himself; he stared. "Sparky, you truly look like a czarina today. You will be the most beautiful woman in attendance."

The deep dusty rose of her satin dress brought out a warmth in her complexion. Although the low, wide neckline could have been inappropriately revealing for a wedding, the gauze bertha covering her collarbone restored the frock's modesty. The fabric of the wrap over her arm must have been woven by the same mill that produced the gauze for the bertha because both were printed with an identical pattern of pale, English roses. She was even carrying a matching pair of crocheted pink gloves. Erasmus smiled at the idea of her wearing those while piloting an airship.

Sparky returned his smile, "I certainly hope you're wrong on this occasion, Erasmus. It would be unforgivable to outshine a bride on her wedding day."

"Right you are. I only meant to say that the ensemble becomes you. Shall we go?" He held the door for her.

When she reached the curb, she was pleased to see that he had hired a proper carriage rather than a hansom. As much as she eschewed fancy dress, it would have been a shame to expose the lovely frock to the insult of London's open air.

Once they were underway, she commented, "I must confess that I resorted to the superior skills of Miss Pogue."

"She may not know her spying or science, but her expertise with fashion is unparalleled."

"She also has a gift for subterfuge. The design of the future Mrs. Howgill's wedding dress is a better-kept secret than Monsieur Punaise's presence in Carlisle. I'm trusting that she won't have subjected Sarah to the indignity of being festooned with so much lace and ruffles that she looks like an infant in a christening gown. I've never understood the attraction of decorating the bride as if she's been attacked by sugar-crazed bakers and confectioners."

"Dr. McTrowell, I detect that you have strong opinions on this subject," Drake winked at her. He held her hand as they rode to St. Paul's. He hoped she wouldn't notice the faint tremble in his. Facing down mad scientists with electrical discharge pistols was considerably less daunting than the mission he had set for himself today.

"I've never attended an event at St. Paul's Cathedral," she mentioned.

"Neither have I."

"I find that a little surprising. Haven't you lived in London a good deal of your life?"

"Yes, but St. Paul's is not just any parish church. It is the seat of the bishop of London. It is quite an honor to be married there."

"I hadn't realized that Mr. Howgill was such an important personage."

"I do not believe he is. I suspect that the arrangement was a wedding gift from a grateful sovereign."

"Ah." She smiled warmly at him and then turned her attention to the view up the Thames toward the center of the city as they crossed the London Bridge.

Once inside the cathedral, they were directed toward the bride's side of the church, where they were pleased to see that Edmond and Yin had already arrived. Drake consulted his pocket watch. "We still have a bit of waiting. Have you been here long?"

Pogue replied, "We rode into the city early this morning with Esmeralda. She's making last minute modifications to Miss Slate's gown, so we had a lovely stroll and tea. Delightful!" Sparky saw a brief smile cross Yin's face accompanied by a twinkle in her eye. "If you'll excuse me, my sister is not the only Pogue who has official duties today." He slipped out of the pew toward the side aisle and headed back toward the entrance.

The organ struck up a tune, and the guests obligingly settled down. Drake leaned over and whispered in McTrowell's ear, "John Stanley's Trumpet Voluntary." Charles Howgill entered from a side door and took his place in front of the altar accompanied by his best man. Although Sparky didn't recognize the other man, his likeness to the groom suggested a brother or first cousin. She was struck by Howgill's calm demeanor. Most grooms she had seen projected excitement and anxiety, as if they were both delighted and terrified by what was about to happen to them. More than anything, they always seemed utterly without a clue as to their future. Conversely, Charles Howgill bore an air of sanguine certainty, a man who knew exactly what he was about and embraced the opportunity.

The officiant entered from the other side of the altar. He was wearing a mitre. Sparky leaned over and whispered in Erasmus' ear, "Is that …?"

"Bishop Blomfield? Yes," he whispered back. They raised their eyebrows knowingly at one another: a very grateful sovereign indeed.

The organ struck up a lively march, signaling the congregation to rise. They did so, turning expectantly to look toward the nave, awaiting the arrival of the bride. Erasmus added helpfully, "The Prince of Denmark's March." When Sarah entered the light, a collective gasp arose from the guests.

The bodice of her dress shimmered iridescently between ivory, gold, and sky blue, all in perfect shades to highlight Sarah's fair skin, blue eyes, and dark hair. It reminded Sparky of the inside of an abalone shell. As she marveled at the fabric, she realized she was looking at another application of Sarah's visionary fabric design skills. The cloth must have been a cross between the stealth fabric that camouflaged HMA Britannia and the composite armor worn by the Royal Aerial Marines. The sleeves, skirt, and short train were silk satin jacquard, also undoubtedly woven at Howgill's mill for just this occasion. As Sarah and Edmond passed by the end of the pew where Sparky stood, she noticed that the pattern woven into the fabric was the interlocking daisies she had seen in Sarah's notebook.

The low, draped waist made Sarah appear taller and accentuated her trim figure. The wide stand collar trimmed with embroidered lace framed her face. There was just a hint of a bustle. Enough to be fashionable but not so much as to detract from Sarah's grace. The veil, trimmed with the same interlocking daisy lace as the collar, was affixed to her upswept coiffure by a pearl tiara. A wedding gift from Charles? Perhaps a loan from one of Esmeralda's well-to-do friends? It mattered not; it served to complete the elegant effect perfectly. And to those who knew Sarah best, the dress was a testament to the fruitful partnership she had already forged with the man who was about to become her husband.

Sparky thought she and Drake were probably the only ones in the church who noticed Dr. Pogue walking Sarah down the aisle. Well, perhaps Yin noticed. When they reached the altar and the march ended, the guests took their cue to be seated. In the attendant shuffling, Sparky commented to Erasmus, sotto voce, "Remind me to have Miss Pogue design my wedding dress." Drake's heart skipped a beat, and he had to grasp the edge of the pew in front of them to keep from falling over. Did she know? Could she really be that perceptive? He spent the entirety of the ceremony trying to calm his nerves while memorizing every detail he could of Charles Howgill's comportment.

When the organ struck up the cheerful recessional, Sparky leaned toward him, "And what is this piece?"

"Um, Handel's Hornpipe from Water Music."

"Why, Chief Inspector, I'm surprised by your extensive knowledge of wedding music." She winked at him. He felt the blood drain out of his face. He was grateful for Edmond's interjection as the newlyweds passed.

"Shall we share a carriage to the reception breakfast? Mr. Howgill has bought a new home for the new Mrs. Howgill in Camberwell. I believe my sister had a hand in that as well." He smiled broadly.

Erasmus took advantage of the chatting, scuffling, and footsteps of the congregation exiting to ask Sparky, "My dear Sparky, may I have a private word with you at the reception?"

She looked at him quizzically, wondering what could be the cause of his solemnity on such a happy occasion. "Of course." She took the arm he offered as they reached the aisle and gave it a squeeze as if to say, "Whatever it is, everything will be fine."

There were considerably fewer guests at the reception than had been at the wedding. It occurred to Sparky that many of the people missing had been business associates of Mr. Howgill's. The breakfast gathering appeared to be mostly family and close friends, or in Sarah's case, her close friends who had become her family in London. McTrowell spotted J.B. Fox for the first time.

"Good morning, Sergeant. I didn't see you at the ceremony."

"I was observing from the back."

She took a sip of her tea and laughed softly, "You make it sound as if you were standing watch." He didn't flinch. Well, she supposed she shouldn't have been surprised by that response. She looked around for Drake. He was standing in the foyer having an intense but low volume conversation with an older gentleman she didn't recognize. She inched closer as nonchalantly as possible.

"How did you find me here?"

"Your landlord told me, but it doesn't matter. I need your help urgently."

Drake spotted McTrowell close at hand. He tried to smile at her reassuringly but suspected his facial muscles had failed him. "Can this matter not wait just a bit? I have some urgent business of my own." He patted his coat, checking that the small box was still safely in place.

"No, it can't."

Sparky's face registered concern. She put down her teacup and began to approach purposefully.

"I am sorry, Edwin, but I really must attend to this other matter first. It has waited long enough." He closed the distance to Sparky and took her hand. "Dr. McTrowell, would you please join me in the garden?" Without waiting for her answer, he led her across the room and out the back of the house. He didn't notice his other companion follow them out and secret himself in a corner under the eaves.

Just as he had hoped, there was a small bench so common to English gardens. He guided her to the bench and made as if to sit next to her. Once she was seated, he pivoted around in front of her and bent down on one knee. As smoothly as he could manage with his shaking hands, her extracted the small box from inside his coat, opened it, and presented it to her.

"Dr. Czarina Llewellyn McTrowell, will you do me the great honor of becoming my wife?"

She stared at the ring inside the box, unsure what to do next. She was unclear on the correct protocol as she had never had the foresight to ask another woman how this important event should proceed. Was she supposed to take the ring first? Agree first and then take the ring? Perhaps she was supposed to accept, and then he would put the ring on her finger. Surely there was a splendid kiss forthcoming. Poor Erasmus looked like he was about to drop dead from anticipation, when she realized that she should just say yes and see what happened.

As she opened her mouth, she heard screams and shouts coming from the house. She and Drake jumped up simultaneously, looking toward the sound of the commotion just in time to see two enormous men with the dark complexion and broad, flat features of Pacific islanders dash through the same doors they had exited just moments before. The two intruders stopped, scanned the area rapidly, spied the observer hiding in the corner, and snatched him. He put up a struggle, but between his age and their size, he was no match.

Drake dropped the box into McTrowell's hands and ran to the aid of his adoptive father. Before he could reach Edwin Llewellyn, a pair of ropes with hand and foot loops dropped from the sky. The kidnappers grabbed ahold, taking their human cargo with them. Sparky turned her gaze skyward in time to spot a swiftly departing airship as she expected. Just before the ropes were pulled out of reach, Drake executed a flying leap, catching the end of one tether, and dropping his top hat to the ground.

Fox charged out of the house just in time to see Drake hauled out of view, narrowly clearing a gable of the house behind the Howgills'. Sparky shoved the ring on her left ring finger unceremoniously and pointed at the disappearing vessel, "We need to follow that airship!"

ABOUT THE AUTHORS

David L. Drake and Katherine L. Morse are the award-winning, San Diego-based authors of "The Adventures of Drake and McTrowell – Perils in a Postulated Past," a serialized steampunk tale detailing the adventures of Chief Inspector Erasmus Drake and Dr. "Sparky" McTrowell. The duo's many adventures are provided in penny dreadful-style episodes on the web (www. DrakeAndMcTrowell.com). They have produced four novels since 2010: "London, Where it All Began," "The Bavarian Airship Regatta," "Her Majesty's Eyes and Ears," and "The Hawaiian Triple Cross." Drake and Morse won a Starburner Award for the radio show based on their first story, which has run multiple times on Krypton Radio.

When not cosplaying their alter egos at conventions all over the West, they are both research computer scientists specializing in distributed modeling and simulation. Mr. Drake is a nationally ranked foil fencer. Dr. Morse is an internationally respected expert on standards, but prefers to be recognized for her cookie baking skills. They throw awesome parties if they do say so themselves.